The Electric Affinities

— Also by Wade Stevenson —

Ice Cream Parlors in Asia (as Steven Wade)

Beds

The Little Book of He and She

One Time in Paris (a memoir of the 1960s)

A Testament to Love & Other Losses

THE ELECTRIC AFFINITIES

WADE STEVENSON

A NOVEL

BLAZEVOX[BOOKS]
Buffalo, New York

The Electric Affinities
by Wade Stevenson
Copyright © 2014

Published by BlazeVOX [books]

All rights reserved. No part of this book may be reproduced without the publisher's written permission, except for brief quotations in reviews. This is a work of fiction. Any resemblance of characters to actual persons, living or dead, is purely coincidental.

Printed in the United States of America

Interior design, Cover Design and typesetting by Geoffrey Gatza
Cover Photo by Charles Marks

First Edition
ISBN: 978-1-60964-148-1
Library of Congress Control Number: 2013942420

BlazeVOX [books]
131 Euclid Ave
Kenmore, NY 14217

Editor@blazevox.org

publisher of weird little books

BlazeVOX [books]

blazevox.org

21 20 19 18 17 16 15 14 13 12 01 02 03 04 05 06 07 08 09 10

BlazeVOX

Acknowledgements

I would like to thank Geoffrey Gatza, for his invaluable support and enthusiasm, and Donna White, for her understanding and incisive editing. My gratitude to my wife, Lori, for her love and patience. Special thanks to all those who were close to Maria during her last days, especially Marie-Françoise Maupaté, Micky Engel, Sylvia Lorant, Sylvie Morini.

To the memory of Maria

Preface

The material on which this book is based was handwritten, in notebook form, in 1969/1970. At that time I was living in Paris in an artist's studio at 31 bis rue Campagne-lrè, Paris 14. When I returned to New York ten years later, I left all those notebooks behind me, stashed in an old steamer trunk in the basement of that building, what the French call a "cave." My girlfriend stayed in the apartment. When she died in 2011, I returned to dispose of the books, artwork, and furniture. I was told that there had been some basement leaks, water damage, so it would not be wise for me to descend into the "cave" and to look for that streamer trunk and its contents. Actually, I was afraid to, because I didn't want to find all my writing turned into an illegible mass of dirty paper pulp. Nevertheless, on the last day I ventured down with a flashlight and found the trunk. Nervously, I opened it. Much to my surprise, the notebooks were neatly stacked together, intact, much as I had left them. I had the trunk shipped back to my home in Buffalo, New York. I edited the notebooks, shaping and rewriting as necessary. The result is the book you are about to read.

The Electric Affinities

In chemistry and atomic physics, the electron affinity of an atom or molecule is defined as the amount of energy released when an electron is added to a neutral atom or molecule to form a negative ion

$$X + e^- \rightarrow X^- + \text{energy}$$

"All beauty is making one of opposites and the making one of opposites is what we are going after in ourselves."

—Eli Siegel

"I live, I die; I am intense and I drown."

—Louise Labé

PART I:

UNDER THE RED, WHITE AND BLUE

Chapter I

It was the fourth of July, the first official weekend of summer, and the broad lawn at Ben Steinberg's house in Sag Harbor was crowded with editors, artists, writers, architects, decorators, models, and movie and theatre people. Andre Cordier, a film director, was speaking. He was a burly, rather aggressive young man in his late twenties. "The fireworks ought to form a pattern like, let's say, the American flag, red, white and blue, unfurled, exploding against the night sky. I see the image lasting for an instant, and then being torn apart by a rocket shooting through the center of the stars."

Ben moved about his guests, his arms around the shoulders of Robert Lord and his girlfriend, Carolina Cook. He introduced them to his friends, saying, "They're just back from California and are going to spend a few days with me. They're the most charming couple I know!"

Over the bay, the sun was about to drop into the slot of the horizon like a flaming coin. The light floated, fine, superb. Guests talked loudly, confidently, gaily, discussing new projects, plans, and mutual friends with the faint arrogance of those who have earned their holidays. There was no hint of anything wrong, of anything that could possibly go wrong.

Satisfied, yet seeking more pleasure, the guests swarmed around the food on the buffet table like hungry birds. Laid across the table were plates of tiny meatballs, Virginia ham, and several varieties of paté. One of the guests commented wryly, "Americans don't like their innards; they sell them to the French who sell them back to us as paté!"

The arms of the handsome, young caterers rose up and down as they pumped drink after drink out of endless bottles. Under the shadows of the century-old trees beyond, people were sitting in a circle on the lawn, quietly talking. A curious American tree with some of its limbs lopped off towered above them. There was an abundance of pretty girls, their faces masked by sunglasses, all perhaps desiring to meet that man who could unmask them or take away that slight edge of superiority their dark glasses gave them.

Cars streamed up the long driveway that wound through bushes and trees. All those who could afford it and many, who could not, had left the city and found their way here. They greeted each other with quiet, formal gestures of welcome. There were many quiet, friendly, young men, wearing colorful clothes, with a vaguely hippyish appearance. Small, well-toned, pretty women talked eagerly and enthusiastically. Ben did his best to point out his friends to Robert and Carolina.

"There," he said, "is Irving Salzman, the decorator. That lovely Japanese woman putting a drink to her lips is Fumi-Fuigi Tofuiji, Buckminster Fuller's assistant." Blonde, fragile, bubbling with her airy laughter, Carolina teased, "Fuigi or not to fuigi…" Robert helped himself to another vodka. He noticed that everyone had the rather modish appearance of watered down, slightly stylized hippies.

Ben steered Robert and Carolina toward a particularly stylish couple, "Do you see that tall, lean man with the serious but friendly face speaking French with Louise? He's one of the editors of 'Vogue'. He has thirty people working for him and lives alone near the Creek." Robert was about to ask which one was Louise, when Ben divulged, "She's a French woman from Paris, spending the summer here with the most interesting woman on the island." Before Robert had a chance to find out who "the most interesting woman on the island" was, Ben was talking to Louise, telling her that she "ought to find herself a guy."

Louise, apparently, was very excited. She had put on a see-through knit dress. Her hips, thighs, breasts could be seen without any difficulty. Although her proportions were modest, she was very well shaped, curvaceous and compact. After Ben had introduced them, Louise asked if her costume flattered her? Before Robert could answer, she added, "But the shawl isn't mine, it belongs to Maya."

For the first time since he had come back from California a few days ago, Robert felt excited, free, tuned in. The lovely Fourth of July party on the lawn, the sun sinking over the bay, the presence of the flashy guests, the kindness of Ben, the fact that it was the beginning of summer, the Polish vodka - all had gone to his head. He forgot the horrors of the Vietnam War. He forgot Carolina and the difficulties he had with her. It was as if he had jumped out of his skin and mind and begun to live.

Standing nearby, Ellen, the editor of "Architecture Today", was getting quite drunk, wobbly and tough. Her woman friend, who lived with her, had grown even tougher and smarter with her tongue and was telling Louise how much she hated the French.

"But, oui, I agree," said Louise, astonishing everyone. "You know, I much prefer ze Americans to ze French. I came to America in search of a 'new life'."

As the old sun set, the bay shone with light atomized in the evening vapors. The party drifted, flowed; groups broke apart, reformed. People permutated. Ice clinked in glasses. Upon the porch two well-known pianists began to play a duet. The air, breezing over the water was cool and refreshing. Jack Mandel, head of the Vietnam desk in Washington, was trying to defend the disaster of "Hamburger Hill", where 241 Americans were recently killed, to some of his weekend friends. More and more liquor flowed as the lights over the bridge to Sag Harbor flickered.

Carolina took in the extravagance of her surroundings. Swinging her bag absentmindedly she watched as Norman Mailer engaged Jack Mandel in a vigorous debate about the war and whether the U.S. was right to bomb Laos. Suddenly the chain handle broke and her purse fell to the ground. "Oh no," she exclaimed. "Robbie, look, it's broken." He grabbed for the bag before its contents could spill out. "A screw came loose. I'll fix it. You stay with the guests." He headed off across the broad lawn to the house. In the kitchen he used a knife to replace the screw. He was just finishing the job when it slipped and cut his finger. It came so quickly, the blood, he thought, as he hurried to the bathroom for a band aid. He hoped it wasn't an omen for the summer.

He came back outside, down the porch past Ben's bronze Giacometti-like sculptures, past the gay piano players, into the deep, exotic evening that, as a bough with fruit, seemed to be laden with promises and expectancies to be plucked for the simple asking. Fruit with selections of French cheese was being served for desert. As he walked past various guests, he overheard bits of their conversations.

"Where should we put our plates?"

"Why doesn't someone bring out something for the garbage?"

A stunning, serpentine girl approached Robert and asked, "But what do you think of God?"

"If He's there at all, He's probably laughing it up with some woman right now," Robert responded and watched with pleasure as the discomfited lady slithered away.

Carolina, her funny Turkish pants flapping in the breeze, stood out on the edge of the grass near the fence where the apple trees grew, eagerly scanning the horizon that glowed with darkness, as if looking for some sign. No matter what she did, Carolina always managed to be like a sentinel on the outpost, the frontier of things. She never let herself be assimilated to any group. 'Carolina' wasn't even her given name. She had chosen it because she said it sounded "free".

Nearby, in the illumined waters of the swimming pool, a few daring girls, anxious for publicity, had stripped and were leaping nakedly around, giggling.

Ben grabbed Robert. "There, take a look. Have you ever seen a woman with green eyes and six bracelets on her arm? I damn sure never have. Come, I want you to meet Maya. Aside from you and Carolina, she and Andre are my favorite couple."

Maya was wearing a white lace vintage dress that accentuated her willowy, elegant figure. On the stem of her neck, she wore a black velvet cameo choker. The moment Robert saw her, from the very first glance, he felt troubled by her in a way that he had never felt before. She did indeed have gorgeous green eyes and wore a kind of extravagant, curly wig that crowned her head and gave her an imperial look. She had a way of constantly inventing herself with a fantastic allure that had the effect of a bomb upon those who saw her for the first time.

Robert would later learn more about her incredible sense of theatre, of disguise, combined with the airs of an empress, something regal and superb that mocked itself through play, that delighted in creating a series of illusions and sleight-of-hand appearances, so that you could never tell where she began and where she ended, what was her and what was not her, or if she even existed at all. But Maya did exist. Behind all her lacy camouflage, there was something precise, joyous and powerful.

Robert hesitated, hung back; it looked as if they were interrupting a scene. Maya, the girl with the green eyes and the exuberant wig, was saying, "Andre, I beg of you, will you please be quiet!"

The film director, using his fingers like claws, raked his nails into her flesh above her stacked bracelets. His angry mouth blasted words into her ear, "Suicide, despair, luxury of the rich, you say! You know damn well we're all just wolves prowling around the fire, looking for something to warm us. Now that we've got the summer ahead of us, why not be free?"

Superb, without moving, with a proud and savage serenity, Maya answered, "If you think I'm going to be your sheep ---!"

Seeing the others approach, Andre stopped. They both stood in an uneasy truce, fiercely glaring at each other like animals at bay.

Radiant spokes reflected from under Maya's lashes. She sneezed, held her nose so that the sneeze was choked through her mouth. "Pardon me, all the flowers, scents in the air…"

Ben introduced Robert; Carolina appeared; Andre drained his glass, trying to muffle his rage. Maya said, "Would you excuse me, please, I would like to wash my hands." There was a droplet of blood on her arms. Her eyes glistened with moisture, the radiant spokes of the fake eyelashes becoming undone.

"Do you have a repair kit with you?" asked Ben. She laughed. "No, absolutely nothing!" Eluding the encounter, anxious to be alone with her own feelings, Maya bounded away, stooping to pick up some lavender flowers.

She struck Robert with the impact of a revelation. He had never seen a woman who united within her such grace, extravagance and dignity. He had already decided: I must have this woman; it is absolutely necessary to my life that I have her and make her mine.

The dark pool waters hid the dangerous nudity of the girls. Tirelessly they swam back and forth, as if celebrating some forgotten ceremony. Maya came back out, turning her head sideways. She looked washed, refreshed. Her long Nefertiti neck rose up. Was it possible that she loved Andre?

Ben was conversing with some famous writer who summered in the Hamptons when Carolina snapped, "For goodness sake, let's stop talking about the meaning of art and literature. We've been stuffed with that fare for more than two thousand years. Let's just enjoy the air, the sparkling water, the evening, and the delicious company of ourselves. No need to go any further. We are here, we are 'it', we are what's happening, baby." The summer of 1969 had begun; the people around them were chattering a lot about revolution and discontent and Vietnam and the unliveableness of the cities.

Gradually the evening settled and the first fireworks were arched up in lovely, incandescent, multicolored expanding parabolas. Over and over again, above their upturned heads, far out over the bay, burst parachutes of convulsive color. Carolina kissed Robert; she hugged him and sighed and whispered into his ear, "What a sexual thing, just think of a man bursting like that inside a woman!" Detonated mushrooms of diamond and emerald glitter deployed, floated and crashed into infinity. Snugging her warm little nose into his neck, Carolina murmured, "When the world blows up, which I think will be soon, I hope it happens like that."

Chapter II

After the party was over, the last lights blossomed in the sky and the cars disappeared down the driveway. Ben took them all to the local clam bar in Sag Harbor. Luckily the jukebox was broken so that it was quieter than usual. Eight or nine fat, solitary men, squatting on bar stools looked up as they entered, laughing loudly. Immediately, Andre said in a provocative tone "Look at all those asses dripping over the stools. What an image for the Fourth of July! Think of all those fat, lonely asses on the stools stretching onward, expanding like tombstones into infinity."

"You bore me," said Maya.

Andre was already quite drunk. When drunk he resembled a blind bull. He turned round and round upon himself and never stopped talking. "Once I was working in a garage in Detroit. I'd just come to the States and needed to make a little bread. One night I took some girls out and they asked me what religion I was and I said I was an atheist. The next day the boss called me into his office and said, 'Look, I know you're from France, but stop teasing these girls. I know you're not an atheist. It was a joke, wasn't it?' Crazy! A week later, you know what? My boss went home to dinner one night and his wife was undressing in front of the window and across the street another guy was watching her and jerking off. The boss picked up a gun and shot him dead! He went to court and was acquitted! Public opinion was for him. Of course this was in 1958... Still, I'd be happy if Maya inspired someone to amuse himself...."

Contradiction! Bells should have rung. Maya did repeat, "You bore me!"

Andre didn't seem at all jealous of the electricity that had begun to crackle and flow between Maya and Robert.

On the wall behind the door Ben stopped to inspect a painting of an old whaling ship, rendered with acute detail. "There's somebody home there," said Maya. "And that coat rack in the corner is quite lovely too," she remarked. "It's like a Brancusi sculpture. So much better than all those modern minimalist sculptures you see."

In the back of the room there was a billiard table; the year before, Ben said, there had been a bowling machine. Ben had been drinking quite a lot and hadn't eaten anything at his party earlier. It was impossible to know how much liquor he absorbed during the day but it was a substantial quantity. Although he had had undergone several detox cures, often drinking nothing but water for six months, Ben had a way of falling abruptly back into alcohol. At such times he would say, "I heard yesterday that Bunuel, the famous Spanish film-maker, is alcoholic too. But he does pretty good stuff, don't you think? All the more reason, I tell myself, to go on drinking!"

Upon that particular night, Ben already had a good head start. He kept talking back and forth with Maya and had obviously fallen under the influence of her extraordinary, high-pitched charm. "You know what, you're my little sister!" he kept trying to convince her.

At the same time, in front of both Ben and Andre, Maya was engaging Robert ---who was not slow to respond ---- openly, without reserve, as if to show her independence, flaunting her liberty. It wasn't certain whether Ben knew what was happening. Andre did. Vexed, he stomped, stalked and fumed. "Quit playing these games," he demanded.

"What for?" came her quick retort. 'I want to live everything."

"You better leave now if you want to live."

Again her ironic, savage, "What for? It's the Fourth of July festival. Once a year, you know, everything is permitted. I'm having a good time; I'm amusing myself. If you're not, you're free to leave...."

Was it the presence of Ben, of the others, that kept Andre from slugging Robert, attacking Maya? Or did he feel that his control of her was such that he didn't need to worry about physical possessiveness? As masters sometimes allow their dog off the leash, was he condescending to give Maya a moment of unleashed liberty?

Carolina hadn't wanted to come, but had finally let herself be persuaded by Ben. She would often say, "I don't like cocktail parties; people are always so self-promoting. If they had a good relationship with their dog, they wouldn't have to go there." Now she was managing to make the best she could of Robert's antics. She was all too willing to give him this liberty and had often encouraged it; she was totally against the kind of jealousy and possessiveness that pushes a man and woman to devour each other. Carolina felt there was complicity between them that went beyond whatever he might do. Still, it did hurt her to see him cavorting so openly in public. Did he have to use her presence as an arena in which to prove his independence?

Louise sat next to Ben. She had become very quiet and demure, playing a humble, defensive role. The atmosphere of the evening, the bright gaiety of the party, the fireworks that for a moment had cut the sky to ribbons, had triggered something deeply in all of them. The summer had begun with a bang and already it seemed that this evening would serve as a launching pad for everything that was to come later.

Robert too, felt a terrible need to go outward, to expand himself. The volatile moods of protean Carolina, their constant oscillations, all encouraged him now into a great openness. There was a moment when life had to be seized, when a man, like a trapeze artist, had to leap without knowing whether his outstretched hands would catch a bar or fall through the nothingness of space.

What did it matter anyway? He was sure they were all so drunk and delirious that by tomorrow everything would be forgotten.

Ben, ebullient as a "godfather" surrounded by his adopted family, ordered another White Label and soda, followed by a round of clams on the half shell and clam chowder for all of them.

The clams were small and exquisitely fresh. They ate them before the clam chowder and then again afterwards; it was a little like having desert. How pleasant it was, after the hot chowder, to have the clams return; Robert said they tasted like ice cream from the sea.

"Let's have some more," Andre urged.

Ben called the waitress over and asked her to bring another round of clams. "How long have you been working in this joint?" he wanted to know.

"I've worked here all my life. I'm the fisherman's daughter."

"That puts you in your place, Ben," Maya said. "Stay there!"

"Right, right," muttered Ben, and became quiet for a moment.

"How can anyone know what their 'place' is if they have to stay in it all the time?" Carolina wondered, glancing at Robert.

Robert paid no attention. He felt a rare spark had flashed between Maya and himself. Some sign had identified them as belonging to the same nervous family. Maya stretched her body out sideways on the seat, like a panther exercising. Robert moved against her. He was mad for her. Under the table he tried to play hide and go-seek with her hands. She moved them away.

"They're like children; they're just playing," Carolina said to Ben.

Ben made a movement with his hands as if brushing flies away from his head and announced he was going to have another drink and then go home; he had just driven out from New York City that morning.

Leaning over Robert's shoulder, Maya announced to no one in particular how much she loved this local bar. "It's wonderful," she said. "It's classic Americana."

Andre then jumped up on his chair and, his voice half-drowned in the din, amusingly crooned:

"This is America, America, America,
Land of highways, hotdogs and lights,
Of cash, commotion and chaos,
Motels, churches and communist fears,
Kids touch-footballing on the White House lawn,
Salesmen groaning in front of empty doors,
Fantastic sounds breaking through space,
Waw jaw faw caw cat cool man dig hip yeah super wow!!!"

Everyone in the clam bar laughed and clapped.

At the end of the bar a squat, sturdy blonde woman stood up and jeered raucously. "In my country, in certain bars in Marseille, you can see the same thing," Louise remarked.

"This ain't nothing but a local bar in Sag Harbor," said Ben, "and you gotta keep the proportions right."

"Hey, baby, don't forget this was a whaling town," Maya answered quickly. "That's what I'm looking for, the great, white whale!"

"Funny to hear you say that," Ben laughed. "I always had you pegged for an Egyptian sphinx."

Seeing how the delirium was spreading everywhere, Carolina began to laugh; her laughter spread out like a Japanese fan, cool, soft and gracious.

Bored with the nonsense, Maya knocked her head against Robert's.

He realized what he hadn't wanted to admit: like a car going faster and faster, the evening was escaping their control. They were no longer acting so much as being acted upon by other forces and atomic states of mind. All this is a test, Robert thought, nothing but a test, and you must somehow endure it and move into the space beyond.

Ben, by now infected too, was looking up at Maya and imitating her gestures, her bright laughter and the swift, lively movements of her hands. Putting his own hands to the side of his face, he let out a loud squawk.

Ben poured himself another drink and mumbled something; he clearly had had too much. But his lapses only seemed to stimulate Maya. Quite superbly, she kept slashing at him with her brilliance. Robert was stunned; this was a side of her that he hadn't seen.

At the end of the bar, next to the raucous blonde woman, Andre skulked. Carolina rose and joined him. Every now and then Andre shook his head in disgust.

Louise broke her silence to announce, "It is very crazy, no, how busy this bar is tonight?"

True, it was the Fourth of July, but in such a small town as Sag Harbor, at past two in the morning? The door didn't stop opening and shutting; brawny, boisterous men swaggered in and out.

"It's because of all the activity down at the fishing port," Maya answered. "The fishing boats going in and out and the fishermen coming in for a drink." She paused. Ben and Robert both knew the port was closed down during the night; there was absolutely no fishing activity at all. But Louise was so curious that Maya continued, putting her on, "It's on account of the whaling activity, too, you know."

It wasn't clear whether Louise had understood, but Robert and Ben broke up laughing.

"That's not bad," Ben kept saying. Admiringly, he glanced across the table at Maya.

Maya blinked her eyes and hid her head for a moment behind Robert's shoulders, squeezing his arms as she did so. Robert felt full of her light, of her energy, but fearful of the consequences --- certain acts being irretrievable --- and suddenly became aware how he must be hurting Carolina.

Something felt twisted and broken inside his stomach. He withdrew slightly.

Ben must have sensed something too, for he stopped drinking, and looked up solemnly long enough to say, "It's a little bit late for you to be coming on with such charm, isn't it, baby?"

Maya smiled but said nothing. She turned and started whispering rapidly to Louise. Ben sank back, a little resigned. "All right, Maya," he murmured. "All right, you're not too bad."

Something in this family reunion of exiled souls that had adopted each other was going sour.

Too late, Ben realized what was happening. "My god, you're a pretty intelligent girl," he said to Maya. His tone changed, became somber. "Don't be stupid. I don't think you and Robert should be so close together: your heads are too strong. And you and Andre are such a good two-headed animal."

"What do I care for your morality?" countered Maya, impetuously bumping her head against Robert's.

Robert felt a new emotion stir inside him. He knew he had entered the danger zone.

Maya could do whatever she pleased. She had won the night for herself. In this game, she had triumphed. Like a beast in a labyrinth, lured now here, now there, Robert struck out at melting mirages, fantasies that faded as soon as they were formed. Carolina was far away, watching them with amused, ironical indifference. She thought: if he truly belongs to me, he'll be with me. If not, he won't.

The bar began to spin like a merry-go-round. The walls shrank and Maya's head was enlarged as if projected upon a screen.

Although Louise tried to restrain her, Maya got up suddenly, pulling Robert with her. "Let's go and see the billiards."

Only too happy to leave the table's oppressively ambiguous atmosphere, Robert rushed to the smoky rear room with her. Maya pranced up and down with excitement. For her the night was just beginning to unfold and its hidden possibilities emerge.

The moment they were safely away from the table, Maya stood on her tiptoes, threw herself against him, almost collapsing Robert with her embraces. Of course, he responded; how could he get himself to say "no" at such a moment? Even if he had had the willpower, he couldn't have done it. After the cool arabesques and oriental harmonies of Carolina, he was recklessly overjoyed to abandon himself to this hysteria.

It didn't matter that they were both giddy. It didn't matter that everyone was looking at them. It didn't matter that Andre was murderously smashing the billiard balls. It didn't matter that another night would come and another and another and another...How could their fury be contained? Or sustained? At bottom, Robert was as desirous of losing himself in Maya as she was of losing herself in him. Together could they vanish?

The old theme in Robert's head surfaced: throw yourself away; fling yourself like a match into the barn of a woman. Life's nothing, particularly today, so hard to have a dignity.... nothing but a grain of sand, pouring away along with all the other lost grains... Good. Who cares? What difference did it make? He kissed her, enjoyed the feeling of letting that part of himself flow into her.

Carolina herself once said, "Throw yourself like a knife into the trunk of a springtime tree. If you don't vibrate, you're other than you're supposed to be!"

Andre stood with his cue raised, poised menacingly in his hand like a spear. An obese, sloppy-shouldered youth slouched over the tattered green table and racked the bright-colored balls. They jumped together with a military clack. Effaced in the corner, half-hidden in the shadows, Carolina laughed. "You all look like soldiers. Why don't you challenge each other to a duel?"

Then it happened. Robert shot first. The white ball burst into the fixed triangle, exploding it. Balls scattered in every direction; a red one dropped in a pocket. Maya squealed with excitement. Andre was serious and enraged. Robert stroked the cue again. Maya cried out. There was a bewildering whirl of aimless motion. Andre lurched over the edge, drew the cue carefully, painstakingly back between his arched fingers, and let loose.

"Wow!" Maya cried.

The spinning balls disintegrated in a profusion of bright, cool color. Maya's body careened into Robert's. On that crazy evening, were they not all like billiard balls, ricocheting off the slightest impulse of their feelings into each other? Maya pressed against him, dancing, her face and eyes lit up. Robert let his lips run across her cheeks, trying to convey to her quickly, as in a telegram, how wonderful she was. He didn't have much time, when, his cue held up like a sword, Andre lunged at him. Robert leaped aside. There was a brief, intense scuffle. At the back of the room, Ben and Louise sat observing them. She didn't know what to say or do. Ben's face had changed. It grimaced with discomfort as he pleaded with them to stop it all.

The few blows Andre had thrown didn't satisfy him. Curiously, he didn't seem angry with Robert anymore. All his fury was directed at Maya.

Snappily, she spun on her feet as Robert grabbed her by the arm, and they strolled back to the table. They sat down. Ben didn't say anything. He got up, ordered a beer. Carolina hung back in the shadows, feeling a stranger to everything. She couldn't understand what was happening or why Robert was deserting her like that.

When the waitress came over with the check, Maya told her how wonderful the clams had been. Noticing her accent, the fisherman's daughter looked at her curiously and asked, "Where are you from?"

Maya hesitated, hating to be put on the spot by such a typically direct American question. "Over the hills," she answered.

It was a fine reply. Even Louise laughed. The waitress was perplexed. "Where? Over there? What hills?"

As if nothing could be simpler, Maya repeated, "Over the hills!"

The waitress turned away, perplexed but seemingly resigned to her confusion.

The tension dropped. At four in the morning, people start thinking of going to bed, even in the Hamptons. Carolina yawned. She took Robert's hand. Ben passed his beer around. For a moment, it was almost as if nothing had happened.

But Maya leaned over and whispered to Robert, "You know, when I was talking about the whale, I just meant: the search for the impossible!"

How well he knew that! The impossible, the absolute! Totality of a passion, unity of two minds, harmony of a love or a life! The forever inaccessible. What had they been doing all evening long but searching, each in his own way, for that absolute?

Softly, with an agonizing sweetness, Carolina kissed Robert. Ben put his arm around Louise, who stiffened uncomfortably. Maya told her to stop acting like that. Louise retaliated by rolling up two white fangs out of paper, putting them in her mouth, and grinning with them like Dracula at Ben and Maya.

Maya, overcome with laughter, rested her lovely head on Andre's shoulder, and Ben said they looked so well together.

"Don't lie to me," said Andre. "Tell me what kind of game you were playing."

"Don't bother to forgive me: it wasn't a mistake."

Louise whispered into Robert's ear, "She's so strong, so terribly and dangerously strong. Why is it then that the only thing she puts any value on is succumbing?"

"Bitch," Andre snarled as Louise gripped Maya protectively. Ben paid the bill. The bar was being closed, an iron grill lowered over the lines of whiskey bottles. "Fantastic," said Carolina. "It's as if they're putting the alcohol animals back in their cages."

They walked out onto Sag Harbor's deserted main street. In the diagonal parking strips, there were only a few white police cars. All the fireworks had long been buried in the deep beckoning majesty of that early July night.

Like a little puppy, Louise trotted behind while Andre dragged Maya off. She was too weak to protest as Andre pulled her by the arm, but she managed to murmur to Robert, "I felt so comfortable with you, for a moment…"

"But that's marvelous," he began to say, but she walked off with Andre, and he cut himself short with a rebuke, "Idiot" he muttered. What a fool he was to have let himself get so excited for such an illusory spark of feeling.

In the Volvo station wagon driving back over the bridge, Ben said, "But things are simple, aren't they?"

"I don't know," said Robert, shaking his head.

Carolina hugged him. "I hope you found the truth this evening."

"What's the 'truth'?" he asked, more out of weariness than a desire to hear anything about the "truth", whatever that might be.

"The truth," said Carolina. "You don't have to look for it. It's inside you. It's THAT. It's a laughing cow!"

Chapter III

The explosions and tensions and vagaries of the preceding night rippled away in the plenitude of the sunlight that appeared the next morning. For ten days it had been damp and rainy, but now the first generous bursts of light and heat came into their own.

Andre lay in wait, hoping Maya would get up. He didn't know whether to talk to her about the evening before or pretend that nothing had happened. The danger of course was that if he said nothing, it might happen again, maybe tomorrow. If he said something, she would defend herself, but he was sure he could master her.

So sure? Somehow the ends of the rope that had lashed their bodies and hearts together were beginning to unravel. Andre couldn't reshape himself, couldn't get himself to feel like the July summer, generous and fresh. Too many things had happened, too many incidents that, singly, could be forgotten but, taken together, could not be ignored. Andre was too proud to humiliate himself by pretending to be blind. Hadn't he been the first to insist that each man had his own truth, which he had to live, and that no one could help him in doing so? But what was his?

Their lives were getting more and more scattered, diffuse. Contacts were rare. Talk was sparse. Was it possible that the forces he had done so much to ignite in the flesh were fading? It was true that love moved at such an astonishing speed. How could any connections be made between what they were when they started and what they were now? How to measure the distances traversed, the indescribable intimacy of the journey?

On each leaf of the willow tree in the garden the brilliant sun managed to repeat itself into infinity. The blue teeth of the air had raked the sky clean of clouds. A magnificent morning, clear, soundless, and without stain. If only Maya would appear to dissolve his uneasiness with the grand and beautiful forgetfulness to which she had the key! If only he didn't feel like a bundle of wood and the cord holding the bundle together had broken. Andre felt so much death inside his body that, like dynamite ---more and more of it stacked up every day --- was just waiting to be lit.

The Long Island light lacquered the leaves, the grass, but the silent and relative obscurity of what was happening made Andre feel insecure, and things were made even more complicated by the presence of Louise. She always arose punctually at eight, and he could hear her now stirring in the kitchen, washing and cleaning. Andre decided not to go and get a cup of coffee. He hated Louise. She had the mentality of a servant.

Maya woke up toward sun-tossed noon. Barely greeting Andre, she descended and had lunch with Louise on the porch. "How marvelous it is to feel fresh in the morning! I can't remember a thing of what happened last night. Tell me, was I very crazy?"

Andre, convinced of her sincerity, said nothing. How could you talk to a woman who never remembered anything at all? Knowing the fantastic life she had lived, her friendship with Man Ray, who had photographed her, or with Marcel Duchamp, with whom she had played chess (and won), Andre was always amazed at her total forgetfulness. To think that she couldn't even remember where she was born, that she didn't know and didn't care. How rare, how extraordinary even, to find a human being not limited by a particular condition or situation. He recalled when, last night, the waitress had been indiscreet enough to ask her where she came from. She laughed and said, "Over the hills!"

What a glorious response! Andre knew he would have loved her for those words alone, even if he never had the chance to know her in any other way. No less extraordinary was the way, each night when she slept, waves washed through her mind, cleansing her of everything that had happened before, so that each day her mind, like a blackboard, was fresh, each night moving over her like a gigantic eraser. What a fantastic way to live, to be free. The heads of most people --- weren't they like the ledgers that accountants keep, filled with petty additions and subtractions? Wasn't it in their natures to tally up each encounter as an exchange? "I'll give you this, if I'm sure you'll give me that?" Horror! Andre grimaced. What an example Maya was, a real statue of liberty, monumental and unseizable. If only he could have achieved her state of being, could have forgotten, for instance, the details of his own father, who had died penniless of alcoholism in a nursing home.

Silence. The sun shone, the air glittered; a few butterflies were inviting the flowers to waltz. Andre strained to say something to Maya, but wasn't able to interrupt the breezy, chatty conversation she was having with Louise. Why remind her of the night before? Why do anything but live in the present, if he could?

After lunch Maya and Louise decided, as usual, to go to the beach. The sun had preserved its great intensity. Maya took off her lace blouse. She was wearing such a small white bra that it seemed to be a delicate verisimilitude of a real woman's bra. It held her breasts firmly and softly, making Andre think of them as knobs embossed on her chest. How he longed to touch and to turn them!

Andre sat, burying his eyes in Maya. Louise began getting authoritative. The moment Andre failed to act --- or just relaxed --- Louise moved in and occupied the space. "Shouldn't we go out now and profit from the sun?" she urged.

Andre was determined Maya and Louise should not be allowed to go to the beach together. He protested. "It's not a good idea for you two to do that." How could he have any idea what shenanigans they might succumb to when, removing their clothes, they isolated themselves in their "little hole" carved in the dunes? It was maddening to think about.

"Why don't you come along?" Louise suggested gaily.

"Shut-up," Andre growled. "You know I hate the beach."

It was true: Andre did dislike the beach.

"It's so flat, boring, monotonous," he liked to say. "I can't stand it. Gives me hallucinations all the time."

Andre was a man who had a need to consider everything from the optics of the night. A double Scorpio (born in November with a Scorpio ascendant), how could he possibly find joy in something so simple as the sunlight and an open space?

Maya slipped into the bathroom. As she was getting changed, he ran up and shut and locked the door behind her. His approach frightened her.

"I don't want you to go to the beach," he said firmly. He grabbed her arms and forced her to sit down on the edge of the bathtub.

"Why not? Why not?" she insisted, puzzled and indignant.

He lied: "Because it will exhaust you and later you'll be too exhausted to ----"

She saw right through him. "Because you'll get too lonely and anxious waiting here in the cottage for me. Egotist! Come with us then."

He let the invitation drop. "If you just want to sit in the sun, there's plenty of it here outside on the grass. Besides, I want you take a look at this new film script I'm working on."

With a certain satisfaction Andre could hear Louise murmuring outside the bathroom door, "But aren't we going to the beach?"

"There seems to be a slight problem."

Louise ---he could have cursed her for her ignorant innocence --- answered, "No, Maya, chérie, there's no problem at all."

"She's right, you know," said Maya, more to herself than to Andre. "It's stupid to make problems. If you don't want to go to the beach, don't go. I'm going."

It wasn't the first time that Andre felt like putting his hands around Louise's throat and choking her.

Maya put her white lace blouse back on.

Disgusted, Andre watched them as, disguised with oil, sunglasses and bikinis, they mounted their bicycles and pedaled to the beach. He lit a cigarette, leaned against a tree, and watched with a mixture of desperate jealousy and casual contempt as the figures of the two women in profile --- one tall, gracious, svelte, the other small, compact, business-like --- glided past the fields, the cows, the farms. Above the crude, brownish texture of the potato fields, goldenrods blazed. A cow mooed its melancholy. Until she disappeared at last between the sky and the trees, Andre watched intently as Maya's bare thighs rippled up and down, her feet alternating on the peddles.

Maya was wearing high red stockings that came up to her knees and she was clasping some letters to be mailed in her hand; she looked absolutely like a schoolgirl. There was a faint promise of promiscuity that the presence of Louise, as a chaperon, accentuated.

Andre grimaced thinking that he was about to lose her --- that perhaps he had lost her already.

Like a cat, Andre lurked around the house, waiting for Maya and Louise to return. It was strange: unless Maya was there, physically present, he couldn't do anything, yet if she was there, he had no desire to do anything. He hated it when she was gone. The worst was when she went away with Louise. From his own experience and from what his "spies" told him, he knew they climbed up into the "little hole" where, if the sun was hot enough, they sat or lay naked.

The trouble was that when Maya lay in the sun, it was as if the sun were her lover, and she abandoned herself totally, ready for anything, to that solar power. With Louise there… plus the fact that no one could see them in the nice niche they had found for themselves in the dunes… If only the sun would evaporate, go up in a puff of smoke, or a black cloud slide like a blanket across it! He found it odd, how Maya was never alone. Was solitude as difficult for her as it was for him? She was either with him or with Louise. He wondered how involved Maya and Louise really were?

While nervously waiting for them, Andre walked out several times into the garden to test the sun. What he wanted to know was: was it still warm enough for them to remove their clothes?

Two hours passed. The sun no longer glared; it shimmered, the light floated. Andre couldn't work. For the first time in his life he had the backers, the funds, a few well-known actors. Everything was waiting for him, dependent upon him, yet he couldn't get himself to put the whole project together.

He had done it before, had done it once on Broadway and more recently at Lincoln Centre where he had staged a successful production by three black playwrights. But now --- was it the summer heat, his own lassitude and the deterioration of his relationship with Maya or his own spiritual crisis? Somehow he couldn't bring himself to make that final effort that would have brought his new project off the written page and set it before the whirring cameras.

He knew he had to do it --- it was as important for his future as it was for his life now; in effect, he was broke, having quickly run out of the advance and option money he had been paid more than a year ago. If the new film wasn't started by September, he would lose the option and all control. Obviously the time for idleness had passed. Yet, Andre talked and talked but couldn't engage his mind in that straitjacket of discipline, the tangible results of which had caused so many critics five years ago to hail him as a young director of brilliant promise with a beautiful future.

A future without Maya was inconceivable, but if she persisted in going to the beach with that idiotic and petty-minded Louise… Strong undercurrents of jealousy, dominance, fear and possession bubbling in his head turned Andre's brain into a simmering broth.

He resolved to make her pay for these brief absences that tortured his mind by the sufferings he would impose on her flesh.

Left to himself, Andre couldn't remain still; he couldn't even stay seated or stand for more than a few moments in one place. Nature bored him. He needed others upon whom he could exercise his will, test his powers.

The sun was warm. There was no wind. The leaves didn't dance above the road. He sat in the back of his old car, lay down, and looked through the window at the sky. He thought of the Scorpio brooch he had given her. She had always worn it, pinned to her lace blouses, next to her heart. He hadn't seen it in a long time

A while later he was woken up by the sounds of Maya and Louise returning, chatting gaily under the tree as they clambered off their bicycles. He ducked into the house and arranged the objects on Maya's desk as they had been before. She would have been horrified if she had known how he spied on her.

Maya was coming upstairs. Andre rushed out to seize her but stopped. Struck. Capped in her sunbonnet, face shining, her eyes clear and without makeup, she looked startlingly exotic. The sun and the sea had blown all feeling, all disruption or disorder, away. Nothing had been left but the essence of Maya.

He grabbed her and squeezed, trying to inflict something of himself upon her. She responded by running into her room. He chased, caught her, and swung her off the ground. Had anything happened between Louise and her?

He ran his fingers over her eyebrows.

"Sweetheart, so glad to see you! Didn't like your absence."

"Didn't like my absence?" she mimicked cruelly, twisting away.

"No, not at all!" he shouted. "I went out on the damn road, looking for you. I searched, searched all the time!"

She touched him and was serious. "You knew where I was; you could have come."

She had stirred a sore spot. It was true he could have come. Why was it he preferred suffering to trying to alleviate the sources of the discomfort? Why was it that what most interested him in love were the obstacles on the path to fulfillment? Was that what Maya had meant when she told him once that what he loved most was "disequilibrium"?

"I couldn't come because it would have interrupted my work," he protested.

She smiled. The same old song and dance. How could he expect her to believe it when he knew himself it wasn't true?

He lifted Maya up and carried her with unusual softness back to the bed, where he deposited her with gentleness strange for him, as if he were putting an egg in a nest.

She didn't move. She looked at him with eyes he wanted to crush. He lay on top of her. Her bare belly was still warm from the sun. Her shoulders were oily, her hair tangled and salty, and he could smell the salt behind her ears. The warmth of her belly beneath him felt comfortable and good. It was a little bit like lying on top of a warm, oceanic beach.

Andre's experience with Maya had led him to the point where he couldn't act anymore. She encompassed him so completely, had led him so far into a new territory, that he had need of nothing else; indeed, everything else seemed skimpy and miserable by comparison.

With the sunlight floating through the lace window curtains, she observed him slowly, indolently, (with a hint of scorn?), out of her cat green eyes. Andre felt as if he had no weight, was empty, and something flew out of him into her.

What a miraculous thing it was that this woman could transform the angry, raging bull of his body into a feather. Yet she didn't vibrate or flow with him as she once had in her swift, springing enthusiasms. She just watched him, inert, indifferently passive, and calmly immobile.

Stretched beneath him like the sea, at one with herself, Andre realized she didn't need him. Perhaps she never had needed him. He felt himself growing coarser, more abrasive, his instincts rougher, and he tangled up in them. Her silently voluptuous peace, her impenetrable reality, the silence in which she hid, carried him back to what he knew best: his own unmanageable self.

His lust rising, he came into her forcefully, holding her head down with one hand, slapping her buttocks hard with the other. Why, for Andre, was love itself always an act of force? If he had walked out and assaulted someone on the road, he would have been less violent, less criminal, than he was now. It was monstrous, almost inhuman.

Yet Andre didn't see it that way. For him there were only two choices: either he cast himself mentally as a sexual imperialist, or else he resigned himself wearily and drunkenly to being impotent. How else could he think of love but as an intrusion, a territorial violation of the other? If for one moment he let any respect, tenderness or nostalgia he might have felt for Maya influence his feelings, he was dead. And this thought, though he knew it was false, haunted him: she wouldn't have accepted it.

Andre felt a burden to himself; his body blocked him from becoming what he was. How to think of Maya? As a Ferrari for his sex? He had abolished himself in her momentum, hurtling beyond all speed limits.

Most remarkable was that no matter how many times he had "killed" her, she never died; all the more vigorously, as if refreshed by the assassination attempt, she bounced back.

Andre's sex knife was ready, hard and blunt. Religious sacrifice? As the waves pound the shore, so he battered and slapped her, coughing his rage, spitting himself into her flesh. About to be redeemed for all his miserable moments of waiting, he felt close to triumph, ready to burst and break out into the great "beyond".

The startling and insolent passivity and indifference of her body didn't annoy him. On the contrary, he was too furious, too carried away with his feelings of "love", to care whether she responded or not. He revenged himself upon Louise and the night before and everything else. As for Maya, she was too proud to even groan or complain. Like a trained dog, she knew the tricks too well, and when Andre slammed into her with the force of a man trying to grind a woman into hamburger meat, the lonely spasms of this man she refused to recognize, only amused her.

The last shadows curved on the window curtains as the sun sank. From the road outside came nothing but the silence of the countryside.

For Andre, it was now or never. Here were the split legs, the wound, the gaping sex that had to be penetrated. He had to bridge the gap between him and her. Live or die.

Their bodies collided. As if heaving a harpoon, Andre threw himself as violently as he could out of himself. She was his absolute passion, his white whale. He sensed that Maya was jarred, that she was shaken off balance. She had to yield to his power.

Another man would have been satisfied. But Andre, who was never satisfied, who didn't seem to know what satiation was, who could never make himself drunk enough, continued in this game beyond the point of ordinary exhaustion. What was ironic was that he tried to "kill" her, yet he invariably was the one who ended up being annihilated.

In the final throes, he howled like a kamikaze pilot. Maya would have laughed but she didn't want to give him even that satisfaction. She was so tired and he was hurting her so much. His imagination may have been working wonders for him, but it didn't do anything for her.

Still, it took Andre a long time to finish his need, quench his thirst. She felt free. Her belly was warm and slippery like melted butter. What she wanted to do most was to get up and wash herself.

He kept stroking her, his fingers running down to the cleft of her beautiful buttocks. Simple, non-possessive caresses didn't suffice. For Andre love was an absolute: it had to be everything or it could be nothing. Andre saw no other way of reaching fullness but through certain violence.

His head swam with the memories of all the different ways he had consumed Maya, of how he had opened and penetrated her until she had cried, "No, no, stop! I can't take it any longer!" While with another voice, the silent voice of inner passion, he felt she was begging him to be stronger with her, to continue, no matter what she said, no matter how she protested....

His violence destroyed his anguish. His fury muted his anxiety. Losing himself in her flesh, he rid himself of the terrible memories. When he woke up much later, the light had faded. It was dark all around him, and Maya was no longer there.

Chapter IV

From downstairs in the small medieval vault of the kitchen, where candles were already flickering, Andre could hear the steady, simultaneously reassuring and annoying, chitchat of Maya and Louise. It was incredible to him that they never ran out of things to say to each other. Andre had never heard a silence between them that lasted longer than a minute. Louise was one of Maya's oldest friends. She had met her during her modeling days in Paris. Maya had invited her to spend the summer with her, Andre guessed, to help her resolve her relationship with him.

What had caused his downfall? The need to go far, to always go further, to push Maya beyond endurable human limits, so that she now turned to Louise to find some small happiness in a narrow, easy tranquility? She had retreated to a "safe" zone. For such a long time they had been bright, gay, joyous, one of the most beautiful and explosive couples in the New York City art scene. They had mingled with Andy Warhol and Ultra Violet and all the pop stars. Wasn't it the nature of beauty to be convulsive, to push farther and father, to seek what lay beyond the last limit? He knew in his blood that Maya had understood this, had lived it with him. All the more reason for him to feel bitter; the mediocrity of her friendship with Louise seemed to betray that ideal. It hurt him to think how he and Maya had shone together with the acute intensity of knives. Maya had told him frequently how happy she was. "No bottom to my happiness," she had said. "No beginning, no end." And now, was it over?

It had happened quickly. One morning after a love scene, in which Andre had perhaps demanded too much, a sudden, brusque storm had set in. Her heart throbbing with a strange panic and new desperation, Maya had screamed at Andre to get out, to leave her alone.

"I can't stand love anymore!" she cried. "I can't stand anything about it! I want to unlearn everything I know. Please, will you be gracious enough to let me go as quickly as possible!"

Maya had never spoken to him like that before. Was it the beginning of a nervous sickness, the sad and bitter and final result of their vertiginous illuminations?

This time it was Andre's turn to wrap himself in silence. He pretended he had not heard. A dialogue of the deaf. Maya's voice rose in silence, becoming bitchy, tough. "There's no more discussion," she kept repeating. "Absolutely nothing more to be said."

To Louise she confided, "I just can't stand it when a man becomes like an occupying power."

To appease her, Andre took her on a weekend trip to Maine. The distances travelled might delay and soften the impact of her nerves. In the great forests she was silent; she said the forest spoke to her. The cool darkness delighted Andre; he took to the woods as Maya did the beach. She chased the "happy end" of her suns, he his doubtful midnights. The only problem was he had let Louise come along too. Another concession. But he knew it made Maya happy. Also, it saved him from being totally alone with her.

Her face terrified him; in her eyes he saw the knowledge that they had broken all the laws. Also, the hubbub of her outrages and insults, the mental tohubuhu she at times seemed to return to…. Andre tried to flee that hysteria by reaching new roots into the body below. Every day, magnificently, triumphantly, he demonstrated his manhood to her. But in doing so, had he also lost himself? He knew now, more than ever, that the physical contact they had shared, the bridges they had thrown from one to the other across whatever chasm was separating them, could collapse at any moment.

It was chilly that evening in Maine. Andre huddled for warmth in the little white room where he had set up his worktable, lighting one cigarette after another. What a fool he had been to think that a promise lurked somewhere in Maya's taut, sensual energies. He had taken her perpetually renewed desires as a sign that nothing in their relationship was ever destroyed. He lacked the patience to learn this game of perpetual beginnings. What could he do now to keep the life he had lived with Maya from becoming an illusion? He had permitted himself the luxury of thinking he could settle and establish a life with her. He was sure he had found a permanent place to be. But it was quickly becoming apparent that he had hoped for too much. The boom would soon be lowered. The guillotine of another love that hadn't worked out would come crashing down on his neck.

He thought that, like a donkey, man carries his wretchedly small cargo of love, which here and there, he unloads at the feet of certain magnetic women. Soon the day comes when he has to pack everything up and begin the long journey again.

Taking his clothes off, Andre shivered apprehensively. His body was throbbing like electric guitar strings with the pain Maya had given him. How could a woman be allowed to create such suffering? What gave her permission to act with such sudden impetuosity and abruptness? How, from being so soft, had she been able to become, without any warning, so tough?

All these questions demanded answers that he couldn't give. Nor could he cry, because this was the fate he had chosen. After all, he could have been with his ex-wife in New York. She had once written him bunches of letters, telling him in detail how much she loved him and how she was still waiting for him to come back. Now several months had passed since he had heard from her.

Chapter V

Long, narrow bands of light broke over the beach where Robert walked alone trying to separate his fate from the people in whose hands that fate was involved. Carolina, first of all, and Ben, who had been like a father to him, and then perhaps Maya, with whom he had shared a spark he couldn't forget. Mussels lay blindly in the sand. The sky was bare, pure. At this early hour the sea had yet no color to it. Everything was empty.

Unable to sleep, Robert had slipped away from Ben's house, from Carolina asleep in the bed next to him, and had come down to the beach to think, alone with the dark jumble of his desires. Water slopped lazily on the shore over the edges of the sea bowl. Slowly things stirred as they moved up toward the light that soon would become clear and intolerably dazzling. Robert wished he shared the same fate as the dawn - that somehow he could converge toward color, shape, clarity. If only he could erase the war memories!

Out of the milky white summer mists that still hadn't vanished, a figure emerged running toward him: an athletic young man in a grey football jersey. Upon his shirt was the number sixty-nine. Things were what they were. The foggy distances down the beach soon swallowed up the solitary, stocky figure with the driving legs. A strange brief encounter, almost surrealistic in its simplicity. No sound but the unfailing whoosh of the waves. The world seemed visible, legible. Behind its signs nothing else was to be read. What was, was. Absolutely. Carolina would have loved that.

In this emptiness, this beautiful return of things to themselves, the sand was modulated, finely textured. It was as if someone had carefully attuned it to the exact vibrations of that morning. Although the sun had hardly risen, the air had an unusual calmness and fullness to it. The surf lapped. Carolina would have been happy here, he thought. She would have felt at "home."

Robert walked down the beach with Ben's golden retriever, Bruno. On the wet sand, Bruno ran, sported, and cavorted. He was a golden retriever puppy. His tail erect and quivering, he dashed down the beach, sniffing out shells and seaweed, overturning with his teeth the carcasses of crabs. Robert envied him his springing vitality, the naturalness of his desires and the harmony he had with them. Sometimes he would pick something up, a piece of driftwood, and bring it back to Robert, strutting, his nose in the air, joyous and proud of what he had found.

Robert kept moving --- it was the only way he could keep in sync with his own thoughts. Wasn't that one of Carolina's complaints, that she could never make her body go as fast as her head? Bruno the Magnificent, as Robert called him, jumped up and down and nipped at his hands, yapping as he ran round his legs like crazy. His nose felt cool and wet and sandy when he thrust it up into Robert's hands.

Robert looked at the rocks, wondering how all this life rose up. There were layers and layers of sand, sediment, and colors. All this sand was interleaved, interwoven, with other forms of life. That life moved microscopically around him in small hints, refinements, and nuances. How could he get close, get more into it than he was?

The Atlantic was awakening too, becoming noisier, rougher. It was not snarling yet, but it had a sort of fresh, glittering clarity. It growled and barked and bit at the shore and took joy in the simple expression of itself the same way Bruno did.

Robert thought: last night in the Sag Harbor clam bar, I met and sparked with a woman who for the first time gave me a sense, a hint, a clue, of what grandeur, majesty and plenitude could be. I must not miss this chance to live! To bring myself through her to the point where I resemble myself, to free myself through fulfillment. To the degree that I am a man, I must not lie to myself by letting her elude me.

He looked around him. There was no one. The retriever ran eagerly sniffing, flipping over crabs. The light played up and down the beach, which looked as if someone had hammered it like metal, putting dents and indentations into it. What craftsman but himself at some future date could straighten out, hammer and polish the unwieldy mass of his bulky desires?

His bare feet crunched over the pebbles the tides were forever dragging, smoothing, eroding. Time did that to a man, too. If only Carolina had been capable of giving him even a temporary tranquility. She was always accusing him of being "too anxious," yet she herself was often the cause of the anguish he felt.

Life seemed to grow up around Robert in columns. Their masses spiraled up, becoming thinner as new forms emerged. Light came out of the shadows. He thought of the paths from the old to the new, all the fat that eventually winds itself around the basic thinness. He imagined columns of men moving forth in the night through the darkness. Light. Day. Mixtures of light and darkness. Salt, you are my salt.

Maya had kept him awake. Tired now, Robert moved slowly, with uncertainty. His mind sank back into prenatal darkness, shallow womb times. The more the day defined itself, the more he felt vast, unformed spaces floating inside him. Little animals worked around his heart, urging him on, shaping his instincts. Here he was, all alone with Bruno the Magnificent by the sea, dreaming of Maya the Majestic.

Out of the blank space the sun rose, splendid. A million suns, a million summers. Out of the depths of time, fragments of life surfaced, lived and dreamed. Where did life begin? When did he start? On this bare beach, alone with his clashing desires and the sea that kept on murmuring in order to say nothing, it was simple to sniff eternity. The hard core of will blazed powerfully within Robert, urging him to desire more than what was given. The life of every man, Carolina insisted, centers on the "nowness" of the moment he is living. "I try to think more and more," she said, "that I have always been, that I am of all time." But when, Robert wondered, did the first "now" begin? How much of his "I" belonged to that universal "I"? And what, Carolina had asked, did Robert have to be afraid of if so much of what was, was already a part of him? She had warned him, "Stay clear of things. Don't let them cling to you or accumulate. Be bare."

Just as life had begun slowly that morning, unfolding in nuance after nuance, layer after layer of color surfacing across the sky, so Robert tried to live slowly, moving in slow motion from one state of mind to another, an art in which Carolina was a master. He wanted to go back as far as he could to the sources, and by going back to that point he hoped to go far ahead. He wanted to go out far out, toward the ocean, and also far inland: he hoped to do both. All the tenderness of his past love, of his deep and painful love for Carolina, he wanted to see emerging around him so that he could touch it.

"Let me go back to the abyss, find my true face. Let me spread out and become deep."

What was Carolina to him that perhaps she could be no more? What were the memory traces burned into his brain with which he would forever identify himself?

He shook himself out of his reverie; Bruno licked his hand. Where was the summit where he could live? What love would reveal to him what he was? "Tell me, tell me," an inner voice urged.

The waves, always the same, repeated themselves. Like the song said, "Bring him back, bring him back, to where he once belonged."

He whistled to the dog, which was rooting with his muzzle in the foam. What did the sea taste like in the morning? Salt and spray. The risen sun bit the surf, which rolled to get away.

Bruno trotting ahead as Robert walked back down the sandy, narrow road, past the diagonal parking stripes, to Ben's house. He liked the careless, almost accidental, way in which these access roads led up to the beach. He wondered if his own path would take him somewhere less predictable and more open to chance.

Chapter VI

Carolina was dreaming. A hirsute young man with horns on his head was chasing a naked woman through a field. At first he stumbled over drowsy picnickers who looked up, startled. Eluding him, the woman ran in and out between the bushes like a white rabbit. Imposed upon this, came the sudden image of a terrified rabbit zigzagging wildly to escape a pack of pursuing dogs. As the rabbit ran, its form changed, and slowly she recognized herself.

The geography shifted and she was back in California; California-dreaming, she was lying on a huge white stone that curved gently outward above a pool, her body relaxing, getting farther and farther into a trip not so much toward nature as toward naturalness, ease, calm. How beautiful!

All morning long she had spent climbing over the rocks or wading through the rock pool. Her body, nakedly moving up and down along the rocks, was a flower, was a ribbon, and was simply pale light. At times, seen from above, she must have looked tiny, a flashing shadow, almost effaced against the rocks. The wind rippled lightly. Her body seemed naturally created for inching in and out between the huge, ancient rocks. As she stepped to and fro on the clear, strong layers of stone, it was almost as if they were inviting her to sink into them, become one with them, immobile and illumined She found a space between the monumental rocks where she could escape the sun. From above the water sprang sparklingly down. She lay down, lying sideways on the great warm stone slabs, the contours of her nude body curving outward, merging with a timeless moment.

What was she looking for? She knew in her heart: above all, a great ease with everything and with herself.

How wonderful that morning had been, so much had been done, felt, experienced, yet nothing had been said, nothing had been broken or hurt.

Blindfolded with an American flag, she came out of a Boston subway. In the street before her shone a huge crystal globe. Some people stood in awe before it, others sat; some touched it with their fingertips; others sprawled around it. But for Carolina, approaching the ball became a religious act. She performed it with great slowness and ceremony and precision.

Waiting at Logan Airport, she saw the airplane appear and with a jump she was already on it. Down below she saw lakes swollen to the proportion of gigantic fishes shining. In a moment, she was back on the ground; the plane was approaching, floating down, wings aglitter. It never seemed to land; it just kept coming in, endlessly approaching, wheels lowered.

After an interminable moment, the hatch at last opened and suddenly people were pouring off the plane and going through the lobby to wait for customs inspection. She looked for Robert.

How strange it was to see him again, standing behind the glass panel, gesticulating. He had a duffel bag with the words "Property of U.S.

Army" written on it. How taut, alert and nervous he looked. How happy and warm and soft and full of welcome she felt!

Carolina wanted to glow luminously with her welcome. She wanted to be nothing but welcome and harmony and joy. She wanted more than anything to show how much at home she felt with him, how glad she was of the freedom they knew how to give each other, the grand freedom of being able to go away and come back and find each other again.

"Hello, Sweetie Pie," she cried. She danced around him, singing, "Good morning, Sweetie Pie, good morning, welcome!"

"Good morning," a voice said above her.

She awoke suddenly.

With her eyes, at once large, frank, she looked up at Robert, who was bending over the bed.

She closed her eyes again and murmured, "I was just dreaming… so beautiful. I was back in California, on the rocks by a stream in the country, and then I flew to Boston and was coming out of the subway, someone had put an American flag around my eyes, I took it off, and in front of me was this huge mysterious globe that looked as if it had fallen out of the sky, and then…"

"Hello, my treasure," Robert said.

But she sensed he was far away, must have crept out from her during the night, been on the beach in the morning.

Slowly, she remembered. A week ago, coming from the airport, driving down the rocky, austere coast to Gloucester, where they had found a room in a nice, private house with windows on the sea. It was there that they had spent the first night after his return.

"Good morning, precious. I'm glad you made it," Robert was saying.

The night for her was always a test, a difficulty to be surmounted; her dreams were barriers, obstructions she had to leap over somehow.

"I'm glad you made it too," she said, calmly, trying to figure out who this man was and what she had meant to him. As he looked down upon her, it was as if she were seeing him for the first time.

"Hi, Saucer Eyes," she went on, continuing the game. One of the things she had always loved most about Robert was his fantastically dilated pupils, which were like black olives.

She waited. When he didn't do anything, just stood above her, gazing into her eyes, she said, "Hey, cold fish. Can't you embrace me?"

"Mmm," he went with an ambiguity that seemed calculated. "Mmm."

This didn't satisfy her at all. "What does your 'Mmm' mean?" she asked.

How difficult it was for Robert to respond. How could he possibly repeat to her the intimate conversations he had been having with himself on the beach that morning?

He said nothing but put his arms around Carolina and squeezed.

She had been lying with her long, fluted back, buttocks, pressed against the wall. Now she turned over and lay slightly across him, against his shoulders.

With a deep and tearing sadness he realized that it was too late to learn to love her, as she needed to be loved. He had never been very good at it.

There was a sort of silence. His eyes wandered over the room, at Ben's paintings on the wall, the light-dappled curtains, their bags strewn over the floor.

"What are you thinking of?"

His mind, which had gone off in another direction, jerked itself together. "Nothing."

Aware he was lying; she pushed him for the truth. "What are you thinking about when you think about 'nothing'?"

He didn't answer. She waited and let it go. "You're all sandy. Do you want to take a bath?"

"No."

"I'm going to take a bath, ok?"

This was a change. Carolina had always hated baths. He thought this must be related to her new desire for self-purification.

Carolina got up. She had slept in a white robe. As she moved through the apricot light that streamed in the room, she looked like a deep, fragile phantom that belonged neither to sleep nor to waking life.

As if magically aware of the images she aroused in his mind, she stopped, turned, smiled curiously at him and said, "Life's haunted, like a house. But who cares about the past or the phantoms? We have to live. What counts is the 'now'."

How true! Looking at Carolina, Robert realized that her robe made of her a priestess. She said she slept in the white robe at night because for her, confronting her dreams was a sacred act. During the day, however, she was often dressed in black. Then she looked simple and austere but never solemn. Her natural gaiety and wit shone through the black outfits.

Robert regretted that she never went to bed naked anymore as she had in the old days when they were truly together. That was obviously one of the parts missing from their relationship. At night and in the morning she was always dressed in a long, white robe.

What struck him that particular morning was that she was getting more chaste and pure than he had ever seen her before. It was almost as if she wished to return to some original virgin state. The vibrations that came from her desire for purity and transparency had become so strong that they terrified him. He didn't want to lose her but he didn't know how he could stay.

She was removing her robe, getting ready to step into her bath. "What are you looking at?" she asked him sharply, noticing his hard, piercing regard.

She turned around, half-naked, and faced him. Her pale skin was calm and soft and cool. He saw her as if enveloped in a layer of freshness and whiteness.

"Just you," he said. "Just you."

He lay down on the bed, yawning, hands behind his head, while she stood, absorbed and intense, next to the claw-foot bathtub. He liked the way the light fell across her nudity, reflected off her curved, slender haunches.

Suddenly she ran over to the bed and flung herself upon it, her head with its cascading blonde hair snug against his shoulders. His enthusiasm, aroused by her quick move toward him, didn't last long.

"Please be patient with me, Robbie," she urged. "I've been trying so hard to unlearn everything I've been taught, all the stupid education I've been burdened with since my childhood. It takes time to learn to be child-like again."

"That's obvious," he answered, irritated by the innocence she was trying to achieve.

Yet what had he been doing on the beach that morning if not trying to get back to the original sources? His nostalgia, his inner craving that Carolina couldn't satisfy, was for a "cosmic" woman, a woman spread before and beneath him like the sea, in whom he could cosmically re-unite himself. Whereas in Carolina's quest he sensed something curiously asexual, and he remembered her saying to him, "I think there are very few women who can make love without feeling some sense of shame."

He saw it clearly now, as she took a long bath, in her emphasis on purity, ablutions, being clean in body and mind. He understood it but it went beyond him. He couldn't connect with her feeling. He felt heavy and dark. Upon his back were strapped all these terrible desires, this horrible horde of instincts that Maya had ignited in him, heaped upon him. There, in the old claw-foot bathtub before him, was Carolina doing everything she could to make herself as empty as possible, as free, as clear, as light.

"When I see you like that," he said, "you really remind me of a very young girl."

"It might be better to say free spirit," she answered. "And what's so bad about that?"

Sunday afternoon they went to the beach. He watched Carolina cavort playfully, ballerina-like, on the sand. His head was filled with more serious problems: in a few days they were supposed to be leaving Ben's Sag Harbor house. He had decided he didn't want to leave.

It was difficult to think in the freshness and ardor and warmth of that blueness threaded through the sky at the beach on that mid-July afternoon. They had gotten there late because it had taken Carolina a long time to decide what she wanted to do. She had reclined on the hammock on Ben's lawn, musing and dozing.

"Let's get going," Robert said, but she refused to be hurried.

As he sat by Ben's pool waiting for her, legs dangling in the water, he imagined she was running across the grass; just as he was on the point of catching her, he tripped and fell. When he rose again, she had disappeared.

Now she called him, "Look at those trees. The pattern of the leaves."

A slight wind was blowing, ruffling the bay down below and making the sailboats happy.

She walked up to the edge of the pool and sat beside him.

"The other morning I decided to go on an acid trip. I wanted to confront myself. You know each kind of acid is different. I remember I came over to the window and looked out at those trees. What fantastic shape they had! You see the way they're waving lightly in the wind now? If you look at them long enough, you can even enter into their substance and movements. Well, let me tell you, I've never seen such lovely trees. Incredible! They swirled and danced. They opened up and all these wonderful shapes started coming out of them. It was as if they had been reborn as Indian dancers. Such crazy, fantastic patterns. If you look carefully at the trees now, perhaps you can get a glimpse of what it was like. But you can't recapture the whole thing."

"Ok, I'll look at the trees with you." He turned to observe the incessant, infinite motion of the tossing leaves, on and off of which the sun vibrated, click click, like the shutter of a camera.

Carolina took his hand and said, "If I look at it long enough it becomes a kaleidoscope and all these new forms keep pouring out of the trunk into the sky."

Robert could only think that love was a kaleidoscope, a slight turn and a new pattern appeared. He was looking for that new pattern. He wanted it, needed it, his whole body cried out for it.

"You ready?" she asked. "Let's go."

She threw off her sandals and jumped into his big Buick convertible. They drove to the shore.

She started talking about the days she had passed at the beach as a child, "tower days," as she called them, because they had been so high and splendid. She had the same yearning to go back to the state of her childhood, as he had to get away from it, to forget everything about it.

The waves that lazy July afternoon were long and soft and slow, the sea shone as if it had been polished by the wind, and Carolina said, "That's how I see the world sometimes when I close my eyes, nothing but sparkle stretching into infinity…"

Against the deep, blue sky, gulls chivvied and chattered; the waves churned. Robert watched her bare feet as they pranced playfully over the sand. He was afraid because he sensed that something was about to end. He knew that she wanted to spend what was left of the summer in Vermont with her friends, and that he was going to insist on staying here, seduced by what?

Rising up from the sea, he imagined the slow birth of foam-cupped breasts. Would his desires be his doom?

Thinking of their past and all that they had already shared, he hugged Carolina, so strongly that for a moment she seemed to melt into his hips.

She smiled; her eyes sparkled. "It's wonderful how crazy and childlike we can be."

"Yes, I know," he said. "I wish we could just stay that way."

"Oh please, yes! Just a little bit longer!"

Did she already know it was impossible? Robert wondered. What did they know in their hearts that they could never tell each other?

The long flat expanse of beach stretched before them and looking at it was like remembering diamonds. The sun glinted everywhere. They walked on, hand in hand, alone in the togetherness of their feelings.

"I'm so happy we finally came to the beach," she said. "It's like entering this bare void just filled with light and color."

The day was dying, the light beginning to decline. They walked separately now, she taking fancy, comical steps, pretending to waddle like a sandpiper, dancing up and down. The space widened between them. They were each dancing by themselves now, in separate spaces. They moved a few hundred yards. The last wave of heat came down and they felt it. "I'm hot," Carolina said.

There was hardly any wind, the dunes scarcely rustled. The setting sun shone with the relaxed wisdom of something that has endured for a very long time. Farther away, people lay passively aligned in curious patterns that resembled bodies after a battle. Along the shore, distributed at random, even the pink and white seashells seemed asleep.

They lay in the warm sand and watched the waves. A cloud of silence passed between them. Robert was certain they each were thinking about the events in the clam bar. He sensed that she felt threatened and wanted to protect her. "Don't be afraid," he said.

"Who knows what's going to happen?" she sighed in a tormented way. "I just want to leave. Jump out if necessary."

"You can't just leave," he said stupidly. "You can't jump out of what is."

"The things here are too old. The land is too flat. Just the beach and potato fields. All the artsy people are nice but boring, like members of a big family. I want to keep going. I've got the impression that I've gone beyond, outdistanced so many things. More and more I'm getting to be really alone. Alone as I've never learned how to be."

Her words struck a blow deep in his gut. It was his turn to be afraid for her. But he turned it into a joke and said, "Too bad they don't teach those things, like how to be alone, in school! That's the kind of knowledge that would really come in handy!"

Carolina smiled, her big blue eyes wide-open, a trace of bitter irony on her lips. "Seriously, when are we going? Where are we going? It's been nice here, and Ben's party was lovely, but I feel.... well, like I'm rotting, falling apart inside. I don't care about the summer, all the high ego talk of the artists and writers bores me I really don't like the beach. I just don't want to sit here one day after another and rot. There's too much talk here, too much thought, too much art. I want to go beyond all that and embrace the world in another way, my way --- maybe one day I'll even write my own Kama Sutra."

She laughed, smiling slyly, mischievously.

"In other words," he continued, "what you want are drugs and magic."

"No," she replied sharply, tapping him on the shoulder. "Why do you always have to be so categorical? Can't you be open like me? I just want new and different realms."

She looked at him intently, as if trying to read the answer on his face. In her warm regard he did feel an invitation from her, a "come hither" gesture, a kind of embarkment for Cytherea. It was clear she wanted him to get on her boat, follow her on her trip. She seemed to be promising so many things.

Could he join her in her experience? Or was it all a mirage, another illusion flickering in front of him, out of reach? He looked at her, as if trying to grasp the simultaneous reality of her body and mind. She seemed so fragile and delicate, a golden girl, a fairy-tale dream of a woman, her body attuned to the music of a higher sphere and aquiver with minute vibrations. How could he say no to her beckoning call? How could he say yes?

A few nights before at the clam bar he had encountered a furious, vigorous, coruscating presence, a woman whose name was Maya, who radiated a sense of savage, defiant happiness. How could he deafen himself to this call? What was the right thing to do? As a man, he should know. As a human being, he didn't.

Carolina's clear appeal rang out to him again and he shuddered. She sensed he was troubled and moved closer to him. Her pale body lay over him in the darkening sand, as she caressed his hair with her fingers.

"Look," she whispered in his ear. "See how fantastically supple the sand is, how it adjusts to my movements as I move against you, clinging to whatever shape you desire. That's the way to be, my lion-hearted darling."

Chapter VII

The next day he asked her to come back to the beach with him and watch the sunset and she agreed. Robert felt that time was running out and that he needed to share the maximum of special moments with her that he could. At the same time, like Carolina, he felt exiled in time and space, torn apart. He had this yearning for a great re-integration. How and when it would take place he didn't know. What he did know was that an unknown woman the other night in the clam bar had let the hint drop that it was possible.

When they got to the beach they didn't speak, neither of them willing to risk breaking the silence that hung between them. It had been that way for more than a day now. At best, they made small talk. The larger issues, they were afraid to confront. That morning she had showed him a photo of himself he had sent her from Vietnam. He was standing shirtless, smoking a cigarette, a rifle slung over his shoulders, in front of the door to a straw hut.

Robert lay and looked at the void of the perfect blue sky. Children cried, gulls circled, waves crashed. He tried not to think of anything. He didn't want to say anything.

Carolina came over, kneeled down, and started caressing his shoulders with her soft smooth hands. "Massage, massage," she murmured. "It works wonders."

She worked on him with her hands patiently for a long time as if trying to drive the demons out of his flesh.

The light westerly wind, threaded with dwindling sunlight, rubbed the waters. Was each wave that plashed a sigh of contentment? This day was coming to an end, another day that would never be repeated.

But not even the deftly working, soft hands of Carolina could assuage Robert or calm his nervous tension.

"Listen," she started to say in the tenderest voice, almost in a whisper, "if you think you're so in love with her, make a rendezvous with her by yourself --- you'll see ---."

He really didn't want to talk about it. But now that she had brought up the subject, there was no point holding back.

"Yes," he admitted. "You know I felt something for her, I can't describe it, but ---"

"Do you realize how cruel you were to make a play for her when your own woman was present?" she interrupted. "I was so angry with you I felt like cracking you over the head!"

He knew she was right. He bowed his head, letting some sand trickle through his fingers.

"I'm sorry. I couldn't help myself."

"Tell me what you mean exactly."

"It was stupid. I went crazy."

"But what did you see in her that you like?"

He felt tongue-tied. What could he say? He didn't know how to answer. He hardly knew Maya.

"So, what is it about her that you like?" Carolina insisted. "What is it about her that you even know?"

"Well, I know she's a Ram," he said dumbly. "Her birthday's in April."

"Hah!" she laughed. "Come on, is that the best you can do? Are you trying to copy my style?"

He shrugged. He felt like putting his head in the sand and burying it there.

"I think she's vain," Carolina went on. "She's always twisting and turning, trying to draw attention to herself. Of course that pleases you, of course! Any man likes to see a woman behave the way she does! But it was just terrible the way you were acting with her at the clam bar, chasing her down with your puppy-love eyes! You know, it just wasn't nice. It wasn't the right thing to do. If you want to see her, go out and see her alone!"

"Listen, my dear Carolina," Robert pleaded helplessly. "I wasn't running after her. I wasn't trying to do anything."

"Oh no!" she cried. "Of course not! You're just Mr. Innocent! Why didn't you wait at least until you were alone with her? Why did you have to carry on with myself there, and Ben, and Louise?"

"For sure, I wasn't planning to."

"You can't plan things like that. You ought to know!"

"But I don't know," he answered, rolling over onto his back "I don't know what it is. I don't know if it's anything. I just felt happy and crazy."

"Why? Why? What's she got? You know, nobody even knows where she comes from. They say she's an orphan, born in Berlin."

"She's got flame!" he retorted, at once feeling ashamed for defending her. "There's this inner fire, almost volcanic...."

"Well, I have flame too," Carolina insisted with defiance.

A little too cruelly, Robert answered, "But not like Maya. It leaps out of her, quick, direct, impulsive, like her laughter, something she can't control. It's something that assaults you, really. Once you've felt it, it's difficult to get away from."

"And what do you think it felt like for me? It's very uncomfortable being there in a position like that, with no one to talk to as you carry on. None of the damn evening interested me anyway --- the party, the bar where everyone stuffed themselves with clams, the crowds of local people, and you running after Maya, eloping with her at every possible instant, giving her all your attention!"

"Stop it!" he yelled. "Can't you be kind? Can't you ever give me some liberty?"

"No, I can't! It's just not nice what you did, trying to make love to Maya in front of all the others. At least be a little discreet!"

"You're the one who says the only thing that counts is being spontaneous!" he replied.

"I was just so irritated by what you were doing, the little children's games you were playing, exchanging glances, going gaga-eyed back and forth." Her voice sharpened.

Robert nodded his head. Some children down by the shore were holding hands and dancing round and round in a ring.

"All Maya had to do, or you! was look at my face to know how unhappy I was. You should have known!"

How could Robert tell her what he did not know? Could he put his encounter with Maya down as a caprice, a brief obsession? If he said that to Carolina, would she believe him? He knew she had been very hurt and all he could say now was, "I'm sorry, darling."

She sighed heavily. "I guess I'm just going to have to find someone who thinks I have a flame."

"You do," he affirmed quickly.

"How do you know?" she answered, and left him hanging upon a silence that burned.

Some time passed. Flakes of light dotted the horizon. Balanced just above the waves, the sun flared. People were now streaming off the beach. They got up. Carolina laughed and took his hand. They walked along the shore where the sand was dense and hard-packed.

"Don't worry," she said, with a smile he felt was too cheerful to be true.

She broke into a little song she had made up, "Don't be proud, look at that puffy cloud, it's been here a moment, it's about to go away."

She sang so sweetly, trying to be gay and positive for him, that Robert ached. His "I'm sorry I hurt you, darling," sounded awkward and stupid. An agonizing pain clawed at his mind. How could he make amends to this woman, not only for what had happened but for what was about to happen too? How do you apologize for the future?

"Don't be so proud, look at that cloud, it's been there a moment, it's about to go away," she danced and sang down the beach.

Carolina's words floated out over the sands and faded away in the salt air. Simple as they were, Robert saw a whole philosophy behind them, a complex way of being that represented Carolina so well that something pulled apart inside him.

She was so fragile, evanescent, ephemeral, he thought of her riding on the backs of seagulls, soaring high above the waves. An exquisite pain arose within him, and he wanted to embrace and hold onto her, almost afraid that, similar to a cloud, she would drift away the next instant.

How, he wondered, could he have treated her so badly? How could he have been so ignorant of who she was, her true nature, so as to let himself go as he had with Maya?

In that moment he reached toward Carolina, overcome with a desire to smother her with embraces, to wrap her around him, to hold her, to keep her from falling, from going away.

But at the very instant that, full of tears, he stretched toward her, she proved inaccessible. She swerved aside, bent down with the sure instinct of a gull swooping down upon a fish.

"Here's a flower for you."

Carolina put a wooden flower in his hands. It was a beautiful driftwood flower she had found among some seaweed.

"Look," she offered, "it's a tulip born from the sea."

He held the sea-worn wood in his hands. It felt natural and delicate, full of a secret sense and a labyrinth of meaning.

"The waves must have carved it," she said.

Cool fragility was written into every line of the petals. Carolina laughed. Robert looked at the strange, beautiful wooden flower she had found for him and laughed too.

At the end of the beach some children were building sandcastles. The sun had sunk and the sky was blue-grey and calm and low.

They came to a wire mesh garbage can stuffed with empty soda bottles and popular magazines. She remarked how it was funny to see all the images and mythologies of modern civilization crowded and crushed into that bin on the beach.

They walked back slowly in the broad, empty evening. They were alone now. The waves bursting like grapes covered the wetted shore every few seconds with their foamy wine. Carolina ran ahead of Robert, flapping her arms, pretending she was a seagull.

Suddenly she turned and shouted, "I love you! I don't even know what it means! I must be nuts."

Chapter VIII

Vico woke up and uttered a great, barbaric "Yawp!" He was a piano player, motorcycle rider, professional weirdo, and Andre's best friend. His Italian wife, Benedetta, had a motorcycle too, and they led a very free, open existence. Vico took off whenever he felt like it. He never had any fixed destination in mind. Sometimes he left for a week, sometimes for a month or more.

Maya had met him by chance on the beach one Sunday afternoon. At once he had invited her to hop on the back of his Harley and go to the stock car races with him. With the same childish mixture of enthusiasm and fiery delight she always had on such occasions, Maya leaped on the back of the motorcycle without a second thought.

Stranded on the beach without her, Louise, her self-appointed "guardian", was dismayed. "If you get on that motorcycle," she warned severely, "you're going to have a hemorrhage."

The previous week she had taken Maya into New York City for an abortion. She had tried in vain to talk her out of it. "My own childhood was so horrible, you have no idea," Maya would say. "The thought of bringing another being into this world terrifies me. Please just forget that subject."

Framed by the perpetual sea, her black hair rolled up in neat bobs around her head, Louise had no choice but to watch, desperately flailing her arms, as Vico vroomed the big bike and sand flew up as it rocketed away.

Maya, her bare skin glistening wet in her scanty Ken Scott bikini, a shawl hurriedly flung by Louise over her shoulders, clung to the hips of the lanky, Viking motorcycle man.

Overjoyed by this surprise encounter, Vico whooped, "What a marvelous roll of the dice has brought us together! It's a woman! It's a bird! It's Maya! She comes from the dawn; she's far-out, new, amazing, fantastic! Yeah!"

Maya's laughing voice trailed off in the wind behind them.

Louise stood alone and bewildered on the shore, wondering how Maya could ever be stopped. For her, Maya was the equivalent of the life force, and she loved her for that, as much as she had ever loved anyone. Louise had even told her, "I don't know what I would do if you were not here.'

She had responded, "If I die, I don't care. It has to end somewhere."

That was one freedom, Louise knew, that Maya would never give up: the freedom to die.

The stock car races in Bridgehampton were sold out; it was impossible to get tickets. "C'mon," said Vico, "we'll head through the woods."

He gunned the bike, they swerved off the dirt road in a dust stampede, bouncing over the ruts; leaves and trees flew by.

Branches that snaked out in front of her face tore Maya's shawl from her shoulders. She paid no attention to her bare arms, which were cut and bleeding as they roared out again into the sunlight. Before them, banged-up jalopies zoomed sonorously behind a low green wooden barricade. Maya shrilled, "Fantastic!"

Vico gunned the bike, as Maya, hugging him from behind, screamed with laughter. How she loved his crazy intensity, the whacky way his lanky, loose-limbed body lit up with energy when he leaned forward and became one with the speed and the wind.

Around them the benched galleries were saddled with noisy Sunday afternoon people scrambling and shouting. Everyone was struggling to get his share in this sun-drenched moment of violent happiness and crowd and machine delirium.

"It like going to the moon!" Maya cried, and Vico added how happy he was that they had the best seats in the house and they hadn't had to pay a dime.

The light flashed off the metal of the multi-colored racing cars that seemed about to liquidate themselves through the jolts of speed. The roar of the motors swirling around them resembled a mechanical sea.

Vico, his sunglasses reflecting the scene, stood straddling his bike. Maya hopped off and lit a cigarette.

"Wow," she said, "What a splendid area for these cars to duel themselves to death. It's like a bullfight."

"Incredible," Vico agreed.

Three bikes burning a curve stuttered to a stop in front of them.

"Take a look at those curly hairs," Vico whistled derisively.

Three guys took off their helmets, their matted hair flowing down to their shoulders. Their attention for a moment seemed riveted on some spot just below Maya's bare navel.

The men approached Vico, fists raised to ready position as they came to more serious business. "Scram! You're not allowed to be here!" Out of their pockets they pulled police identity cards.

"What geniuses the pigs are at disguising themselves!" echoed Vico as they beat their way back through the woods.

"What bastards," said Maya. "Do you think they wear wigs? I thought they were coming to ask us for a joint and instead they tell us to turn."

"Yeah, turn, turn, real fast," said Vico.

Excited from their tussle with cops masquerading as freaks, they tore back to the cottage. Maya tossed back her head, surrendering her body to the swift whoosh of their passage in the same way that she offered it to the sun on the beach. Vico grinned so broadly his teeth shone like a row of white tiles.

Louise waited on the road like a nervous mother for Maya's return. As Maya swung herself off the motorcycle, Louise pounced, saying sternly, "Maya, you should never have done that. In your condition! After what you've just gone through! You could have been killed. Look at your arms!"

"It's life; it's just life!" Maya exulted happily. She thought the whole adventure was funny. More than that, she thought it was fantastic. For Louise's benefit, she described in detail the fabulous ride through the forest and the arrival of the curly-headed pigs.

Vico was still standing by his bike, a big silly grin on his long tanned face.

Maya ran up to him and tossed her arms around him. He towered over her. She kissed him.

Louise stood back, her hands clenched, as if waiting to hear the impact of their two unequal but incredible bodies. She didn't know whom she admired or envied more at the moment, Maya in her unconcern for her bleeding arm, or Vico with his easy, casual, reckless freedom.

Andre barreled out of the cottage; he embraced Vico, clapping him on the shoulders. Louise quickly hustled Maya in her ripped shawl up to her bedroom.

That night around a bonfire on the beach, Vico enchanted them all with stories about a healer he had met in Africa, who had introduced him to "bulabula" pills that were supposed to give you visions of the future.

"Great idea!" said Andre. "Why don't we import them into the States, we could make a fortune."

"No, that's not a good idea," cautioned Louise. "What would happen if children took them and were poisoned?"

"Tomorrow you might walk across the street and get killed too," Andre snarled at her.

Evidently, according to Vico, you go to this healer, and he's sitting there with this mirror in front of him and tapping upon it as if it were a typewriter. "His fingers tapping up and down, quickly, like that," said Vico. "That's his way of looking into the future. He tells your future and then looks up and down and says, 'All right, that will be $2.'"

"Of course," Vico went on, "no one really believes in him. They think he's funny. On the other hand, the natives believe bad dreams can make you sick, that certain dreams are a disease."

"Freud thought that too, but he wasn't the first one to draw parallels between the modern psychiatrist and the primitive healer."

Andre thought of Maya and wondered if their love had been nothing but a dream-like disease of their minds that had descended, entered into and haunted their flesh.

Vico got up and did a fire dance around the glowing embers, his limber body silhouetted against a clear night sky full of stars. Maya clapped her hands and cried, "Olé!"

Louise was staring at Vico as if in a trance. Suddenly, in the mist of his weird, silent, rhythmic shadow dance, he turned to her and said with that total frankness which was his way, "Hey, woman, you want to ball?"

Louise couldn't have understood, she hadn't been in the United States long enough to have picked up the slang. Yet through osmosis, or the regards of the others, she must have sensed the meaning because she lowered her head and blushed. While she grimaced and Andre grinned, Vico applied the finishing touch, the coup de grace, with: "You're missing a piece of good meat!"

Before his response had sunk in, before Louise had time to react, he returned to his shaking, bobbing, twisting motion around the fire. Just as in the dances of primitive tribes, it looked as if some divinity had come out of the night skies and literally seized control of his soul. He shook, his head thrown back, and Maya rose and began dancing with him, vibrating to the exact measure of his movements, shaking with him. There was no peace to their dance, nothing but frenzy, delirium and divination. On the shore the waves beat like drums, crashing. Above them the crescent moon maintained its deadly gleam. "It's a cosmic sex symbol," Andre said, looking at Maya.

The beautiful summer, which they had just begun to live, unrolled before them like a song that incessantly demanded to be played. Who could tell how it would end? Andre squatted on the beach, watching the fiery forms of Maya and Vico weave back and forth in front of the flames. He wondered how it was they saw the world, how they thought they could master it through rhythm and dance and love, and yet were so lost within it. In that obscure night, into the fabric of which the crescent moon seemed inserted like a sliver, despite the contempt he felt for her, Andre was almost ready to press himself against Louise and search for warmth in her meager fires.

Andre believed only in what was fragmentary, explosive. Like so many young men of his generation, he didn't believe there was any point in trying to create something durable. He shared a common belief that the future was blocked. There was no exit, no way out. Life was bad, rotten to the core, and would soon collapse whether they did anything or not. Both positive and negative actions were equally superfluous. He had chosen exile. What do you do when you're in exile? You try to amuse yourself, to make the best of a bad deal. But Andre's amusements always verged on the suicidal. He had far too much scorn, irony for himself, to want to live simply for the sake of living. He threw himself into life because life was perishable, he didn't have to worry about anything; it was known in advance that he wouldn't last.

Her hands stabbing the night air, her head thrown back wildly, her magnificent hips gracefully twisting from side to side, Maya looked phantasmagorical. She might have danced through the fire, conquering the flames. She sparkled with images that spun off of her in the darkness; she looked as if she had fragments of gold in her loins, impassioned ingots of heat and fire. How long would she be able to keep moving like this, he wondered, until the clear silver moon froze her?

"Wow, I feel wild! Wild!" shouted Vico, his arms rotating like pinwheels.

Maya kept dancing around him, taunting him, always staying just out of his reach.

It was all too much for Andre. He felt as if he had hornets buzzing in his head. He jumped to his feet, shivered like a dog coming out of water, groaned with jealousy.

Soon the suicidal spasms of his energy had surpassed the movements of the other two. To Louise, they were fading out, blurred on the far corners of the night, moving indistinguishably together. They were momentarily all part of the same thing, the same blind force, the same cosmic impulse that shot through them, making them indestructible.

Maya, Vico and Andre were soon thrashing in the surf foam, their bodies leaping in and out between the curling waves like shark fins. Louise only hoped that Maya didn't catch cold. Louise didn't know how to participate in their frolics. She sat alone, feeling abandoned and mournful, swallowed by a night from which she couldn't separate herself.

Shivering, her smooth skin sparkling, Maya pranced out of the noisy surf. Vico ran around her, romping, playful as a big puppy. Maya flung herself on a towel on the dunes.

Louise came toward her. She felt responsible for Maya's health and wellbeing. She hovered around her until Andre pushed her away.

"You look crucified!" he said, standing above Maya, his hands on his hips, looking down at Maya, who lay on the sand on her back, her arms spread out, as if she were dead.

Maya laughed. "Crucified in the sand by the moon!"

Andre shook his head. Louise just watched.

Suddenly Maya cried out, "Oh! My big friend has stolen my ring!"

A look of horror came over Andre's face. He glanced down at her fingers. The precious sapphire ring he had given her for their marriage was missing.

"Who's your 'big friend'?" he asked accusingly.

"The sea, you idiot!"

Andre barreled back down the beach and plunged into the ocean. Vico chased after him, trying to restrain him. Andre dove into the shallow surf, desperately trying to find what had once united him to Maya.

Maya crawled on her hands and knees over the sand, groping blindly for the lost sapphire ring. Louise dropped to her knees and followed along, groping too.

"It's lost, I'm sure," she sighed.

Not giving up hope, Maya and Andre kept raking their fingers through the sand.

Louise tapped Maya on the shoulder. "Would you like a hot bath?" she whispered. "I'll run you one when we get back to the cottage."

Maya shook her head. "No, no, I've got to keep looking."

An hour later, discouraged, they walked back, Maya between the arms of Andre and Vico, repeating in dismay, "It must have been fate because my big friend swallowed it."

Chapter IX

Vico swung into the kitchen. Louise put a cowboy hat on his head. He grinned and sat down. "I've been having conversations with myself," he said. "I always do that before breakfast."

"Oh, I see," said Maya. "You're trying to figure out how to arrange your day."

"No," Vico answered, friendly and grinning. "The moment you do that you're dead."

Louise poured him coffee.

"I mean, I have conversations that come out of my dreams that continue when I'm waking. I love to awake slowly, watching my mind doing acrobatics with itself. Don't you think that's a fantastic time for acrobatics, early in the morning?"

Maya agreed instantly, with that tremendous burst of enthusiasm she always showed for everything she felt was poetic and fine. But she felt terrible. "What a hangover! Oh my God," she groaned.

Vico wolfed down the omelet with garden herbs Louise had made.

Andre drank black coffee and paced nervously up and down in the back of the kitchen. Last night on the beach with the bonfire had been splendid, but the sapphire ring was lost and this morning he had to face up to that hard reality. Maya had said she was planning to go into New York with Ben. Originally Ben had been planning to leave on Thursday, but after learning Maya was looking for a ride on Monday he changed his plans. Would Maya like a ride that afternoon?

Why had Ben changed his plans so quickly? Andre, whose jealousy made him suspect everyone, sensed that Ben was trying to get Maya for himself. Everything about her suited him completely, Andre realized with horror. Who wouldn't be seduced by Maya's style of life, her naturalness, her great sense of taste and form, and her beauty? Ben really needed someone who could help him recharge his batteries. The fervor that had inspired his early work was simply no longer there.

Louise, playing the part of the secretary, intervened. "Your friend Marthe called. She said she wants to come out to the cottage. Could you possibly pick her up in New York?"

"I read a really hip book last night, man," interrupted Vico. "'Clockwork Orange.' Fantastic slang. Must be invented from the Russian or something. I haven't been able to sleep in three weeks anyway. So I stayed awake and finished it. I didn't know Anthony Burgess had done anything as really good as that. Wow!"

"All that slang in the book," said Andre, "is totally invented, but much of it comes from Russian sources. Maya should know; her mother was a white Russian. Still, it's quite an accomplishment."

To invent language, to create an idiom or an image that has not existed before, what an achievement! If only Andre had been capable of doing something similar in his own life!

"Yet," continued Vico, "the slang in English can be pretty fantastic too. Words like cock and shit. And the use of connectives…" He waved his hand." Also, the way they invent words, not what you'd expect at all. The way the say, 'Darling gorgeous'."

Maya laughed. Andre whispered into her ear, "Just remember, you're my 'darling gorgeous.' And I want to gobble you up whole, eat you alive!!"

"Gobble gobble," Maya murmured. And then: "Oh my poor head!" she sighed as she slumped back against the chair. "Last night was just too much." They had really gone over the brink.

Louise was thinking: she's so delicate, such a sensitive creature, that one drink can destroy her.

"Problem is, when you woke up, you should have taken a lot of fruit juices," Vico told her. "How do you think professional alcoholics keep so sober in the morning? That's how."

"So sorry. I just forgot to take the fruit juices." Maya felt simply terrible. And that afternoon she was supposed to go to New York with Ben.

Then Maya was laughing uncontrollably as she watched Andre and Vico eat liverwurst on bread for breakfast. Louise smiled in her tart, knowing way. Maya covered her sandwich with sweet pickles, for which she had a real passion. When she had been pregnant a few weeks ago, she had devoured dill pickles as if they were peanuts.

Louise was always shouting at her that at the rate she was going, she would soon be pregnant again. The last thing Maya wanted was to bring another human being into the world. Now she was laughing because Vico had neglected to trim away the white rim of fat from the liverwurst.

"Should I cut it away?"

"Yes, yes!"

"No," Vico replied. "Don't you know, everything can be eaten!"

However, as soon as he got the white stuff in his mouth, he was quick to make an unpleasant, wry face. "Oh," he said. "Oh. Guess you're right."

Vico, his rangy shoulders bent over the table, sat cutting the white rim off. He refused to use a knife and doing it with his fingers proved awkward, slow and comical. Maya was still laughing. She tossed her head back. Her tanned, bare shoulders were pressed against the back of the chair. Her head tottered.

"Oh hahahaha!"

The nonchalant way in which Vico ate upset Louise.

"You see, the reason I'm eating this way is that I've lived in India for awhile, where meals are a slow affair," Vico tried to explain.

"Oh, so you have spent some time in India?" Louise asked, interested.

"No, no, I've never been to India in my life," Vico answered, grinning, as he clumsily worked with the liverwurst, picking it up and watching it fall apart in his hands. He stuffed it into his mouth and chewed eagerly. His big, healthy appetite for life annoyed Louise.

And Vico's deliberate slowness, the fact that nothing seemed to bother him, irritated Andre. Yet what really upset him was the fact that Maya was driving into New York City with Ben. Could he trust Ben? Could he trust Vico? Could he trust anyone?

Andre was intelligent enough to realize that the problem lay not with Ben or the others but with himself. For some time things had not been working correctly for him. His body functioned as it should but something was off in his mind. He could not think beyond tomorrow, could not establish plans, or stick to a schedule. His work in the film industry fell far short of his intentions. The enthusiasm he formerly felt, that great marvelous enthusiasm and sense of exaltation that had carried him on its surge for three years with Maya, was dwindling invisibly but relentlessly.

Where was his creative fertility, where his savage explosions? Where was that inner strength that can push a man to renew himself and go forward? Had Maya simply exhausted him? Squeezed him like an orange? He had never felt so lacking and so unsatisfied. Sometimes he saw himself as a lake being gradually dried up by the burning sun.

As a film and theatrical director, Andre turned to ritual and gesture, using their sense of primitivism and innocence to break down language and societal rules as a way to examine the heavy price people pay for leading the lives they lead. Andre knew that sensual happiness could be stolen --- it was like a fire, always calling for another Prometheus --- that the basis of love was its very precariousness.

He had tried to hold on to it too much, tried to guarantee himself against loss. That was what little by little was killing their happiness. Even at the time of their marriage, he had known better, that the very nature of love was its perishable fragility. But with Maya he had discovered something he hadn't found anywhere else, a life so beautiful, rich and deep, it had finally seemed worth living, the game worth the candle. He had taken that chance.

But then he thought there must be a way of getting beyond that chance, of possessing a woman more safely, without fear of loss. He wanted the love he felt the first day for Maya to be perpetuated into the next, somehow to be spared the difficult burden of having to recreate it anew.

How strange to think that happiness with a woman is only really established when that woman is living beneath your roof, when you know where she is, almost what she is doing on a daily basis. Love, which by its essence sought to escape the limitations of the self through the union with another being, began with such a limitation: under the same roof!

How stupid he had been to depend solely upon a woman for the hope and success of his life. Yet it was Maya who had given him the strength to destroy and conquer. He had enjoyed a big success on

Broadway, introducing dangerous nudity on the stage for the first time, giving actors a chance to perform spontaneously. Andre knew his excesses, which at first had enchanted Maya, had finished by frightening her. But it was her own fantastic exuberance that had given birth to Andre, allowed him to become who he was. He had slowly begun to resent her because it was she who had shown him the path. Then, when she turned slightly against him, afraid of his outbursts and inner rage, he felt judged.

He would never forget that day when she had cried out at him, "You bore me! Boring! Boring! And you know what, if you bore me, you bore the world!"

What would happen if he left Maya, if he simply packed up and walked out? She had even urged him to go. When he had looked into her eyes for confirmation, he realized how absolutely difficult it would be for him to ever say goodbye to her, to renounce the life he had made with her. He realized he needed her now more than ever.

It had started out to be a foggy morning but it was clearing up and getting brighter. The clouds were wandering away from the sun.

Vico was still talking: "I went for a walk this morning on the road very early. Everything was covered with a milky mist. I could hardly see anything. It was silent, very beautiful. Living in the city you get so un-used to things like that. It really was terrific. Wow! And you got such soulful fields around you."

"That's why Ben decided to go into the city this afternoon. He's an artist, he couldn't see anything, and he couldn't work."

"But now it's clearing up. Maybe he can work and you don't have to go," Andre suggested.

"Do you think you can get high on aspirin?" Vico suddenly asked. "Pot's in such short supply." Vico said he had smoked all the pot he had with Maya on the motorcycle yesterday. On the back of his helmet Vico had painted the sign, "Be friendly."

"What about bulabula pills?"

"I tried to give Maya three aspirins this morning," said Andre. "But she hid the third aspirin in her hand and would only swallow two."

"Ah, what conditioning!" Vico laughed.

Curious, and always anxious when it became a question of limits, Louise wondered, "Do you think it would hurt you if you took an overdose of aspirin?"

"Baby," Vico answered, "people don't know what aspirin is. Even the people who make it don't know how it works. They don't understand the first thing about it."

Andre went upstairs and came down with a bottle of Bufferin. He handed Maya a pill. She refused to swallow it. She put it in a bowl of milk and let it dissolve and then sipped it on a spoon. Her face grimaced. "Bad taste," she said. "Bad taste."

It amused Louise to watch her. How silly Maya could be! It was all because she hadn't lived in America as a child and didn't know how to do some of those natural American things like taking Bufferin.

"You take aspirin like Vico eats liverwurst," Andre remarked. They all laughed.

"You'll have to excuse me," sighed Maya. "I have to go 'dodo' some more."

Louise had to smile. 'Dodo' was a French expression meaning to take a nap, go to sleep.

Andre's heart leaped forward when he heard Maya's footsteps finally going upstairs. They would have a chance to be together on the bed and talk about her proposed trip into the city.

How Andre hated himself for allowing Maya to turn into a religion. He was a fanatic. But he disliked spying on her, opening her letters, listening in on her conversations. But Maya was like that. She inspired fervor; she aroused devotion. Her friend, Salvador Dali, had said something she liked very much and which she often repeated: "I never see anything in reality which inspires me. I only am inspired by inspiration."

Andre, who detested reality, let himself be inspired by Maya. He was the kind of a man who couldn't live without an "elsewhere." Maya, and the fantastic environment she created around her, had become his necessary "elsewhere."

He followed her upstairs. Maya was simply too tired from their prodigious night at the beach to be angry with Andre. She didn't have the heart to tell him to go away. She let him make quick love to her in his own frenzied way. Then, moaning from her headache, she fell asleep, and Andre wrapped his arms around her fine sleek body and tried to infiltrate himself into her sleep, into her dreams. Coiled haphazardly around each other, merged together by some blind force of love, they dozed like stones.

Ben left for New York City alone.

Chapter X

Andre awoke, his mind still reverberating with the cosmic vibrations of his dreams, his interplanetary skull chase. Next to him Maya, the woman who haunted his head, was still sleeping. Looking at her, half-naked beside him, he felt a little like a robber surveying his booty. What was he, a thief of life and stealer of love? How was it that the night had gripped both of them and then the morning came and showed them how alone they were?

Andre realized now that he would be alone whether they left each other or not. Possession couldn't save him from solitude; he saw how little his "victory" over this woman meant. Nothing could stave off the inevitable disaster of that final rendezvous with himself. Love would not work as a substitute; Andre began to grasp that beyond love there was something else that had to be lived.

Maya woke up at about ten. The morning was wonderful; the light had no time, no space, connected with it. Golden, free, it floated through the delicate shades on the window.

That splendid summer every morning brimmed with possibility. Nothing would surprise them, keep them from laughing, or risk throwing a shadow or stain on their happiness. Even Andre's grief over possibly losing Maya subtly changed into something else and became part of a total luxury of feeling. He was ready to accept the idea that everything that happened outside of him was meant as an interior test. Finally, what did it matter what happened? Or didn't happen? In those summer mornings, at least, it was impossible not to be relaxed, not to feel good...

Maya clearly felt much better. She was back to her real self. Of course it was she! Andre recognized her once again, her exuberance, her joy, her keen sense of life. As he lay propped on the bed looking at her, how stupidly exposed he felt! What was his desire for her worth? Upon what scale could he weigh it? For a miraculous moment he felt carried beyond desire, subsumed into the slow majesty of her mornings, when Maya floated so freely and nothing could touch her, not even he.

He had been afraid she would wake up in one of her moods, regretting everything that had happened the night before, saying bitterly, angrily, "I hate your violence and your kindness, which hardly exists, has never meant anything to me either!"

Each morning for the past few weeks there had been this dilemma: should he pack his suitcase and leave? Or should he risk everything by daring to stay? Was Maya perhaps more attached to him than she thought? Was she no more capable of letting go of a relationship that had made them both "belong" than he? How far could they push each other without breaking all limits and wrecking themselves? No sooner had she come back from her difficult abortion in New York than she had defiantly urged herself upon him and they had made love. What folly! What magnificent delirium!

If Louise felt contempt for him, she certainly had her reasons. It was she who said, "You could have killed Maya!"

Maya had responded, "If I can't sleep with a man when he desires me, then for me life's not worth living!"

There was no murder, blood or destruction in the calm, sunny air of that morning. As if to dispel any doubts, "I'm feeling so much better," Maya said.

Andre was thinking: the battle's over, she's going to give us more time to work things out. Stay of execution.

"That doesn't mean things have changed that much either," Maya added.

She smiled, moved her delicate head with her long flowing hair back and forth on the pillow, changing position. She moved a little closer to him. Was she planning to test his "promises"? He had said he would be "sage"; he would be cool and in control and almost chaste. No more wild giving in to these instincts, no more self-destructive love, no more throwing himself at her as if Maya were a lifeboat destined to carry him out of the tumult and help him defy fate.

Tomorrow he would leave, escape to pursue another destiny --- or he could stay and kill her, use his strong hands to strangle her. The village police would come and arrest him; Louise would be hysterical with fury. He saw the whole scene in his head. "My love," he felt like saying, "you drove me to this; you have made me crazy!"

"Louise, Louise, can you come up?" Maya called.

Andre reached out to touch her, to caress her hair, to make sure she was real. She lay without moving on the pillow and looked up at him as if he were a total stranger.

"Louise!" Maya called again.

Andre knew how Louise spent her mornings, fussing around in the kitchen, waiting for Maya's call that, like an alarm clock, would set her off jangling with joy. Instantly she appeared and Andre was excluded. Whatever intimacy there had been between Maya and him, whatever new promises, went up in smoke. He just wished he could tell Louise to her face how he couldn't stand her.

She skirted evasively around him. He lunged at her, pretending to grab her. Frightened, she scurried a few steps away. "They say you're a lesbian," he sneered under his breath. "I hope it's true --- for your sake! It's better to be something than nothing!"

Like birds their voices rose in a chorus of morning welcome. Louise could hardly contain her excitement. Marthe had just arrived on the early LIRR train and she had a young English boy, Hoppy, in tow. Marthe had been one of Maya's closest friends during a rough period for both of them in New York. Maya told Louise to put Marthe and Hoppy in the guest room on the other side of the cottage, where they were welcome to stay as long as they pleased.

Andre called Vico and together they went to the beach. Andre hoped the ascending sun would blot out his body for a while, efface his nascent anguish.

Marthe and her boyfriend moved into the guest room. They said they didn't know how long they would stay, perhaps until tomorrow, perhaps for the whole summer. The old wood-shingled cottage, built in the early 1800s, was full of women, Maya, Marthe, and Louise.

That afternoon they joined the men on the beach. The sun printed the air with light; the pages of the sea kept turning over and over.

Compared to slender, fiery, fragile Maya, Marthe seemed plump, robust, almost monumental. Like Vico, she lived her life with a total freedom, caring nothing for tomorrow and even less for yesterday. Hoppy and Marthe clowned together; they pretended to crawl on the sand like crabs; they stood on their heads. Something in the ample, abundant presence of Marthe's body reminded Andre of one of Niki de St. Phalle's sculptures of women. Marthe's rich, vibrant laughter, thick as soup, seemed her basic response to life and the things that happened to her.

The most touching thing about her was her devotion to Hoppy, a rather skinny, blond, young man with curly hair. He spoke in a soft, slow voice. He seemed shy, said little, and smiled constantly, as if he knew some joke the others didn't.

Marthe, Maya explained to Louise as they lounged on the shore, had been married to a very established architect, a friend of Ben's, in New York. She had lived in a fine apartment on Gramercy Park and moved about in all the in-circles. She was an intelligent woman, but at times her intelligence failed her, or seemed to have gaps, and in those moments she became absolutely like a child. Although Maya and her friends tried to stop her, Marthe stubbornly ran around having lots of stupid, crazy affairs.

Eventually Marthe left her husband, the architect. They divorced and because she had left him, she lost custody of their child. This was a tremendous blow; Marthe's son was her life and she couldn't stand the thought of being separated from him. "Maybe it finished her," Maya said. "Or, maybe it was that which liberated her."

Marthe had had a breakdown and gone through several stages of despair. More and more, despite her intelligence, she seemed absolutely incapable of taking any responsibility for herself or her life.

Once she had confessed to Maya, "I had this need of going down to the bottom and only then perhaps, I could go up."

But soon it became obvious that neither going down or up meant anything to Marthe anymore. She was beyond that.

Maya was astonished to find out in what miserable, desperate conditions Marthe was living in New York. Although her ex-husband was rich and famous, he gave her absolutely nothing. "That's the price of your playing around," he had told her.

Maya found her in a bottom-of-the-barrel hotel filled with drug addicts and more-than-strange people. Maybe it would have been all right for a man, but it was impossible for a woman. In short, the result of this was that Maya had invited Marthe to come and stay with her in her Wainscott cottage.

Marthe, however, could not so easily give up the habit she had of acting quite impetuously, taking off on impulsive whims à la Vico for long weekends in distant places. Maya would ask her, "Where are you going?"

"We're taking off." And she would be gone.

Maya liked Marthe. She had grown to respect her. "She's the only American woman I know," she confided to Andre, "who has truly freed herself. She has no constraints. No limitations."

"She just likes to screw around," said Andre.

"Yes, she lacks the style of love, which to me is most important," Maya added.

Andre remained suspicious of Marthe. Her sexuality, so apparent on the beach, was too overwhelming, too blatant. As he lay there in the hot sun looking at her, he could imagine her big breasts slowly turning into ice cream cones; it was a short step from there for him to imagine her haunches as gigantic lollipops. Andre wanted either real perversity or genuine innocence, not the in-between ambiguity of Marthe. Carefully he kept away from her.

On the other hand, he liked Hoppy at once. They sat beside each other, smoking joints on a driftwood log. Gradually their minds detached, and they felt themselves beginning to float somewhere between the sand and sky.

The sun glared elaborately. He could hear Maya breathing beside him, her body clothed with light. He looked at her and suddenly was jealous of her navel, one hole he had never been able to penetrate.

"Where'd you learn how to smile like that?" he asked Hoppy, envying him too.

Hoppy shrugged and smiled. His smile had a wry gentleness and he seemed to possess no anger, no hatred, no illusions. He lacked the extravagances of Maya and the boisterous energy of Marthe, who came over and flung her arms around his neck, pulling him backwards and almost choking him.

Before them, white as cheese, a fat man with a balloon belly stood for hours letting the waves caress his toes.

Marthe got up to leave, Hoppy following her. He nodded briefly to Andre, as if to say, "Thanks, man, for the nice moment, but I have to go."

"A beautiful trip!" sang Marthe. Brimming with energy --- as if she could draw the sun's energy directly out of the air --- she skipped down the shore, splashing through the whipped cream surf.

"I really like Hoppy," Andre remarked to no one in particular. "He's tired of everything and anxious for nothing."

"And so what?" Maya retorted. "Frankly, I don't understand what Marthe's doing with him. There's no competitiveness, no aggressiveness in him. Where's the life? The spice? The salt?"

As usual, Andre ended up by giving in and agreeing completely with her. He decided that actually he didn't like Hoppy. How could that cool, relaxed life style compare with the beautiful craziness he and Maya had lived?

Luminous troops of children trotted down the shore. The sun, which wavered back and forth over their heads like a pendulum, didn't stop glittering. This ultimate sign of fire renewed itself on its own combustion throughout the ages, burning in order to burn, being burned in order to burn more. Didn't it reflect the network of sparks and smoldering intentions that circulated between them all?

The sudden buzzing of a caravan of Navy helicopters as they cut the sky in half, disrupted Andre's reverie. Vico commented with his perpetual grin, "God, there are a lot of birds today. The army must be testing their Vietnam pilots. Suppose those noisy things crashed into the waves just as they were breaking…"

Marthe skipped ahead, dunking her head in the sea froth, a bright, happy doughnut of a woman. The cheese-white, fat man locked his arms about his belly like iron bands about a barrel and watched the diamond sun shatter on the curling waves before him.

Flies buzzed around the dark smooth gleam of Maya's bare skin.

Suddenly Vico tugged on Louise's arm. She was as startled by the touch as she was by the abrupt enthusiasm that it ignited inside her. A tiny force like a knot grew tight somewhere between her belly and buttocks.

"Come on, let's go!"

He pulled and she followed. It was too late to squirm away. Besides, she had no desire to.

Louise had spent the last ten years of her life waiting on the platform for some powerful train to arrive and take her away. She had no illusions as to Vico's being that train, but why not enjoy the moment as it presented itself?

As the clouds shifted, the sunlight became diffuse; they ran hopping and jumping over the bodies of bathers who, neither dead nor alive, had simply become sun-sponges. The kids rode the waves, in and out, up and down, as if they had toboggans underneath them.

Vico scrambled up and helped pull her over a rather steep wall of sand. They found themselves in a hidden niche cleared out behind the dunes. As the clouds dispersed, the sun bombed the landscape with light. Vico looked at Louise, enjoying her hesitation and uncertainty. He had decided to give her one of the thrills of her life.

He couldn't exactly throw Louise down in the sand, make her roll over and over; he couldn't give her a tumble but perhaps he could give her a tingle that she would remember. "It's so hot up here," he said. "Even hotter than down there. Why don't we take our clothes off?"

Louise, always happy to receive an order, obeyed instantly. She turned and stripped off her one-piece bathing suit. Let him see my buttocks first, she thought. She would guard her sex, her ultimate favor, to the last. But Vico confronted her immediately with the full force of his ripe, lank manhood.

His flanks lean, pinched in, his body superbly hard and smooth, Vico squatted down next to Louise, who had nothing to hide from him anymore. If they had been dogs, they would have sniffed each other; being man and woman, they sat uneasily, suspiciously, next to each other. Vico hummed; Louise smiled vaguely; she was beside herself with joy. She had never been this close to a man in such a long time! A naked man! What an intimacy, all the more remarkable for its spontaneity! Little fibers of nervous light woke up and stirred inside her. If Maya could only see her now!

Louise felt her libido stirring and tried to conceal her emotion from Vico, who sat immersed in the procedure of rolling a joint. With his shaggy, shoulder-length hair, Louise thought of him as a Viking god. It was men like him who had conquered America, ploughed its fields and fertilized its women, she mused.

Conscious of the impression he was producing on her, Vico stared silently at Louise, knowing how his gaze excited and embarrassed her. It was true he didn't desire Louise --- she was too tart, enclosed too snugly within herself like a nut in its shell, but it stimulated him to be next to her, teasing her nudity, tantalizing her, watching her grimace with a pleasure she wasn't sure she could accept.

Louise didn't budge; a curious smile that wavered between pleasure and distress was fixed on her face. Vico took advantage of the moment to slip one of his huge hands over her thighs. Louise barely cried out. She opened her mouth but nothing came out. She tried not to move, to show that anything had happened to her. She felt she was brave to accept his touch. Vico's hand, just grazing her flesh, burned deep, like an imprint of sun, into her mind.

This beautiful naked immobility might have continued until sunset if it had not been suddenly interrupted by a wild cry, like that of an animal bursting out of its cage. There was an explosion of laughter as Marthe, her surf-wet body sparkling with sun, appeared over the cliff. The sight she saw made her toss her head back; then she peeled off her bikini and flung herself down on the hollowed sand next to Vico. She wrapped her arm around his shoulder, almost provocatively. Vico withdrew his hand so discreetly poised on Louise's thigh.

Louise did not forget about the moment so easily. That night she dreamt of a phantom giant hand floating above her skin and, bubbling like a child, she declared in the morning to Maya, "Guess what? Vico had his hand on my thighs, on my ass! On my bare ass, we were naked, haha! Can you believe it?"

Chapter XI

Robert had not seen his grandmother in five years. Mrs. Mellon lived about thirty miles to the south of Ben in Southampton, in a great, gabled, grey house called "Sunny Hours" that had belonged to one of her late husbands. She was one of those rare people upon whom life, in an excess of caprice, fantasy, or simply an absurd burst of generosity, had bequeathed a great deal. Born at the turn of the twentieth century, Mrs. Mellon could remember riding around Lake Agawam in a horse-drawn carriage. She could recall the vendor who came once a week and sold penny candy from a cart; she could remember the installation of the first pharmacy on South Main Street, the building of the old railroad station, the arrival of the first Ford Model-Ts, all the amazing developments of the century.

Now, at the end of her life, she lived in a blissful, balmy ignorance, safe in a sunny little corner of reality she had made entirely her own. She had made no attempt to understand modern life, to even come close to grasping its complexity, confusion, and chaos. She heard it around her, like the sea -- the ceaseless shuffling and restless turning over, which she could easily hear from her bedroom window on clear nights. And it bothered her, really, no more than the sea.

Mrs. Mellon liked to say to her bridge friends that she was proud of the fact she knew nothing about Picasso, had vaguely heard of Vietnam, and thought that all of China was a little island off the coast of Asia.

She read only the local Southampton paper, mostly the obituaries. One of her sayings was that most people don't know enough to be intelligent but too much to enjoy the benefits of being stupid. She felt that she was one of the few who breathed "clean" air. She allowed a TV in the house for the benefit of the maids. Since the death of Mr. Mellon four years ago, her life had been regulated with the unfailing precision of an atomic clock. In the mornings she gardened (she was known for her rare roses); at eleven-thirty she went to the beach club (the "Southampton Bathing Corporation") where she swam three lengths of the pool. Promptly at one-fifteen her lunch was served on a pink tray in the blue patio. At two-o-clock she either went out or a small group of her friends arrived and they played bridge and canasta for high stakes --- it was not unusual for Mrs. Mellon to win or lose five hundred dollars in an afternoon --- interrupted only by iced tea with mint leaves and a few tiny plates of dainty watercress sandwiches, the crusts cut off, served at four. By five her friends had left, then Mrs. Mellon retired to her room, where she bathed and rested until six, when Lizzie, the Scottish maid who had been with her for twenty loyal years, helped her to dress.

She had dinner, often alone, in the big formal dining room at seven, after which she embroidered for a while, and then returned with her needlework to her bedroom where Lizzie undressed her and drew her bath. Then, lying in bed with her sparrow-like head resting on a rose satin pillow, she would read modern gothic romances (Victoria Holt) until ten, at which time, putting on her black blindfold so as not to be awoken by the early morning light, she turned out the bedside lamp.

"What I give her really high marks for," Robert told Ben, "is her ability to pass time well." She was one of the few women he knew who could stand to be alone for a long time. She had a way of arranging her life so that the passage of time didn't seem to touch her. What was her secret? Was it her life style, or the fact that her last husband had died so suddenly in Florida and left her a widow? Robert didn't know. He hadn't seen her in five years. Many things can change. He hoped she was the same.

Robert hadn't been planning to see her. Of course he was aware that sooner or later he would have to come to terms with this easy-going yet despotic lady. He had thought of her often when he was stationed in Vietnam. He knew that he loved her. But as in all love-relationships, absence played a very important role. He had even developed a special name for her. He called her "the Olympian" since she seemed to live in another world that was so apart from and above the ordinary concerns of men.

Mrs. Mellon had had one daughter, his mother, Mary Louise Mellon. He had a picture of her as a golden-haired beautiful debutante just before she was crippled by a severe case of infantile paralysis. She never recovered the use of her legs. This sickness, from which she nearly died (she had been treated in an "iron lung"), had put a crown around her daughter's head, an exquisite, intangible radiance which, at a society party toasting her honor in New York on the event of World War II, had attracted the eye of a young naval lieutenant. While he awaited his Pacific orders, they spent their honeymoon in Warm Springs, Georgia, where his mother became friendly with the future president of the United States, Franklin D. Roosevelt.

Robert never knew his father. The destroyer he had been commissioned on was attacked and sunk by kamikaze pilots. A few months later, Mrs. Mellon's polio-stricken daughter died in a New York hospital shortly after giving birth to Robert. His grandmother told him that he had come screaming into the world attached to a body that weighed seven pounds and ten ounces.

Mrs. Mellon rarely spoke about her daughter now, nor even about her own father, a strange brilliant man who had once owned major chunks of Manhattan real estate, but had died in bankruptcy. Whatever she had lost, she projected onto Robert, whom she at once took fiercely in hand. She liked to say she had lost so much she couldn't cry any more, she was all "cried out." But she was determined to take control of her grandson.

Until the age of ten he was helplessly at the mercy of this rich woman whom, he stubbornly insisted, would never mean anything to him, as she was not the "real thing." It was true; she tried as hard as she could to turn him into the image of what she had lost. Once, on his eighth birthday, she had dressed him in skirts, then stood before him admiring, saying, "It's incredible how much you look like your mother!"

Robert stiffened with pride and retreated into himself. The fight wasn't over: Mrs. Mellon's Scottish maids, knowing how it pleased their employer, continued their efforts to disguise him, to dress him up in feminine costumes as much as they could. One day Robert simply revolted and crawled under his bed like a dog where they couldn't reach him. He and lay there on the floor, helpless and writhing, sobbing furiously, and resolved with that brutal and fixed determination of which only children are capable, never to be had by a woman again, never to let himself go to any of their caprices. Nevertheless women were to taunt and tempt him for the rest of his life.

Is it possible for a man who has no mother, who has never known a mother, not to launch on a search to find her, and by extension, himself? Was this what made him so obsessed with a quest for personal sources from such an early age? Robert considered the pathetic and touching tendency he had to view all women as connections to his identity. He imagined lifting their mysterious veils to reveal a sudden and splendid reflection of the original face he had lost so many years ago. For Robert, a host of magical sensations accompanied the very word "woman" and love acquired the mystical quality of a force capable of leading him on transcendent, illumined breakthroughs. Men dreamed of and did go to the moon; Robert was romantic enough to think love could take him just as far, spinning him off into some world of divine, cosmic purpose. Love would be the key that would help him to resolve the enigma of desire.

Curiously, Robert never experienced the same reactions toward his father. The face of that man, blown to bits by an exploding Japanese plane, rarely came back to haunt his head at night and make him wonder what he was. In the universe where he grew up, surrounded by his grandmother and her bevy of crisp black-and white uniformed Scottish maids, men didn't count for much. His grandmother married three times, survived all her husbands, and grew rich on her inheritances. Man was an accident at worst, at best a tool to be used and exploited.

All the attention, love and care Mrs. Mellon gave--- had hoped to give--- to her paralyzed daughter was interrupted by her death, and was diverted toward Robert. What a struggle it had been to avoid succumbing to those sugary caresses, that prodigious, if misplaced, honey love! Some kids might have been permanently crippled, ruined for life. Looking back, Robert often wondered if his mother's own paralysis had not finally, in some obscure way, been a physical expression of this same mental reality?

Do not get paralyzed! Like a tension wire running through his mind, this guiding thought sustained Robert throughout many dark days. He made it a goal to stand upright and resist victimization by nannies and maids who tried to master him. Finally, he must depend on no one but himself. Whereas Mrs. Mellon acted out her love for him through her lost daughter, he would rely on himself, for himself alone. His grandmother always sent her help as ambassadors of love to that foreign country called Robert, that strange, nervous, high-strung boy who refused to call her "Grandma" but always Mrs. Mellon.

In this struggle against the love she imposed upon him and his fight to escape the daughter image she wished him to resemble, Robert became what he was - his love of solitude, that need for independence, for freedom at all costs, every trait that characterized him later on. He learned to battle the phantoms of his family, the servile yet terrifying presence of the maids, the awesome presence of Mrs. Mellon who, like a hidden goddess, pulled the strings that made the others, marionettes, move.

In fighting all of this Robert discovered himself, discovered all that he could be and everything he wasn't. He discovered too, that life had to be made and the moment you stop making it, you become the victim of what others said you were or wanted you to be.

One of the reasons he had gone to wage war in the jungles of Vietnam was to escape the sweet but sticky claws of Mrs. Mellon.

He had fought, he had been lucky enough to survive, and now he was back.

Friends marveled at his background - the bold steps he had taken, all that he had dared. "To think that you came from that ---!"

Robert liked to think that his past meant absolutely nothing to him. He had been born with it. It had happened. That was all. It wasn't worth more than that. He had escaped it as soon as he could. He had taken his walking papers and hadn't come back. Like so many children, Robert had had the simple dream that he had fallen down in a basket tied to a cloud from the moon. Lacking a real mother, he sought a mythological, mysterious one. Why not the moon? Certainly not Mrs. Mellon.

It would have been dangerous to return before he knew exactly who he was, before he was formed. Vietnam and his travels had done that for him. He took far too much pride in his independence, his self-createdness, and his lack of attachments, to want to risk being claimed by Mrs. Mellon as something belonging to her. Even Carolina --- they had found each other, had helped to make each other --- was basically another way of remaining unattached. Carolina and he insisted so much on their personal freedom that it was very difficult to say what bonds existed between them. Ben was not the only one to have remarked that the complicity between them seemed, at times, almost incestuous.

Chapter XII

"When are we leaving Ben's?" Carolina wanted to know. "The summer's almost half-over."

"I can't leave until I've seen my grandmother," Robert would answer.

"Well, what's stopping you? Just do it."

Why couldn't he bridge the gap and drive the fifteen miles that separated him from his grandmother's house in Southampton?

There was no reason to feel bitterness or blame anymore. He knew the time had come for him to go see Mrs. Mellon, to reconcile himself with his past. For a long time he thought there was something fixed, immutable, almost eternal about her life. Now it scared him to think that she might die tomorrow and he would never see her again, never have the chance to try to make his peace with her.

He worried he was condemned to treat Carolina in the same way he had been treated, perhaps the same fatal pattern was destined to work itself out in all his future relationships.

How often Carolina had accused him of blocking her development, limiting her movements, tripping her up! It was the same reproach he had cast at Mrs. Mellon with such furious rage, long ago. Wasn't there some way of escaping this dreadful psychic scenario? If he confronted his past, if he went to see Mrs. Mellon and everything he feared from her turned out to be nothing but a scarecrow, then he would be released, free.

The desire to see his grandmother pressured his mind. Meeting Mrs. Mellon might bring him a step closer to that lost face he had been searching for. Could she tell him something that would spare him many painful detours?

How had Carolina put it? "Grow quickly, travel rapidly, and don't get stuck. That's the only thing that counts." Robert wondered if he could obey that exigency. Or did life slowly come with its quicksand and catch the feet of even the swiftest of men?

"Just because your grandmother could never accept who you are or how you live is no reason to feel guilty about it," Ben had said.

Robert hoped that perhaps enough had happened that he and Mrs. Mellon might be able to accept each other.

Meanwhile Carolina kept pressuring him to leave Ben's house with her and return to Vermont.

"What are we waiting for?" she asked impulsively. "And what are you dragging around here for? What do you possibly expect to find?"

He shook his head, afraid to tell her the answer he felt in his heart.

"The land's too flat around here," she declared. "It bores me. I need mountains to be happy."

He came close and tried to hug her.

"I feel like I'm just rotting," she sighed. "That I'm not going anyplace, and we're just wasting our time here in the Hamptons in this stupid, stagnant summer."

"You can rot anywhere," he reminded her.

"True. But there's too much money here. It's too rich."

How could he explain to her all the reasons that were pushing him to stay, forcing him to linger, when he could hardly explain them to himself? It was almost as if he had embarked on some secret mission and the purpose of that mission was precisely to find out what it was. To leave now would be to learn nothing; he would be doomed to being exactly what he was with Carolina and no more. If his relationship with her had been fuller, if there had been some kind of a sensual plenitude, then perhaps… But the freedom he had with her, and from her, bored and exasperated him. He was tired of their discordances, asymmetries, of their jagged edges. Something else had to happen. A shadow would step out of the corners and reveal itself. A promise lurked in the air, a happiness vibrated that had to be seized.

"You can stay here as long as you want," Ben had told him. "I like your company. Your girlfriend makes me feel so alive."

Robert knew he could just hang out, linger; perhaps nothing would happen. There was no guarantee. He had no definite goal. As Carolina said, the risk was to rot. Maybe his exaggerated desires deceived him. Or the bursting sun of that young summer made him drunk, made him see mirages. But he had to give himself a chance. He couldn't cheat himself by cutting short on an experience that seemed to promise so much.

Probably he would never be able to explain it to Carolina; she would die not ever knowing what had happened to him. It wasn't just the emotional backwash of his war experiences in Vietnam. But it would be ridiculous to tell her that he suddenly found himself in the presence of "magnetized forces. Abruptly, for no reason he could see, life had been "charged." Positive or negative, life or death? It was too early to say.

He felt he was playing out his life here, that something of the utmost importance was about to occur. Two or three times in your life perhaps --- if you are lucky --- you reach a point where you can switch the tracks you've been running on, when a vital change, a new direction, can take place. Robert felt they had accidentally stumbled into a zone of metamorphosis and it was important to stay and give the change time to work. Whatever happened, he was sure they would not depart from Ben's the same people they had been when they arrived.

Carolina too, suspected that something fatal was in the air for both of them. With that way she had of sniffing out the future, she said, "All my senses tell me so. It's as if there's malaria around here. Do you think your grandmother can really do anything for you? Do you actually think she can help you go forward? What do you want to stay here for? For that woman, Maya? I don't trust her at all. I tell you, I feel death in the air and we should get out of here while we can."

Carolina talked about sibyls, about young virgins who are shut up in caves, about goat's blood and sacrifice and various processes of purification. Like Cassandra, she prophesied doom if they did not leave immediately. Despair came over her when her words failed to arouse an instant reaction in Robert.

"I can't leave until I've seen Mrs. Mellon," he repeated. And it was true. Yet he knew that these words were only a pretext for something he couldn't name.

One night, when they were having dinner again at the clam bar in Sag Harbor, Carolina said bluntly, "Look, if you want to go to bed with Maya, go to bed with her. But don't be the dupe of your desires, the clown of your feelings!"

That angered him so he almost slapped her. Was he the puppet of his own desire? Was he simply intellectualizing an experience that at the bottom was of the simplest? Or was there something else at stake, of a more profound, deeper nature?

This ambiguity itself became a lure, a merciless temptation. It festered in him and he wondered how he could possibly resolve it.

Ben had given them the spare rooms overlooking the garden at the back of the house and told them again they were welcome to stay as long as they wanted. He was busy preparing for a retrospective of his work at a major Madison Avenue gallery in the fall.

Carolina began to do everything she could to provoke disaster and trigger departure. She tried to shame Robert, accusing him of cowardice. "You're afraid the moment we leave we'll be out in the street again and you'll be wandering around, a wounded warrior! Are you dumb enough to think that staying in Ben's house gives you a place, some position?" Her voice, with its ironic, sharp tone, harassed him.

She blamed him for copping out, for seeking an illusory security. Sometimes he broke down in tears as he thought of these desperate efforts she made to defend herself, to pull him toward her, to re-unite what had been broken. He knew she didn't want to lose him, and the fact he could do nothing about it touched him all the more deeply.

He just stood there, repeating stupidly, "I can't go now. I have to live this to the end. I simply have to go as far with it as I can."

He realized, when she answered, that it didn't matter what he said; he could have said anything: one shield, one defense, was as good as another.

Carolina pressed her attack. She did everything she could to overcome his inertia, or whatever had glued him to this one sunny spot. She tried to distract him, "Life is going on in so many directions. Just put your antennae up in the air and feel!"

She always wanted to see and feel more. He knew it bothered her that her senses were less acute than those of any animal.

Then she spoke to him frankly, "If you think waiting around here is going to win you anything, you're wrong, you fool! Maya will never go to bed with you, not Maya, not with me here, not with Andre around, not in such a situation. Are you ignorant enough to think that night at the clam bar really meant anything? Of course not! She was just testing you, playing with you. If you really want to have her you've got---" she stopped in mid-phrase. "Besides, I think she's afraid of me. I spoke to her very sharply the last time I saw her."

"It's not Maya," Robert heard himself saying. "It's really Mrs. Mellon. She's living so close by and I haven't seen her since I shipped to 'Nam and ---"

"Haha!" she interrupted. "Some four years go by and you hardly speak about her and now she pops up - this big thing in your head. I can't seem to figure it out. One of the reasons I fell in love with you, you idiot, is that you're one of the few people I've met who seemed totally free of family influences. Do you realize what a terribly important thing that was for you? You never had a family, never knew your mother or father - do you even realize what a fantastic chance that gave you to be free?"

"Or the slave of everything I didn't have," Robert murmured drily.

She tried another tactic. "You know, when certain animals are surprised or frightened by something they stop dead and don't move. You are being like that - either that or you're just playing dead like a dog. God only knows why."

"There's no play here, Carolina. I'm serious. I didn't know it when we came here, but I know now I can't go away from here until I've settled all the accounts I have to settle."

"What accounts?" she asked. "And since when did you become an accountant?"

"I can't explain it," he shrugged. "You're either with me or you're not."

Carolina embraced him with a sudden violence that was unusual for her. "Oh my darling, all the freedom I can give you, I want to give you now."

Her kindness disconcerted him. He would have preferred to fight. When she became soft, something viscous and sticky appeared in her softness, like a mixture of honey and glue. A blonde, fragile figure, she clung to him, embraced him. He felt that she was sticking to him with her sweetness, her incredible desire to give him everything she had, more perhaps than she had.

He smiled sadly, held her, and stroked her head, her long flaxen tresses.

She pulled back and said, "You stroke me exactly as if I were your cat or your dog."

He didn't know what to answer. There was nothing he could tell her that would save her or him. He felt powerless to alter what was happening. The dice had been thrown. It was almost as if they had nothing to do but sit back and await the results.

Maybe Carolina was right: he was afraid of leaving Ben's. Ben was famous; he had a spacious, superb house, with a constant flow of interesting people. Ben liked Robert and was perhaps, secretly in love with Carolina. He wanted them there too, didn't want them to leave. In the years before the war, and even in the jungles of Vietnam, time had meant nothing to Robert and he had lived without any special regard for the day or the season. Somehow this particular summer had enchanted him with its images of luxury, ease, and freedom.

It's true he could have told Carolina, "I just want to do nothing, to learn how to do nothing," and she would have agreed, smiled and been pleased.

Robert felt at home at Ben's. He liked the casual artistic atmosphere, the clever people that came and went, the late nighttime talks he had with Ben about art and life. He didn't want to be flipped back into the street like a fish, promised to a succession of long car rides and one night stops in cheap motels, and finally some cabin on top of a mountain in Vermont.

"I'd love to be a gypsy," Carolina said as they sat on Ben's screened-in porch one early August evening. "I could live in a tent. I wouldn't care," she said gaily.

"You're right," Ben said, "I often think of getting rid of this big house. I'd love to be like Cezanne, take a notebook and my pencils and crayons and go right into nature. Maybe live in one of Bucky Fuller's geodesic domes."

"Wow, that's it!" said Carolina. "A tent is best - no materials, no possessions, not weighed down by anything. That's my idea of living free."

"That's for sure," Robert said ironically. "A tent will solve all the problems."

So their time was prolonged. The summer stretched out lazily before them. The brilliant blue sky droned. Carolina did her best to make herself an accomplice of Robert's waiting. Robert tried not to think of Maya and assured Carolina that they would leave after he had had his meeting with Mrs. Mellon.

"When would that be?" she wanted to know.

"Maybe tomorrow," he said.

Chapter XIII

Ben was the "head" of the "family." The real family, he said, should simply be people who try to live together as if they made up one body, as if they were parts endlessly restructured into a shifting wholeness that had no center because the center, at any moment, could be any one of them.

"What a great idea!" Carolina said.

"A real family you choose. A blood family you're born with."

A few afternoons ago Carolina had gotten them all to play tag on Ben's lawn. Suddenly springing at Robert, she had shouted, "You're it! You're what's happening, baby."

"I know that."

"I know you know it. But it doesn't matter how much you know it. It only matters when you begin to live it."

A brutal memory from Vietnam flashed in his mind: his unit had lined up some innocent villagers, women and children, and ordered them to run for their lives. 55mm rounds from his buddies' machine guns had cut those who were too sick, or too weak to run fast, down.

He shook his head in disbelief. Ben tried to cheer him up. "Come on, snap out of it, kiddo. Let's live the moment, like Carolina says. Let's be one big happy family."

Ben had no proper family of his own. His ex-wife, an alcoholic, had fallen asleep with a lit cigarette in her Park Avenue apartment and died of smoke inhalation in the subsequent fire. His one son was locked up in a mental institution. He really had no one. Another reason he wanted to keep Carolina and Robert orbiting close to him as part of his "real family."

As an architect, Ben was known for his sleek, sinuous, weightless buildings. When he was a kid he would draw on anything he could find, even using his fingers to sketch in the air. His drawings were based on floating combinations of strong colors and vibrant curves. "Everything comes from the curves of a woman's body," he liked to say. "I learned that the first time I went to a brothel in Paris after the war. Thighs, hips, breasts, that's where life is!"

He had power, wealth, wit, a studio in New York City, the rambling house on the bay in Sag Harbor, and yet none of that soothed his chronic sense of isolation and loss. Although he always seemed to live with people around him, he was rarely able to escape his inner solitude. It was true, he drank, sometimes as much as a bottle of Johnnie Walker every day, but drinking didn't seem to affect him. If anything, it made him more lucid.

When Carolina on her inner trips, touched the farthest frontiers of herself, she was always surprised to see that Ben was there, that he had kept up with her. Alcohol, instead of dragging him down, made him buoyant, so that he could fly as far and high as she.

When he went in for a check-up, the local doctor told Ben, "Mr. Steinberg, when I take into account how much you say you drink and smoke, it's amazing how good your health is. It's almost an insult."

Ben Steinberg was an artist's artist, a man's man. He had piloted bombers in World War II. He had gotten his start studying art in Paris on the G.I. bill. There, he had met Carolyn, an heiress to a pharmaceutical fortune. Their one son, Max, was autistic. His condition worsened after his mother died in the tragic cigarette fire. Ben often would tell Robert how he hated the "bourgeois" idea of the "ordinary family."

"It's like a disease you catch as a child," he was fond of saying, "that your mother and father infect you with, and from which, most of the time, you never recover."

He said his own mother had been one of those devouring ogres who probably would have been far better off in a circus sideshow. At least that was how Ben saw her. He had never been able to get over the terrible duality of the woman as vampire, as a destructive mother monster, and of woman as pure spirit, as soaring idea, as arching curve, as dancing motion.

Once he confessed to Robert, "If Carolyn became an alcoholic, I think it's because that's what I wanted her to be from the beginning. The moment she started drinking --- and she'd start in the morning --- then of course she wasn't there for me as a woman, and she posed no problem. What a rat I was!"

Ben spent his childhood in Romania, in a little town that had since changed its name and re-baptized itself with the American name Ben had chosen for himself when he first arrived in the country as a young teenager. Despite the honor his natal village had shown him, Ben said he never thought of going back there. He didn't even remember much, he said, except how cold the winters were and as a child always having to put his hands in his pockets. He laughed, thinking that if he hadn't left he probably would have been a peasant there, at best a bricklayer.

Since then Ben had become something else: quite simply, one of the best architects in the world. He built churches in Italy, an art museum in Brazil. He described his working habits to Robert, "I try not to do anything. Finally I get bored and I start amusing myself."

Once at one of his parties a guest was propounding, "In the future nothing will count but the computer and statistics; the individual as we've known him is dead."

Violently, quickly, Ben interrupted, "That doesn't mean we stop living. No alibis."

One of the things that attracted young people to Ben was that he wasn't the dupe of anything, neither of Socialism or Capitalism or any other "ism," not even of Love ("It can be beautiful for a while but the most intense pleasures get dull, and nothing has struck me as more sordid than the way certain couples live together.")

About the United States, his adopted country, Ben readily admitted, "It's pretty bad, but find me a better place."

One afternoon Ben took Robert and Carolina in his jeep into the sand dunes to the north. Cloud shadows covered the dunes. There were thick, heavy odors, and around them the relentless buzzing of insects. They roamed the shore looking for exquisite shells that Carolina joked they could use as earmuffs in winter. By chance they stumbled upon a strange, haunting sculpture: someone had carved the rough forms of a woman out of a driftwood log and then propped two pieces of wood together upon which she was "crucified."

"Looks like she's missing a sex," said Ben, and picking up a handful of seaweed he stuck it on the magic triangle on her grainy, hollow groin. Robert burst out laughing. Nonetheless, that image of the crudely made driftwood woman with the seaweed sex, "crucified" on a deserted beach sunk deeply into his head. He wondered if that woman had at last found something she could believe strongly enough in ---love --- that she had been willing to die for it.

Ben remarked, "Do you know that painting where the lean fasting monk is kneeling before the Cross, praying to Him to deliver him of his evil desires? And suddenly above the Cross, in a cloud before his startled eyes, blossoms this marvelous Venus woman?"

Robert laughed, but Carolina, tagging along behind them, said, "It all goes to show that you have to live your desires if you don't want to be crucified by them."

Thus another idea penetrated them that, like a harsh and savage melody, was to float through their minds for a long time. Expand or expire. Fold in on yourself and die or fling yourself outward and be fulfilled. These were the cruel but basic laws that Robert felt, awkward as school children, they were just beginning to learn.

Another afternoon they went surfing. They weren't very good at it, kept toppling off the boards. Ben said he used to be good at it, but hadn't done it in such a long time. Finally they gave up and just sat on the beach, feeling friendly, as together they watched the surfers trying to catch the cresting, curling waves.

"You know," said Carolina slowly, "it's wrong to think that there are no correspondences between the inner and the outer world. Look at those surfers. Everything makes part of the One. We're all waves, part of the same ocean. I feel we're coming closer and closer together, despite our differences. It really doesn't matter what we think. Basically we all know. And our thoughts, like the light, all come from the same place."

"I've often thought that if people ever saw how much they resemble each other in everything, they would kill themselves," said Ben.

"Of course," Carolina quickly agreed. "Because from the very beginning they teach us how different and unique we are. That's why I dream of being without memory, because without memory you could be anything, could belong to everything."

Robert had to smile. There was Carolina again trying to forget everything she knew or had lived, so that she could become more herself.

Ben just nodded his head sagely. He seemed to understand. Was there anything he didn't understand?

"I knew a man once," he said, "who could forget everything ---"he paused, "except his amnesia."

They laughed; the sky laughed. That afternoon there seemed to be echoes, swift, lovely connections between everything, the sky, the sun, the sea, themselves, the solitary figures of the surfers shooting down the white slippery slopes of the long-distance waves. It was easy to forget the disaster that would soon set them violently against each other. They enjoyed a brief moment of intimate peace, of radiant repose.

One blonde child was trying to bury another. He had him covered in sand up to his shoulders. Other gleeful kids constructed sandcastles that the purring sea kept licking away.

They lay there, and for a moment Robert thought the sun was cooking, stirring them, warming all of their instincts and making them ripe. For what?

Carolina said, "It's fantastic the way the surfers catch the waves. Just at the right moment. Not a moment too late or too soon. Life is such a question of timing! Then they ride it as long as they can until it collapses."

"Or they fall."

"And then it's finished," she said sadly, drawing wistful figures in the sand with her fingers. "They have to go back and look for another wave to carry them some more."

"Es la vida," said Ben.

"Si, si," she sighed.

Ben stroked her silken hair, which he wound out in the sun around his fingers. Robert watched nervously.

"I think I could love you, kid," he teased.

"I think anything can happen at any moment, kid," she answered, tit for tat.

"I'm sure of that. If not, what would life be worth?"

"Why do you always want life to be worth something?" Carolina struck back, vaguely petulant. "Life just is."

"I'm sorry, kiddo," said Ben, without having the air of apologizing for anything. "That ain't enough for me. Otherwise we could just sit here."

"I'd like that. It's peaceful."

"Yeah, peace is nice," said Ben, without conviction. "But too much of it bores me." He got up.

Carolina shrugged. Robert took her hand. He agreed with Ben. He felt there was something he should say to her but he didn't know what it was. He said nothing and stepped away.

"Why does everyone need to be so aggressive?" She wondered out loud.

"So that's your truth for the day, huh?" said Robert, irritated at the distance that had suddenly sprung up between them.

"Yes."

As if disgusted, or anxious to get away from Ben and himself, she picked up her sarong and ran ahead of them back to the Jeep. He ran after her, calling her name, but it was no use. Her sarong fell off her shoulder, he picked it up. Was that all that was left of love, one sarong? It anguished him to think that he had been with her for over three years and still felt as if he didn't know who she was. When she wanted, she could be so simple and lovely. Her innocence stabbed at him and his heart writhed in his own deep, bitter knowledge. He stood on the shore, his hands shaking, watching her walk away.

Behind them trailed slow, languorous voices.

"Mommy, Mommy, I'm not going in the water!"

"Here's a ladybird!"

Some man cracked, "I like 'ladybirds' better than I like Jackie Kennedy."

Chapter XIV

There was nothing pretentious or extravagant about Ben's house in Sag Harbor. Everything in it hit exactly the right note of a refined and superb taste. There were beautifully carved Moroccan chairs and Dogon sculptures he had brought back from frequent visits to Africa. In the entrance hall, over a surrealistic hat rack, he had draped a magnificent six-foot long Indian head dress, which hung suspended, as if waiting for some phantom body as gorgeous as itself to return to it. This prompted Carolina to tell Ben of her search to find a Mescalero Indian guide in Taos, New Mexico.

Ben, teasingly, said, "What kind of a tourist are you if you need a guide to explore your own head?"

"Here, look at this." He held up and offered her a strange vibrating instrument from Nepal. "Shake it gently and you'll see, some strange, very complex, vibrations are released."

Carolina did as she was told. A weird humming arose in the air, quivering in subtly changing nuances.

"Wow, it's like a tuning fork of the soul."

"They must use it in some religious ritual."

Carolina was delighted to have it. She said it set a beautiful series of spiritual correspondences resonating in her. "I won't use it all the time," she declared. "Like about an hour a day. It's like tuning yourself into a certain wave and staying there. In short, prayer."

"Yes, it's guaranteed to put you in touch with the deep vibes in yourself," Ben teased her again.

"Thirty days to psychic success with this hi-fi religious tuner!"

He also gave her a book, which proved a strong influence on her thought at that time: "The Book of the It" by George Groddeck.

Ben had the knack of seeing people's paths, their future directions, before they themselves saw it and, through a hint, a gift, a word, helping them toward it.

Carolina started reading it at once. "It's one of the few books that's really excited me," she told Ben.

"Make of it what you want. I read it a long time ago and I think there's a certain truth there. I mean, I think we do create what happens to us. Whether it's cancer or a love affair, whatever happens is an expression of us. I think we deserve what we get; our fate is ours."

Robert knew that Ben was not denying freedom, simply asserting that man was free to become whatever he was, to realize what was inside him. At the same time, didn't that idea go back to the classic American belief that with force of character and a will to work everything is possible, even the moon? It was true for Ben: more than forty years ago he had arrived on these shores as an immigrant and through his art had forged himself into what he was. Would Robert be able to do the same?

Carolina took "The Book of the It" with her everywhere she went, to the beach, even to parties. Like a dog, it had become her faithful companion.

She tried to explain her thoughts about it to Robert. "I think everyone has this thing in him. It's there, you can feel it, but how can you bring it up, make it part of a total expression of yourself, so that nothing is hidden?"

Carolina wanted to be all surface, completely transparent. Perhaps the image she set before her was that of Ben's weightless buildings: perfect lucidity, balance, proportion, all the parts constantly shaping and re-forming themselves into a wholeness that could never be fully achieved because the weight of it could be felt so equally everywhere. Was Carolina a psychic guerilla? Robert felt they were all trying to come up from the bottom of themselves, to liberate all the hidden energies, to burst into the sunlight.

Robert and Ben shared the same birthday, November 1st, which in France was always celebrated as the Day of the Dead. "You're typical Scorpios," Carolina mocked them, "you're both devious, full of doubts and dark thoughts. Not like me; I'm an Aquarius."

"I think this astrological thing is so much hogwash, doesn't mean a thing," Ben answered. But he added, "I love Scorpios. They're beautiful, passionate and deadly people."

"Beautiful no, passionate perhaps, deadly certainly!" Robert replied, thinking of Andre, who had the wretched, almost grotesque, misfortune to be a double Scorpio.

It was Thursday. Robert sat in Ben's Volvo station wagon watching the trees slip by as if in a parade. On Wednesday, Ben had driven over to a garage in Riverhead, the only one that repaired Volvos. They had put on some new parts but hadn't adjusted them well enough. Now they were driving back to Riverhead to have the repairs repaired.

Ben had the same problem with airports and taking planes as he had with cars. Returning from a recent trip to Italy, where he had a big show in Milan, he had refused to depart with Air France because of the excess baggage fee they insisted on making him pay. "This has never happened to me before in my life," he muttered angrily, ordering the porter to carry his overweight bags over to the Pan Am counter. There, nothing was said about the excess baggage, but the girl told him he needed a vaccination.

For tax purposes Ben had put the Sag Harbor house in his wife's name. They were divorced, and shortly afterward, she died in a tragic fire. Now Ben's son, from whom he was estranged, claimed possession of the house in which he was living. "It's a complicated mess," Ben said. "When I'm working, I forget about it. When I'm not working, it really gets to me."

That morning, driving to Riverhead to fix the broken Volvo, Ben told Robert, "I feel that everything I've done doesn't concern me anymore. My buildings have their own life and what am I? What's left? I feel I have to build myself again but maybe it's too late."

Stunned by this confession, Robert didn't know what to say.

Ben continued, "My work, as you know, made me famous at twenty-five, when I had my first show. Then I went through various stages of myself until, one after another, I abandoned them and finally came to settle on the one I am now. Sooner or later you find a 'self' that works and then you exploit it like a mine until it runs out. And then?"

"And then?" Robert echoed, not knowing what to tell this man who had always found and invented all the answers he needed for himself.

"I just don't want to repeat myself," said Ben. "I think a man should know how to shut up if he has nothing more to say."

"Nothing is more difficult than silence. That's why I fell in love with Carolina. She's teaching me what I'm afraid I could never learn by myself."

The logical outlet for Ben Steinberg might have been to go back into the past, to retreat into time. But he was too smart to do that. What he did was very simple: he isolated himself in his airy, magnificent house in Sag Harbor; from there he could contemplate the bay, the flat marshlands, and think of how it reminded him of Holland, of Rembrandt, of something eternal. He built a solarium for himself and Roman-style baths; he spent his time gardening or playing with his cameras. From time to time he flew to Paris or Florence, or went to Nepal, where he knew the prince, or spent winters in Bali, where he absorbed the great naturalness of a life where people have no name for art but simply say, "We're doing the best we can."

In the summer, in the voluptuous spaces of the spacious white house with the balconies facing the bay, he surrounded himself with his well-populated solitude, with the ease of a life in which he became a god. It was marvelous to see him coming down the road, a splendid Buddha-like smile covering his entire face, stopping to lovingly examine his trees, apple, peach, pear.

The one thing Ben couldn't do, was decide whom he loved more, Carolina or Maya, Robert, or Andre. Beauty, whether it came from a young man or woman, struck Ben with equal force. It was something that he needed, a fluid.

Ben loved them all as if they were his sons and daughters, but as always happens in a family, the focus could change, and now it was Maya who played the prima donna, now Carolina; now it was Robert upon whom Ben's affection fell, now Andre. Ben was the nucleus and they orbited like particles around him.

Trying to be clear, Ben continued to Robert, "There's only one important thing in life and that's to know whether you want to live or die. If you want to live, you live. If you want to die, you die. It's as simple as that. It should be as simple. With me it happens the moment I get up --- what a fantastic moment! In five seconds I know."

There was a time when Ben had not known so well. Moments of excess, of delirium, of extravagant parties. Robert remembered a night when torches surrounded his property, casting their lights far out into the bay. Fake jungle animals had been perched in the trees, where hidden microphones produced real jungle noises. Silver helium balloons floated mysteriously up and down between the trees. The doors of the huge house had been flung open and rich, pulsing music poured out into the night. Boys dressed as medieval pages stood before flickering entrance ways. Clad in leopard skins, beautiful, blonde-haired, young men came prancing barefoot over the grass. There were fantastic travesties: two men disguised as nuns slipped by like shadows, whispering love words into each other's ears as if reciting religious devotions. They sat murmuring to each other all evening long until, at the end, the hands of one slowly began to slip up the thighs of the other. Farther away, a "panther" lady was coiling herself like a vine around the trunk of a tree.

Discreet, infinitely polite, debonair, witty, Ben Steinberg mingled among his guests, but somehow he didn't fit in, wasn't able to join in the carnival atmosphere. Nothing excited him; what he wanted, he no longer knew. He drank and went up to his room shortly after midnight, letting the others amuse themselves until dawn.

Driving to Riverhead with Robert, Ben remembered that night; they teased and joked about it. "I remember," said Ben, "that this guy came up to me and asked if I would like to meet this really wealthy art patron, Mr. X. And I said, very politely, no, I had no desire to meet Mr. X. I much preferred to drink."

"Here's Riverhead," Ben interrupted. "On the way back we'll drive through Southampton. Doesn't your grandmother live there?"

"Yes."

"Are you ever going to see her?"

It was through his grandmother, who had sponsored a charity art auction some years ago, that Robert had met Ben.

"I don't know. I'm thinking about it."

They stopped at the garage. The mechanic had a pet monkey that kept jumping from his shoulders to the gas pumps and back. It was funny to watch. He said it would take an hour to "repair the repairs."

They went to a nearby dinner to get coffee and sat talking.

"In everything I've done, I've always wanted to go to the end. Whether it's drinking, making drawings, making love, or living life, I always had the feeling that I had to go beyond the last possible limit. That's what I did. I had success, and it worked, but now I feel I've come to the end of something, and I don't know how to get myself going again and go beyond. That Carolina of yours really troubles me; I have to tell you. She's got so many different personas, you never know which one you're going to meet. She's so unpredictable, and God does she amuse me with all her clown-like antics."

Robert wondered why Ben was telling him this. What did Ben expect him to do or say?

"You know what Carolina said to me just last night?"

Robert shook his head.

"She told me I would never catch the carrot I was chasing until death ended the chase."

That was true, Robert thought. Ben just kept turning round and round upon himself. It was impossible for him to follow the path of Carolina, to change, to flow.

"I guess I'll just have to keep looking for something," Ben said. "I don't know what it is, maybe I won't even know when I find it. But I can't stop."

"What you should stop," Robert advised his friend, "is all the booze. I mean, last night you went through a whole bottle of Johnny Walker."

"Oh come on now, kid," Ben said scornfully. "That's not very much, is it?"

Robert didn't answer.

"It's so simple," Ben said, as if talking to himself. "If you want something, take it. Or forget it."

"It's that easy?"

"Anything's possible that you can make possible."

"Is that what you did, Ben?" he asked.

"No, hell, when I was a young man I hesitated all the time. Never knew what I wanted or couldn't pay the consequences of it when I did. I was very bourgeois, you know. I still am. I had a wife and there was no playing around. Once I remember I wanted to see this woman desperately. Life or death, you know. The day was difficult, the night more so. What could I do with my crazy craving? Well, I made a rendezvous with this dame for nine in the morning. I would get up at eight-thirty and shave and put on a coat and tie and stand in front of a mirror and primp and get ready to see her. If my wife woke up and asked me what I was doing, I had it all figured out: I'm taking the dog for a walk. She took one look at me and cried out, "You mean, you shave and put on your best suit to take your dog out at nine in the morning!"

Robert burst out laughing. What a farce!

"So you see," finished Ben, "I know. Remember what you do belongs to you. I'm not judging anyone. Either we're all free or, if we're not, what are we talking for, right? But at least have the courage of your desires. Step out and control them, don't lag behind waiting for them to pull you."

"You're telling me all this because of Maya, right?"

"Look, pal, I've chased women too. You think you're hunting her? You're really just pursuing yourself. Anyway, I think I've gotten over that.

You obviously want to get into it. What can I say against it? Even demons can be useful if you know how to make them work for you."

The garage man came out with his pet monkey's arms wrapped around his neck to say the Volvo was ready, the repairs repaired. The air held the familiar gas station smell of spilled oil and burned rubber.

Ben paid, lit a Lucky Strike, and settled himself on the well-worn leather seat. If I had to describe him physically, Robert thought, I'd have to say he's a mixture of John Wayne and Henry Miller. The cigarette that was always on his lips, his authoritative manners, and brusque way of talking, accentuated this. Ben had been like a father figure to him. Robert loved him because he was a man who said exactly what he thought and went to the end in everything he did.

They took the back roads home and soon they entered Southampton and drove down wide lanes past the great estates with their manicured lawns guarded and concealed by clipped boxwood hedges. In one of these lived his grandmother, Mrs. Mellon.

"I see you've got a monkey on your shoulder," remarked Ben, almost casually.

"What?" said Robert, thinking of the monkey at the gas station.

Ben seemed slightly annoyed. "Do I have to spell it out for you? You've got Maya."

Robert evaded the question, which of course, was another way of answering it. Was Ben judging him?

"I don't have anything. Sometimes I think I hardly have Carolina. The 'Book of the It's got her."

"Dead wrong. Nobody has nobody. Your 'It' has probably got you. Do you know what you want?"

"I'm trying to find out," Robert pleaded.

"Do you think summers last forever?

"I'm trying to have the courage to let things happen by themselves. They do, you know."

"Just don't wait too long, or what you want may not be there," Ben warned.

Was Ben trying to free him of the illusions his desires had created by urging him to tackle them?

Robert felt similar to Ben: he had reached a certain level in his life; he had found a "self" that worked, but how could he go beyond?

He didn't know what to say. He felt a dread; something filled him with anxiety yet at the same time a nervous anticipation. As the highway back to Sag Harbor lay before them, so did the rest of the summer stretch ahead, asking to be discovered. Not to do anything, of course, would be another way of doing something, but Ben had urged action. There was no perfect moment, no right time. Carolina, like the surfer, would lie in wait for the wave that would carry her (and that might never come). Ben said you had to make your own "waves."

"Welcome to the crew cut capital of America," he announced.

They were back in Sag Harbor.

Chapter XV

Robert was walking along the shore with Louise. Remember, remember. Walk, taste, smell. Dots in his mind, rectangles of dunes, red snake fences, motion. A kid ran ahead, carrying a kite, jumping with joy. Once Robert had been like that. Before Vietnam, before the mud jungles, before the senseless killing in the villages. It was clear he would be what he had been; and what he was now he had been before. Ben had said, "There's no escape from ourselves." He had added, "Yet no man can live without his 'elsewhere'."

How things remain. Nothing in life is ever ended. Perpetual presence. Over the Atlantic that day a flood of light was suspended like a magic carpet.

There are some people who don't seem to exist by themselves, only by virtue of what they belong to. Louise was of that family. She had left her little fashion shop in Paris and come to America with the old dream of its being the new world.

"I have this feeling that America will solve all my problems," she liked to say.

Robert wasn't so sure. It seemed to him that Louise was drifting around with no clear purpose in the uncharted spaces of her own life. It was true she was charming and kind; she would do anything for you; she would have given her life for Maya. With her short, dark, hair, her compact, curvy figure, she was pretty in a mysterious way.

"I'm thinking maybe this winter I'll go to the Bahamas and open a boutique," she was saying. "Then next summer I'll come back and stay with Maya again."

Louise always put a special spin on her intonation when she said the word "Maya", like a devotee speaking of the object of her adoration.

"What I'm going to do depends on so many things," she sighed. "Right now I'm just sleeping, going to the beach, to the post office, trying to help Maya sort out her life."

"Maya's lucky to have a lady-in-waiting like you."

"Oh, how I would love to go back to the seventeenth century," Louise said.

"And Maya?"

"Oh, she would like to go back even further. She's a thirteenth century girl!"

Robert thought of Carolina who, half-jokingly, had once said she suffered from future nostalgia.

"You know," Louise went on, "Maya really is a medieval lady. She has that gothic character. She soars into the sky like the steeples! She's outside of ordinary time and space but that, I tell you, is the big danger."

What danger was now lurking that he needed to be aware of, Robert wondered? He had come back from 'Nam; he had escaped the horrors of the war. The fantastic exuberance of 1968 was also over. Days of reckoning were ahead, a return to hard realities.

"Look at that woman there, draping herself in a blue and white towel with red stripes. It looks like a flag," Louise remarked.

Robert turned his head away. After what he had seen in Vietnam, he wasn't sure he could look at that flag, at least not right now. Too many of his comrades had been killed.

"Why did you call me this morning?" Louise wanted to know. "Carolina, she doesn't mind?"

"No, she's not the jealous type," Robert said, wishing it were true. When he told her that he was going out for an afternoon walk on the beach with Louise, she had warned him, "Don't get mixed up with Louise and Maya. Andre's made Maya so disgusted with men that she's taking her revenge with Louise and that revenge could last a lifetime."

Robert felt he had no choice but to take his chances. He needed to try to find out from Louise what was really going on with Maya. But Louise was cagey; if she knew something, she wouldn't say it. All Robert could do was smile at her, as she looked at him ambiguously, both of them troubled.

The sea crashed, endlessly breaking its back; opposite, rose the beach grass-dotted dunes. Behind, half-hidden like icebergs, loomed the huge white beach houses that fascinated Louise.

She ran away from the curling surf. "It's too cold for my toes!" she shrieked.

Louise tripped and almost fell. Robert had to reach out and catch her shoulder, steadying her. He could not help but notice the tight, taut curves of her behind.

A dog jogged by them, trotting through the foam. A breeze blew through their hair. The sun was magnificent, calm and cool; the wind seemed to be blowing down from the sun. Robert had a sudden intuition that perhaps Louise really did want to talk to him about Maya. She also was in love with Maya and that pain was deeply inside her, troubling her. She took Robert's hand and they walked along the beach together.

Robert couldn't help but feel that he and Louise were slowly ascending a pyramid that soon would lead to some intolerable climax of life. At the summit, poised at the peak, Maya sat enthroned, gazing down defiantly at them with her wild ardor, her keen, high-strung enthusiasm, that peculiar volatile quality that made it look as if she were going to explode from one moment to the next.

Was it that magic force that now suddenly united Robert and Louise, turned them from friends into accomplices, kept them walking so closely together, their bodies brushing against and bumping into each other? By what strange fate was Robert's hand intertwined in hers?

"It's very funny," Louise began "My relationship with Maya is no longer so clear! We were once so close, you know. Her mother was Russian; my parents were Russian also, did you know that? And I met Maya when she first came to Paris and started working as a model for 'Vogue'."

"Wow, I didn't know you were so close."

"Yes, but now I think it's finished. Maybe because of Andre. He's a real demon of a man! We all live together in that beautiful cottage and no one can relax or be themselves. It's very strange, very bizarre! I don't even feel like I'm a guest there anymore; I'm a stranger! Andre hates me for sure. He knows he's going to lose Maya and that makes him want her all the more for himself. It's nerve-racking. Maya's a very strong woman and Andre can't get away from her. She dominates him completely. Maybe you could handle it. You must be very tough with Maya. She needs someone like that."

"I'm not that tough," Robert said. He thought of the war, of how he had come to hate it, of how passionately he felt that his country should never have become involved in that bloody quagmire.

"When you are with Maya, there's one thing you must always have," Louise told him. "That's a lot of energy. Yes, you must meet her energy with your energy! No doubts, hesitations, or detours! We say in French, she's the kind of woman you have to show your fist to, your blood. No milk! No childish maneuvers! You've got to show her that you've got a heart of tender steel, that you don't give a damn for anything else but her, and that you're not just some other lost guy trying to find a home for his heart!"

"And what about you?" he asked.

"Yes, I want her too. I want her as my friend, as we used to be. Before Andre. Before all the craziness."

Louise had made it clear: Maya was their common goal, the target that absorbed their attentions. For a second Robert doubted that Maya even existed, perhaps she was just another fantasy or fiction in their minds. What did it matter? If they wanted to live so intensely, wasn't one pretext as good as another? Maya became real.

"I'm just so tired of Andre," Louise continued. "He's so destructive. He got her pregnant and because he wanted the baby he said, if you want an abortion, go get it yourself, I'm not going to help. Can you imagine? So I had to take her there."

Robert realized that she couldn't resume her old relationship with Maya until she found a way to get rid of Andre or to replace him with someone to whom she felt much closer. She needed him as much as he needed her. Near them the ocean roared quietly like a slumbering giant. The usual chorus of beach voices floated abstractly around them. "Does anyone need a ride? What time is it?"

"I don't know, honey. You'd have to ask them back there."

"It's almost five o'clock already, Brad."

"Them white things, you see them out there, what are they, birds?"

Birds.... Caressed by gulls, the sea laughed. It was a pleasant afternoon, full of sun and wind. The waves were high and strong and when they crashed they didn't so much crash as chop down with a great bang. Then they quickly flattened out and foam was flung up, wetting their faces. Louise had an unusual face. It was small with sharp angles and her dark eyes gave it an attractive intensity. It was curious that Louise never truly smiled. Her lips came apart and the corners of her mouth turned down, somewhat sourly. Robert thought that kissing her would be a little like putting a lemon on one's tongue.

While the shimmering afternoon light hung over the sea like a stage curtain that could be lifted, revealing something else, Louise began talking to Robert in that intimate tone people use when they are bound by a common cause, telling him all about her troubles with men.

"I get too dependent so quickly," she said, "and then I become enormously possessive! My heart is always creating impossible situations for me."

She looked at Robert and smiled, making him wonder when was the last time she had had a relationship with a man. Was it possible that she was flirting with him now? Was sleeping with Louise the price he would have to pay if he wanted Maya?

Louise confided that, years ago, she had lived with some French gangster in the south of France and more recently, Bert, "the well-known con-man who peddles his jewels to rich ladies in California", had showed up to stay on the condition that Louise "care for him."

"What an imbecile!" Louise exclaimed. "He took me for a nurse. It was pretty disgusting too because he insisted on pulling down his pants and showing me how his thighs were filled with artificial veins. He'd just been operated on. He couldn't walk too well on account of his artificial veins; he needed a cane."

"So what happened?"

"Well, I refused. And Maya showed up and sent him packing."

"I guess that's a good thing," Robert said, wondering if Maya was jealous enough to want Louise for herself.

"My whole life I've been saying 'no' to men," Louise confessed. "Because when I yield, I yield too much. I lose control; I become like a slave."

"Yes, sometimes it's more difficult to give in to desire than to resist it."

The light, ebbing away, clung to the plashing waves as if reluctant to leave. The burning day dwindled. Images of Carolina flashed through Robert's mind, the way she was like a child, spontaneous, innocent and playful. After what he had experienced in the war, it was a welcome relief.

"Maya didn't have much choice when she was young," Louise was saying. "She was thrown into life in such a brutal way it made her renounce all hopes of having a personal life of her own. I don't know if she told you that the Nazis killed her parents. She grew up in an orphanage among strangers. It was so difficult for her that she couldn't even notice herself growing up, to see what she was becoming. Completely guileless, somewhat stupid, she rocketed toward the age of eighteen. It was then that I helped her, gave her a chance to rest, to become herself. But her life has never had much organization or equilibrium to it. She was waiting for someone to come along, someone strong enough to stamp her with meaning, to give her a life, use her capabilities. She thought it was Andre. But it wasn't. He wasn't enough for her; he couldn't control her."

Louise sighed, more out of exasperation than sadness. They turned around and started walking back. Near them, a baby had a tiny blue shovel, which he was churning around in the wet sand. His mother called him. The exodus from the beach began.

"Did it! Touched you last."

"Hey, cut it out."

Their kids in tow, people left slowly, patiently, wobbling a little, a trifle intoxicated by the sun.

"What's your phone number?"

"Can you remember that?"

"Yeah, I'll scratch it in the sand."

"Can you carry the surfboard?"

"I'll meet you down there."

"It's a long walk, boy, you better believe it."

A gold, diaphanous laziness tainted the late afternoon.

Unexpectedly, Louise turned and faced Robert. A queer, difficult smile cut across her features. She was shaking slightly when she said, a few moments later, "I'm so unhappy."

Kicking a striped soccer ball ahead of them, some happy bathers trotted along. Robert put his hand around Louise's bare shoulder. He didn't know what to say. An act was required, a simple gesture.

Did his hand on her shoulder suffice? He wanted to say something meaningful to this thirtyish woman, cramped by life, taunted by promises that were never fulfilled.

"But suffering is hardly new, Louise," he heard himself saying. "What do you think all the revolt is today but an expression of the inner suffering which obsesses everyone?"

His words sounded horrible, pretentious; he was hateful. Yet he knew that if Louise was suffering, it was on account of Andre.

"Revolt!" a grotesque, acid, indignant laugh escaped her. "My family had enough revolt in Russia to last me for a life time. It killed them! If you think anything is going to happen in this country that will make it better than what it already is… The parakeet revolution!" she sneered softly, and then slumped into a silence that shot her quickly back into herself.

Louise squirmed sideways and after a moment, almost resignedly, she repeated, "Every time I've fallen in love with a man I've become his slave, totally and completely. I prefer to be alone, or possibly with another woman, than with a man, who turns me into a slave and makes me helpless."

Robert pained for her but said nothing. He was walking very close to her now, his arm around her waist. Her cute, curvy buttocks suggested a forbidden sensuality. He wondered if she was even aware of it.

It was strange to think that she had no family either. Did any of them have any roots they could trust or count on or love? The answer was no. Like children they were all marked, haunted by what they had missed, the childhoods that had escaped them or to which, like Carolina, they were trying, rather desperately, to return.

"You know, we only have each other," Robert said. "There's nothing behind us, no family, no past. There's just you, me, Ben, Carolina, Maya, Andre. That's why I feel it's so important that we can come together now, that we be well and whole together, like a 'family' at least for this summer, before autumn comes and we all go our different ways."

Yet old desires, stirred to life, as disruptive as ever, were already tearing them apart, and he knew they were falling into disputes and Byzantine intrigues.

A dog barked. Robert could have cried from the sorrow of his awareness. If only the sea with its endless lapping could have lulled their minds!

Robert leaned toward Louise; he felt a sudden ache in his heart, a desire to touch her. If it would help her at all that he touched her, if any of them could have been saved by a simple caress! The long evening sea wash flowed back and forth between them. Upon this lonely beach that dusk was emptying who would ever know what they did or care what happened to them? Robert took Louise in his arms, pressed his throbbing head against her own. It was stupid, but he felt himself leaning toward her lemon lips.

The sea no longer hid within it any radiance. In the darkening light, it was flat, open, calm and revealed; it could be charted like a map.

Louise twisted away, refusing to give herself even to the compassion that was behind his desires. In a second she had recovered her equilibrium, and it was as if nothing had been said or acted upon between them. Did she see that he was hurt? Or did she simply want to help him understand why his clumsy attempt had been thwarted --- as if in another situation she might have been more than willing to accept him --- for she said, "Robbie, you know that I'm forbidden to you because you're reserved for a higher destiny."

It was not a question but a statement, and the way she put it made Robert laugh. Was it true? Was he promised to something that he didn't know yet but that would inevitably happen and become part of his life? What was funny was that he felt that in their long walk on the beach together, Louise had revealed something of her true self. But now, listening to her, he felt mystery surrounded her more than ever.

As if sensing his thoughts, Louise went on, "I live in myself but there's no meaning to my life. I love Maya dearly, but she's so irritable these days. She tells me to shut up, so I retreat back into myself. Sometimes I wish I could just go away, find something that would really interest me, live some great passion. But that's not to be."

Robert knew she didn't expect an answer; besides, there was no answer to be given. Within the last half hour many subtle changes had occurred. The sky was lower, heavier, cooler. The brilliance of the last light had spread out evenly across the western sky. The beach was already filled with shadows and deep, dark indentations.

"Try not to think about the end," Robert said finally. "That's the fatal carrot that's been leading on and killing the donkey for centuries. Besides, there's no future anymore, we're already living the future today. Try to feel the 'today' intensely and forget about tomorrow."

"If I think about what's happening today," Louise said, "I'm finished, dead, done. Because nothing ever happens today. It's just like this beach, empty, empty, where we're wandering."

Ahead on the endless beach, old plains of sand were now turning brown in the slow darkness.

"Oh, I wish you'd tell me what to do, Robbie!" Louise implored. "I'm in such a delicate, difficult situation."

Trying to cheer her up, Robert jumped around here like a dog, going "Woof! Woof!"

Louise was hardly amused. They walked back to their bikes in the parking lot and then left each other, each hoping that by returning to their own darkness they could forget the inscrutable darkness of the other.

That strange afternoon was to prove decisive. Everything of course depended on Maya's reaction to Louise's going out with Robert. Did Louise herself realize that she was being used as a decoy so that Robert could attract Maya? Robert was certainly aware that Louise was employing him as an instrument to dislodge Andre.

The very next day Louise called and laughed and said that Maya was "burning with rage" to think that he had stolen Louise from her! Nothing else was said, but it was clear that if Maya wanted Louise back, she would have to do it through the intermediary of Robert.

Therefore the only real question was: how long could Robert and Louise successfully continue their completely "fake" relationship.

Carolina couldn't believe it, "That Louise is so far out it isn't funny. She's really dull and boring. How can you stand even to talk to her? I thought you wanted to go forward in your life, Robbie. I thought that was the very sense of our being together, that we could each help each other to travel quickly ahead. But now it looks as if you've put your tail between your legs and are beating your way backwards as fast as possible! I'm really disappointed in you!"

Carolina told him that he must be a victim of bad visions, from which he would soon emerge, startled that he had ever let himself be seduced by such "a bad trip."

Meanwhile Robert called Louise faithfully every day, which made Maya furious. "If you're going to continue talking to Robbie, I'm going to forbid you to use the phone!"

In order to have some independence, Louise was forced to rig up a little room between Maya's cottage and Marthe's apartment, where Robert could safely call her. What started out as a "fake" situation began to come true: Robert developed an intense affection for Louise.

Were these no more than summer games, innocent pastimes that autumn would cancel, or were they a breakthrough into a new life, another reality? Was Robert truly promised to a higher destiny?

It didn't seem that way when, a few days after their beach afternoon, Louise called him, "Oh, hello! How are you? It seems like such a long time since I've seen you, Robbie. I send you the fondest kisses. When can we see each other again? I have something very important to tell you. Tomorrow? Perfect."

"Can you borrow Maya's car?"

"Well, perhaps, but ---"

"Then I'll pick you up at two. I'll take you to the village. We'll look at the shops, then the sun, the sea…"

143

"Ok, kisses. But tell me, why didn't you call me yesterday? I was so upset I didn't hear from you. What were you doing?"

"Why do you ask me that?" he wondered. Was she afraid he might have arranged some secret rendezvous with Maya? Had Louise doubled her activities by becoming a spy? In the heart of a luxuriant summer when most people demanded only to relax and to have a holiday from work, it was strange to think of the complex net of sinister forces accumulating around them. He saw them as particles moving in a magnetic field, now attracting, now repulsing each other.

They spent the afternoon together. Before he went to pick her up, Robert had smoked a few joints with Carolina.

"All these intrigues - you, Maya, Louise, it really is ridiculous," Carolina reproached him.

He had to admit she was right. If he wanted Maya so badly, why was he wasting precious time with Louise?

That afternoon, once again there was a vibrant, healthy, apricot sun. A progression of laughing girls, nearly naked, parading down the beach, made Robert's mind sway slightly. Louise bought a pistachio cone from a white ice cream truck.

"That's another one of my problems," she told him. "Gourmandise. I drink a milkshake every day for lunch. I'm absolutely crazy about American milkshakes."

While her tongue flicked lizard-like around the edges, she savored her cone. A boy darted past her, shouting, "Charlie! Charlie! I have a machine gun. Now start running or I'll shoot you. In ten seconds, 1,2,3,4,5,6,7..."

The sun distributed a high, intense, burnished brilliancy as the hot ritual of the beach repeated itself.

"Tell David to come back down here."

If anything, the sky seemed more blue, purer, fresher and warmer than it had been the day before. Each day, in fact, seemed to be leading them higher and higher, toward what explosion, apocalypse, or illumination?

"Stay out with Suzy for awhile. I'm gonna go in."

This was a medley kind of beach with a hurdy-gurdy crowd. It wouldn't have been out of place if an organ had played and a black-tailed monkey jumped up and down on the sand.

"I guess I just don't understand your Carolina," Louise said slowly. "I suppose I dislike her."

"Why do you say that?"

Louise said she thought Carolina had been ruined by her "careless impetuosity and mystical desires."

"Are you telling me I should leave her?" he wanted to know.

"No, I'm not saying that. It's clear that she's so much in love with you. It's really my problem. It's just that I feel I'm not capable of such a great love myself."

Robert had hoped he would hear something about Maya. After all, hadn't Louise lured him to the beach with the promise of telling him "something important"? Yet she didn't mention a word about Maya until they were about to leave. She had kept Robert prisoner all afternoon just so she could have the pleasure of telling him, "What I wanted to share with you was... I finally realized that Maya really loves Andre very much."

Robert couldn't believe it. "But I thought it was settled they were going to separate?"

"I thought so, too," Louise groaned. "Don't think I encouraged her to keep him. But the thought that they're going to leave each other has brought them closer together than ever. Andre spent all last night begging her not to leave him and swearing to her how much he loved her and that he would kill himself if she left."

Robert was stunned. "We have to do something. This calls for a desperate rescue operation." At least now they could intervene. Robert could save the beautiful maiden in distress from the hands of the suicidal egomaniac!

Louise was too sad and depressed to focus on solutions. "Maya has no use for me anymore," she lamented. "When I tell her something, she orders me to be quiet, as if I were stupid. She acts so regally toward me and then to him she's docile as a lamb. What can I do? I feel my presence in that house is completely superfluous."

"What can we both do?" Robert murmured, suddenly gloomy. The hidden hope that had been supporting both of them had now vanished. At that moment, it was as if someone had stuck a needle in the blue bubble of the summer sky and punctured it. The high-tension wire that had been running through him now sparked in vain. He had been caught in the net of his own longing. He had played the game but there was no reason to play the game anymore since the stakes had just been removed.

He and Louise looked at each other dumbly. They both seemed to realize the same thing at the same time: there was no reason for them to be with each other anymore.

The frothy sea panted. The five-o'-clock wind picked up and scattered some sand. A few children flung themselves toward the dunes, and with piercing cries, scrambled away.

"Don't you want to have a last swim, Paul? Come on in, Paul."

Louise looked at him. Her face was stern, heavy, as if sculpted out of rock. Did she feel guilty for egging him on, for having dangled Maya like bait in front of his eyes? No, he was responsible. Whatever happened, he had deserved it.

Louise had nothing to say but "I'm going. Are you coming?"

"No, I want to stay by myself and think for awhile."

They felt disappointed like robbers who, having planned an intricate hold-up, come away empty-handed. There was no need to do anything now. Perhaps as Carolina had been urging him all along, he could now just relax and begin to be.

The peaceful waves sculled over the wet sand, dragging up pebbles. In the indifferent sky, colors faded, leaving a silent blue. Robert watched without curiosity as Louise, walked slowly in the shadow of the chipped, red sand fence, and gradually vanished down the beach. Two young girls, both with pony tails and tight zebra-striped bathing suits, disappeared in the same way. The beach, vortex of distances, drew and sucked them all up.

Chapter XVI

Robert was shocked: Carolina had "mutilated" herself.

It was almost the end of July – the doldrums of mid-summer, when they seemed sunken more deeply than ever in themselves and what was around them. Although nothing definite, decisive, had happened, everything had happened already. Would they have the courage to draw out the implications from what they had started to live, or would they remain fatally incomplete, unachieved? Louise's last conversation had seemed to suggest there was one less issue, another path closed. Yet talks with Ben had made Robert realize that there are no given paths, only the paths that you make.

In a few days the first astronauts were scheduled to land on the moon. Ben exaggerated his pessimism. "I'm afraid this is the end of everything we've known up until now!" On the radio they listened to the psychedelic sounds of the "Jefferson Airplane." In the Big Apple, the film "Easy Rider" had just opened.

Coming back to touch base with Carolina --- they had always been able to come back to each other, find each other --- Robert was astonished to find that she had profited from his absence - his afternoon at the beach with Louise - to go through a surgical operation no less drastic than if she had "lifted" her face: she had amputated her hair, chopped it all off, even cut her eyebrows. At the very moment their love might have been reborn, she had chosen to symbolically kill herself. He had come back to find her and she had already escaped. For shearing off her gorgeous volume of long golden hair, was more than mutilation: wasn't it a way of making herself untouchable?

This concrete act, the cutting of her hair, the fruit of many minute feelings, which refused analysis, bewildered Robert and made him aware of the distances travelled. More, the new nudity of her face, when he first saw it, was numbing. Her bare, austere features left him dumbstruck.

He didn't know what to say.

Carolina smiled at him ironically. "Why do you want to keep me from being myself? This is the way I feel now. Why won't you let me be it?"

Carolina made a slight bow, as if introducing someone on a stage, and said with that faintly sardonic bitterness he had detected before, "Here, darling, here's my new 'me'."

He controlled himself enough to say, "All right, we always said we'd give each other as much freedom as possible. Still…"

"Of course you don't like it. Men have always loved long hair on women. It's something they could grab onto."

"Just to make the point you had to cut your eyebrows too."

"Yes, I want to be bare. This is my new self. Since we're so independent, and you're off on a woman-trip with Maya…"

Robert grimaced, scowled. How could he tell her about his talk with Louise? That nothing had happened and he considered their reality unchanged. By scissoring her hair, he felt she was resigning from her role as a woman, taking her chips off the table, so to speak, and no doubt forcing him to do something that otherwise he might not have done. Her radical action, with no warning, was certain to create responses, ripples. This de facto declaration of independence had changed something between them that, despite their differences, might have remained the same.

Carolina had broken an unstated rule to say in effect, "Look, I've chosen to become like this in order to give you the liberty to go and be like that." What generosity! Yet what terrible scorn! Robert writhed. He reached out, tried to cling to her bare head, but there was nothing to cling to. She had made herself untouchable.

They sat on his screened-in porch. A Django Reinhardt record was playing in the background. Ben was drinking Johnny Walker Black and smoking a cigar. He had not been as surprised as Robert when he saw the "new" Carolina. "I think cutting her hair was a sexual symbol, a vindication for herself. To be honest, I don't think it's as bad for her as you think. It makes her more what she is, brings out the lovely, luminous, childish simplicity of her face, and gives her more power, too."

"But it looks so naked," Robert said. "It frightens me." He remembered how in the villages in Vietnam the soldiers had cut off the beards of the old men.

"She's still your woman," Ben was saying. "She loves you. You know that."

Yes, it was true; he knew that. Carolina had a way of looking at him as if she knew everything about him, as if she could foresee all his future acts. In her regard, too, there was something of a tender, profound understanding. It was as if, from the heights where she dwelled, she looked down upon him, ready to pardon whatever he did, whatever childishness he wished to commit. How could they come any closer to each other than they already were? Yet when she had looked at him with her cropped head, her gaze had burned into him, and he had turned away.

"I don't know if I can deal with it," he admitted to Ben. "When I'm standing in front of her I feel as exposed as if on an X-Ray sheet. There's nothing I can say that can make it good between us again."

"No explanations," said Ben. "There never are."

If his words were now useless, what about his gestures? If he could make love to her once again as they had done so many times! Even if the lovemaking was not as good as before, that might be the simplest way of bridging the distances between them.

"I do love her, you know."

A love so overwhelming he didn't know where it came from took possession of Robert. He wanted to fold this precious, troubled woman delicately and softly in his arms, stroke and caress her until she shone.

"I don't think she's judging you either," said Ben. "No accusations."

"But I can't help thinking that I'm the one who did this to her, who made her so bare, austere, remote, stripped down. If only I could bring her back to how she was!"

The image of Carolina's face defied him, defied their love, whatever had held them together since they had met in his senior year at the summer study program at St. Paul's School. Her radiant features loomed out at him as at night from a tree the yellow eyes of an owl.

Ben got up and poured himself another drink. Half the bottle was already gone.

"Do you want some?"

Robert shook his head. Why should it be like this? He wondered. It was she who had at first urged liberty upon him, almost against his will. It was she who had declared how ridiculous it was to be living in the space age with more or less the same set of emotions that motivated the cave men. It was Carolina who had said that if they wanted to survive, they had to evolve toward new forms of feeling and being together, surpass the old limitations of jealousy and possession, break down the barriers, and eliminate the rotten categories of love that had made man such a prisoner of himself up until now.

Only a week ago, while they were having dinner with Ben and still talking about the crazy night in the clam bar, she had said, "There are several ways in which we can love, in which we can be with other people. Why should we limit ourselves to one of them for a lifetime?"

"Why should we limit ourselves to one of them for a lifetime?" For a long time, these words were to echo in Robert's head. For the moment there was nothing he could do, despite the foolish impulse he had to pick up her cut hair, glue it together, and paste it back onto her.

"It's death to keep certain things," Carolina had warned.

"So you know what I finally did with her hair?" Robert told Ben. "I swept it all up and flushed it down the toilet."

"Good for you. There's no way you can rewind the tape, restore the original condition."

"Remember how she was always saying she wanted to get back to some kind of Garden of Eden innocence?"

By cutting her hair, Robert thought, hadn't she deprived herself of the sensuality that might have made such a return possible?

Louise stopped by a little later to ask something of Ben, and when she saw Carolina, even though there was no special friendship between them, she cried, "Oh, what have you done? You've ruined yourself!"

"That just shows how little that woman understands about me or about anything for that matter," Carolina remarked to Robert when they were alone. "You know what, I feel great. I feel like I'm becoming more and more myself, freer and freer, more and more conscious. Cutting my hair was simply the first step in new, much bigger, directions."

Robert wasn't sure. He knew in his heart that something had dramatically changed. Where it would lead to was anyone's guess.

There was a beautiful sun that afternoon. It wasn't westering at all, just hanging there, whole and clear above the fields and the bay. Lovely long purple flowers were growing up beside the water, and Louise stopped to pick up some for Maya.

"Do you think she'll like these?" she worried. "Perhaps they'll rub her the wrong way and she'll throw them back in my face."

The way Louise held Maya in deferential awe troubled Robert. Don't we attribute to people the emotions we ourselves desire to maintain toward them? Theirs was another master and slave relationships. Robert realized this was exactly what Carolina was trying to get away from. He was ashamed of being so angry with her, of having hesitated to accept her no matter what she became.

They sat out in reclining chairs on Ben's sloping lawn. Closing his eyes --- close your eyes in order to see what you love! --- Robert saw Carolina garbed in her austere white gown, carrying a torch, leading the procession of all of them through the succulent, summer darkness, alive with appetizing mysteries, closer and closer to Oneness.

He remembered the night in New York City - how she had hated it; she said walking on the pavement "jolted her stomach" - after seeing "La Strada" at a movie house on 59th Street. Carolina had completely identified herself with Giuletta Massina. It was true, for she had the same innocent clownishness, the same fugitive and frightfully open soul, brought into relief now, made even more apparent by her cropped hair and eyebrow-less face.

Louise left at last with a bunch of freshly cut flowers, larkspur and Queen Anne's lace, spilling over her arms. "I just hope Maya likes them as much as I do!" She turned to Ben and said, "Right now, I have the most powerful craving for a chocolate strawberry milkshake. Is there, by chance, an ice cream parlor in Sag Harbor?"

The calm sun, which seemed immobile, as if this suspended moment they were living was destined to continue into all time, flooded the bay with silver light that occasional vagabond clouds interrupted. Robert felt empty of energy. From time to time Carolina pulled him over and told him that she loved him. Yet he couldn't accept this love. Its very offering hurt him, wounded him terribly.

It was all becoming so serious. Carolina tried to change the tone. She clowned, "It's a dog's life, ain't it so? I isn't even curious anymore."

She sighed. The afternoon yawned. The light wavered over the quiet bay. They sat looking straight ahead, as if they had blinkers on. It was hard for Robert to look at Carolina. He felt he could see the evidence of what he had done to her clearly written on her bare face.

"Why can't you be happy here?" he asked. "I can't think of a place more comfortable than Ben's."

Carolina kept striving after something else, lyrical yet inaccessible.

"Nothing much to do these days," this pure child of the spirit hummed. "Just sit back in the hammock, look at the changing sky, talk to the birds."

He didn't answer. He was too busy thinking about how her beautiful blonde hair had once tumbled over her shoulders like a waterfall.

"Guess that's what man's problem has always been. What's he gonna do with himself?" Carolina went on musing in her funny way.

"You could go fly a kite on the beach," Robert suggested, hoping the cutting irony in his tone was less than apparent.

With her cropped head it would have been hard for a neutral observer to tell whether she was a man or a woman. Perhaps just a protean spirit.

Although it was warm sitting on the lawn near the garden and the inclined steps that led to the solarium, every now and then a troop of clouds marched across the sun and it was suddenly cool. Alternating patches of light and darkness fell on the century-old trees around them.

"Look over there," said Robert. "Do you see that black cat? Isn't it fantastic the way it slinks through the tall grass?"

His remark piqued Carolina. Hidden irritations burst to the surface. "Don't you understand that I'm sick of looking at things? You're always pointing things out to me, trying to manipulate and grab my attention. More possession! Let's just be quiet and go into our feelings. It's so peaceful here."

He frowned. From up at the solarium, clear and detached against the drowsy air, came the garbled sound of voices, a joke: "What did Robinson Crusoe do with Friday on Tuesday afternoon? Forget it, Mr. Moonstone," followed by a spray of laughter that died before it quite got to them.

Carolina didn't fall asleep, as he was hoping she would, since her waking presence anguished him. Instead, adrift in that odd lull that occurs between four and five-o'-clock, she lolled her head against his shoulders and murmured with a self- indulgent dreaminess, "Robbie, I love you so much."

Robert shuddered, as if a bullet had grazed his flesh. He knew that her love was indeed flowering. Never had he seen it greater, more expansive, more sublime. Never had it tortured him so much either. An ache had lodged like a hook in his belly, and he squirmed silently, wondering how he could possibly ever be free from it. The tremendous pressures that had been accumulating made him feel dopey and drugged. The summer, dulling his senses more effectively than wine, had it turned him into a somnambulist of love? When would the release come, when the awakening storm? Gently he stroked Carolina's bare head.

How far would she go in her feeling? How long could this magnificent love he didn't understand support and keep her spirits in such an exalted state?

"I'm so unhappy here," she murmured softly, not knowing that the very gentleness of her words was tearing Robert apart. "Can't we go someplace else? Anywhere. You promised we'd only stay here a short time and it's already dragged out to more four weeks. Just think, we could be at the Indian festival now, the coming together and meeting of tribes in New Mexico."

The only way he could hide his ravaged feelings was to reply sternly, "I've told you that I can't leave here until I've settled certain accounts."

He knew how horribly vague he was being. He knew he had given her no reason to love, and nothing to make her love him. Her own love, being totally self-generated, was all the more astonishing and beautiful.

He had loved her for her free spirit, her fine body, her flowing palomino hair. But was that enough? He wondered if it was not the essential nature of love to embrace the whole, instead of fixating on the parts. Did he renounce Carolina because she refused to have secrets, because she so ardently desired that enlightened wholeness without mystery which was perhaps, finally, the greatest mystery?

She sensed where he was. "If you loved me at all, you'd take me away at once. But no, you've never loved me; you've only been in love with a certain image of me you have created. Did you think you had me? No, not yet anyway! You only had your phantom!"

On the peaceful lawn her accusations crashed against him with that sickening, splintering sound that signifies a reality collision. There was no way to get out of it, words wouldn't have worked; he was strapped into his seat. She had a perfect right to heap upon him all that he deserved. Yet this idea jarred his mind: could cutting her hair have been a way of making herself a scarecrow for his phantoms?

Just a few moments ago, when she was telling him how much she loved him, he had wished to transform himself into a monster so that he could escape the terrifying presence of that love.

Robert couldn't say anything, couldn't defend himself anymore. He just sat there, a perfect target, a stupid sitting duck, as the waning light of the falling sun did a last ballet over the bay.

Did Carolina realize she had him cornered? All the long frustrations of the past mounted to her head; here was a chance for her to liquidate the sum total of what she had suffered. Redemption? Release? It was rare for her to lose the lovely easy calmness in which she floated. She took aim and attacked.

"You don't know how to dance. You never knew! We never could dance together. You never cared what was important to me. I waited for you when you were in Vietnam. I wanted you so much, now you're back and you're not there. You're rigid and rectangular and I want the curves and soft, flowing shapes of the future. You never knew how to keep up with me and I'm oh so tired of having to drag you along in my wake! You're not flexible or supple or pliable, you don't know how to move, to tremble and sway, to quiver according to every slight modulation or hint of the wind!"

"No, damn it, I'm not a cotton pod!" Robert yelled, furious now too.

Startled bathers started clambering down from the solarium to investigate the source of the screams. What did Robert and she care? They were already miles away, isolated on the plains of their own bitter, locked combat.

Maddened, Carolina really exploded; she wheeled like a serpent and hurled at him, "You cripple! You emotional weakling!"

Robert reeled, his senses spinning under the impact of words that shattered like shrapnel against the back of his brain.

She thrust again, "You paralytic!"

As if she had squeezed drops of lemon into his eyes, Robert winced. How was it possible for him not to think of the polio-paralyzed mother he had never known?

At that moment, as if lightning had burst in his head, he saw a direction opening before him; he saw the path he had to follow. He glimpsed destiny. In other words, for a moment he saw the future of himself.

But she had him now, and she continued with a brutality that masked a pain that was killing both of them, "You don't even know how to make love!" She paused. "If you want a drug, if you want a woman who serves you as a drug, you've got one. Me!"

Carolina didn't mean to be cruel: she was just telling him the truth. How clearly, with what poignant accuracy of feeling, he realized that! She had been his drug, his alibi, his scapegoat, the sacrifice he burned in order to save himself. He knew that what she had really meant was: "You don't know how to make love to me."

This truth stung him. He had never learned how to approach her, never had the key to her gentle blonde doors. The few times he had struck the right combination he could count on the fingers of one hand. It wasn't much.

"Go on, don't stop now," he heard himself saying. He wasn't going to try to dodge her blows. He just hoped the agony would end and her fury subside in the evening calmness that was already beginning to stretch out, long and lovely, around him.

But he wasn't prepared for the new intensification of brutality to which her momentum carried her when she turned to him and screamed, "You don't know how to fuck!"

The short, four-letter-word had an explosive effect he could only answer by echoing, "I'm warning you, bitch, watch out!"

It might have been better if he had simply said, "I'll show you!"

He restrained an impulse to hit her. Their words had already degraded them enough.

She waited for him to shrivel up, to show some sign that he was hurt. When he didn't, she followed up with these hard jabs, "You're not able to go to bed with me. You're a child; you've turned us both into children in a desperate attempt to recover the childhood you never had. I don't know how you are with other women, but with me you're weak, incapable, useless. That's the truth, Robbie. I'm telling you how I feel. We didn't make it together, baby, we missed it." Her voice went weak. She stared at him helplessly. Something was about to crack.

He shivered in the immense cold solitude of their being alone together, phantoms, scarecrows propped up in a desert of their own making. It all didn't mean anything anymore. They had loved each other too young. The war hadn't helped. Later it might have worked out but not now.

"I'm so sorry, my precious," she sobbed. "But you never knew what to do or what to say or how to talk, not to me anyway, and that's what counted. I feel so used, so awfully old, as if you'd pounced on me, preyed on me…"

Her words shot out like random arrows, but a few of them struck him, hit home, hit nerve. How wrong, how criminally wrong, it was to have tried to call love this fear of emptiness and death and the dark! He had needed to be loved more than he wished to love and the balance hadn't worked. He was guilty. He would always be guilty now before Carolina. He stood with his head bowed while she lashed him through her streaming tears.

"You couldn't follow me in my dreams and you were always asking me to take care of you in your life. I'm so weary of these tensions. I just want to live peacefully and calmly, at one with myself, at one with… the One. When I wanted you to be soft, you were cruel. When I wanted you close, you were detached. When I wanted to sleep, you were upon me. When I did something on my own, you were jealous. And if I stayed with you too much, you said you needed your precious solitude! Oh my darling, what a contrary beast you are! How can I live? Tell me, tell me, how can I live?"

Her anguish tormented him. But her laments had transfigured Carolina. Her groans had put a kind of glow around her bare head; she suddenly belonged to that long line of women who deserve to be crowned.

He could spend the rest of his life making reparations toward her, and what she was suffering made him love and hate her more than ever. Her suffering was a part of their love; it was "their child." What was the fatal law that condemns men and women, however different they have become individually, to keep repeating the same pattern of relationship the moment they are together? Carolina and he were doomed because they couldn't become "new" to each other, because no matter what they became, they would always be the "same" to each other. Here was one love they couldn't reinvent because it seemed to have pre-existed, preceded them, and would continue to exist, outside of space and time, no matter what happened to them.

Bare, stripped, revealed, with nothing left to hide and nothing to show, they stood confronting each other. Robert reached out to touch her, to make some appeasing gesture, but Carolina turned away.

Around them was the simple melancholy of a late July dusk: another day ended.

Chapter XVII

In the mornings it was easier to be gay. How pleasant and wondrous it was to wake up free, washed of the day before. All the storms were forgotten. When Robert lay next to Carolina, it was as if her dreams were being transfused all night long into his body. It was no surprise when they woke up amid the flowery coverlets and pillows and she said she had just dreamed the most marvelous sensation: she was riding a surfboard and had just caught the peak of a gigantic wave.

"I felt so calm, so calm. I didn't know what was going to happen to me. I didn't even care if I fell down. I just knew in that moment there could be no such thing as death, and I felt so happy, still and serene in my knowledge of it."

The ripe summer swarmed just outside the windows as if anxious to enter; the air was young and light and luminous with the sun. For a change Carolina dressed in black. It gave her a solemn, prophetic and distant look, a little bit like that of a priestess. Since Ben was busy, they climbed into the super, blue, panoramic, travelling car and went into town for breakfast.

They sat for a while in silence over coffee. Having said --- spilled --- everything to each other the day before, there was nothing left to say, only perhaps the tenderness of an understanding which Carolina accented when she said, "Robbie, I think it's best if I go. We're just blocking each other here. You'd be much better off alone and it'll be much easier for you to do what you have to do. Then when it's done you can come up and join me and perhaps we can begin to live again."

Robert nodded. What she said sounded so natural and inevitable to both of them that it was almost accepted without discussion. Perhaps all the harsh violence of yesterday had simply been a means of preparing and softening the ground to attain this today.

Almost perfunctorily, as a matter of form, he asked, "But where would you go?"

"Vermont, where we planned to travel, don't you remember? I have friends there, really beautiful people, and I will wait for you. Anyway, anything would be better for me than here, which is so civilized and cultivated that it's nowhere."

"Sounds like when you're up there you're going to be waiting for me to get out of jail."

"No, it's more like giving you a chance to become free."

"Free exactly for what?" he wondered, knowing she was right. Instead, he reprimanded her, saying, "You know very well there's no 'nowhere'. There's only 'here'," he went on, mocking her style. "That's our fate, you see, just to be 'here'. Perhaps if we could get enough of our 'hereness', we might begin to get 'holy'." He grinned, pleased with his parody of her way of thinking.

But Carolina was quick to put him down. "Ha-ha! We'll never get too whole just waiting around here like scavengers, lost among these rich people and these sandy flatlands." She paused, she smiled --- one of those quick smiles that are like a sudden flash of sunlight on a lake. Once again, did they understand each other?

"The only nice thing," she said, easily laughing, "is watching the clouds. It's summer and they're out of school, they're on vacation and they're having a good time."

Thus it was decided without further ado that in a few days Carolina would leave.

It was the first definite decision they had reached since arriving at Ben's and it made them both feel good. At least something had happened. Out of the obscure mass of feelings and sensations that surrounded them and in which they were floating, something concrete had emerged. It didn't matter what they thought; what was happening was infinitely more complex than anything they could think about it; and when Carolina said, as he drove the car to a popular diner where they often came, "We're still together, aren't we? But from now on we'll just continue our paths parallel," it was simply her way of saying, "I accept that we're leaving each other for a while and I think it's for the best."

In the old-style diner with the shiny nickelled counters they sat at a booth in the corner next to the jukebox, out of which occasionally burst the sounds of "Good Morning Starshine" or "Spin and Win."

"Those are two songs I like," she said.

Somehow the knowledge of her imminent departure had made their tensions disappear, and again they were easy and relaxed with each other. There wasn't much time left. This fact made them each feel a subtle happiness too fugitive to be real.

While they waited for their orders, and the saccharine sound of "Good Morning, Starshine" kept repeating itself, suddenly Carolina pointed and said, "Oh, look at the butterfly."

Through the window Robert could see a butterfly with exquisitely fine scarlet and black wings resting on a leaf. From time to time its wings moved up and down.

"It's a libellula," Carolina told him. "It only lives for one day, you know."

"Oh," murmured Robert, distracted by the waitress who was presenting them with their pancakes. While he spread the butter pats evenly and smoothly over the fluffy textures, he looked at the maple syrup and thought of Vermont, into whose mountains Carolina soon would vanish.

She ate with a hunger unusual for her. The decision they had come to was actually a monumental piece of work. They felt as exhausted as if they had spent all day digging ditches in the sun. Carolina remarked, "The cook must like me: she gave me such a lot of bacon."

Abruptly she changed the subject. "Why don't you try to be like the butterfly, Robbie? It doesn't do anything. It has just one day to live. It does its thing."

Her small bright voice rose against the jukebox chaos. It was funny to be sitting in the grand western diner and to be talking about oriental-graceful butterflies. Robert thought: in comparison with the earth's time, we live less than one day. As we are to the earth, so is the butterfly to us. Looking at things from this angle, it was impossible to take anything seriously. Robert began to laugh. Carolina looked at him and laughed too.

In the booth opposite them a fat red-faced woman was sitting next to a man with a white beard, dressed in tennis shorts. Voices burbled. "Did you get anything?"

"I got the newspaper but no check."

"What you got," she said smartly, "was a big slew of sausages."

The man, puzzled, frowned at the enormous quantity of sausages on his plate. Then he picked up his fork and started to polish them off.

Carolina sipped her coffee and her hands nimbly leapt over the polished table's breakfast clutter. She reached for his hand; he pulled his away. She was always calm; he was always agitated. Carolina always knew what to do in her calmness, whereas Robert never knew what to do in his agitation.

"Be like the butterfly," she urged him with an imperious tenderness.

Why couldn't he accept? Why did he have to push her with his "Why?"

She didn't lose her cool but responded with a superb ease that mocked his uncertainty, "Because the butterfly doesn't waste all its time building up houses of cards."

Was that, then, what she thought he was doing: erecting houses of cards by the sea, friendly illusions that made life luxurious for a while? Was love just a house of crazy mirrors? Was Carolina right when she said, "Most of the things that we live or that happen aren't that important, yet we waste our time pretending that they are."

The lyrics of "Good Morning Starshine" repeated again and again in the diner. Outside the window the butterfly, poised perfectly on a leaf, only contributed to itself, its own being. Carolina was right: it didn't try to squeeze, it didn't grip, and it wasn't possessive.

"Be like the butterfly!" Carolina had commanded.

Robert glimpsed the world fluttering in the scarlet and black depths of some infinite butterfly. Clear and simple, Carolina's voice floated around him. In that moment did they guess each other's fate?

"The butterfly doesn't write anything. Since he has only a day to live, he doesn't have time to go around writing about what he's living."

Robert gazed at her with that special tenderness we have for things that we know are about to die. It was as if they, too, had been butterflies together, had lived their day in the sun. To get away from this gloom, which could have grown heavier, he teased her, "But suppose the butterfly is writing? Suppose he's writing on the leaf, on the pages of the leaves?"

That amused her. She had finished her coffee. Something had ended. A beautiful child in a blue jumper suit rushed into the room and shouted, "Good morning!" There were no more pancakes. Robert reached over the plates and folded his hands over hers. In the opposite booth the big white-bearded man whose head was out of proportion with his neck, leaned over his syrupy sausages, examining them.

"Suppose," Robert said, "the butterfly is writing his life story on the pages of the leaves."

"Imagine he's dreaming about us," she said. "Our butterfly lives."

The butterfly zigzagged away. They paid, walked out of the diner into the afternoon light.

"Look," she said, "the clouds have changed."

They stood on the hot sidewalk for a moment and embraced. It would be the last time he truly kissed her. Like ballet dancers they had struck a position that could only be held for a certain number of seconds before it collapsed. So often they had talked to each other but their hearts had been shut. Now, with Carolina on the verge of departure, they opened their hearts and walked away and said nothing.

Chapter XVIII

A few days later --- it was the second weekend in August --- Ben gave a farewell party for Carolina.

"I'm sorry you're going, kid," he told her. "You know how I've grown accustomed to your face! But if you've got to go, let's do it right with a big send-off."

It was Carolina who insisted that Maya and her friends should come. "It's wrong to think that we can't all be well together," she said. "We began as a family, let's end as a family."

Carolina preferred the group to the individual, another reason for her haste to get to Vermont, where the conditions were more primitive and many young people were eager to share her "butterfly philosophy."

"I think you're nuts," Robert told her. "We should just have a quiet simple dinner with Ben."

But "quiet" and "simple" was not exactly Ben's style. So everyone came. It was a disaster.

The day had begun rainy, clearing up toward the late afternoon. The guests started to arrive around seven. They were all enchanted with Ben's house, the gardens around it, the fantastic fragrances that had sprung up after the rain. Approaching the house, they could smell honeysuckle and orange blossoms; it was dusk; inside there was an even more enchanting smell of herbs cooking.

As if conscious of the theatrical aspects of the evening, the sun came out clear and strong and was putting on an even more glorious performance than usual. The sky was an opera of colors. Ben hugged Carolina, who was sad. She wasn't sure she wanted to go now. Despite its luxurious surroundings, she loved Ben's house, the healthy, rudimentary sense it had to it, such as the copper utensils hanging simply on the kitchen wall, or the fountain Ben had built in the garden, with its labyrinth of stony layers, over which the water so soothingly dripped. She had to admit that there was a great contact with life, an enormous simplicity. On the point of leaving, she knew she would regret it intensely.

Robert was sorry too, yet it was clear to him that it was impossible to go back. The old life was over. He felt free, as if Carolina had already gone.

Still, she looked marvelous that evening. She was wearing a psychedelic outfit she had made which Ben said had wonderful feeling and depth; someone else said it exposed and brought to light primitive patterns of consciousness. Garbed in dazzling colors that lifted her up and brought her hurling like a cannonball to the center of the mind, Carolina reclined in the large, easy Italian rocking chair she adored.

Although Ben often worked with glass and aluminum, there were very few modern objects in his house except the Italian rocking chair, two chairs by Mies van der Rohe, and a "joke chair" which was built in the shape of a translucent woman: you sat in her "lap" and your back rested comfortably against her "breasts."

"You think I'd live in what I build?" Ben joked. "Don't be foolish. Work's one thing, life's another."

Then Maya and her troop arrived and the grim, unspoken, deadly duel between herself and Carolina began that was to last the entire evening. Andre and Vico escorted her across the lawn; she came at them gracefully, superbly, like a mirage floating out of the evening forest where the sun was sinking, like a statue from another time.

How many mental photographs did Robert snap of that majestic moment when Maya was reaching the porch, flanked by her glorious freaks. Vico had his perpetual grin; Andre looked somber, violent, explosive; Louise happier than she had been in days, her face positively alive and shining, because Andre had to go into the city tomorrow and she at last would be alone with Maya.

Maya's hair was lifted, bouffant, into a series of baroque, convoluted curls. Out of her, above her, it shot like an electric aureole, giving her a royal, charming, exquisite energy. On top of it she had fastened a white orchid. Her completely crazy, superabundant look contrasted brutally with the bare, shining, psychic simplicity to which Carolina had reduced herself by shearing her tresses.

The combat between the styles of these two women was ferocious; Robert imagined them for a moment as lady wrestlers, or wolves, tearing each other apart.

Maya was wearing a pale white and blue Courrèges dress, full of marvelous details. The orchid on her hair set her off, ennobled her, and made her seem even more distant, miraculous. Between Andre and Vico she moved gracefully, almost as if stepping in a ballet.

"Look at her!" Carolina whispered with apprehensive savagery to Robert. "I really don't like her. Look at the way she's always masking, disguising herself. What is she hiding from?"

"The Great Clear Eye," Robert said.

Carolina laughed. "You're right. That's the 'I' that I want to see!"

Once again, seeing Maya approach, Carolina attacked. "What does she need such masks for? What could be more of a mask than a naked face?"

Beyond Maya's shoulders over the bay the sun hung suspended in the pale slipping sky.

Carolina stood her ground beside Robert as Maya came toward him. He felt split between this terrifying innocence and simplicity, at one with itself, and the baroque exuberance and sensuous masquerade of Maya. In their own way, they were each otherworldly. The shock of their coming together triggered harsh, violent vibrations.

Maya did not deign to acknowledge Carolina. She cast her a kind of scornful look and stepped aside. Louise followed in her awake, along with Vico and Andre, Hoppy and Marthe.

Looking at Maya's regal presence, Robert realized how little she had to do with the daily life of most human beings. Carolina was engaged up to the hilt in the "Now" --- whatever that was --- but Maya was totally "elsewhere" --- wherever that was. Vico had expressed it more simply: "Maya, like she's far-out. But Carolina, she's so far-in I can't even see her anymore." Ben, with his superb politeness, asked Maya, "Will you accept a glass of wine from grapes a farmer friend of mine grows?"

"Why not? I'm a peasant myself!" she replied.

"We need a beautiful woman like you," Ben said, "to protect us against the weather."

It was the first day when the summer had seemed unsure of itself, undecided, ready for change, with a yearning for autumn.

"I'll go get some more wine."

The wine that Ben brought warmed up Maya and she quickly forgot Carolina and felt more and more at home and at ease in the atmosphere. She grabbed Robert. "Let's go into the kitchen so we can talk."

Old-fashioned peasant baskets from Mexico, hanging on the white walls, created smooth harmonies. Through the door there was a glimpse of a few other rooms, with high ceilings and white walls, very symmetrical.

Unexpectedly Ben wandered in and found Robert kissing Maya, playfully pressing his lips against her forehead. He sensed the fire in her body, inhaled her perfumed scents. He drew back instinctively when Ben came in. Ben laughed and said, "Go on kissing her."

Then Robert saw Ben moving toward Maya and realized that he wanted to kiss her too.

"But I'm private property!" Maya cried shyly.

"Oh, private property," Ben said. "I thought you were with Andre."

"I'm not," she answered defiantly. "But I'm still private property."

"She belongs to me!" Robert heard himself saying, with a completely reckless and idiotic impulsivity.

"Hey, how come is it you have so much property?" Ben questioned Robert, thinking of Carolina.

Before Robert could think of an answer, Ben answered his own question. "One needs a woman for every mood, doesn't one? For the rain, for the sun, for different kinds of weather. A woman in every place. Now wouldn't that be nice."

"Like records," Robert said sarcastically. "You choose the one which suits your mood."

"If you guys want to talk about property, you can do so by yourselves. But this property is going!" Maya interjected angrily. "Guess what, Ben? We've just had our first fight!"

"Oh Maya, my dear, our first fight!" Ben was genuinely touched. Once again he became the indulgent father. He bowed, kissed the back of her hand, and walked out of the kitchen.

Maya was still furious. "I thought Ben was freer than that. As if I belonged to anything! The only thing I care about is being happy and nothing else."

That grand imperative, "Be Happy!" rang out so clearly and loudly in her voice that it couldn't be forgotten or denied. They would spend the rest of the summer trying to assume it. Robert wondered if Maya's energetic cry, "Be happy!" was the same thing, finally, as Carolina's calm and deep "Live in harmony with the One?" Didn't happiness have to be stolen? Thieves of happiness, they had robbed a quick kiss in the kitchen. Carolina would have said that harmony was true happiness, that it was all around you like the air, and all you had to do was make an empty space in yourself and listen to it.

Robert didn't have time to develop this thought any further because Maya asked for a cigarette and another drink. The homemade wine tasted stronger than ordinary wine. It was almost like vermouth. Ben came back to check on the veal roast in the oven. He had wrapped it with spices and herbs and now those odors rose and filled the kitchen. Maya sniffed the air and smiled. She whispered that she was just in the mood for having a big meal.

As they were walking back outside Maya suddenly squeezed him. He felt it was almost perverse, because she knew as well as he did that Carolina was departing, and that soon there would be no obstacles between them. At the same time he realized that his feeling for her, which had begun almost casually a month ago, on a chance encounter, had now reached a very dangerous point. It was no longer: take a taste of me and leave if you don't like it. It had already become, with a solemn, unspoken gravity, all or nothing.

They were, in a very literal sense, gambling on themselves. This knowledge gripped both of them with a sense of the absolute. As Maya leaned into him, she murmured, "Be careful. I'm so afraid… You know what I mean, we might be engaged with each other."

"How can you be afraid of being engaged? Isn't that exactly what you want, total involvement?" Robert flung out as a challenge, issuing a check that perhaps later he would have to make good.

Over the inlet the sun was setting very slowly. Yet every minute it was going through modifications, changes. "What a trip the sun is," Vico remarked.

He was sitting out on the lawn with Marthe, Hoppy and Carolina, grooving on the sun, which looked as if the surrealist painter had invented it, Max Ernst. Vico was talking about a friend of his who had just gone to North Vietnam on a peace mission and come back with the startling news that the North Vietnamese were wonderful people, full of bravery and humor. And the underground hospitals were "really fantastic."

"Perhaps," Andre suggested, "the sun is singing an elegy for the U.S. of A., this dying giant."

"How can you say that?" someone else argued. "What about Apollo 11? Didn't we just put a man on the moon?"

"I'm telling you," Andre went on, "sooner or later there's got to be a sacrifice, a huge burning, a conflagration all the more beautiful in that it doesn't have any purpose. That's the moon shot, man, a fantastic sacrifice of money and energy to bring back a few shovelfuls of moon shit!"

"How boring!" Maya interrupted. "Don't they have anything else to show us? If you want to see something, just look at the reflection of the sun in the window, for starters."

"Look, look, look!" parodied Carolina. For Maya had a habit of saying things over and over again, so that she ignited a feeling of enthusiasm, of quick, jubilant emotion.

Across from them Louise was seated at such an angle she could see no reflections in the window at all. Above the bay, magnified on the glass, the sun streamed. Maya and Robert looked at its engorged reflection in the window and were nearly blinded.

Ben came over for a moment and the talk for some reason rambled on about diaries. "Most diaries are like those that sea captains keep, aren't they, limited to descriptions of weather and food?"

"Exactly," said Robert, who kept one himself, "but it's only when you get beyond weather and food and conversations that real life begins."

"That's why the summer can be so important and interesting," continued Ben. "It's a very special time, perhaps the only time when man has a chance to become free. The weather doesn't bother him, and there's a short moment, at least, when he doesn't have to work. His needs aren't so great, he can live simply, and he has a real chance of getting free and being fulfilled. Of course he has to be able to escape the conditioning of the other ten months but the chance is there during the summer and it can be seized."

"Of course, of course!" cried Robert, enthusiastic, for that was exactly his idea as well, and another reason for not going with Carolina to Vermont. He thought the beach, the sea, and the sun provided an extraordinary framework for freedom and for once, instead of talking and meditating about life, it was possible to jump in and act and live.

Carolina stood up and faced the sun in a moment of silence. "It's dying," she murmured. "Its head is about to be chopped off." Solemn, austere, she saluted it with rapt attention.

Others came and the talk swung to Hemingway, Tolstoy, and the way the theatre changes from one country to another. Maya mentioned dills, and the talk went on into Neufchatel, katydids, tomatoes, and tomato plants that grow more quickly if you talk to them; Switzerland, which Maya hated because it was so organized, and the village in Romania where Ben was born, how he had changed his name and how in honor of him the village had adopted his new name.

While they were talking, Robert found out a little bit more about Maya from Louise, who was wearing a blue and brown embroidered Mexican dress with a belt made of silver scalloped shells. "Her mother was Russian, like mine. She escaped to Berlin and married a brilliant Jewish engineer. They knew they'd be arrested, so just after Maya was born, they had a friend smuggle her across the Swiss border in a suitcase. She was raised in an orphanage on Lac Constanz. Later the German government gave her a scholarship to Oxford as war reparation. . She's very shy about this, says she doesn't remember anything, and refuses to talk about it. Please, Robbie, don't tell her I told you. Besides, her past doesn't come up to what she wants to be, to what she expects of herself, so she forgets it."

"I can see why. It must be really difficult to have no past, no family, nothing."

"But she does have one thing, this great style, this extraordinary sense of life. I'm warning you, it's difficult to resist it, to remain yourself. Andre, for example, was completely stylized by her love. He's completely dependent upon her; he's a love-addict. Be careful. She wants to leave him but he's going crazy. Love can be a drug, a powerful hypnotic. Or maybe it's because I'm not capable of such love that I don't know anything about it. But watch out, I'm telling you."

Her words made Robert feel that his encounter with Maya was a challenge that he absolutely had to accept. Hadn't it been promised to him since his childhood? He owed it to himself to accept this rendezvous that sooner or later every man has to face.

Carolina wasn't saying anything. She sat quietly, inhaling the essence of one of her last summer nights on the Long Island shore. She had a vague feeling that she was going to die, that not only was she going to lose this night but Robert as well, and she didn't care. She had a few happy images in her head and a peacefulness that rippled outwards from her inner being, and what else mattered? She had lived a special love with Robert, a unique closeness that could never be repeated or imitated. They had somehow become even more intimate than lovers. She remembered the day she had run down the beach, feeling at one with the surf and the sea. How she had loved the blue dome of the sky, reverberating with its harmonious totality, with its dazzling noon-time emptiness which was perhaps another way of being full; and she remembered telling Robert, "The sea is just like me, it's always moving, changing, fleeing."

He had replied in his usual intelligent yet critical way, "But it flees inward, toward the shore, whereas you flee outwards, toward infinity."

"Stupid! Who says your 'outwards' is not my 'inwards'?"

There was always this slight misunderstanding between them, this gap of words and communication that could never be narrowed. Why had they never been able to truly make it together, yield to each other? He had once accused her of being "asexual" but in his heart he knew he was wrong. He simply didn't know how to take care of her body. Since he returned from Vietnam, it hadn't been the same. Never before had she been so obsessed with the idea of having a lover. How to make physical and mental love go together, that was the haunting question. How to live together and be one, simply and wholly?

The nude pure truth Carolina longed for should have been able to conquer the baroque grandiloquence of Maya, who was really letting herself go now, as she launched into a riff about --- of all absurd subjects --- peanut butter!

"It was just awful, absurd! I was sitting at this big formal cocktail party before dinner, lots of businessmen, you know. Suddenly everyone begins talking about peanut butter --- I've never seen anything like it ---- it was absurd, absurd! I was sitting there, hardly able to control myself, just splitting my sides laughing --- and no one around me saw, realized what I was doing. They went on talking about their peanut butter! The whole kit and caboodle! And I just sitting there laughing, rocking my head off! You wouldn't have believed it ---it was unimaginable!"

"What about penis butter?" interjected Andre.

Laughter. "How disgusting!" cried Louise.

"You're all neurotics," Carolina mouthed to herself. She knew it was true: they were all outside of themselves, even Ben. Bars as implacable as those in a zoo cage separated them from who they really were. Somehow she had managed to make it; she felt 'within', and her words were vain attempts to calm their agitated simian efforts. How tired she was of it! She would have been much happier with a band of children, who at least would have taken their play seriously.

How could Carolina understand the tender, tragic feeling Maya aroused in Robert? He sensed such a quality of lament coming out of her, which her peanut butter story disguised and yet revealed; he felt all these emotions smothered in her, flashing beneath the surface, ready to burst, looking for an outlet, an opening. Maya was obviously another one of the motherless ones. Was this what had attracted him? There was something in her quick, bright, nervous laughter that touched him deeply, aroused feelings that he hadn't suspected, foreseen, or known he had. They were all orphans that summer, circling around Ben and each other, unstable, volatile, ready to come together or break apart, washed up strangely together at the end of a fabulous decade that didn't look as if it could maintain itself, its force, fury or fantasy into the future, little streams looking for a river, rivers hunting the sea, haunted by it.

Ben said dinner was at last ready. They moved inside, out of the darkness deep as a well where it was getting slightly cool again and looked as if it might rain.

The roast was delicious. Ben had also mixed salad from his garden called "runculo." It had a slightly sharp, tart, earthy taste to it. Maya put leaves between her lips and chewed them. Warm plates were put on the table and it was nice to touch hands to them since it was getting damp and unpleasant outside.

At a certain point during dinner, which was exquisite, Andre turned to Ben. "Don't you think that women are like some of your furniture: they're transparent. I've spent most of my life groping for their bottom."

"I've never found their bottoms so hard to find," guffawed Vico. The two men started clowning around like intelligent idiots. There was a harsh, raucous laugh from Marthe at the other end of the table. Carolina was silent and Louise smirked.

"You're drunk," Maya said to Andre. "How can you try to be so serious when you're drunk? You're too little serious except when you're drunk and then you get too serious."

"What do I care for your 'serious'? Listen; let me tell you what sex in America is like. When I came to Detroit in 1962 and started working in a gas station --- to make some bread, right? That was something else. It was hard to get girls at that time, boy. I was panting like this... Finally I managed to get this girl --- her parents were originally from Austria but she'd adopted all the uptight American ways of the 1950s' ---- well, because I was French everything that I did was wonderful. So one day when we were in bed I took my shoelace off and tied it around her ear and she cried that was so wonderful, where did I learn to do such fantastic things, and pretended to come ---"

"She must have been a real idiot!" Maya cried.

Ben interrupted them, raising his hands with a commanding gesture. "The only woman I could ever live with is Maya. She is really fantastic. I tell you, I've seen all sorts of life and been through all the stages, but the stage she's at, wow!"

Maya made a joke of it all, "Hahaha I'm on no stage, baby!"

Louise, suddenly afraid for her, hugged her. She had her arm protectively around Maya's shoulders.

Robert felt the whole thing was a comedy, being put on for whose benefit? He glanced at Carolina. She refused to look at him. It hurt her so much to see the insane way they were all acting. This wasn't what she had planned.

Andre was snarling at Maya, "You make a terrible mistake when you try to connect morality with art. What does it matter how I've lived my life? It's like saying: if Van Gogh had lived a better life, he might have painted better paintings. Nonsense! If Van Gogh hadn't existed, we wouldn't even know what real painting was."

"I don't care a French fig about Van Gogh," Maya said. "He chose to be unhappy. That's his business. All I care about is being happy. Here, give me some more wine. I love it so much."

Outside it had started slowly to rain.

"Wet on the inside, wet on the outside," Maya said, bringing her glass to her lips. Andre laughed. He loved her quick, pinpoint observations.

Ben brought out some Havana cigars he had just brought back from a trip to Cuba. They started talking and joking about the Havana cigars, comparing them to other cigars that could be bought. Ben mentioned how cheap they were in Moscow.

"Let's all go to Moscow and buy Havana cigars," Maya suggested. Anything seemed possible.

"Why don't you stay with us for awhile?" Ben shouted down the table to Carolina. "There must be enough cows in Vermont to keep your friends company for awhile. Look what a marvelous time we're all having together."

"Yes, I think it's lovely," added Maya, who no longer seemed in control of what she was saying. "Stay with us, Carolina!"

Boisterously, Marthe threw her arms around Carolina. "I love you so much!" she gushed.

A confused chorus of voices urged Carolina to remain. Robert alone was silent, believing that no matter what they said, they could not change the reality.

Finally Carolina responded, "No, there's too much evil in the air. We're not with each other at all. I thought we could be. But we're all against each other, fighting each other all the time like wolves. I'm sorry, it's too tough for me."

What she said went unheeded and was forgotten as a new center of conversation popped up. Andre attacked Maya. "Oh come on," he blasted, "how can you say such a thing? What do you mean you don't like Van Gogh? How can you possibly say such a thing? Are you trying to be chic?"

Carolina tugged at Robert's arm, whispered to him, "There's something telling me to leave. I must go."

There was urgency in her voice as if she were rushing off to some fatal secret rendezvous with herself.

"Then go," he said.

"I'm not going without you."

But Robert wasn't ready to leave.

The aroma of the cigars drifted away. Andre had begun to monologue: "Sex has become so stupid. A thing for idiots. How to make sex intelligent, difficult again? What we need is a new Roman Catholicism in love: ceremony, rites, pomp, terror, and mystery. But the only thing everyone is interested in is getting down to the facts as quickly as possible. Sex, life, business, everything with its technique, its time, its place, how boring!"

Andre threw his words like sparks into the air. They flashed for a second, and then burned out. He kept talking, making a desperate attempt to light them again, to re-ignite the love between himself and Maya, which had failed and was flickering out for whatever reason, by the force of things, or because they had lost their sense of the Great Terror.

Louise was talking to Ben about life in the American suburbs, saying how big some of the houses were on the inside, even if they did look all the same on the outside. "Anyway," she said, "it's much better than Europe where people are still trying to imitate what the Americans did fifty years ago."

Andre turned his attention to Carolina for a moment. She had always annoyed him because he had never been able to find a way of approaching her. "Finally, what do you want?" he was saying. "In other words, where's your head at?"

"I've got a new head," she replied honestly. "There are many things this 'new head' of mine won't accept, such as more romantic devotions."

Was that why she had to leave then? Robert puzzled. Because she couldn't accept the bond that once united them any longer?

Carolina repeated what she had often told him, "My 'new head' wants to live in such a way that all my acts just don't end up by becoming another mirror of myself. No," she added, "from now on I just want to be personally honest, free from material possessions, and free from seductions of whatever nature, even from love."

Overhearing this, Ben immediately asked her, with perplexed admiration, "But how do you manage to be so ethereal?"

Voices rose. Andre violently accused her of "being stuck half-way between Maoism and mysticism."

This provoked a storm. Robert defended her, shouting at Andre that he was just "another trite Tarzan, a fake wild man society can't digest making himself martyred for his refusal."

"So what do you want me to do?"

"Find another role for yourself or shut-up."

"You think you're so big just because you fought in the goddamn war. Well, you know what, you're just a petit-bourgeois faggot," Andre growled furiously.

They were about to come to blows, but Ben intervened, pushing them back, saying there was no point in carrying on a conversation if they were just going to insult each other.

"It's really terrible how all your people's heads are fucked up," Carolina sighed hopelessly.

"Right, we don't need any more heroes or martyrs," Robert said.

Andre extinguished his cigar butt on the back of his hand, which Ben immediately doused with whisky. Andre swore. Others laughed. They continued to drink, smoke, exchanging jokes, winks and sarcasms with one another.

Robert noticed that Maya's shoulders were shaking; she was covered with beads of light sweat, something was happening. She tried to reach out to him. "Please help me," he heard her say.

At once he forgot all the others. A suspicion, stronger than ever, came into his mind that they were going to love each other, afflicted with the burden of that love already.

The other guests were crowding around Maya like beasts of prey, waiting to see her fall, collapse, the first traces of blood shoot up.

Robert sensed something in her, illuminations of some tragic difficulty. Maya was talking absolutely without any control now. Her words came out of her against her will, hiccupped, almost vomited forth. Robert, no greenhorn himself, had never seen anything like it. He shoved a cigarette between his lips. He wondered what he was getting into, where he was going.

Maya was trying to talk about her past, her mother, Russia, their estate, the flight from Russia, the escape to Berlin, Hitler, the war, her mother's refusal to leave again and then… Maya broke down, she couldn't speak; she couldn't cry, she couldn't talk. Alterations, modifications in her consciousness began to appear. It became clear that there was nothing solid about Maya. Her character was a surface, stretched into a tight mosaic of diamond-hard fragments of being.

Robert longed to touch those fragments, to collect them, but he couldn't, they were coming too fast. With a kind of majestic, magnetic defiance she let her life fall, bric-a-brac, around her. Then it all became too heavy, she stopped and spun around. Robert stared at her. Her green eyes became clear for a moment. There was an instant of mutual recognition; their hidden desires leapt out.

At the end of the table, in another world, Marthe sat diligently rolling joints, packing them largely, thickly, rolling them tightly.

"Andre, will you roll a few for me?" she asked.

"I can't. My fingers aren't nimble enough and I've been drinking."

Finally she rolled one that was so tight you really had to drag on it to get anything at all. She handed it to Hoppy, as if entrusting it to the hands of an expert.

Hoppy leaned back, took a long, deep drag. "I don't like it," he said. "Puffing's much too hard work!"

Marthe passed the joint to Carolina. "You try it."

Marthe was emitting a lot of good vibrations. She smiled and looked radiant. She and Carolina took turns inhaling. They started laughing together, in a rather silly way, for no real reason at all.

Pushing her hair back, Marthe moved to the sofa, where she reclined, holding the cig high in the air. "I'd love to be a bum. Live off the track."

"You'd like to be a bum? Me too. I'm pretty close actually. I've been begging Ben to make me an inflatable dome."

"I could really get into being a bum. I'm getting closer too. I've only got a few possessions. And half a brain!"

Marthe's rich, rollicking laughter vibrated.

Robert thought of Carolina, of her desperate flight from her womanhood --- into a greater womanhood, she had insisted, freer, grander, but finally into a liberation that had nothing to do with womanhood. Carolina affirmed she was moving more and more toward life. Was she? Or was it death?

Maya, tottering in her extreme weakness, began to slip off the chair. Andre lunged for her. Drunk himself, he missed and ended up on the floor. Hoppy giggled but made no move. Ben tried to help Andre back on his feet. Andre spouted, "I feel my head bursting!" It was ugly.

Gracefully, with the movement of a dying swan, Maya became one with the floor. Separated from her by the table, Robert couldn't reach over and grab her, seize her shoulders. It was an awkward moment but Maya made the best of it. She lay on the floor laughing amid the shouts and groans of the others. The orchid had fallen out of her hair.

It was then that Robert noticed what an incredibly long neck she had. It rose up from her cleavage and delicate collarbone like a long, fluted stem. All of Maya's moods, her joie de vivre, her repressions and tensions, were reflected, thrown into sharp and occasionally agonizing relief upon her swan-like neck.

Robert called it her "Nefertiti" neck.

Carolina, observing the scene, felt a weary sense of repetition, of old things being done over and over again until they lost all their meaning.

Lanky, limber, devil-may-care, Vico wandered around, making rather lousy jokes such as, "What is your sexual Dow Jones average?" or, "Industrialize your dreams!"

Louise busied herself with Maya, who was becoming more and more vague, excited, and incoherent. No one could understand her now. It was almost funny. Ben started to laugh. Andre gurgled, "My darling, how I love you when you are like that!"

Louise, furious, kept trying to put her body between Andre and Maya.

Andre began tugging, yanking at her, finally punching her with little blows on her arms. "Let's come to the facts," he bellowed. "I hate you, you bird-head, you petty vulture!"

"Don't you dare touch her or me," Louise snapped, hard and angry. "One day all that hate in you is going to get you everything you deserve," she menaced.

Helplessly Maya moaned, "Stop it, stop it...."

"For what?" Andre blubbered like an idiot. "I want to know for what?"

Louise turned bitter and sour and silent. Her face curdled like milk gone bad. She hung back, hesitated, as if waiting for Maya to call, to summon her.

When in doubt, Robert thought, Louise retreats. She blots herself out.

As if covering up for Louise's ineptitude, Maya began to laugh and giggle. She buzzed and beeped with strange signals.

Pathetically Andre bent over and crooned, "Maya, my earth-moon-woman, please come, come…"

"Are you all right?" Ben, more serious, asked.

Maya shook Ben off, went on laughing nervously and shrilly, amusing everyone. Robert tried to listen to her, to understand her. Marthe rolled another joint. Not knowing what to do, Ben paced up and down.

This thought ran through Robert's head: Maya is shining in a mad brightness that could be the beginning of an enormous clarity.

Andre, pulling himself up, stretched out easily and comfortably on one of the leather chairs. He sat there, calm now, eying Maya with the silent patience of a psychoanalyst who knows that sooner or later his patient will crack.

Robert hated him for that distant attitude he had suddenly taken, the cynical humor that protected him from everything Robert saw coming to the surface in Maya's eyes.

Yet Maya paid no attention to him. Her eyes, shiny, feverish, were lifted elsewhere, directed to a new focus. It was very difficult to look her in the eyes, to sustain that regard. There was such an intensity of being united and centered in her look. Robert tried to maintain eye contact.

From faraway, beneath her silent glances, he could hear Carolina crying out, "Come back! Come back, Robbie!"

What an appeal! Thrusting her away from him was a crime, and the remorse --- the violent, boundless nostalgia he would soon feel --- anguished yet excited him as much as the crime itself. If he could only do the right thing and stay with her! But he couldn't. He felt the sort of grim happiness of a man who's purchased his airline ticket and is ready to go. There was the tough pleasure of having committed himself. That had to be done. Robert felt inexorable toward himself, hard, cruel. And yet, and yet, if only he could have known what he loved, what it was possible to love...

Outside in the blood-black darkness of the bottomless August night the rain splashed sonorously against the porch and trees. "The sky is trying to kill itself," Andre remarked.

As everyone was leaving Louise leaned toward Robert, whispered, "Come over tomorrow. I'll take you to Maya. We'll be alone. I promise."

Chapter XIX

Andre's first experiences with women in America had disappointed him. He had come to think of women as screaming, fat, hysterical sex-goddesses. He thought of the rather ugly, falsely voluptuous kind of women one sees in pornographic movies, or even between the covers of "Playboy", women who have been fattened, thickened, decked out with sex like geese about to be slaughtered. He saw them comically enlarged, looming up before him as monsters on a movie screen, omnivorously devouring, multifarious in their appetites, a huge albatross of green dollar bills hung around their neck, obsessive, neither good nor bad, immediate, jealous, greedy, terrified of the instincts in themselves they have suddenly discovered, sick of being ignored and anxious to capitalize on having been ignored for so long, more vegetable than female, full of malice toward men. This was more or less the kind of woman Andre thought he had known during his time in Detroit.

That was why too, he had been so glad, infinitely, joyously exuberant, when, shortly after arriving in New York, he had met Maya. He sensed at once that she had sparks in her. He could only guess at what enormous amounts of fire and simplicity and life-affirmations she had stored up beneath her skin.

True, her past, the tragic sense of her own life, could bring Maya down on her knees, weeping; Andre had seen it happen. But one way of her getting beyond herself was her sexuality: she was utterly and absolutely intense. Sleeping with her revealed another Maya, adding multiple dimensions. For Andre she had come to be like a streak of white fire, fire that flickers, that flows forth, that stops, flares up, begins again, runs up and down the walls of her white room, terrifying him. But it was a beautiful terror, almost sacred. Never before had physical contact been more important, more essential. For Andre, this was all the more fantastic as he thought that today all forms of eroticism had been made so cheap, so public. He told Maya, "Guess what, the other day four women undressed themselves in the gardens of the Museum of Modern Art and began to imitate the poses of the bronze statues."

"That's absolutely beautiful, absolutely perfect, absolutely the way it should be," she surprised him by commenting.

From the ubiquitous displays of it, Andre had the impression that in America, nudity was an end in itself, a product. It was as if once a woman had removed her clothes, there was nothing more to know about her. What could be further from the truth? For him nudity was only a beginning, a platform from which one jumps and springs and dives. Andre had found the freedom he was looking for in the arms of Maya. At last it seemed to him, he had discovered truth in love through her body electric.

How it hurt him now to let her go. How it pained him to know that he himself, through his own intensity, had destroyed that truth. He had lived so much with and for Maya that, little by little, he had lost all sense of himself. He didn't know who or what he was anymore, and somehow the answers he had once found in her no longer worked or helped him. Andre had preferred perfection in love to progress in life; and the history of their love, which his demands of perfection had made static and frozen, now mattered to him much more than anything that could possibly happen in his own life. Out of a fear of the future and of breaking apart he was deadlocked in meaningless repetitions. Their lovemaking had become a ritual assuring them that life would go on when in reality it wasn't going on at all.

Andre was one of those men who cannot accept the relativity of everything to everything else. He had to find some stable, meaningful subsystem underlying the world and tying it together. The relativity was there but it had to be rooted in something and he believed it could be rooted in his love for Maya. Therefore, he had begun to identify himself so entirely with that love, that he didn't resemble himself any longer.

At that point, Maya (one of whose favorite expression was, "It's relative, no?") had gradually ceased being interested in him.

This, in turn, raised the interesting question: could love be a vice? Was it possible to love too much? Was it possible that by letting himself go too much in his love for this woman, he had let himself be destroyed? Certainly Andre had believed that he was strong, powerful enough to assume this woman and all the baggage that went with her. Yet in the end he saw himself perched at the height of a burned out love in a derisory glory, a pitiful splendor.

Now Andre had to leave for the city to talk with producers. He was broke; he needed money. Maya had exhausted him physically, emotionally and now economically.

Louise was even more derisive: "I doubt if he'll be out again for a few weekends. He doesn't have enough pennies to pay for the train. Poor guy!"

Andre left with Vico and that acid-stoned blonde kid who kept going, "Whooey, whooey!" They rode two motorcycles back into the city, wearing the helmets with the "Be Friendly" signs lettered across them.

Andre took his film cameras. He said he had been making an intimate film journal. His task? "To film every day the details of that crisis which is my life."

"I'm only interested in mental reality from now on," he added. "The sensations that come from the head, that take us beyond the wall of what we see." Or he would say: "I'm a witch doctor. I try to tease the spirits that lurk in the flesh to appear on the film of the mind."

The rupture he felt was coming with Maya hurt him so much that he began to write her letters, three, four or five pages long, in which he talked with a certain poetic delirium about his loss, his sense of abandonment, his regrets.

Even when he came back to the cottage, he continued to write her letters, as if somehow, through them, he could hold on to her.

Their conversations, when they occurred, grew bitter, accusatory. Sometimes in the middle of them Andre would shout, "How can you forget those nights, my crazy little sunflower? How dare you betray everything we've lived together by talking to me as you are now?"

Maya, always maintaining her dignity, wouldn't listen, would walk away.

Andre would yell after her, "Just wait till your next lover has a chance to learn all about your cruelty in love, your black and white choices!"

He felt like a bull, lured into, and lost in mazes ---- the sense that once he had had the key to where he was going but now he no longer had it. Was he infected? With what? Had he made an error? But what error? Love? Was it just the mistake of having followed his instincts? In taking a risk, leaving what he knew, venturing into something he didn't know at all... He had given up his life. This woman was his cross, against whom he was stretched and nailed. Did he do it in order to gain the understanding that only came from having given it up? Perhaps you lose your life to know what life is; at the moment of knowledge you realize your loss and it is terrible… It was terrible for Andre now.

The man-woman battle continued. Andre's efforts to renew himself resembled those of a burned out meteor. He told her he was writing a book about her; bragged and boasted about it so much that one day she took the unfinished manuscript to the seashore and watched as the scattered pages floated and drifted down into the foaming waves.

Andre pretended not to be upset. "Wow," he told her. "What a homage to our love, that nothing of it should remain, no written records!"

If Andre accepted them with joy, Maya's extravagances frightened Louise, who kept calling Robert to tell him how dismayed she was. Yet Andre took them as the most culminating point of their love; Maya couldn't be wild enough for him; and in his own surrealistic way he declared, "I love the grandiose deaths you prepare for me every day."

Once Maya might have said, "We really are living, aren't we? We're not vegetables for sure!" Now she merely laughed at him, finding in him a terrible caricature of everything she was. Does love's bankruptcy begin the moment a couple cannot take each other seriously, when they see to their horror that even the ecstasies they created with such joy have now become a disguise, an alibi for something that is no longer there?

What was most terrible for Andre was the way Maya and Louise had begun to wait. Out of their silent waiting grew a suspicion. They watched, observed him, as if stalking his departure. Once he had been "king"; now he had become an intruder. Maya would never tell him to leave; she was not capable of shutting him out of the cottage. It was up to him, on the basis of the overwhelming evidence she gave him every day, to make that decision himself. So something very ironic happened: Andre, who had always forced other people to confront their solitude, had to begin accepting his own.

Louise took him aside and said boldly in frank French, "If you had any balls, you'd get your ass out of here!"

Maya added more discreetly, "If you were a man, you would go."

Louise even went so far as to call him her "pet shopping bag" because he accepted everything, even though he inwardly raged. There was nothing left to reveal to them what they had once been. Andre felt like a man who has discovered the source of life, then lost it. There were no trail markers to guide him back.

One night Louise came running into Andre's room in a panicked state, saying there were big spiders under her bed. Andre refused to help. "You're the spider," he retorted, "just waiting to weave your web with Maya the moment I leave."

Finally and simply, there was no money left. It became too humiliating for him to have to keep asking Maya for help. Vico spurred him on, saying, "You're not going to solve anything by hanging around here."

That really was the question: how to resolve his life? He had tried to live out his great love to the end, to see it through. Instead he had been seen through. The two women paid him for his efforts with the united front of their disapproving silence.

The afternoon Andre left for New York City, he was again yelling at Louise. Vico had to pull him away from the front of the cottage. "Get on your bike, man! I don't dig all these performances."

Capricious as a child, Andre squatted down on the grass --- the huge shiny bikes were standing like horses under the linden tree --- crossed his arms, refused to budge. "Do you dig how I sit here any better?" he quipped.

Framed by honeysuckle vines and flowerpots, Louise stood on the porch observing, laughing her head off. Her features vibrated with happiness as the landscape of southern France shimmers with light. After two weeks of being treated worse than a rat, she could come out and her love for Maya could burst into the open. Her face resembled a pomegranate, burned by the sun, ripe, yet difficult to eat on account of all the tiny seeds.

Incapable of remaining immobile for more than thirty seconds, Andre jumped to his feet, announced dramatically, "I'll be back. It's not finished; it's far from over. I'm not done with you yet, you French country bitch!"

Exactly like a bull, his shoulders lowered, breathing hard, he tore off around the house, seeking Maya, who had wisely slipped out the back door, hopped on her bicycle and pedaled off in direction of the beach.

Happy-go-lucky Vico caught up with Andre and said, "What the hell are you doing, man? I hate this egomaniacal bullshit. Do you want me to have to knock you down?"

Farther away, under the tree by the road, the blond kid, Hoppy, sat twiddling his fingers and murmuring, "There are submarines floating through my mind."

Believing that Maya was still inside the house, Andre tried to break down the porch door. When that didn't work, he spurted across the road, hacked down the wires on the fence, and let the farmer's bulls loose. Uncertain, swaying its massive horned head, a big black bull rambled across the asphalt road and trampled into the garden. Louise gave a quick, panicked cry and fled through the bushes into the potato fields. Vico, after collapsing with laughter, recovered himself and thrust Andre onto his motorcycle; he yelled at the blond kid with the submarines in his head to hop on behind him.

The bull crashed through the herb garden as they gunned the bikes in a circle and curved away. Andre shook his fist and shouted, "I'm not finished with you yet, you bitch!" In a nebula of speed, dust, confusion, and jubilant cries, they roared down the country lane.

Chapter XX

Robert drove his faithful Buick down a narrow road past a clean, white space of fields. Everything here was so open, flat, accessible and beautiful, and he was taking Carolina to the airport, away from it all. Turning to him, she smiled in her quick, enigmatic way and said, "Isn't it funny to be changing our skins like this?"

"Yes, it's so funny, so odd, so fucking unbelievable even, that I really don't know how to answer." He slowed before the entrance to Route 27 and tried to let the simple act of driving galvanize all his attention. There was no use trying to resist or to think and he forced himself to succumb entirely to the motion of her going away. He tried to think that she was already gone and there was nothing he could do about it.

Fields spread out before them in evenly split rows like fractured crystals. He thought, if only everything were as simple, clear and apparent as these fields. For the first time Robert had doubts about what he was going to do once she had flown off. Carolina had, by her very presence, opposed a resistance to his desires. With that presence removed, would his desires simply collapse? Suddenly it seemed stupid and ridiculous for him to linger on as if the dwindling summer bore some secret message or gift for him. He envied Carolina --- her liberty to leave, her freedom from the illusions of the demanding ego. If he could have looked inside her, he felt he would have seen something similar to those fields, something calm and simple, open and manifest. He felt embarrassed and something in him tightened.

Carolina sang gaily, trying to make her departure easier for him, he who had initiated it all! Sunlight, liberty, freedom, love, air ---- were they anything but words he had invented in order to be alone? His precious solitude! But if freedom lay in the possibility of making errors, was the error he felt they were making now by leaving each other a measure of their freedom? What would happen to her in his absence? Would she be safe? Would she indeed wait for him as she had waited for him patiently during the war years?

He grew fearful, apprehensive. She sensed his mood and said, "You know, Robbie, the only real freedom is death. You don't become free until you're dead."

"That's true," he answered stupidly.

He felt ashamed that he had been unable to get closer to her in her great bareness, her simplicity and austerity. He tried to think of death, of all the deaths he had seen, but he couldn't; all he could think of was the "little death" that was going to take place at the airport, for which he was responsible. Was he killing her or sending her back to what she loved most, her freedom? Or was she secretly giving him what he most deeply desired: her absence?

An airplane floated above them, far out over the fields, an ominous sign. They had stopped at a traffic light. He lit a Winston. On the street corner a young man had halted his bicycle in order to zip up his fly. His legs looked awkward as he straddled the seat struggling to zip up his pants. What was really funny was that between his teeth, to free his hands, he was clenching a shopping bag, loaded with consumer articles. They had a brief laugh.

Carolina said, "The other day, coming out of the supermarket, I met this sixty year old man who said to me, 'People just aren't helping each other anymore. They're doing more and more to hurt each other, to grow farther and farther apart!"

The light changed and they moved on in this trip that, every moment, was widening the spaces between them. Robert's heart beat like that of a hooked fish. The miles ticked off. For her sake, he tried to hide what he was feeling from her. They accepted their decision to leave each other as a kind of fatality; it hung above them, guiding them, like the plane that had now vanished from the sky. They passed suburban houses, cool neat quadrangles of lawns. Robert wondered whether the time would come when tears and sorrows would be considered indecent, obsolete? Since the Renaissance, hadn't man paid too much attention to himself? Hadn't he assumed too much? Could a new humility be regained? Could the "I" be eliminated? Would it be possible to escape from the pleasure-seeking vicious circle of the self?

"I think it's possible," Carolina said. She was going to try. She felt that if she loved him, it was her duty to set him free. If he truly loved her, he would come back.

Carolina was gazing idly out the lowered window at the passing sights. He thought: she can't stand to look at me. She knows what's happening as well as I do and she thinks I'm a coward. It was true: he didn't have the courage to accept the consequences of a love that had gone beyond his understanding. Pushing her away, he found himself repellent. Even Ben had warned him, "Maybe you're just obeying some inner law of your own that I can't see, but it seems to me that your life is about to get pretty messy."

Relentlessly Robert accelerated toward the highway, the smooth road to travel ahead, hoping to make the speed of the car outdistance his thoughts.

Easily, fluidly, Carolina said, "Hey, look at those flowers over there. They have a funny name: hydrangeas."

Robert jumped at this chance to shift his mind back to something simple. "In Paris we used to call them hortensias. Don't you remember we didn't like them very much then? We thought they were ugly, bourgeois, cemetery flowers."

"That's because we saw them in pots. Here, natural, they're wonderful. It's beautiful the way they grow up into the bush and color it and shape it. It's very rare, too, to see such a blue flower."

"Why? Irises are blue."

"Yes, but not the kind of blue these hydrangeas are, a perfect sky-blue or baby-blue."

Cerulean, sky-blue, baby-blue, dark azure, how the hydrangeas had swollen into such a beautiful blue bouquet was a mystery, a sweet lovely mystery --- Robert remembered sitting at Ben's complaining about the symmetry of one of the rooms, how he felt that all the parts in were so well locked together that there was no room for a human presence. "Relax," Carolina had said, "there's room for you. Just look out the window. Do you see the blue bush?"

Now he said to her, "Blue is the only color that we don't eat," and she laughed, this woman of blueness, airy and ethereal. It was as if Carolina had special lenses on her eyes that made her capable of seeing an intense, infinite blueness in everything. In less than an hour she would be on the plane in the sky.

He recalled the last time he had tried to make love to her. In an effort to take her, to drag her "floating blueness" down to the earth, he had grabbed her and dumped her brutally as a sack of potatoes on the ground. She had showed surprise, disbelief, astonishment. He had been desperate, it had been such a long time; he hadn't known what to do. He had hovered around her half-clothed body like a black vulture. She just lay there without moving, neither waiting for him nor rejecting him, just whimpering a little. Her hair, spread out on the ground, had looked like a pool of honey. Then she laughed, and it was her sudden, irrational gaiety that had truly annoyed him. He had drawn back, she still laughing and flapping her hands at him as if to scare him away.

As they joined the stream of traffic that finally eddied around the airports and broke against the city, he had a desire he couldn't suppress to antagonize her, to separate her violently from him, to make her glad to be rid of him. He said, "So, what do you think of Maya?"

She was taking everything so calmly that he was curious to know whether she would take that calmly too. He knew he was provoking her but he justified himself thinking that he was doing it for her own good.

Carolina responded in a second, "Poor girl. Wow. She's really miserable."

So that was it? Why it was so easy for her to leave? She was judging Maya from the scene at Ben's party and didn't imagine Robert could possibly be interested in her. She was going to let him stay here and be bored while she went up to Vermont and tuned herself in with her hip young friends. If he stayed too long, he would die with the dinosaurs - that was what she thought!

"I believe many of our sufferings come because we misjudge people. Here's a good way to see each person: of how much do they make you aware? How much new do they put into you?"

The conversation had become heavy. He weaved in and out of traffic, anxious to get to the airport.

"Can't you see why I'm against Maya?" she continued. "Because that's where everything started, a month ago, at that Fourth of July party. It was when you saw her. She disrupted everything. If it hadn't been for her, I wouldn't be leaving now."

It was funny how she, who was the complete opposite of Maya, blamed everything on Maya. Maya was fire and ice, whereas she was clarity and calmness. But he thought he could give something to Maya and there was nothing he could give anymore to Carolina because they were both too full of the same vibrations. He hated the knowledge she had of him. It was only too obvious why they were both pulling apart from each other.

Billboards gleamed above them, as the traffic grew denser. One blazoned: "One of the major causes for crisis in our society is that the protests of the young and alienated are not being listened to. Lend an ear." Around them was the roar and quick zip of cars. From time to time he glanced at her fine, delicate profile. It was impossible for him to forget for a moment the gravity of what they were living, the courage she had, and the way her face was pointed toward the future like a prow. There was such a marvelous and touching light-heartedness to her, as if she didn't know how to be unhappy. He couldn't stand it. His hands tightened around the wheel. They approached the airport.

She began to sing a sweet, soft, song. She seemed so sure of something, so radiant with nothing in particular, what was it? Love? Was it their love she was thinking of, the fact that maybe one day they would come together again after he had his experience with the mystery of Maya? He felt sick and tortured. If only it were ended! Wasn't his biggest problem finding a way to make her die? Worms crawled around his heart.

She caressed his shoulder. "Don't worry, Robbie. I'll protect you. I'll be with you. I'll follow you from faraway. We'll always be together just as we are in this car now."

These beautiful words he could not accept made his brain spin. He could hardly control the car. "Let's stop and get some gas."

"Gas, gas," she murmured. "Even gas can be a contact with life. Lifting a tube and putting gas into the belly of a car. You see; it's as simple as that."

But it wasn't so simple and he was already elsewhere. "Listen, when you're in Vermont don't just sit in some lousy cabin on top of a hill. Get out and have a good time."

They got back into the car. But she paused. "Don't you think I can have a good time just sitting alone by myself?"

"I guess," he muttered.

Carolina looked at him with a curious, hard stare, as if to say, "Why don't you wake up to what you really want to say."

He said nothing.

"What you really mean is you feel guilty you're not spending as much time with me as you should, and you feel anxious about this and you try to compensate by telling me to go out and have a good time."

He half-nodded, half-shook his head.

She pressed him, taking another tack, "In the past you always accused me of my going away. But you never stopped long enough to find the deep, profound causes of it. You never asked yourself: why does she do it?"

He knew exactly why she was leaving now: because he wanted her to.

"I'm with you," he said, putting his hand on her knee.

Now that she was drifting away, he desperately sought to make her his own, to prove that she could be his again, that they could be together as intimately and as beautifully as they once had been.

In less than five minutes they were at the airport.

It was a horrible night. The sky had suddenly burst open and rain lashed the pavements. Robert thought for a moment of spending the night in a motel, of talking things over. But what was the use of doing that again? Why torture themselves? Nothing would be resolved. She had to go.

But she wouldn't leave without his promising to join her.

"I will, I will," he repeated. "I'll join you in a month."

He knew he was lying. He felt sick to his stomach. He knew at that very moment that he would never see Carolina again, never again be with her as he had been up until now.

There she stood, with her beautiful bare face and chopped hair, the "independent" woman, staring at him, supplicating him with her look, with her eyes, with her whole being. She started to cry.

The emotions of departure were too strong; she said she didn't want to leave him. Hugged close to him, she mumbled, "There are so many problems."

Robert was unbearably brutal. "Tears in your eyes, that's your only problem."

It tore him apart to be so cruel, but there was no other way to be. He felt if even for a second he let himself be soft or understanding, he would collapse.

"Please," she urged him, "whatever you do, don't be 'fixed'. Don't let yourself be magnetized."

"What can I promise you, dear Carolina?"

He held her numbly in his arms. He thought: this sorrow hurts so much it ought to be smashed with a brick.

They stood in the harsh glare of the arc lights. Outside the rain roared down on the parking lots, the buses, the circling cars.

"Remember the day I spent at the gas station, sitting around on the tires, talking to the men? Then you came and I said, 'The only thing that counts is our being happy.'"

Carolina looked at him with that sweet, smiling sadness so peculiar to her. She still had tears in her eyes.

"Nothing is lost," she said finally. "Do you know that? Nothing is ever lost." Her words fell like the rain.

The plane left in an hour. Robert knew he would never be able to wait that long. "I'm going."

"I understand. Go, go quickly." She seemed almost happy now. Soon she would be on the plane, flying through the night to Boston; all the dirty work Robert had not been able to do would be done slowly by time.

"Go to the beach," she said. "Look at the children, listen to them, how they play…"

He kissed her for the last time.

"Go to the end of what you want," she whispered. "For once live your desires instead of talking about them. If you don't, you'll die."

He hushed her, wincing. He could have screamed. Here she was, on the point of leaving, giving him helpful advice! Trying to assist him! As if nothing were wrong between them and they would inevitably find each other again in a short while.

He turned and without looking back, he dashed through the building and started to run through the rain, ducking under the fence and into the parking lot.

Chapter XXI

Robert knew what he had just done was enormous, unthinkable, almost heinous. He had sent the woman who loved him away. He had done it almost in cold blood. If he had murdered her, he would be in prison. But was her departure any less of a crime? He knew he had not wanted to hurt her. At the airport her tears had made it impossible for him to say anything to her. He had thought they would die there together. He had come away in the thundering rain with his stomach ripped apart.

Carolina had offered him the complete sacrifice of herself and he had rejected it. She had waited patiently for him while he trudged through steamy tunnels in Vietnam in search of an elusive enemy. She had met him in Boston when he returned. The breadth and depth of her loyalty surprised him. It was as if she had finally made up in her mind what she wanted. What she wanted was him. She had to stream through him in order to become herself. At the same time she hated the fact she had to flow through him. She had tried to make him abandon himself, his body, and his ideas, in order to flow through her.

And he couldn't.

That was the way he saw it. Perhaps he was wrong, but he was nonetheless happy to be alone as he drove back in the hammering rain.

Even the fact that windshield wipers hardly worked didn't bother him. He was free.

As he approached Sag Harbor the rain stopped and the moon came out, a lush, full moon hanging ripe and solitary over the fields. Robert stopped the car, got out, and took a long piss by the side of the road. He leaped over a ditch, ran into the open field, stood there and let out a wild, yapping howl. Then he jumped in the car and drove with great joy back to Ben's. For the first time in more than a year, he had no one to dispose of but himself, no one to worry about, to think about, no one even to love. It was a strange sensation.

Robert arrived at Ben's before midnight and was astonished to find Louise standing behind the wrought iron gate on the driveway. What was she doing there at this time? A cold shock went through him. That afternoon on the beach, when he had tried to embrace her, she had talked about his "being reserved for a higher destiny." He had never suspected that, on the heels of Carolina's departure, she would come to make good on her promise and deliver him toward it.

It was weird. She stood on one side of the gate, he on the other. They greeted each other uneasily.

Louise was wearing a white dress, a black knitted shawl flung around her shoulders. A faint lemon peel of a smile was on her face. Surprised, still under the impact of the trip to the airport, Robert felt that Louise was a devil sprit who had come to fetch him.

"I just finished playing chess on the porch with Ben," she said. "He won and went to bed. He told me you'd be back soon so I decided to hang around and wait for you."

All Robert wanted was to be alone, to enjoy his new freedom.

"I must talk to you, Robbie," she said. "You know very well that Maya is the star here, the 'vedette', and I'm just like her caretaker, but I want to be a good caretaker, and that's why I need to talk to you."

Robert felt guilty, a little nauseous, and the way Louise smiled at him now made him suspect that it was she who subtly and secretly was engineering the whole relationship. Could there be something at stake much more important than he had guessed? Louise knew he had just come back from driving Carolina to the airport and yet she had said nothing about it. Wasn't that odd? Although he was too tired to think clearly, Robert knew he had to be careful. He stood on the verge of something exciting and dangerous, what it was exactly he didn't know. But, however obscurely, he had wanted it and he couldn't turn his back on it.

There are some people who seem to act as shock absorbers, as go-betweens in life, and Louise was one of those. For all her sweetness and charm, there was still something indefinable about her. The real life she was living was never revealed. It was impossible to tell what her goals, desires and ambitions were, what she was aiming at.

What did she want now? What had she driven over to Ben's house in Sag Harbor for? Robert had a sense of coinciding with old patterns of life that were played out again with slight variations. Wasn't that what Carolina had warned him about? Already the events at the airport seemed to belong to another period of his life that had nothing to do with the realm he had just entered.

At that point, though nothing had been said between them, Louise slid into the Buick, which Robert started and they looped out of the long driveway. It was a wide, lonely night. The crickets were chirping everywhere. The first sad lovely notes of late August were in the air.

The road that led back through the woods was deserted. Robert drove quickly. The moon silvered the leaves. They didn't speak. They were too much aware of what was happening to break the silence.

"I wish I knew what to do with my life," she said finally when they got to Bridgehampton. "I don't know if Maya will want me around when the summer's over."

Robert didn't know how to answer. Maya kept saying how fantastic Louise was, how clever and subtle. But Robert saw no depths in her. He saw Louise as a kind of inverse anchor, floating on the surface, anchoring Maya's depths and nuances.

Louise flicked her head sideways and looked at him askance, that same half-bitter, half-charming, smile on her lips. What did her glances mean? Even as he looked at her she flashed another quick, enigmatic, a trifle ingratiating smile. If only Louise had been able to come out and say what she meant! If only she had been able to make her meaning clear! But everything with her was obscure, shrouded in ambiguity.

It troubled Robert to realize his dependency on her. Were they moving toward death or toward life? He had sent Carolina away to be free of this web of intrigues whose meaning escaped him.

"I'll just drop you off at the cottage and then go," he said. "I'm exhausted."

She said a hurried yes and looked at him and smiled nervously. Had her plans backfired? Robert sensed that she was afraid of him, afraid of what he might do if something went wrong. The headlights illuminated the thick trees one by one; a swollen moon hung low over the potato fields. Their ride was more remarkable for what was not said than for what was. A hidden tension tied them together, smoldered between them.

He wondered if they were united by the fact that they had both just lost something. Louise wouldn't have come and waited for him if she had felt secure in her possession of Maya.

With her glances, what was she trying to tell him? Was it a warning, a sign saying, "Danger, Stay Clear!" or an encouragement?

"You're lucky you weren't here the other day when Andre left. It was terrible! What a storm! You know, he set the farmer's bull loose and I was so scared I had to run and hide in the corn stalks! These outbursts have to stop. Some peace, some kind of understanding, has to be reached, no?"

"Right, but how?"

"You need to take Maya aside, talk to her, convince her that you're not amused by all these insane actions, that you expect a little more of Maya, that's it not quite the big joke she takes it to be."

In short, Robert realized he had to assume a stance above her, not below her; he had to refuse to play court-jester to her joker.

"Maya is like a very difficult horse, you have to come and show her you are the expert rider!"

Robert was called upon, he was summoned; could he accept the challenge? Could he surpass himself and everything that he had been with Carolina? Or was he no more than emergency help Louise had called on because of her own relationship needs?

Louise, sensing his agitation, added, "I know it's late, but let's go up and see Maya now in her bedroom! I called her before we left Ben's. She's expecting us."

Louise had promised she would lead Robert toward Maya and she was doing it. Yet it disappointed Robert to think that the paths ahead of him were inevitably traced. Was he simply the puppet of his own desires? Who was pulling the strings?

Louise smiled. "I always knew you would be my angel. This weekend was just horrible. I can't take it anymore, the nervous strain. I'll end up in a mad house. Andre spends his time running up and down the stairs, watching, and surveying my every movement. Half a dozen times a day he barges into my room, looking through things, trying to find out something. And Maya's terrible too. Instead of being quiet and indifferent, she provokes him. She actually gets him madder. He's wild with rage."

"Like a bull," Robert joked, trying to visualize the moment when the farmer's bull had bolted through the picket fence into the herb garden.

"Yes, exactly, just like a bull. He rampages through the house, upsetting everything. He hides behind doors, eavesdropping, trying to hear what Maya and I are saying. But as I told you before, Maya's so naïve, she doesn't take any precautions. She's always mentioning your name, bringing you up for some reason or other when Andre is listening. She's got to be more sensible, discreet. Otherwise there's going to be death, blood. That's not the kind of games you want to play, is it?"

Into the moon-struck night ahead of them, past the sudden gaps the headlights revealed between the trees, they drove up the road that led to the beach lane.

Now that Louise had spoken, Robert was determined to make her clarify the terms. "Are we both going to go into Maya's bedroom?" he questioned sharply. In a way, he was warning her: I won't accept a three-way relationship. It's you or me.

Louise laughed. "You'll probably end up in her bedroom."

Then she stopped laughing to add quite abruptly in a saddened tone, "Not me. Not me."

She paused. He said nothing. She changed the subject. "I like Ben very, very much. He's a very gracious man, and so smart. And a great deal of charm."

"He's a world-renowned architect, you know."

"Yes, he's quite charming. He has a good smile and he likes very much talking to women. Perhaps too much. His drinking I like less. There's something in Ben's personal life that doesn't work and I haven't yet figured out what it is."

The night was huge, vast, nostalgic, reaching up from the earth to the moon-filled sky with only the trees in between. Robert felt the same limitless nostalgia floating in himself, and wondered how he could turn this tremendous outer space into an inner space. He thought of Carolina, who must have been asleep in Vermont by now, and her search for unity and oneness. Robert realized it wasn't so much love he was after as something that went beyond it and would be at once deliverance and fulfillment and joy. Ironically it was Carolina who had told him once, "How do you become a god? You love."

"You need to talk to Maya, Robbie. You need to have a real talk with her. Things can't go on any longer like this."

Headlights appeared behind them, followed them for a moment, and then disappeared. Louise's face, in profile, looked less hard and set than it usually did. Robert sensed she was trying to help him, to point a way forward. She wanted him to help Maya escape from the inferno in which she was living. She wanted to make sure, too, that he didn't fantasize too much about Maya, that he was informed in advance who she was, so that he wasn't tricked by his own dreams.

"Until you get to know her, you cannot imagine what a special woman Maya is. It's strange, but sometimes I feel I was born simply in order to serve her."

Robert looked at Louise, imagining her in the role of a handmaiden to a goddess of love.

"Don't forget what I tell you," she warned. "Remain in control. Maya needs a guide."

Robert was remembering what Carolina had said: "Don't get 'fixed'."

He lit a cigarette. Louise asked for one and he lit it for her.

"The trouble is that Maya catches other people in the circle of her life, so that she's only ruining her own life, but she's ruining theirs as well."

"I'll make sure I don't get pulled in," Robert said more confidently than he felt.

"You can't give in to her. You're the only one, Robbie, who's stronger than she is, to whom she'll listen. Every time I try to tell her something she tells me to stop interfering with her life. Or she says I'm saying silly things. It just depends on the whim of the moment, how she feels. I told her she shouldn't be at the cottage when Andre shows up. She should go and stay at a friend's. But she just smiles and says I'm confusing her. So you've got to be really strong, Robert, you've got to take her aside and help her get out of the terrible predicament she's in."

Robert frowned. He wasn't sure if he was cut out for the role of the savior.

"I don't have any power over what she does. Maya has to choose for herself. But I think what's happening now, the events of this weekend, are very dangerous and unhealthy for her."

Robert's mind had reached a boiling point. He couldn't wait to see Maya.

"Don't talk to her tonight," Louise cautioned. "Do it tomorrow afternoon."

What, then, was the sense of the visit tonight? Was Louise simply ushering him in, initiating him? With the patient skill of a chemist she was going to put the two of them together and wait and see what kind of reaction occurred. The worst of it was that he wanted it just as badly as she.

He parked the car on the grass in front of the cottage. Louise touched his shoulder. "Before we go in, I want to warn you, Maya's never acted like this before. I've known her a long time, since she came to Paris after leaving Oxford; I've never seen her so agitated. It's all because of that awful Andre. He keeps coming back; he won't give up. He just clings to her and she feels so helpless. She needs a big push from outside."

The house was dark, quiet. A light shone in the sitting room behind the lace curtains. The screen door Andre had kicked in had been repaired. Crickets were crying their hearts out in the fields. Otherwise the night was warm, serenely quiet, tinted with the nostalgia of its being already mid-August.

Was Andre lurking somewhere in the shadows of the honeysuckle vines?

"I feel as if I'm walking into enemy territory," he told Louise.

She laughed. "It's safe now."

"Right, I just don't know for how long."

He felt like an intruder, a thief in the night, as Louise guided him into the silent house. "There's another girl, Marthe, staying here," Louise whispered. "That's good for Maya. Relaxes her."

Louise opened the door to the narrow stairway. She nudged him on the shoulder, telling him to go forward. It was too late to back out. He wanted Maya, yes, but not at once, not so suddenly.

"Go," Louise commanded. Her job was finished; she slipped away. A pale yellow patch of light gleamed on the landing and Robert moved with relentless, excited caution toward it.

His time had come. Everything he had lived was concentrated in this one moment he was living now. He ascended the steep wooden stairs.

He felt he was moving toward liberation, toward dying and being born again. He didn't know how this would happen but he knew now that it would. His life had prepared him for this instant, for this higher stage. He also realized the sweet absurdity of this "mission." Downstairs Louise was waiting and listening anxiously.

Darkness and lovely shadows were piled up in the corner. The room shone with its frank, soft whiteness. Everything was nuance, whisper, murmur. He could hear Maya laughing, welcoming him, and waving a slight, cheery hello, which rose at once to his head like good wine. He was happy because she had gestured and at once they were friendly. It had been a slight, faint wave, a mere flowery wisp of a wave, but he took it as a sign, an indicator, of what might happen later on.

How far would they stay together into that night? Robert didn't want her at once; what he wanted was to lead her to that point where she would offer herself of her own free will. Slowly and steadily, she was bringing Robert into a renewed adolescence. He was burning. His mind was flushed. His nerves jumped up and down at the sight of her in bed like the rear end of a rabbit hopping across fields.

The room breathed delicacy, freshness, and simplicity. Maya was submerged under the white coverlets. The whole room seemed to be in white lace. A series of beautiful vintage patchwork quilts hung on the walls. He moved toward her, succumbing already. She was looking at him and smiling. With a kind of violent gentleness he took her fine head in his hands and squeezed some more laughter out of her delicate, Nefertiti-style neck.

Was it possible that he could take such playfulness seriously? He thought of all his political struggles, the sit-ins in Chicago, the marches in Washington in the middle of winter. Youthful idealism? At first he had thought he might be able to do something, protesting an absurd, senseless war he had fought in but no longer believed in; gradually he had resigned himself to not being able to do anything at all. Had he simply been too weak to glimpse things in an historical perspective? Was what he was doing now in this bedroom anything more important, less stupid, than what he had tried to do in the streets before? Why did he suddenly see a chance for liberation --- to call things frankly by their name --- in this woman who herself had such a grandiose sense of absurdity.

Maya, who had disappeared for a moment, came back wearing a long, lovely, dark blue dress. It was wrapped about her in folds and flounces and curves. She joked about it, saying it was just an old rag, but it was funny to see her wearing it long after midnight. As always, she looked extravagantly elegant.

"Why don't we get on the bicycles and take a ride down to the beach," she proposed.

This slight project seemed indicative to Robert of a future between them that had to be lived.

Stretched out on the couch downstairs, Louise observed their preparations with the watchful eye of a mother hen and warned Robert, "I give you half an hour."

Then Maya came down, clung to him for a moment, laughing, too, at the absurdity of the situation, and they strolled separately out into the garden. Crowns of leaves rose up around the old tree in whose shadows the air was cooler. The full moonlight shone on the grass, the rose bushes. Maya's dress glowed with a somber, beautiful intensity. She walked forward, moving her shoulders from side to side, casting him quick glances.

But Robert was thinking of all the tenderness he had already known, whose fires still burned so deeply within him. Past memories, associations, images, dreams, kept nagging at him. It was so difficult to undo in a night what he had spent three years trying to construct! Part of him still lay with Carolina, and the new part of him, the part he was trying to urge forward out of himself, had not yet come to be with Maya. In his guts he knew that he and Maya were moving forward at a swifter and swifter pace. But were they travelling forward quickly enough to escape the gravity of what was left behind them?

Was he betraying Carolina in obeying this law of dynamic growth that was leading him forward? She had believed so much in the "Now," why should he feel guilty about letting himself be carried along by the momentum of the moment?

What did he want? Why was it that he suddenly felt so full and free, joyous and complete? He had nothing; he was a disenchanted war veteran, and he had just lost his double, his soul sister, his shadow psyche. Even much later in his life, he would never forget this rare moment of exaltation, of being for a second on the heights without any reason or cause, just for the pure joy of being there. Something in him was rising, consenting, saying yes and meeting the marvelous night. The nagging remorse he felt over Carolina only added to the totality of his feelings, and he began to understand how everything could be perceived as one, without any contradictions or discontinuity. Wasn't that what Carolina had been trying to teach him? A cruel thought came over him: that's the way love is --- you learn from one person in order to give to the next.

For a split second Robert did not feel trapped by any future, by any intention, by any magnet of whatever nature. Something in him expanded, his soul flooded up, went out and joined the cricket-combed fields and the full moon, which seemed entirely within his reach.

"Let's go on bicycles!" said Maya excitedly. "Yes, yes!" Her note of triumph, of wild affirmation, only lifted him higher.

Maya ran forward quickly. She always ran so lightly, carried forward by the crest of her ever-present enthusiasms. Yet Louise was right: she was not well, how could she be, when she lived all the time at such an extreme level of tension, openness, danger? The cord of her being was stretched as tight as it possibly could be: small wonder if it broke occasionally. When she snapped, she lost control. Her soul burst into fragments. Robert had seen it happen at Ben's; it was happening now.

Like those surfers he and Ben and Carolina had watched one day at the beach, he had at last found a rideable wave and he was letting it sweep him forward. It was too late now to think of what might not have happened, or whether that wave would break and collapse. Carolina's words of warning lit up in his head, "Flee this woman as the plague, for she is the very image of the eternal devourer you have always feared so much."

Nevertheless, in spite of everything he knew or didn't dare to know, Robert yielded; he yelled his assent; he had to live, she had so much life! To the bicycles!

"That long dress of yours is going to get caught in the spokes," he warned her.

Maya looked at him and laughed. She averted her head slightly to one side --- the moonlight slanted across her, illuminating her --- and became very proud. She hardly deigned to look at him. Superb moment! Setting off into the night as if their bicycles were ships and they at last were leaving the harbor, entering the uncharted spaces whose pounding vibrations had taunted their heads so much.

"This is crazy!" he muttered. "What a soap opera!"

"Come on, up, up, let's go," she cried.

Laughing hysterically, her dress streaming behind her, caught in folds around her hips, Maya rode off into the soft, moon-washed night.

Once again Robert had the impression of really being stung by life, of having no control over himself. His life was up for grabs, open to all the chances.

They glided silently together, their bike wheels almost interlocked; but before they reached the old ghostly farm at the end of the road, Maya suddenly swerved and toppled off.

"Are you hurt?"

"No, just grazed. Oh the bitch!" she moaned. "I'm always falling off and banging up my poor legs. Ha-ha! I don't care, I really couldn't care less!"

Robert laughed, admiring her basic insouciance, her cheeky bravado. Laughing at herself, she lifted up her skirt, pulling him forward to show him exactly what the details of the fall had done to her.

She swung astride her bike, holding up her skirt, and said, "Hey, take a look at my legs, you!"

The little bruises on her thighs only revealed her delicate build. Robert made up a funny song about love, cows, rockets, and tumbling off bicycles. From around them, drenched in fertile white light, came the odor of fields, cow manure, corn, potatoes, flowers, and apples. Maya shrieked with apprehension when the headlights of a lonely car menaced them for a moment. Then they were alone again in the star-tented darkness.

"So few people have a sense of spark, of fire," Maya said. "It's so difficult to be happy, to have something joyous to live for."

"Sunlight, liberty, freedom, euphoria, hahaha!" Robert echoed.

He moved over toward her, grazing her, moving his fingers like gauze over her arms. She kept talking. He felt her quivering slightly.

It was strange to think they were alone at last, responsible only to themselves.

"Watch out," she warned. "Don't come too close."

They pedaled past potato fields that seemed bathed in a clear, silent consciousness. Robert concentrated on how things happen, the slow birth of impressions, how they were each moving together, perhaps about to be interlaced, thinking of the unknown worlds in the other, all that they didn't know, were about to find out, and to which this bicycle ride was a prelude. He was about to say that most people spend their lives looking for something to turn them on, to ignite them, but there were so few real sparks, when he was interrupted by the baa of a sheep.

He waited a few seconds, but the loud, bizarre Baaaaaaaa! repeated, and Maya's laughter, more explosive, rose over his.

"Wow! Those sheep are responding to me. I'm carrying on a conversation with them, they've caught hold of the spark!"

She stopped her bike and solitary, solemn, almost religiously, moved off across the moonlit fields, for an encounter with the sheep whose "Baaaaaaaa" had sounded so magically and heightened the comic diversions in Robert's mind. He braked, straddling his bike, marveling at the way in which the sheep immediately rushed over to see Maya, who tried to feed them. But they wouldn't take the grass out of her hands. Then she tried to feed them pears but no luck. She returned, gracefully, but when she came close to him she screwed up her lips, stuck her tongue out, and said --- looking silly, repentant ---- the sheep had rejected her

Another "Baa" sounded, deeper, and Robert said that sheep was like an old successful banker going "Blaaa! Blaaa! Blaaa" all the time. They laughed.

"I guess some sheep are like bankers, but most men are like wolves," Robert added, a little sadly now.

"Si, si," Maya nodded swiftly, caressing him up and down with her eyes, raking his face, as if looking for the confirmation of some truth. Quietly she began to tell him a little more about herself, filling in details he didn't know. Vaguely she mentioned her first husband, a wealthy Mexican who had an import-export business and was known as the "emperor of sardines." It was a marriage that lasted only one week. She liked his family name and she took it: Alvarez. When she married Andre, whose mother was American, she elected to become an American citizen.

Briefly Robert talked about his grandmother, Mrs. Mellon, how much she clung to life. Maya answered quickly, "Myself, you understand, I absolutely don't care. If I were to finish tomorrow, I would be very happy about it. It wouldn't bother me one bit. I absolutely have no regard."

They rolled on evenly, smoothly, through the vast, scented night, and Robert affirmed, "Neither do I."

Was it a consequence of the war, or of his leaving Carolina that he didn't care any longer what happened to him?

Finally they arrived at the beach, where the sea was shining like a molten sheet of silver.

"Shall we sit down?" asked Maya.

Here was the beginning, the irreversible yet irresistible invitation. Robert thought desperately of Carolina, of everything they had built up and projected. Maya lay back, and started making holes in the sand with her hands. But it was cold. She rose and ran. She tumbled down the shore in the darkness, Robert following.

"I'm going to swim to England," he heard her cry. She swam so far out that he began to worry when he lost sight of her bobbing head. But she came back, shivering and cold, and he wrapped her in a towel.

Nothing else happened. They rode back silently in the darkness. Louise was still up, waiting for them. She had lit a fire. Maya embraced her. "You are so sweet, you are so sweet," she told her.

"I just want you to be happy," she answered, already resigned to her new role.

Robert was glad. Maya's eyes were shining with satisfaction, joy, and pride.

Louise took Robert aside and scolded him for bringing Maya back so late.

"If I told you about the sheep, you'd think I was trying to pull the wool over your eyes," he teased.

They sat around the fire Louise had made. She brought them mint tea fresh from the garden, served in Moroccan glasses. Maya talked about bull fighting, the time she had spent in Spain on a bull farm near Madrid. "I wanted to learn to fight the bull," she said.

"So the matador is the woman and the bull is the man, right?"

The talk shifted to drugs; Louise was, of course, totally against them. Robert and Maya already felt an elevated high. They watched the shadows shift on the walls. Robert sat next to Maya by the fire. He observed her long neck, the delicacy of her collarbone, the extreme fineness of her features.

"I'm tired, my body's so weak."

Louise said it was time for them to go to bed and Robert left.

Chapter XXII

Polish the light until it emerges. Rub the darkness until it dies and light is born, wash, wash, Robert murmured. Softly stoned, unable to sleep, he sat on the beach early in the morning.

Images kept assailing him: he imagined a man with the horns of a bull locked in mortal combat with a voluptuous woman who had the head of a sphinx. Then he envisioned a naked girl with golden blonde hair lying buried in the sand, both of her splayed legs wrapped with remnants of a blood-stained American flag.

The image terrified him. He sensed he had killed Carolina and visions of her were already returning to torment him.

Out of his desire to have something real, solid, tangible, was he inventing Maya?

The sea was flat but rough. The sound was that of wine sloshing around deeply and thunderously in large, dark barrels. The same confusion raged inside his head. Gone were those remarkable dawns of startling and all-encompassing clarity. Perhaps because of the number of weeds, scattered algae and dead little sea-animals, the beach looked shipwrecked, empty, and desolate. There was not much to be hoped for here, nothing to be gained. Myriad patterns of foam checkered the belly of the waves just as they were about to crash. The glum silence of the sky added to the brutal monotony of the relentlessly revolving waves. How distant Robert felt from the exhilarations of the previous night.

As he realized the truth of his life --- he was a killer --- both literally for what he had done in Vietnam, and figuratively, for what he had done to Carolina, he felt himself growing smaller and smaller, shriveling up. As if broadcast over a loudspeaker, in the blue void around him, he heard Carolina's voice explaining to him that there was no such thing as original sin, only the original lie that every man invents for himself. Until he understands this lie, and recognizes the falseness of his ego, he is doomed. But most love is based on a selfish mutual masturbation of that ego…

Yet he could not prevent a few brilliant, photographic images of Maya from popping up in his head. She was swimming in the surf, in the nocturnal ocean glow, tossed against the waves, slippery with joy. Against his will he heard her cries of pleasure, her childish shouts of excitement. His mind ached trying to span her physical plenitude, her sensual promises.

Eroticism: what a marvelous way of escaping appearances, finding miraculous revelations. Bullshit! Yet he had a vision of Maya again: she had daubed her cheekbones with glitter. Her lips opened. Particles of ecstasy danced around her. The moment became electric, and Robert knew, with all the incommunicable longing in his heart, that he wanted desperately to kiss her. He glimpsed diamonds buried in her, a treasure house of intimate intensities. The feeling she radiated, her special joie de vivre, was so rare. Was he worthy of it? Could he accept it and make it his own?

If he wanted her, he had better learn. How to figure out who she was? Who were they, who could they become? He remembered her running across the field in the moonlight to meet the sheep that went "blaa" like a banker. He felt torn between the real, limpid core, the absolute simplicity, of his past life with Carolina, and the new, complex, multi-layered forms of life that Maya represented. He even had looked up her name and found it had many meanings. According to Indian mythology, one of them was "illusion".

Behind him the blades of dune grass hardly stirred. A gentle, azure calm hung in the air that the sun had not yet penetrated. It was pleasant and exciting and dangerous, this moment when life was brimming with latent possibility. Robert was lurking too. The sky sloped like a shallow saucer; its diffused light delicately outlined the contours of objects it touched. The sand was cool, stained here and the by dark streaks; above, the shore birds flew low at the level of the waves.

So many days had passed. July had risen into August, which would soon fade in its turn and disappear into September. It had hardly been a day since Carolina had gone and yet her traces were rapidly being obliterated, and she, who had been determined not to leave any traces behind her, would have liked that. Her presence had been a dancing wisp, light and free and wonderful, but so terribly little of it remained that Robert could hold onto.

The 60's were about to end. Happy 60's. Robert had come into himself, had blossomed, and was reborn. In 1959 he had been fourteen, filled with a wild ache and crazy, awkward yearning. Realizing so little about who he was or where he was going, yet full of rebellious spirit, he had imagined himself unique, not knowing that his revolt had been repeated thousands of times. But in the 60's, he began to recognize he was not alone. After graduating from St. Paul's School, he decided to skip college. He had lived in Paris for a year with Carolina. Then, as much to escape the influence of his grandmother as to prove himself, he had enlisted in the army. The war in Vietnam gave him a vision of global reality such as he never had before. His closest friend from St. Paul's School had died in his arms. He came back to an America obsessed with itself, its own imagery and myths. But he was a different man.

The waves rolled in, attacking the shore, reminding Robert of his generation, which had done what they could, broken some new ground, but were already played out. Those who came afterward would undoubtedly be more engaged, more aware and much "cooler." Lying on the beach all night had cramped his muscles and crowded his head with images. For the first time, Robert felt old.

The sea was receding from high tide, the waves breaking far out now, low and flat and foamy. He rose and wandered down the beach like a white phantom. Softly, he padded along, wrapping himself with pleasure in the bluish mist that still covered everything, digging his bare toes into the damp sand.

Finally, what mattered? As he strolled along on the beach packed smooth and flat by the night wind, he was able to wipe away almost everything that had been before. Suddenly vision was clear. Life seemed calm and simple and marvelously empty.

He tried to keep his mind free but thoughts of Maya surged through him, like a long, painful sea swell. Luckily he had Bruno, Ben's golden retriever, with him for company. The dog distracted him with his frolicking, routing the surf with his nose; he came running up to Robert, panting, his jaws flaked with sand.

How could he forget the fantastic freedom of Maya's sensibility, her sensuality that triggered itself as if on autopilot? Carolina had made the mistake of trying to free herself without passing through the great doors of the body.

Exhausted, he stretched out on the slope of a sand dune and went to sleep for a while. The dog licked his face. He felt himself prostrate beneath the weight of the light which was slowly beginning to invade the beach as the seashell sounds of the ocean lapped in his ears. He saw again the image of the "crucified woman" he and Carolina had discovered with Ben that afternoon a long time ago, and he heard again Carolina's disembodied voice softly and urgently reminding him, "If you don't live your desires, you die."

It was good to lie down, to feel the sand adjusting to the weight of his body, making a place for him. But his head was still heavy from the excitement and ambiguities of the night before. Like an ostrich, he felt like buying his head in the sand, in the depth, coolness and darkness of it. A mild breeze swept up, carrying the fine powder of the sand away from the sea. Tiny yellow crabs made their entrances and exits before the day appeared. Lovely early morning, when no one had appeared on the beach, the sand was hard, flat and dull, and life hummed, singing quietly in the stinging surf.

He saw himself flying through a tunnel further and further into himself; he was spinning downwards, drilling a hole in the sand, spiraling inwards and outwards. With joy he gave up his relentless quest to find his double, his soul mate. He would stop looking for reassuring resemblances. From now on, he was going to learn to live off his guts. But he was living, too, even more deeply than that. All the dirt was being flung aside; he was going down, down…

His fingers slipped through the sand as the first slivers of light penetrated his brain. He was riding an elevator to the bottom of the ocean. No more presumptions or pre-conceived ideas about himself; he allowed himself the freedom of not knowing what he was, or what might happen. Here he was, watching his roots grow into this tremendously organic life he had never known before.

In the middle of the beach wet, darkish clumps clustered. Around them, twigs, branches, sticks shot up in graceful articulations. In the lower left-hand corner of the sky an airplane flew by, very low, creating a high, unnatural sound that soon disappeared as the plane vanished into the pinkish mists that now were coloring the eastern horizon. There was only the sound of the surf roaring obstinately, growing louder, as if it wished to attract attention to itself.

How do you find your frontiers? What are they? Robert wanted to touch the borderline between what he was and what he was not. Explore that no man's land.

It was a little bit as if he'd gotten on a train and bought a ticket for the very last station. He didn't know what it was. No one would be there to welcome him. He'd go anyway. He had to.

There was nothing but the beach, shadows, white light, darkness scarred as if for ages into the hills of sand. Robert sat cross-legged, quietly hallucinating. He was learning to let time pass, trying to live and feel differently. A hard, clear light scattered in the thin air. On the beach below, some men were digging for clams.

Robert lay huddled up. He wondered how he could have sent Carolina away, a woman he had loved more than anyone else in his life. He had been unable to bear her sorrow at the airport; he hadn't even had the guts to stand there and see her cry. Instead, he had turned away and started running, darting back through the parked cars in the lashing rain.

Was it any surprise then that, as a punishment for his cowardice, her phantom should keep pursuing him? Her face shone wet with tears that he had caused and for which, objectively, there was no need. She had obeyed him without even understanding his real motives. Did he even know them himself? She had even tried to help him, to give him advice, to strengthen him in his path. He had chased her away. He had seen her sorrow, and he had run from it. If he had the courage to kill her, at least that would have been simpler, clearer.

Later, driving back, the way he had almost rejoiced in his remorse and nostalgia for her --- what horror! And she, behind her tears, had tried to be happy, to smile at him, to pretend everything was ok, as he was already running away and leaving. Would he ever be able to forgive himself? Would he ever be able to stop thinking about it? Wasn't that a part of his crime too: that he kept thinking about it, the departure, and not about her?

At last he understood something about love: the generosity of her gesture, which he knew he would never be able to match. The time had come for him to face up to his responsibility. He knew already that he had "killed" her and he had to live with the "death" on his shoulders. A little voice that was her voice whispered in his ear, "Everything is in your head. When I fall asleep at night, I feel the stars coming down and nesting in my head. Why is it that when I wake up they have to go away again?"

When he opened his eyes the beach was more crowded. There was an African-American woman, no doubt a model, with a white plume rising up from her hair. A fashion photographer crouched in front of her, snapping. Robert remarked that her face was cheerful, aglitter with the promises of American life. Her long, lustrous hair shone as she strutted and posed. A huge, fat lady with a puppy appeared. The puppy was cute, brown and white, cuddly, breathing affection, embodying kindness, Robert thought, for there was no fear in this animal; he was completely dependent, like a child, a child who will never grow up, who will remain forever dependent... Sweet games of childhood. Robert thought of his own parents, whom he had never known, and a wave of relief came over him, that he had escaped that kind of dependency that families have among themselves.

For the first time in his life he felt attached to nothing, not even any woman, no allegiances. Of course he had his work, his writing, but even that seemed less important to him than it had in the past. It was time to expand.

The morning unfolded itself bit by bit. The beach, waves, dunes, became tired of the spectacle, retreated into themselves, their natural daylight state. Drowsing, Robert fancied he was running down the shore, running for the sheer joy of running; Carolina was panting breathlessly at his heels. They ran and ran. She caught up to him and whispered in his ear, "Scatter pollen over you."

The rising sun had now chased away all the shadows. Robert whistled and Bruno came bounding to him out of the surf. Together they walked back to Ben's house.

Part II:

The Sphinx Lady Waits
For The Minotaur Man

Chapter XXIII

It was the last weekend in August. Ben was busy organizing a big Labor Day party, to which all the artists and writers and famous people he knew would be invited. Robert hadn't seen Maya since Andre had come back from the city. Louise had called him to tell him that Andre had solidly implanted himself in the cottage again. Brooding on his memories, Robert sat and looked out one of the big bay windows in Ben's house.

It was a cool grey day. A fog was spreading over the bay. Bruno was whining, acting strange. He had heard nothing from Carolina. She had left behind such a gaping hole of absence, a deep void, a terrible solitude. He kept the TV turned on all the time, but with no sound. He sat and smoked and looked out the window. Now that Andre was back, would he ever see Maya again? And who would chase away his phantoms? What scarecrow could he plant in his mind?

Was he really responsible for Carolina's departure? By cutting her hair, hadn't it been a way of reducing, minimalizing herself, getting out of his reach? Why had their bodies never been able to find peace? Was pure love never enough? Her absence made him realize there was nothing left to be angry at. There was nothing to grab onto either. Was that what he had wanted?

He spent two days without seeing anyone, wandering by himself alone along the beach. He felt now that he had definitely wronged Carolina; on the other hand, he could not exactly call her back. The words and pledges of her love continued to haunt his dreams. How swiftly she had become a ghost, the terrible woman phantom. Yet when he told himself that life basically was nothing more than direction, an intention, a will toward the future, he realized that that intention for him went through Maya; she was the target. Jokingly Robert thought, if you put a target on your front door, you can be sure that people will shoot at it; Maya was far too reserved and private to hang up any targets. Louise had done it for her, and Robert was shooting.

What did he want? One thing was sure: the last few years of his life, the demonstrations in Chicago, peace marches in Washington, his anti-war activities, no longer satisfied him. He still felt as guilty as ever, which now seemed to him precisely another reason to live beyond his guilt, to do himself well, accept the chance of life, whatever luck he had in the great life lottery.

Very simply, he felt a new call-to-arms: a call to joy. It seemed to him that the time of heavy drugs, mind-blowing trips, fantastic researches on the frontiers of the self, was ending. True, Apollo 11 had just landed the first man on the moon; but there was a limit to how far he could go in the universe, and there was a limit, too, to how far he could go to the outside limits of himself. Robert thought the time had arrived to come back, to assimilate, and to find new centers, new nuclei, around which life again could become possible. Yet he was not for an anarchic, gratuitous joy; even to ecstasy, there had to be limits, otherwise the permanent search for ecstasy risked to become suicide, another way of degrading, destroying the self. He had only to think of Andre.

Carolina had been the princess of the head, of fantasy, imagination, romanticism and dreams; now Robert saw his life leaving that stage and entering fresh and more positive sources of pleasure and concrete fulfillment. He knew a few people who had a great deal of money and still did not live well. They had everything, yet complained they had nothing: they lived in prisons of luxury. Robert felt the time had come when happiness, and not the accumulation of wealth, should be the standard by which the success of a life was to be judged. Maya offered that promise. With her, he might be able to build a relationship that would embody many of the things he wanted and felt he was now ready to live. Wasn't it true that love transforms the lover, and that through love one could become new and, as it were, redeemed? It pleased him to recall the way, in Ben's garden, Maya had picked up the broken stem of a sunflower and said, "Look, she broke her neck trying to reach for the sun."

Robert was floating on all these different thoughts and sensations when that night he received a telegram that shocked him and send his mind catapulting down to the blackest regions: Carolina had died in an automobile accident in Vermont. Evidently, on a slippery rainy night, the road had continued going straight and she had made a soft but fatal curve.

"Why? Why? Why?" Robert cried.

What hurt most was that, at the bottom of himself, he knew why. Carolina, with her psychic tendencies, her love of witchcraft, must have guessed that Robert had wandered away, that he was no longer what he had been. Together they had lived out the best part of themselves; they had already had a rich life; they had created each other.

What had she said? Robert jarred his head, lighting one cigarette after another. Yes, he knew it now: "Nothing ever happens by accident."

Or: "Don't think it's a coincidence if you find yourself pursuing me for the rest of your life."

How young they had been! Tacitly, they had joined their past miseries together in the hope of a joyful present. The trouble with that "joy" was that it had demanded to be endlessly renewed. That had bored Carolina. And the early sorrows had remained, pushing her further and further away.

How they had groaned in their happiness, which had been too great for them, they were too young to endure it. Yet at the same time it was too small: it had left them extended every time they touched it. So gradually they had struggled to resist their joy, which showed them secretly, but all too clearly, the pathetic quality of their existence. However beautiful their love was, it had made them acutely aware of their limits. To Carolina, who hated all limits, this had acted as a spur into other transcendences.

Now, she who had tried to live beyond concern, beyond tragedy, was dead. And wasn't her death, too, indicative of the failure of something, if only of themselves?

He ran outside and down the sandy road and stood in front of an ash-grey, sullen sea and howled --- and found himself idiotic and hypocritical in his grief. He of all people didn't have the right to grieve. For once he had done something that had a consequence to it that could be judged good or bad! He cried. Hated himself for it. And cried some more.

Her dying had suddenly made him as dead; and now he knew that he had death inside him. As the mother felt the child in her belly, so he could feel his own death moving about inside him, waiting for him to make up his mind about what he was going to do.

The summer of 69 was no longer aimless, casual or frivolous. And he had been perfectly right that night at the clam bar, to think of himself as a murderer. The tremendous freedom they had prided themselves on enjoying had led to one death and perhaps, if they were not careful, would lead to more.

Carolina dead, Robert had nothing but memories of her, of which, had she lived, he would have been spared. Was she one of those women capable of dying simply in order to become a ghost, a specter, in a man's mind? Her death had done this: Robert would never be able to forget her, whereas, if she had lived, she might gradually have faded away like an old photograph, in time.

His dreams turned into nightmares. Before he had reproached himself for chasing her away; now, her death rendered a guilty verdict nothing could absolve. He felt "ghosted" by Carolina in the same way as he felt "ghosted" by all his fellow soldiers who had died in Vietnam.

He called Carolina's sister, Ann, who lived in Boston. They had not been close. Her voice seemed astonishingly calm, clear, and cold. Already she spoke of Carolina in the past, as if she had never existed.

He then called Carolina's mother, who also seemed to see in the death a kind of predestined fatality. Above all, her parents were determined not to let it upset or derange their lives. Carolina's death had not only freed her; it had freed them from worrying about her eccentric and disordered existence.

But Carolina's death did have one paradoxical benefit: it brought Robert to his grandmother. He simply felt that, if it ever was going to happen, the time had come for him to see her. Mrs. Mellon had never accepted Carolina. For that matter, she probably would never have accepted any woman Robert was with. With Carolina gone, Robert felt it was now or never. Either he made his peace with Mrs. Mellon or resigned himself to never seeing her again.

Lizzy, the old and loyal Scottish maid, answered the phone. It was strange, even frightening, to think so many years had gone by and Lizzy was still picking up and answering the phone just as she had when he was a child.

"Oh Mr. Robert, oh Mr. Robert!" she exclaimed when she recognized his voice.

It was she who had cradled him when he was a baby; it was she who had held his head between her ample breasts.

Protocol quickly took over as Lizzy said, "Mrs. Mellon is out for the moment. She'll be so pleased to see you. If you come to dinner, would you please make sure your hair is brushed back? You know how sensible she is to that."

Robert snorted. If he were eighty years old, Lizzy would no doubt talk to him the same way. Would anything ever change? He asked who else was coming to dinner.

"Some friends of hers you won't like it at all. You would say they're very conservative squares!" Lizzy laughed.

Robert had never understood the people Mrs. Mellon surrounded herself with. Why did she have to degrade herself so?

"All my good friends have died out," she once explained. "Last year I lost fifteen men! I have nobody left!"

"Dinner is served, as usual, precisely at seven, cocktails on the terrace at six-thirty."

Before Robert loomed a series of tough days. There was the beach, the dog, clear, cool, sunny mornings, a harsh emptiness. From the dunes where he sat Robert looked down at children picking up sticks on the shore. The ocean was a shiny blue, almost violet. Flecks of foam were flung in the air. At dusk Robert set out for Southampton and Mrs. Mellon.

"It's a good thing you're going to see her," Ben encouraged him. "You've got to try to come to terms with your past, you can't keep running away from it."

Robert knew he was right: by engaging with his grandmother, he would reconcile himself with his past, in the same way as Carolina was reconciled with life through her death. The late August afternoon stretched out, revealing one facet of ripe brightness after another. Leaves dotted the air, the potato fields received the light; everything was being born into its final and most complete stage. Everywhere the sunlight winked Robert saw Carolina smiling at him; in death she'd achieved what she'd always longed for. She could alter her shape or size, become large or small. He felt her presence flowing through him, sensed that she had entered a greater fullness. He felt her beneath him, supporting, holding him up, telling him not to feel guilty. Thinking of her as if she were still alive, he drove carelessly, confidently, through the dappled afternoon light, past the duck farm and the roadside signs of "Pick Your Own Strawberries", until an old, dirt-colored station wagon crawling along ahead of him at 25 MPH abruptly slowed him.

Robert pulled out to pass; at the same instant another car coming from the opposite direction swerved out. He cut back in quickly, just missing the front fender of the dirt-grey station wagon. A close call, but no damage done. He gunned the accelerator and drove on, the window down, his long hair blowing in the wind. He thought about Carolina and how, if he ever wrote a book about her, a good title might be, "Pick Your Own Strawberries".

As he approached Southampton Village, the traffic grew heavier. He slowed down, merging with the stream, then noticed that the dirt-grey station wagon had moved alongside him and was trying to push him off the road. A fist pumped at him, and he saw a gnarled red face, furious, bursting like a grape with anger. The guy made as if to pass, but when their wheels were almost parallel, he yanked his vehicle over, almost colliding with Robert's car.

"Horsey, let's beat it," Robert whispered to his car. His shoulders bent forward, he floored the pedal. A wild chase began.

He zigzagged through some traffic, the station wagon hot on his tail. He was determined not to be caught. He had survived Vietnam. He wasn't going to let some angry potato farmer pull him over.

If he could reach the safety of the back roads, he thought he might escape his grim pursuer. He couldn't very well show up at this grandmother's estate in this condition. No sooner had he turned onto an old country road, than he heard sirens and in the rear view mirror saw red lights flashing behind him. There were at least four cop cars coming up fast behind him. He braked violently, spun the car around, and tried to pivot past them on the sidewalk. It was as if the Vietcong were chasing him again and he had no choice but to run and take maximum evasive action.

A wheel snagged in some ditch he hadn't seen, the car spun sideways, he tumbled out, and they were quickly upon him.

"Lie down! Put your hands in front of you," a voice bellowed.

He lay on the edge of the road, his face deep in dust and dirt. They handcuffed him and pulled him to his feet. A few blows landed on his chest. A red fist flashed in front of his eyes.

"We hate your guts, dirty masturbator, communist pervert!"

Their beefy faces were grim with that look of men who believe they are invested by Public Authority and Law.

He was taken in cuffs to the police station in the village of Southampton, where he was booked on numerous charges, including reckless driving, and resisting citizen's arrest. The man in the dirt-grey station wagon who had started chasing him was the town plumber, Peter Petty. If he were convicted of all charges, he would have to spend at least two years in the Southampton jail.

He didn't say anything about his service record in Vietnam. Nor did he tell them about his grandmother, Mrs. Mellon, whose estate was on South Main Street, a short distance away.

But it was Mrs. Mellon whom he called when the Southampton chief of police informed him that he was allowed to make one phone call.

"I've got a little problem," he told her. "I'm going to be late for dinner."

He spent the rest of that day and night alone in a cell in the Southampton jail, staring through the bars with some amazement at the peaceful, quaint village streets, crowded with shoppers, vacationers, and women masked by sunglasses. The next morning Mrs. Mellon appeared with the $1,000 bail.

What a surprise and shock it must have been for her, not having seen Robert since his return from Vietnam, finally to meet him in prison! How it must have confirmed her idea of him!

"You're lucky, Robbie dear," she said, "I've lived in Southampton all my life, I know the police chief by his first name."

Grandmother and grandson hugged and embraced. The sudden strangeness of the jail encounter helped soften and cover up the secret difficulties and warm embarrassment of their feelings.

The affair dragged on in suspense and anxiety for a few days. The village people noisily took sides between the plumber and the suspect young man.

"At least they'll have something to talk about during dinner," Robert told Louise, whom he knew would relay it to Maya.

Robert thought of how funny it was to be in "provisory liberty." Wasn't real freedom always provisory? It couldn't be kept; it had to be discovered and earned.

If he weren't the grandson of Mrs. Mellon, he knew he would have a serious problem. He saw more clearly than ever that the justice you could get was in direct proportion to the thickness of your wallet. His was nearly empty. Mrs. Mellon said, "I'll take care of it. But don't count on anything more from me. When I die, all the money I have goes back to the other side of the Mellon family, who live in Philadelphia."

The lawyer Mrs. Mellon hired paid a visit to Peter Petty. The charges were dropped and Robert was again a free man.

Chapter XXIV

At last Robert came to lunch at "Sunny Hours." How strange it was to be putting his feet again on the great estate, with its spaciousness, immaculately manicured lawns and gardens teeming with roses and exotic flowers. Even the air seemed imbued with the quiet, confident luxury that goes with inherited wealth.

Mrs. Mellon had married three times. Each husband had died and left her fortunes. Her first husband had invented the typewriter. Her second was a brilliant lawyer. Her third and last was a Mellon. She herself came from nothing. If Robert admired her for anything, it was for that.

Her daughter, his mother, had had polio and died in childbirth. His father had been a lieutenant on a destroyer in the Pacific theatre and had lost his life in a kamikaze attack. Robert had spent his early years with his grandmother, taken care of by nannies, and by Lizzy. He had left as soon as he could, determined to seek his own path. Now, coming back, it almost did not surprise him that, after all these years, nothing had changed.

Mrs. Mellon seemed to rule over her over domain like some beautiful queen in a timeless realm. Robert had once had a nickname for her, "The Olympian." She was immune to the troubles of the external world, to the incidents of everyday life. She had a maid who dressed her in the morning, another who took her clothes off in the evening, a cook who prepared her meals. She boasted she had never once been in her kitchen; she liked to say she wouldn't have known how to boil an egg. Her concerns were her gowns, her jewelry, her bridge games, her social friends, and reading the obituaries. She loved flowers and was known for her roses. In her well-tended garden, even the trees seemed to float in a dream.

Mrs. Mellon was sitting comfortably with a few friends around the pool. A man whom Lizzy described as her new suitor, Phillip Poindexter, was bustling around the bar in yellow pants and a pink polo shirt. Robert took an immediate dislike to him. Sprawled on a lounge chair, another hanger-on, a short, fat man nicknamed "The Toad," was discussing the merits of the "Blue Book of the Hamptons."

Mrs. Mellon was dressed in a cool, pale lavender silk gown. Next to her, with her hollow cheeks, a cigarette holder sticking out from her pursed lips, sat her younger sister, Mrs. Coulter Mrs. Mellon now seemed on the verge of a new happiness. She was witty, elegant, full of vitality and warmth, and her younger sister couldn't help envying her and feeling a little jealous.

"You will never guess what I did the other day. My cook was on vacation so I went to the grocery store and bought a ten-pound Virginia ham. But I parked my car too far away, so I had to lug this big ham through the streets. Everybody was looking at me, I had to stop, panting for breath!" she laughed. "I thought I was going to have a heart attack. I had no idea that ham was going to be so heavy."

"Oh my, what an adventure!" the Toad croaked.

Lunch was announced. Robert squirmed.

A procession of maids appeared, carrying silver trays. They served lamb chops "en papillote," tiny garden-grown peas, and soft, clingy popovers. While they passed the hors d'oeuvres there was silence, soon broken by the noise of mouths beginning to chew. Mrs. Mellon finally intervened with, "Well, I'm just glad I won't be living for another ten years. You're welcome to all of it!"

She went on to say how as a child she had once driven down Fifth Avenue in a horse-drawn carriage on Sunday morning, waving to all of her friends. She would wait for hours in Washington Square, in front of the house of a famous actor she admired, hoping to catch sight of him.

Her suitor clapped his hands. He wore canary yellow pants and was at least thirty years younger than Mrs. Mellon. She leaned aside to Robert and whispered, "When Henry Mellon died I said I'd never get married again, but you never know!"

Desert was ushered in, crepes flambés. Champagne was served in crystal flutes.

"Why don't we all go on a trip to Africa?" the Toad was saying. "Wouldn't it be fun to see how the animals live?"

"I'm so delighted you could come," Mrs. Mellon said to her grandson. "We really should see more of each other. You can stay here any time."

Robert said nothing. He knew his grandmother loved him in her own abstract way.

In the room behind the screened-in veranda, filled with cool, green colors, the card tables had already been set up.

She put her hand on his arm. "Stay a little, my dear. I'll even teach you how to play bridge."

Over the delicate demitasses where Sanka now steamed, a certain Mrs. Leonard was explaining her problems, "Can you imagine, I brought over a cook from France whom I pay $25,000 a year and he just left me to go work for Campbell's soup!"

"What flavor is he going to work on?" asked the Toad. "Can we expect a sudden improvement in the tomato?" He chuckled, pulled out a cigar, and smoothed it back and forth several times with his fingers.

They moved into the living room and sat down. Over his grandmother's right shoulder, in a heavy gold frame, Robert caught the somber, gloomy eye of somebody's ancestors staring at him. Whose? Certainly not his. What a joke.

A British maid in a crisp black uniform came and passed a tray full of dainty mints and assorted sweets.

Robert watched as the afternoon light moved over the small, birdlike bones of Mrs. Mellon's high cheeks. The keen, peaked expression of her face changed, widened, as she said, "Toward the turn of the century my father used to come out to Southampton on weekends to hunt. There was nothing here then but Indians and animals! He and two friends of his bought all the land from the Indians around Lake Agawam. That's where we had our first house. A few years later my father went bankrupt. The house had been mortgaged. The day before the bank came to take possession of it, my sister and I went over and carried out all the furniture we could. How we struggled with that buffet table! But I'm so glad I got it because that night the house burned down. Right to the ground. We never learned how the fire started or who set it. We lost everything."

"Bravo!" said Robert, saluting the guts of this great old lady who had always known how to take what she wanted. In his mind he had the image of his grandmother and her sister, dressed in knickers, struggling under the weight of the magnificent buffet table that now stood against the wall in her dining room.

The Toad tried to smile. Mrs. Leonard was still wrapped up in her Campbell's soup story. Mrs. Mellon looked pleased, excited. She turned seriously to Robert. "Let me tell you something," she said. "I've learned life is nothing but there's nothing that's worth life. I do hope things work out for you. Follow your passion. Live your love. That's what I did." She patted his hand. He smiled.

"And keep clear of people like the plumber Peter Petty!" the Toad put in.

Mrs. Mellon went on, insisting a little, "Robert, do something serious. Forget the war, it's over, you can't fight Washington. You did your part, right? Forget the revolution. And no more women, right? Carolina, what a crazy girl, what poison! I feel you're capable of so much, you have so much potential, do something with it, don't waste it on little loves."

"What if those 'little loves' are not so little?" Robert answered with a terrible irony and condescension he couldn't hide.

"If you're looking for a job," the Toad volunteered, "I have a good friend who owns an advertising company in New York."

"I think I'd rather become a cook and go work for Campbell's Soup."

There was no laughter. Chairs were pushed back from the table; they rose. The light faded behind a mass of clouds; the room was somber, deep. The heavy regards of the fake ancestors on the wall made Robert feel he was in flight. Into the future or into the past? Into or out of love? The suitor in yellow pants put his arm around his grandmother's frail shoulders. They moved off conversing toward the bridge tables. The Campbell's soup lady tottered on crutches into the bathroom.

Robert went to kiss his grandmother goodbye. He didn't know when he would see her again. She put her hand on his shoulders and said, "I understand you so well."

"I know you do."

Dramatic silence. Then: "Is everything finished between you and Carolina?"

It was what she was waiting to hear. She didn't want any obstacles separating her from her darling Robert.

He hadn't yet been able to tell her anything about his private life. Now, as if it didn't concern him, "It's more than finished," he said, "Carolina's dead."

She gasped, almost choking. Troubled, not knowing what to say, she looked at him. But his face showed very little. A kind of emotional numbness had set in. He didn't feel like sharing his feelings.

Religion came to her aid. "Poor girl. She didn't believe in anything, that was the problem! She was an atheist will-o-the-wisp!"

He didn't feel it was worth arguing.

Suddenly she took his head and held it for a moment in her hands. "My little darling. We're still together, aren't we?"

"Yes," Robert said grimly. For a second he succumbed to her, to the tender gestures of this grand dame who had somehow begun to remind him of Maya.

They lingered for a moment beyond the terrace, before the curtains filtered with light. Looking at his grandmother's face, Robert tried to trace it backwards into time, connect it with his own roots, both those he accepted and those he rejected. But while he was intently studying her features something horrible happened: her face remained, but a new body was attached to it, that of a sphinx-like woman, Maya. His grandmother's face hardened and became powdery, with white veins, while the body beneath it grew softer and softer, more and more open, supple, expanded with light. Finally her pale, ancient face detached itself from the luminous, floating colors of the body below.

She removed his hands from his head. Anguished with fatigue and a new sort of emptiness, Robert leaned over and pressed his forehead, still burning from her touch, against the wall. He felt dizzy from his vision.

Worried, she watched him. "You've been here all summer. I've seen you not once! Why don't you come by more often? I'm sure we have so much to say to each other. I want to tell you about my travels, my plans, even my marriage!"

Robert ground his jaws together; he bit his lips. He realized she needed him now, his approbation, and she would never be able to give him hers. In fact, she was no longer with him; a dreamy happiness floated over her face.

Powerfully he grabbed and embraced her, his heart grimacing with pain. He owed her so much. Without her he never would have made it. It was true she was the only person he had always cared about. How remarkable it was that she was in love again, that at the age of seventy-seven she was so filled with her projects; what an ability to continue, to renew herself, and to turn the past into a dream that didn't count anymore the moment she had something new to live for.

Robert realized again that she was an "Olympian." Everything that had happened to her had amused her. In her own way, she had triumphed. She had lived on the heights, in style, taking the best advantage of her husbands, her leisure, and her lovers. The pains of other people could touch her, but her own happiness, which she was always inventing, had granted her a kind of immunity. There was something in the ease and gaiety with which she promenaded through life that made her belong to the 19th century, not the 20th. Robert was aware that he loved her but he couldn't talk to her now, couldn't reveal himself. The last time he had truly spoken to her about his problems had been when? When he was ten, or twelve?

Seeing she could go no further with him, she abruptly turned and left and joined her friends at the bridge tables.

Robert wandered back through the gloomy, ancestral hallways. Like apparitions in the doorway, maids appeared, offering him drinks. He declined. A phantom, he wandered in the depths of the old mansion. Here was where he once had romped; there were the corners in which he had hid; there was the bed in which he had cried. The suffocating heat of those long ago summer nights, wrapped around his shoulders like a cloak.

He wanted to say goodbye to Lizzy; he went looking for her in the kitchen. Suddenly he bent over, cramped, nearly vomiting. So much had happened; it all made him feel nauseous, too sick to want to remember. He just wanted to spit it all out.

Lizzy came running to his rescue. She brought a towel, ice; she hovered anxiously around him.

"My dear Robbie," she kept saying. "My dear Robbie."

She had once changed his diapers; she had once rocked him to sleep in her plump arms.

He left, Lizzy urging him, "The only thing you got to do now is come back to your granny's house."

At Ben's, he went up to his room, lay on his bed, turned on the radio, and listened to, "The Giants are now down to sixty-six players and they must pare down to thirty by Friday." A hopeless, helpless wrath seized him. Was he crazy? He felt lost in his own life, adrift in great spaces, uncertain.

The phone rang; a voice said it had to deliver a telegram; then it recited the fact that Carolina was dead.

How strange and horrible that a voice should come back and remind him of what he already knew. If he had killed her by sending her away, for the first time he felt capable of killing himself. If he swam out to a point of no return one night, would it be called "seacide," he wondered grimly?

But Robert didn't want to end anything. The death of Carolina had driven him to a precipice. The problem of ending didn't matter; what Robert wanted desperately was to begin. What should he do now? He didn't know. Carolina had told him she often dreamed of death, of strange, menacing figures and forms, half-man, half-beast. These forms boomeranged into his dreams now. He saw himself as the Minotaur; if he was to survive, he had to fight his way out of the labyrinth.

Carolina's mother called again. "I'm worried about you," she said. But her voice over the phone was cold, matter-of-fact. She talked about Carolina's death in the same way she might have said, "Carolina has gone to Europe for the summer," or, "Yes, it's too bad, Carolina hadn't quite done all the things she wanted to do."

Disgusted, Robert wriggled his way out of the conversation and said goodbye. He recalled how Carolina had always rejected her family's values. Now that she was dead, how foolish and ridiculous to talk of reconciliation. Carolina had never been reconciled to anything, not even to life; she had been one of those rare spirits who are always demanding more, who have this strange thirst that can never be slaked.

Robert had followed her as far as he could. They had lived together and yet they had each had their own lives. They had fooled around, experimented, made their mistakes, and always, somehow, they had been able to come back, to find some truth in each other again. Perhaps even now they would have been able to come back, to reunite. It was stupid to think about it. It made Robert sad and he hated to be sad. Nothing was more stupid than letting oneself be sad.

One thing was sure: things couldn't get any worse. He had touched the bottom that summer.

That night he left for Boston and Carolina's funeral.

Chapter XXV

Ben picked Robert up at McArthur airport and they had coffee in a nearby Howard Johnson. It was difficult for Ben to stop speaking about Carolina. "I still can't figure out how she came to be so ethereal and got to be as far out as she was."

"I know," Robert murmured. "I feel her spirit will always be with me now, whereas before we had our difficulties, and were always so separated."

But was that what he had wanted to say? What he had wanted to say was something simpler like, "Now I realize how I really loved her."

They drove back to Sag Harbor. They got out of the Volvo station wagon and climbed the weathered green stairs, went through the screen door onto the porch where the light was flickering back and forth, and Ben said, "It's hard to accept. She's gone, along with so many things. Each day I feel more and more sober. I've been thinking of all my dead friends, all those who died with big holes in their hearts."

"Come on, Ben. There's no point thinking like that."

"Besides," he mused, "most passion desires its own destruction, doesn't it? It's Tristan and Isolde all the time. As if someone else could ever help us or make us more than we are! We say we love someone and then we try to kill them by reducing them to ourselves. Carolina was one of those who tried to love differently, and maybe she paid for it with her life," his voice trailed off.

"I guess I just wasn't aware how much you loved her," Robert acknowledged. He gritted his teeth. He shook his head. He didn't know what to feel, or if he felt anything.

Ben leaned over, looked out through the sunlight-patterned screen mesh. "Look, the baby birds have gone. I've been watching and taking pictures of them for two weeks."

Robert looked and saw the empty nest half-hidden on an apple tree.

"Just last night I gave them strips of bacon. It didn't take them long to get their flying wings."

Robert wondered when he would get his "flying wings." With Carolina gone, he felt he had just lost one.

"You want a drink?" Ben asked, pouring himself a White Label and soda.

Robert declined.

"Are you still seeing Maya?"

"Yes, I want to. It's not easy because Andre's there, guarding her like a bulldog. He goes into the city during the week but comes back every weekend."

"And it wouldn't bother you seeing Maya so soon after Carolina…?"

This moral reproach, coming from Ben, angered Robert. "But Carolina and I were finished! For a long time now we'd been finished. We just weren't together anymore, not wholly, anyway. When life offers you something new that you want, you should take it, no?"

"Yes, absolutely," agreed Ben. "But you expect too much from women."

"And I guess you don't expect anything at all?" Robert rejoined, taut, sarcastic.

"No, absolutely nothing." Ben paused. "But everything is possible at every moment, isn't it? And if something came along, it would be wonderful. For instance, Maya."

"You've got to be kidding! Don't tell me you're interested in Maya too?"

"I'm not saying no, kid," Ben answered, looking straight at him.

Robert groaned. Could Ben be serious?

Ben helped himself to another round of White Label and soda. "It's true I can't help thinking about her."

Robert felt baffled, a little stunned. He hadn't realized Ben was going to play an active role. Suddenly it struck him with incredible force that there was no logical reason for Ben not to be as interested in Maya as he was. He risked asking, "You mean, you're not happy?"

"Oh, the baby birds made me happy," Ben shrugged. "Come on, don't you know me better than that by now? I'm never content."

Robert smiled sourly to himself, thinking of how often he had said to Ben, "You need someone to organize your life. You need a woman."

And Ben saying, "But woman is really a young man's game, isn't it?"

Now it appeared very clearly that it was his "game" as well. But what was the prize? What were they all searching for? Did any of them know? More and more it seemed to Robert that they were stumbling blindly on a quest for something unknown. How to think of themselves? As lovers without work? Architects who could build anything except what they most needed? Rich, lazy bums, intellectuals looking for something to satisfy their bodies and minds, perched far above the ordinary concerns of men, amusing themselves with Byzantine intrigues? Whatever it was, Robert no longer had any faith in what they were. At the moment, no one was really loved by anyone, and Carolina was dead. Plus, it was already September, and time was running out.

"I'm sorry," said Ben. "I want you to know that I love both you and Carolina. But I know I could love Maya. Sometimes my life seems such a fantastic muddle that I wonder whether I'm living it or someone else is."

He laughed in a self-deprecatory way. Robert felt he couldn't push Ben's hospitality any further. If Ben felt the way he did about Maya, it wasn't fair to him to stay as a guest in his house any longer. The next morning Robert stuffed his sleeping bag into his backpack and left.

Chapter XXVI

Another dawn unfolded itself on the beach, beautiful in its stark simplicity and splendor, with no traces of animal or man, nothing but the mingled sand, the surf endlessly repeating its same old cry, and the light breaking in chromatic waves over the horizon and renewing itself, renewing the day.

Robert lay huddled in his sleeping bag. The fantastic sunrise that morning had filled him with the idea of the perpetual unity of all things, life and death, life and darkness. Perhaps it was simply his over-worked imagination, but he thought he had seen Carolina standing there on the horizon, just where the sea meets the sky, softly urging him not to renounce, not to give up.

He couldn't very well stay camping out on the beach; the few hotels in the area were fully booked. Even though he hadn't lived there since before he had signed up for Vietnam, he decided to go back to his grandmother's house in Southampton.

When Lizzy opened the door, she was delighted to see him. Her heart-shaped face broke out into smiles. "Oh Mr. Robert, oh Mr. Robert!" she kept saying. "It's so grand you've come home!"

Mrs. Mellon was out for lunch and for a bridge party in the afternoon.

In the kitchen the German cook, Brigitta, made him a grilled cheese, tomato and bacon sandwich. Brigitta was a big, busty woman with a glowing, almost obscene, aura of health. During the day she cooked but at night she studied books about astrology and palm reading and numerology. Robert had often seen her coming back on her bike from the Southampton library with stacks of books on these subjects. She had a great love for divination and scrutiny. She prided herself on the way she could instantaneously sense who you were, on being a "seer of souls."

After he had eaten, she offered to "divine" Robert.

"But you don't know me, you haven't seen me in years," he objected.

"Don't matter, don't matter, Mr. Robert. Just trust me, I can see in your soul!"

"Ok, try."

She took him upstairs to her room on the third floor, closed the curtains, lit some candles, touched his palms, and in a strange, hypnotic voice, and intoned, "Aquarians are dead for you. They're too weak; you'll never be with an Aquarian again. A Ram woman --- the only sign stronger than your own ---will be the force against which, ultimately, you will have to measure yourself. You will either be broken by her or made by her. You will either bow down before her in slavish submission, sexual or otherwise, or else you will triumph. She will baffle you, or else you will solve her riddle and shoot through her into a new zone of clarity. She will offer you ecstasy, greater ecstasy than perhaps you have ever known, and either you will conquer and transcend that ecstasy through the truth of yourself or you will succumb. It's up to you, to your most inner capacities. You, Scorpio, are desire as well as death; to be purified of your will toward destruction, you must first be burned in the flame of a leaping Ram!"

"Oh my God!" Robert said, startled. "Can that be true? The Ram was obviously Maya (born in Berlin, April 1, 1940). He had a vision of her leaping forward, horns coming out of her flaming hair. At his darkest moment, the golden clue had fallen. So this summer did possess a secret meaning and he, even against his conscious knowledge, was on a quest. Seeing his reaction, Brigitta clapped her hands and rocked with laughter.

What thoughts the cook had let loose in him, what a stew simmered in his mind! It was clear: he had to meet the Ram, had to lock horns. He realized now what instinctively, intuitively, he had known all along. Besides, it was too late to withdraw. There was no way out, no exit, no door that could possibly take him out of the arena. He had to take the chance, the risk, to live as much as possible. If he didn't, someone else (Ben?) surely would.

Robert felt wound up so tightly that it was no longer possible for him to spend time alone. Something within him, long buried, rose and started to cry out, to demand, "More! More!" He had to take the leap that would transform him and the rest of his life. There were a few moments of whirling chaos. But his mind and body were already expanding so much, rippling outward. Suddenly Robert felt ready for real growth, sudden revelations. If it didn't happen now, it would never happen. He felt dizzy with excitement.

What should he do? Sit and mourn for Carolina? She had once accused him of using her as a drug. Was he then to use her death as a pretext not to live? No, he thought, take the risk of your passion, get out of your darkness, stop standing there like a child waiting for someone --- some secret messenger --- to tell you what to do; there's no law except this: take what you want.

So he decided to be direct: he went to see Maya.

He drove down the wide, leafy lanes of Bridgehampton and turned past the ice cream bar on the corner. Fruit stands gleamed on the roadside. Robert stopped in a rock-and-roll dump for a double whiskey that stiffened him up. There were lots of college kids eating hamburgers. Robert left the dark coolness of the bar, got into the big, blue Buick, and drove off into the warm, bright day. He wanted very much to live and he wanted very much to have Maya: these were the two things he realized now. Robert drove past the potato fields dotted with light; he felt keen, transparent and alert.

A blond young man, his legs crossed, was sitting under the big tree in front of Maya's cottage. His head shook back and forth to some inner music; his fingers toyed with strands of grass.

"Is Maya in?"

Hoppy looked up, smiled. "I don't know who's in and who's out," he murmured. "All I know is that the light is on the leaves."

Robert left him to his meditations and walked past the gate and up the little lawn. One side of the shingled cottage was covered with rose bushes. The sun wavered in the air and delicate green plants reflected the light. Maya was sitting on the porch in a wicker chair, her bare shoulders concealed by bushes, head half-veiled by a turquoise sun hat. A few feet away from her Andre leaned over a Hermes typewriter. Robert was astonished to see him, but he did not seem at all surprised to see Robert. "Sit down," he said. "Let's have some wine."

"I'm working on a script for a rock-musical film," he went on. "It's about the relationship between destruction and eroticism."

"I prefer things that are more positive myself," Robert answered. They stared at each other. A quiet yet violent duel of regards began.

Serene, graceful, like a figure out of some medieval tapestry, immersed in her needlework, Maya sat in the corner, the sunlight flickering through her hat, onto her face. Robert wondered what was the strange glue that held these two beings together? Andre continued to talk about his projects, but Maya said nothing. Without realizing it, Andre slipped into a monologue. "All that interests me now is imbeciles, children or crazy people. I don't want to think anymore: thinking destroys life. And just being isn't enough either, although there are times when I do envy vegetables."

"Like the one sitting outside by the road," Robert jeered.

"Oh yeah, him. That's Hoppy. He's twenty and he's already taken twenty acid trips, so he tells us. I rather like him: seeing no solution to his life, he prefers a state of intelligent stupefaction. In his own way, he's gone to the end, he fulfilled himself."

"Yes," scoffed Robert. "You can see that."

"He's tasting his emptiness," Andre continued, "which most people avoid. Now this rock musical I'm writing is an attempt to make the emptiness that's inside everyone explode. There will be nothing in it with which people can identify. By cutting all contacts with ordinary life, I'll bring people into the heart of real life."

"Which is what?"

"Violence, destruction, consummation, burning," Andre said as if reciting a litany.

But Robert wasn't listening much anymore as he remembered what Louise had told him: in the beginning, Maya had admired Andre for his excesses, his desire to live at all costs, burn the candle at both ends. She had loved him because there was something crazy about him, something original, primordial, without limits, that was constantly inventing itself, and he needed her in order to re-invent himself again. But such splendors, Robert thought, don't last: couples are born and die like stars; the trouble was, even a long time after they're dead, they continue to glow with a love, which isn't real.

Looking at Andre now, Robert had the feeling that the man was flaring out on top of an empty volcano. He saw Maya, with a subtle movement of her shoulders, turn away from this monster she had helped to create. She flashed a discreet smile at Robert, as if suggesting that there were other possibilities in life of which Andre could have no idea.

Andre continued to talk, but Maya interrupted him abruptly, rather cruelly, "If you say another word, I'm leaving."

Docilely, Andre obeyed.

Louise arrived, saying there was a dead pheasant on the road; she had almost stopped to pick it up, since it looked as if it had been freshly killed.

Her preoccupation with the pheasant annoyed Andre, who stood up, cursing, "All she can do is think about details. There's never any life, just details, pheasants and more pheasants!"

"But a pheasant is life, no?" said Maya, taunting him.

"A pheasant killed by a car is a dead pheasant killed by a car," said Andre and stalked off.

"Stay," Maya asked Robert. Her voice was inviting, tender.

Garbed in a gorgeous white gown full of lace and ruffles that could easily have belonged to his grandmother, she disappeared inside for some white wine. Soon Robert could hear the opening bars of "Sketches of Spain". Then Louise whispered into his ear, "Remember, be strong with her. She's so used to getting her own way with Andre. He even thinks like she does now ---- that is, when he's thinking. Everything he is comes from her. Since she's leaving him, no wonder he goes crazy."

Robert felt slightly drunk with victory. He was absolutely sure of two things: that he could handle Maya, and that it was absolutely imperative for Maya and her health that she escape from Andre.

Maya came back. They drank white wine and she sat next to him, very close, and told him how just looking at the mimosa tree that flowered outside her bedroom window made her "super happy." Contact seemed excruciatingly possible, yet Robert felt he should not push an advantage that he had just gained.

Marthe appeared, looking like a lovely tramp, a big, boisterous, woman-baby doll. Hoppy, always smiling, squeezing her hand, suggested they go lie on the grass and look up at the trees.

Louise hovered around Maya more possessively than ever, but in an invisible, discreet way. Her presence could hardly be felt, and yet it was there. Andre did not return. "He's afraid of Maya," Louise said. "He has this foolish idea that if he just leaves her alone, if he lets her enjoy a certain freedom, she'll get over this 'difficult period'. Of course, Maya doesn't want him around. But after all she's taught him, she's trained him to be dependent on her, and she feels benevolent and compassionate, like a teacher."

That evening the sun was orange, a great disc shattered into parts, which became yellow planets that were somehow connected with the white wine they were sipping. Marthe and Hoppy began to talk about the main subject of the day, sex of course. The sun tinged them with color; they laughed; and finally, to amuse themselves, Marthe stripped and Hoppy and Louise began painting her body.

Laughing in that deep, raucous way she had, Marthe lifted her arms in the air and danced, her haunches streaked with bright colors, her big breasts bobbing up and down. Lanky Vico showed up, emitting war whoops of crazy joy. They frolicked. Robert let himself go. They danced on the porch and ran about kookily over the lawn, careening around the trees, wild as children. It was a marvelously unrepressed, free moment. Marthe and Maya had created it. Marthe was earth and Maya was fire.

Hoppy said he had reached the point where, if he looked at a tree long enough, the branches began to turn into flames. "Before I was always running after things, chasing things, now I don't care. My mind is easy."

They plucked potatoes from the fields nearby and roasted them in foil for dinner. Maya chopped up herbs and spices, her hands working finely and neatly over the wooden board.

It grew dark. Standing outside under the great spreading tree Robert murmured ridiculously to Maya, "Your body's like a jar full of fireflies."

"Haha," she laughed. "Fireflies lighting up their asses in the night."

Marthe rolled in the grass with laughter; Hoppy was rolling stuff in the common interest; Louise came and went, a shadow.

"This reminds me too much of too many things," Maya whispered mysteriously. "Let's go to the beach."

They slipped away. They mounted their bicycles and pedaled softly away into the deep, luminous, fantastic night. Hoppy and Marthe ran after them, shouting.

Darkness cascaded through the apple trees; stars came out; they felt bathed in light and cascading darkness. Maya rode her old bicycle gracefully, nobly, erectly; somehow she reminded Robert of those ballet dancers that spin before mirrors on top of musical boxes. The feeling she aroused in him touched Robert deeply, sent convulsive shivers shooting through his body.

Robert curved over the road toward her; riding parallel, they clasped hands. He thought of trapeze artists, leaping and catching each other's wrists. The union lasted for a second. They had started to laugh and then Maya's bike teetered over to one side and Robert was pulled with her, his front wheel locked in hers. He heard a sharp exclamation of, "Oh the bitch, not again, not again!" Tumbling over one another, their bicycles collapsed on the side of the road, they ended up entangled in a ditch.

They lay there, helpless, groaning. It took them only a few seconds to find the accident funny. They squirmed toward each other, Maya clasping her knees. "I'm blue with bruises all over," she moaned comically. "I'm completely covered with bangs."

"Bango," said Robert.

"Bango!" said Maya.

They didn't say anything. They lay there helpless and happy in the sweet rich-smelling ditch.

A pick-up truck loaded with three drunken farmers passed, cranked to a halt, a scruffy head peered out of an open window. Maya made some joke that was met with laughter; the window rolled up; the jalopy swayed off.

They succumbed to the inertia. They lay and wondered how long it would take for them and their bikes to morph into stones, fields, flowers. Looking at the moon high above them on the left, Robert was startled to see that it had been replaced by a gleaming, enlarged image of Carolina's face.

He couldn't look at it. He turned his eyes to Maya --- the bottom of her dress was ripped --- and managed to say, "What a divine emptiness! How little and how much we mean."

But she warned him, "You couldn't be making a greater mistake if you try to make something 'metaphysical' out of me."

There was another long, soaring silence. The moon became the moon. The fields sung. Robert thought of all the insects swarming at that moment in the rich dirt and suddenly love appeared before his eyes as a gigantic insect with huge mandibles.

As if reading his thoughts, Maya said, "Be careful: you know what I am? A spider eagle."

"A spider eagle? Never heard of that before."

He imagined an eagle with a spider riding on its back, an attempt to join earth and sky.

"How about a sphinx lady?"

Above the line of trees that marked the horizon, the airport beacon swung slowly round and round.

"It's looking for someone," said Robert. "It's calling out to all those spirits that are on its wave-length."

A heavy, hollow sadness opened and expanded in his belly. Beneath him the tangled metal of the bikes felt very hard. Yet neither of them had any desire to move.

Farther away from him, Robert saw another image of Maya riding astride a white bull across the fields. The image gripped him with fear. Could she master the bull? Would she be hurt if she fell off? Where was the bull taking her?

The large, cool night air moved over their faces, talked to their bodies. Falling stars flared above them and disappeared.

Maya whispered, "Andre's getting psycho. I don't know what to do. Last week, when he was here, it repulsed me to look at him. And I'm scared. He's gotten more and more demanding. He said to me, 'If you love me, I need you to prove your love for me. I want you to make love to me without feeling anything, as if you were a corpse, as if you were dead! If you make one movement, one single gasp of pleasure, I'll know you have betrayed me. So be very careful: the enormity of our love is at stake. You see, I love you so much, I want you to be all mine. And you can only be all mine if, well, you're dead."

"Extraordinary. But how terrible!" He saw now that Andre, finding no issue for his love or his life, and believing that destruction and violence were the essence of the times, was on a path that could only lead to disaster. He saw shiny fragments of Maya, in endlessly varied patterns, blossoming across the sky. He had to act. If Maya could be saved, it was up to him.

"It's true I did love him," she was saying. "There was such a divine madness in him, such an amazing frenzy. I'd never seen anything like it before. He only wanted to live for me. At first I thought this was beautiful. Then it got so that it was the only thing that interested him in life. This was bad, I knew it was, but what could I do?"

"So in your heart you knew it wouldn't last?"

"I hoped that it would. Because I did love him, you see. But he knew too much about me; he would just sit there, staring at me, inviting me to undress myself. I couldn't get away from his eyes! Was there anything else that he wanted? Sometimes I think I was just a means for him, a kind of trampoline."

"Do you know where he wanted to go?"

"No, no idea. Absolutely none. I never got there myself. I don't think he did either."

She paused; he stroked the back of her shoulders. "And then it finished. It became too much for me. I was sick. He began to drink. He became more and more careless. Simply nothing mattered to him anymore, even his work in the theatre, in films. There was this violence in him, this anguish, because he couldn't get out of me what he wanted, or what he imagined I had. The only thing I could join him in was his laughter. We mocked everything. It was beautiful, sad, laughable. And then Louise came along…"

"And what?"

"She showed me how much the life I was living had nothing to do with life. How marginal it was. Theatre all the time, but like the theatre, there was emptiness all around. All we had to give to each other at that point was our deliriums. It wasn't funny. Louise made my head clear. You know, every time my life has started spinning, Louise has showed up and set it straight again. Louise has been very, very good to me. She's a fantastic woman. And I think she's beautiful, she's got great legs."

To someone bicycling along the road at that moment, it would have seemed funny to see Maya's own bare, bruised legs sticking out of the ditch. They sat for a moment longer in the deep, blue light. Another image came loose of its moorings in Robert's head: spilled on her back, her shoulders resting on the twisted bicycle wheels, Maya opened her lips and called to him in French, 'Viens, viens', to enter her. But a hard constraint he couldn't analyze kept Robert from giving in too quickly. He realized: even if she had wanted to, he would not have allowed Maya to surrender easily. A long understanding had to be reached, and the early sufferings of desire would augment the price of the fruit that perhaps was to fall later.

Suddenly, in a surging, spontaneous burst, Maya flung up her arms and cried, "Ay! Ay! Ay! I want the moon!"

Robert saw himself camouflaged in the form of the moon being sucked through her mouth; the stars were jewels at the end of her fingers; her body the world's map; she was the great woman-idol, Maia, Maria, Maya, sphinx or spider eagle, and like the sun-goddess, she demanded the sacrifice of those who bowed before her.

Extraordinarily attuned to him, as if sensing his thoughts and reactions, Maya cut him off. "I don't think you understand. I don't think you understand anything at all about me."

Robert's heart lurched. What an idiot he was! He had this beautiful woman next to him, entangled in the ditch with him, and here he was trying to turn her presence into something else. If he wanted her so badly, he should just take her. A violent cry rose up in him, nearly came out like a painful gasp.

Footsteps came running down the road toward them. Two forms broke out of the darkness. Shouting, making the quiet star-filled air shake with their riotous laughter and giggles, Marthe and Hoppy dashed past them, crying, "To the beach!"

With remarkable ease Maya struggled free of the ditch and the bicycles and scampered after them, Robert following.

On the beach she stood with her back to the loud ocean, beckoning him toward it; further away, obscurely hidden, Marthe and Hoppy were already rolling and playing in the sand. The night seemed incredibly rich, ripe, and deep, almost on the verge of rottenness. The sea sang as if it had crickets inside it. Maya stood illumined in the darkness over the beach, and the rolling waves did not forget to crash at her feet. Robert answered her appeal, running toward her; the movement had now become irresistible, nothing could have called him back, changed or revoked his momentum. He had to have her, and not only did he have to possess her, but he had to die into her, beyond her. She was beseeching him to do it; she was on her knees.

How she needed him to come and throw himself away with her! But before he could reach her, she had taken her clothes off and dived into the surf. She kept swimming further and further out, as if she wanted to go to England. He had no time to go after her; headlights stabbed the beach.

Followed by Ben and Louise, Andre came rushing down. Darkly, stormily, he approached Robert.

"What the hell are you doing here? Where's Maya?"

"We decided to go night fishing," Robert rejoined sarcastically. "Certain fish leap only at night."

Andre ignored him. He had spotted Maya's head bobbing up and down way out on the moonlit water. He shouted at her and stood on the shore waving frantically at her. The sea was very rough. Ben and Louise approached and started waving too.

"She's going to get sick," Louise said. "If not worse."

"If she doesn't drown, damn you."

"I think what Maya needs is a good spanking," Ben remarked.

She came back giggling, her body seal-sleek and shiny and damp, shivering. On the way out the waves had knocked her down a few times. But she wasn't daunted. "I've never seen such a ridiculous spectacle," she said. "All four of you, standing there, watching me, like idiots! I really should have gone to say hello to England."

Louise wrapped her up in a towel the moment she emerged from the surf. Louise scolded her. Maya put her hand to her mouth but kept on giggling.

"You've been a lot of help," Louise muttered to Robert. "I thought at least you'd take care of her. You're just as bad as Andre!"

"I'm sorry, man," Ben said. "Andre came to my house and asked for my help. He said you'd kidnapped Maya."

"That's bullshit, Ben, and you know it."

Maya was laughing. "You men! It's all so absurd."

They walked back to the car.

"Can I have a cigarette all by my own?" Maya asked Ben.

It was Ben's turn to laugh. "That's great, 'all by my own'. That really is marvelous, 'all by my own'. What a woman!"

He drew out a cigarette, cupped his hands and lit it for her.

"You can't smoke now," said Louise. "Get in the car. It's time to go home."

Maya inhaled a few times then let the cigarette fall in the sand. Louise put her arms around her.

But Andre was jealous. He pushed Louise aside, grabbed Maya, and yanked her away.

"Oh no, please, help me!" she implored.

He picked her up, wrapped in a towel, and carried her back down the beach. Terrified, Louise cowered by the car.

Robert started to run after Andre. Images from Vietnam, of young women dragged out of their villages and raped, flashed through his mind.

Ben caught up with him and held him back. "Let him go, the poor bastard. Now's not the time. You'll only hurt her."

Robert was grinding his teeth. "I just can't take it anymore. I'm not going to let him ruin her life"

"I love Maya too," Ben said. "I love her too much to let anything bad happen to her."

Andre came back, pulling Maya behind him. He jabbed his finger at Robert and yelled, "So this is the man you're leaving me for? Tell me! And tell me why, what are the reasons for it? The whole thing's so horrible. I beg you, I implore you, Maya, tell me!"

He repeated that classic, eternal lament as if saying it for the first time. Robert was stunned, pained. Even in their worst moments, he and Carolina had never been through anything like this.

Maya was shaking, but she remained cool. "You know very well it's not on account of one thing. There's no single fact, Andre. You know that."

He continued to rage. Ben tried to calm him. Almost kindly, Maya repeated her argument. "Andre, you know the reasons as well as I do. There's no sense in my going over all of them again. Why do we have to shout at each other and hurt each other like this? It makes me sick. I don't want to argue. I've had enough of talking to you like this."

"You idiot!" he barked at her. "If I ever see you again with this guy, I'll smash your face in. I'll strangle you, I'll kill you!" He turned and stormed off.

Louise bustled around Maya, trying to console, to protect her. Robert tried to help but Louise wouldn't let him.

"Come on," Ben said gravely. "I'll drive you back to the cottage."

Louise and Maya got in the back seat, Robert in front. Marthe and Hoppy said they would walk. A few hundred yards away, Robert noticed their two bicycles were still lying where they had left them, entangled in the ditch.

Chapter XXVII

Ben called. "I'm not trying to be difficult, but Andre is here, staying with me."

"Andre?" Robert couldn't control the surprise in his voice or the emotions behind that surprise. "I thought he gave up and went into New York."

"Yes, but he came back last night."

"Wow, that makes things really complicated," Robert groaned.

"Well, simplicity is always suspicious and then, on the contrary, there's nothing complicated or difficult. We're all here and it's like one big family. There comes a moment when you can't close your doors and say no to a friend. Andre's a little desperate, but it'll pass."

"That's the first time I've heard someone tell me that being desperate is like having the flu! Just wait till Maya finds out."

"That's exactly why I called and why I think you can help me," said Ben. "You can tell Maya that Andre's here and he wants to see her."

"If she wants to see him!"

"Don't worry. She'll want to see him: they belong to each other."

"I don't know who belongs to who anymore."

"But we're all free, aren't we?"

"That's the trouble: we're all too free."

"It's not like cooking --- there's no measuring cup. Freedom has to be unconditional or not at all. Andre's here, he needs something, and he's the only young man I know beside yourself whose head is not completely addled by drugs." Ben paused. "It's like a restaurant. When someone comes in from the outside, you try to give them what they want."

"I didn't know Maya was being served up for dinner," said Robert acidly. And he hung up.

Louise met him at the "Candy Kitchen" in Bridgehampton.

"Andre's back," he told her. "He's staying with Ben."

"Oh my god, how I know! He showed up this afternoon. Luckily for her, Maya was out. He threw me into a corner and threatened to beat me if I didn't tell him everything. I told him I didn't know anything and it's the truth because Maya hasn't been talking to me. I don't know what's eating her. It drives me crazy. We used to be as close as two threads on a spool. I think she needs rest, peace, silence, even solitude. This thing with Andre is making her a nervous wreck. She won't talk about it but I can feel it. What do you want me to do? I try and guard her but we'd need the State Troopers to keep Andre out of the house. Like a few hours ago, he burst in like a thunderstorm and cornered me worse than the Gestapo. Then he searched the place, turning the bathroom upside down, mostly her intimate things, you know. He says he has absolute proof that she's been making love and I know it's not true --- I've been with her every evening. In the house that is, for she shuts herself in the bedroom and won't let even me come in anymore."

"It's just awful. I thought the violence was over. It seems like it's just beginning. I wish I could do something. Maybe I should come over."

"No, absolutely not! Andre is patrolling the street. He'd make a good cop; he's more efficient than they are. I see him coming around the block - I have my lookout downstairs. Maya went to buy some Mace. She hasn't used it yet but she says she will, if she's pushed. And a locksmith is coming over later to put new double locks on all the doors. You wouldn't believe it but it's true: I feel like I'm living barricaded in a fortress."

"This is absurd, insane. Where's it all going to lead? More destruction?" Robert shook his head in anger. "Why do intelligent people have to live like this?"

"Yes, you are right. To be cut off from Maya has made that man suicidal. At a certain point Maya will have to choose between life and death. Now it's as if she's holed up in some medieval castle, too proud to talk about her troubles."

Louise's hands shook and her black coffee spilled across the linoleum tabletop. A few yards away, a noisy group of children were grabbing multicolored ice-cream cones. Robert wiped up the spilled coffee.

"If it weren't for Marthe, I don't know what I'd do."

"Why Marthe?"

"Because she's adorable. What fun we have! We may be living in a prison but we still amuse ourselves. She has such a need of understanding. Hoppy's a rat. Every time she needs him, he abandons her. And when she doesn't need him, when she's happy, he comes back."

It struck Robert as pathetic that Louise kept getting involved with women. He had urged her to find a man, which is what she herself said she wanted. Had she even tried?

"I'm thinking the best thing for me now might be to pack my suitcases. I should have listened to Carolina. She told me to get out of here."

"Don't go," Louise begged. "I know that Maya depends on you very much."

"But we hardly ever see each other!"

"That's why it's all the more important that you stay. You're like her invisible anchor."

"I'm a little tired of being invisible."

"Tomorrow night, if you like, you can become visible."

"How's that?"

"Didn't you know? Ben's giving a party for Andre. Andre is going to act or do something or other. He's designed the set, the costumes, he's got a few actors, and Ben's giving a sort of a benefit."

"And Maya's going?"

"Yes. Andre says it's very important for his career and he won't put it on unless Maya promises to be there. She feels it's ridiculous to ruin a man's life if she can prevent it by simply showing up. So we're all going to go. Hoppy wants to bring those two bulls in a pick-up truck, tie lanterns onto their horns, and let them loose in the night."

She laughed nervously. Robert embraced her. "Don't forget to come. Maya needs you."

"Stop!" she said.

The brakes jammed, the car skidding toward the side.

"Sorry about that."

Maya had this passion: every time she spotted a beautiful bunch of roadside flowers she insisted on grabbing them. Robert thought: flowers are the blood of Maya; they are the cocktails her mind drinks. He roared with laughter, mocking his own romanticism.

Packed in the LeSabre convertible, pushing near eighty, their bodies rollicking together in the back seat, excited as teenagers out for their first ride in a sports car, already half-stoned, daft, stopping here and there along the fields to plant hats on the scarecrows, they drove over to Ben's. Squeezed in the back were Marthe, Hoppy, and Louise on Vico's lap. In the front sat Robert and Maya.

Maya, wearing polka-dotted stockings, different colored boots, and tight black shorts, had already provoked Vico to shouting, "Viva Maya, Viva Baby Mayaaaa, Viva crazy Maya baaaby!"

Hoppy, stoned to a superior degree, outdid the radio announcer by letting his voice soar, "Return with us now to those sterling days of yesterday when the Lone Ranger rode high and splendid on the plains with Tonto, the original third-world man brought to the service of the cowboy imperialistic land-devouring beef-eating Marlborough-smoking warmongers!"

Vico had his muscular arms around both Marthe and Louise, she positively aglow with the pleasure of the big man's contact.

"Hey, watch out!"

They were barreling down a side road when a rabbit suddenly leapt in front of the wheels. It was impossible to stop. Maya screamed. A glance in the rearview mirror showed the rabbit lying limp and still in the middle of the road.

When they arrived there was already a crowd at Ben's, games on the lawn with tambourines and shuttlecocks, and some woman saying, "Last night I was so tempted by the bluefin tuna I nearly died."

The moment he saw Maya, Ben rushed toward her. Robert's stomach locked. Ben kissed her European-style and hugged her for a long time.

Beyond them, a superb silver light spread out over the bay.

"Are you working?" Ben asked her.

"No, I'm not."

"But you must be doing something," Ben said, a little surprised.

"I'm working at not working. I just breathe."

Her witty reply prompted a detonation of laughter.

No one mentioned Andre. Then beautifully, surrealistically, just as the light was fading, some horses appeared down below in the bay. They were up to their bellies in water, and children were riding them bareback. Shortly after the horses disappeared, a plane swooped down very low in the sky, like a messenger.

Darkness fell over the grass and the water and the crickets were already humming in the mimosa tree. Robert sensed very clearly that this evening would be decisive.

"You want something to drink? What can I get you?" asked Ben.

Gracefully, Maya seated herself in an enormous, Bauhaus-style leather chair. Robert longed to touch her hands, to squeeze them between his own. He had to have her in order to redeem himself from the rather ridiculous situation of wanting her so much. When he glanced around at the other guests so suavely drinking and talking, he no longer distinguished between friends and unknowns; rather he saw machines masked with flesh and animated by desire.

Ben came back with the alcohol, which he said was his drug, his passion, his life; he talked about it with a special fondness, as if it were a woman.

"For a confirmed alcoholic, you look remarkably well," said Maya.

Ben laughed. "When you get to my age, the whole problem is finding something to preserve yourself." He fixed Maya with a strange look. It was obvious he couldn't decide whether to treat her as his daughter, friend, or future mistress. He didn't know what to make of her, where to place her. Did she belong to Andre? Was there something real between Robert and her? Could she possibly belong to him?

The house lights came on, revealing the soft, earthen colors of the porch, the long bar, the buffet, and beyond, a wood scaffolding that had been erected for Andre's performance. With little idea of where it was going, with loose, floating combinations of people, the party kept renewing itself, lavish and magnificent.

Over the bay, on the bridge and in the little harbor, lights twinkled. A chorus of bullfrogs could be heard. "Seems like they're trying to imitate the counterpoint of Bach," Ben remarked.

"I don't like those sounds: they keep me awake. It's as if some harsh, gruff-voiced stranger is knocking at my bedroom door, trying to get in," Maya said.

The conversation, brilliant and fragmented, revolved around Ted Kennedy ("We'll cross that bridge when we come to it") and a rock festival that had taken place in upstate New York: Woodstock.

"I think it's the most important thing that's happened in our time," Hoppy was saying to Ben.

Ben looked up from his drink long enough to expostulate, "Come on, man, time doesn't exist!"

Maya chimed in with, "What a desperate attempt to find some bit of happiness. All those people coming together in the mud and rain, for what? What a waste of energy."

"There must be some better release, some other way out," said Robert. He thought of Carolina, how she would tell him, "No sense trying to impose one's ego on the universe, is there? That's been tried so many times and, has it worked?"

"But," Maya added, "it all comes down to the individual again, to what he feels, to what he can do with himself."

"Everyone's talking about 'liberation'. Words! Words! What rubbish. If you want to be free, the body and mind must become 'other'. They think the transformation can take place through drugs. But the only real way is love," Ben said, ending the conversation.

Down below on the lawn Vico was shaking the tambourines, pretending he was a scarecrow, flapping his arms up and down, and crying out. Of a sudden, he halted his cry, stared provocatively at his audience, then loped into Ben's house, sat down at the piano, and began amusing himself with improvised jazz.

Robert listened for a moment to Hoppy trying to explain something to Marthe: "I think that, uh, that, uh, getting into something is, uh, one thing and, uh, getting out, you know, is another and, you see, last year I was more, uh, interested in getting in but, I mean, this year it's the getting out, uh, that interests me the most…"

Ben went up to Maya with another drink in his hand. "Tell me, how are you getting along now without Andre? Poor guy. He's in such a bad way. I just wish you could help him. I've never seen a man struggle so hard to get back on his feet, and to think it's only a failure in love that's knocked him down."

Ben would have gone on and on, gesticulating in front of her face with his hands, if Maya had not cut him short with, "Ben, I like you, but I don't like lawyers who plead for lost causes. And you've got to stop using Andre as a pretext for trying to get something yourself."

Ben looked around him, a little dazed. On the couch at the end of the porch Hoppy and Marthe were sitting together, making out. Louise, pretending not to be watching, nonetheless observed them with a furious eye. Suddenly she cried out, "It's too much, it's just too much!" She ran back into the house.

Robert circled up behind Maya, laying his hands on the back of the chair while she reached softly up with her own, laid her fingers over his, enveloping them completely. Robert felt he had almost possessed her.

Suddenly the projectors lit up. Ben told them to be quiet; the show was about to start. Everyone knelt down, tried to make themselves comfortable on the grass. Robert noticed that a few theatre directors from New York were seated next to them. In a dinner jacket riddled with holes, Andre appeared on stage.

Maya turned away. "I can't stand him when he's like this," she whispered.

Next to Andre on the raised platform was a scrawny girl who couldn't have weighed more than one hundred pounds. She had a pail full of rubber hand grenades next to her, which she pulled out one by one and began throwing at the spectators. Then she threw herself down on the ground where she rolled about convulsively, wrapping herself up in a torn American flag.

Maya leaned to Robert: "Why does he feel this need to attack the audience before he begins? It was all right against the bourgeoisie in 1910 in Moscow. But now --- what pompous morality!"

Robert nodded and watched. Beating his chest, his voice bellowing cries, Andre played the part of a Neanderthal man who has just discovered Surrealism. Vico, who had squatted down next to Maya and Robert, began to joke, "Whew, man, great balls of fire!"

"Shh! Darn you! Durn you!" Marthe laughed stridently.

Up in the spotlight, waving his microphone like a revolver while over a tape recorder burst the sounds of pigs being slaughtered, Andre chanted deliriously, "Whore cities of the United States, filled with men drunk with death and dreams that haven't been fulfilled, to your rifles I oppose my dreams! I attack your dollars with my delirium, and into your guts made flabby with waste, I stick my mad sword and show that the bodies of even the best dressed bankers are nothing but sacks filled with shit!"

"Hey, Ma, what wuz that?" Vico wondered out loud.

Marthe 's earthy laughter rolled over everyone, like a refreshing bath.

But aside from her, no one laughed or cried or even seemed moved. Robert saw Andre as Don Quixote attacking his image in a mirror and not being able to get beyond that image. Little groups of people rose and started to trickle out. The skinny girl had arched her body and with her head thrown back was supporting herself on her arms and legs. Clapping his hands, his feet beating the ground, Andre danced around her in a primitive ritual. He wanted to be the "homo sacer", the sacred man.

It was the most intense moment of the strange performance. Robert sensed that Andre was playing himself, enacting his life. Circling around the arched, pale body of the woman, a dagger in his hands, Andre cried, "I'm exchanging my life for the death I can find in you. Say yes and affirm my death! My heart's beating like a locomotive as I rush into you.

I've got you now, baby, destroying you is the last possible way for me to avert destruction!"

There was no applause. More people rose and discreetly tiptoed away. The theatre directors disappeared. Robert could hear someone murmuring, "That's the worst thing I've seen in a good many years."

Maya said, "It's just stupid. It's so easy for him to be cruel. He's been doing nothing but that more and more for the last three years. It's become a facility."

"I guess there's only one thing left to do," grinned Vico.

"What's that?"

"Holler your joy to the hills, son!"

"It's certainly better than hollering your despair."

They didn't stay much longer. If Ben felt compassion for Andre, Maya was outraged. "Where does he get the nerve?" she demanded.

"He was doing it for you, you know," said Ben.

"Sorry," countered Maya. "His 'you' no longer has anything to do with my 'me'."

Ben looked troubled. Maya tried to avoid his glances and get away as quickly as possible. Not knowing quite what to do, Ben shambled after her, a drink in his hand. On the stage, the girls had lit torches and whirled around Andre. Tied to a pole, he was about to be symbolically burned. Louise moped after Maya, who held herself proud and erect and tried not to hear Andre screaming behind her.

On their way to the car Vico and Marthe let themselves go in outbursts of laughter. Vico cried, "Lay your rage on thick, boy! Don't be afraid of women and don't be scared of blacks or young pot-smoking revolutionaries, those gawddamn gud for nothing, worthless varmints! I keep fergettin' myself, wonder what in hell a man's worth these days, Sam.

Where's the purity of the past, uh, er, uh, yeah…" His voice trailed off in peals of cosmic laughter.

Robert drove off alone with Maya. Just as they were leaving, Ben came staggering over the lawn and touched Maya's arm. He didn't say anything. As Robert backed up, Ben pretended the car had run over his toe. He bent over, groaning. "He's faking," said Maya. "What's real he'll never show."

The lashes under her eyes enlarged her face; her eyes, with their liquid, pale-greenish transparency, became dominant, almost vertiginous. For a second she looked slightly like a gangster's moll, a baby doll… He pulled her toward him, scrutinizing her eyes. She averted them and moved away from him, looking demure, serene. Suddenly she reminded him of the Lady of the Unicorn, or some quite extraordinary high Renaissance figure, in pursuit of her own clarity, her own dream. It was amazing how quickly she could change.

They were driving down the highway. Cars hooted by. She crept close to him again, her arms draped around his back. He whirled past trucks. Blue and red lights flashed on the road. "Sing me something," she said. She whispered into his ear. "I'm a woman, I'm full of dynamite."

He laughed; he caught her arm.

"I'm a sphinx lady, a spider eagle."

He pulled over. She responded by jumping toward him and biting him. He pressed his lips toward her and kissed her gently, almost furtively. Every brief kiss now was the sowing of a seed that would ripen later. Her lips came shyly toward him, she seemed to be becoming softer and softer, more and more luminous, when suddenly she bit him again, more savagely this time, and said, "I'm going to hurt you very much."

She dug into him with her nails; there was a second of intense pain, so intense it was almost delicious. Then she said in a different tone of voice, "But I hope I don't do evil to you."

He shook his head. Whatever happened, he was engaged, he had to go to the end. He felt he was floating through a space that hadn't been defined, he didn't know what the limits were, what the rules were.

"Go on singing," he said.

She sang in a small, gentle voice, "I'm not going to hurt you, I just want to come and say 'bonjour' to you." Without warning she changed tone. "And put my dynamite in your ear!"

She squeezed him; she was his. Robert felt he was being burned, slowly consumed, by the simple possession of her presence.

She draped one arm around his neck, poking the other between his legs. She held it there for a long time, igniting him with her warmth, making him flare up. He was driving very quickly now out on the far left lane, the big blue car rumbling and rattling.

Two terrible thirsts were gathered together, vibrating and beaming in the darkness.

"Are you ready?" Robert asked. The words escaped him; he didn't know exactly what they meant.

"I'm always ready," she said. "I don't believe in anything."

She moved over, crushing herself against him more forcefully now, moving her hands with a microscopic, pounding rhythm against his thighs. She almost touched the power of his sex, sending instantaneous screams through his head.

Maya, Maya, veil of illusions and enchantment ---- Robert felt he was giving up himself, diving inside the forms of Maya to find his self again. Yet he knew that the moment he found it, the form would change; the search would begin anew.

He started telling her about his fortune-telling session with the astrological cook.

"I want to see the astrological cook!" Maya implored.

"I always felt some guiding line in my life," he told her, "some force of destiny urging me forward."

"No such luck," said Maya. "Nothing but chance for me."

They never made it to the divinatory cook. Robert stopped the car in front of Maya's cottage and they sat quietly in the shadows of the huge linden tree looking at each other.

"Look at those trees," Maya murmured. "They remind me of that Spanish artist, Gaudi."

Some time passed. Again Robert had the painful sense Maya was riding a dangerous bull, that she did not know how to ride very well, that at any moment she was liable to fall off and die.

Suddenly, wildly, they were embracing each other, trying to sink into each other. His heart was going with a fever and he reached out across the miles of seat to touch her and she gave, she yielded... He reached over and drew her closer to him. Christ! How her flesh was perfect, and how he became alive at her touch. He leaned over nibbling for crumbs behind her ears and she started rocking back and forth. She had a precise, almost surgical, presence, honing his desire, making it sharper and stronger. He touched her hips, urging her; his hands of their own accord shot out and caught her smooth, taut buttocks. He tried to capture her with his mouth and he swooped down with his hands, plunging his fingers between her thighs. She let her face fall on his lap. Her belt slipped off, her hips began to sway back and forth.

Then the rain tumbled down, dancing on the roof in a delirious ballet. She looked up and said, "I'm afraid."

She had never felt anyone embrace her like that, with a violence that was all the more striking and startling and painful for the tenderness it included, out of which it arose. His kisses were cries. But he wasn't asking anything for himself, rather trying to rip himself open, give as much as he possibly could of himself to her; and it was the pain of loving like that that made his kisses seem like cries. She liked the kind way he expressed his steely power.

He was surprised to hear she was afraid. It hadn't occurred to him she might be feeling this way.

"Of what?"

The next words were even more of a surprise. "Of you."

She hesitated, and then spoke quite smoothly, "Sometimes I think it would be very difficult for me to do without you."

In the rainy night he pulled her out of the car and they ran into the cottage. While the terrible thunder and rain vroomed outside, they submerged into themselves. Robert didn't leave the next morning or even the morning after that.

Chapter XXVIII

Sunday lunch. Mrs. Mellon sat at the end of the mahogany dining table, her crystal bell in front of her. Every now and then she lifted it and tinkled to signify the end of a course. On her right, participating in this time-honored ritual was Robert. He had come back to grab his suitcase.

Silently, precisely, the uniformed maids passed the sterling silver serving plates. There was Long Island duckling, fresh corn and garden-grown baby green peas.

Phillip Poindexter, his grandmother's new suitor, remarked when told Robert was leaving, "That's youth, isn't it, always looking for greener pastures."

Mrs. Mellon tinkled her crystal bell to get everyone's attention. "The most extraordinary thing happened last night," she said. "My lawn was invaded around midnight by a motorcycle gang the police tell me are known as the Hell's Angels!"

"What a shock that must have been for you, poor dear!"

"Yes, as you know, it was a stormy night, thunder and lightning, and suddenly I heard the angry roar of a dozen motorcycles outside my bedroom window. I was terrified. I knew I should have equipped my gardeners with guns! Of course, I never bring my best jewels to the country.

I heard they like drugs, so I started to throw all the aspirin from my medicine cabinet out the window at them."

Robert could visualize it: the huge machines, the leather jackets, the roar of the motors, the headlights spotlighting the century-old trees in the back of the great mansion, the bikes churning up and down the manicured lawn, running over the croquet wickets, the lights going on in the rooms as the maids awoke, his grandmother tossing aspiring out the window; then, suddenly as it had come, the terrible vrooming of the bikes disappeared, joining the thunder, the rain, the night.

"The next thing you know they'll be invading the beach," groaned Phillip Poindexter.

"At first I was scared, then I thought I was dreaming that the Russians were invading us, then I realized it was a joke, all those motorcycles going round and round on the lawn, what a noise! Reminds me of when you were a boy, Robbie, and you had all those model airplanes." Mrs. Mellon's voice cackled with rich laughter.

Robert flinched. His childhood was something he could do without. He had no reverence for it, no feeling of warmth. It was true he had liked to build the balsa wood planes, to watch them take off and soar. That was the trick, he thought: to get high, to stay off the ground.

"It's funny," Phillip Poindexter was saying, "that the motorcycle invasion happened when it did because I was thinking of getting one myself. But now I feel so depressed by these ragamuffins, these hooligans who arm themselves with machines." He sighed ostentatiously.

The other lady --- permed hair, hunched shoulders, shrill voice --- spoke up, "It's simply terrible. Nothing's sacred anymore. Your back lawn becomes a public park. Have the young become insane? In my generation it was different ---- I'm telling you! Then we had a feeling of what we were supposed to do. We knew what was right or wrong. If I ever spoke badly at the dinner table, my father would beat me over the knuckles with a spoon. And it hurt --- I tell you. It hurt! But there are no laws anymore. These kids on their bikes think they can show up anywhere - do anything!"

His grandmother didn't agree. "That's life, progress. It goes forward. We know it and pretend not to. When I was a little girl we rode around in horses and carriages. Now there are jet planes flying over the beach every afternoon. Phillip has a new idea for a computer company that will tell people what to do in their leisure time."

The excitement wore off. Lunch ended. There was a certain tension. Phillip approached Robert. "In spite of everything, I'm fascinated by the young - how a young man like you can live freely, without any concern…" His voice changed; he became serious. "Perhaps you'd like to work for me. I've got an idea to offer 'computerized cosmetics' to the American housewife. By submitting complete information about herself and subscribing for a year, the housewife will be able to dial a number every morning and, sitting in front of the mirror, listen to the computer cosmetic center inform her --- taking into account such variables as changing weather, styles of fashion, etc. --- exactly what she should do to make herself more beautiful and attractive on that day."

"I think it's a marvelous idea," said Mrs. Mellon as she sipped her Sanka from a demitasse.

"The marvel," said Robert dryly, "remains to be seen."

At the end of the long table, with Phillip's arm now around her, his grandmother said, "Don't you think it's time you started to do something? I know you served in Vietnam, but now you can't just be an anti-war protester all your life."

"If you don't like the cosmetics idea," chimed in Phillip, "I've got the idea for another company, a computer center for art that will make galleries obsolete."

"So what are you waiting for? "Robert asked.

Phillip didn't answer. Suddenly Robert realized: he needs my grandmother's money. He's waiting for that.

Saddened and horrified, Robert turned to leave.

"Must you go, Robbie dear?"

"You know that I can't stay here. I have another life to live now."

"I heard about that sphinx woman!" Mrs. Mellon cried. "Do you understand that for me that's zero? Zero!"

Robert said nothing. He didn't want to hurt her.

There was an anguished moment. Mrs. Mellon's frail shoulders sagged. It looked as if she was about to break into tears. Phillip Poindexter was trying to hold her and comfort her. "Breathe deeply, breathe deeply," he kept saying. "I told you you'd feel so much better and relaxed if you'd start doing yoga with me."

Robert grimaced and squirmed away. Lizzie, the old maid, was waiting by the door with his suitcase. He hugged her and left.

Chapter XXIX

"Hotdog! Ice cream!" Vico cried, swerving his bike to the side of the road toward a glass-enclosed ice cream parlor. Surmounted by two gobs of ice cream, it looked like a pop imitation of Byzantine cupolas in Istanbul. Straddling the rear seat Andre had a vision of a hotdog emerging from an ice cream cone. As Arab tribesmen on camels, on Vico's Harley they roared through a desert crisscrossed with plastic houses, hamburger shacks topped with steer heads, and highways. Vico yodeled, "Yeow, yikes! Back to the hills, man!"

The wind flashed past their faces; Andre wished the wind would run in his head, sweeping it clear of all the images of love that had slowly begun to rot there.

They were rushing into New York, a city that for Andre, was a whore, torn apart in every direction but still managing to give itself to those with money generation after generation. Vico was moving because he couldn't stay in any place for more than one week, and he still earned his livelihood by playing the piano three nights a week at a jazz bar in the village.

Andre was going because Vico was going and he couldn't stand to stay any longer in the emptiness that infested Ben's. As an intercessor to

Maya, Ben had proved useless; he had threatened to "spank" her but even that had not happened, and the days hurtled by.

Ben was working on plans for an airport in Algeria that would resemble a gigantic glass bubble. In short, through his work he kept discovering reasons to live, and was working for the future --- blueprints, projects, consultations --- which Andre couldn't have cared less about. Space whipped by him: to tear at life the way the air tore at him! He clung to Vico, who grinned and laughed.

Andre thought: nothing can change our lives but the progressive insinuation in us of forces that destroy us. What were those forces that had crept into him and blown him apart, so that he felt he was living a life over which he no longer had any control? The evening at Ben's, what a bomb! He knew he had disgusted the people, outraged and disappointed them; yet didn't they understand that he had to break down the barriers, change their ways of feeling and thinking, make them see their lives as affairs of total chance where everything ought to be risked? He couldn't explain anything anymore, couldn't talk to them nicely --- he felt the old psychological drama had had it --- the only way to get at them was by striking them directly in the gut, hammering them with blows to the stomach. Then they might realize something, might have the chance to be carried up to the summit of some transcendent experience. He wanted to tear down the "fourth wall" that separated the audience from the actors.

On the wings of Vico's amazing machine, they whirled into the eye-crushing heights and blazing sirens of New York City.

Andre had no clear idea what he was going to do. Evicted --- for disorderly conduct? --- from the house of love he had suddenly become an exile. He gritted his teeth, crossed 14th street, and passed a pretty girl hurrying desperately into a pharmacy. Something doubtful in his appearance caused a cop to approach and give him the ominous order of "keep moving." How did they want him to be mobile when he had nothing to move for? The springs seemed broken in his legs. He had lost Maya. He declared himself bankrupt. That was easy. More difficult was to arrive at that state he had so often proclaimed as a goal: be proud enough to do nothing. No forced labor. In an obscene society of abundance wasn't it almost noble to be a scavenger?

Smog eclipsed the sun. After a few brilliant moments by the sea, in the sun, in the presence of the loved one, Andre now walked alone between vertical rectangles of glass and steel. A thin, sickly girl stood next to a black tree, skipping rope. Andre felt shadows were watching him, he saw doors mysteriously opening, closing, but he could see no one entering or leaving. He realized that, except for his father, he had only loved one other person in his life, Maya, and that was undoubtedly not enough to keep him alive now. The afternoon petered out like a tallow candle, the city encircled by vast stretches of tarnished silver light. Where was the infinite? How could he become a little closer to what he was already? Beneath the emptiness he knew so well, he felt another emptiness that took him by surprise. At the moment there was not any bitterness in him; that would come later. It grew dark. In the East Village, Vico was already playing his piano gig. Andre went to find him.

Andre rubbed a cigarette stub out in an ashtray on the bar counter at Nina's Club. Next to him some dude with a beard down to his collarbone was trying to explain the meaning of riots. Before them pitchers of beer were smothered in bursts of laughter and noise. Musical sparks, remarkably clear, easy and free, shot up from Vico's piano. In this "in" place of New York, merriment was the rule of the evening. Vulture-eyed, perched on a stool, her voluminous breasts propped on the bar, Nina awarded tables to the lucky few.

The bearded guy was saying, "Everyone today hates what they do. How do they escape? They get together and perform a riot, or they do a sit-in, or do drugs. Then they go back to being what they are, miserable, bored, frustrated, fed-up! Overwhelmed by things they can't understand, the world, the war, kids. All they can say is 'Yes, sir' or 'No, sir', you know what I mean?"

Andre knew. But how tired he was of these people talking like parakeets about revolt and liberation. Certain words were on everyone's lips. Another facility. Andre felt he had lived it, put himself out on a limb, and wrecked his life for it. How many lives had been sacrificed to hopeless causes, drained and flushed away by time and history. His father, the legendary cyclist, used to say to him, "What's needed, boy, is discipline! If you want to win, you've got to keep your legs pumping!!"

That horrible afternoon, after a few drinks with Vico, his own agitations and uneasiness had made Andre's head turbulent with images. On 42nd Street he had seen a student try to set himself on fire. No one had moved, tried to intervene. The kid had cried, "Americans, what have you done to us?" While nearer to him he had heard someone munching on a hotdog, go, "Ummmm!"

He had visions of fires bursting out, of horses charging; he saw firemen swarming over ladders into buildings, handcuffed people emerging, smoke everywhere in the streets; he saw men in suits whose smiles were conditioned by a ten point rise in the stock market. In his mind everything was burning, flowing together in flames. Then came Maya, bareback on a horse down the beach, a priestess queen garbed in her elegant gowns, raising a knife in her hands.

He had once asked her, "What does a grand lady do in a time that doesn't have any grandeur?"

Her reply had been simple, swift and deadly: "She kills herself."

But she hadn't killed herself; she had gone on living. He had thought of killing her; he was still thinking of it. United in life, united in death --- the impossible dream.

Some other dude at the bar jostled him, and asked abruptly, "What do you do?"

He mumbled an answer, "I'm in the theatre, and I make movies, events, performances that reflect the disasters of the time, signs of love, passionate aggression --- a few months ago we killed a chicken, poured the blood over the thighs of a woman, who became a goddess, dominating us all…"

"What the hell? Are you crazy? What kind of a crazy thing are you into anyway, buddy?"

They were about to come to blows when something tugged at him. Vico had come over and was slapping him on the back. They clinked glasses. The conversation grew weird, fragmentary. Vico was rambling, "Ice-cream cones and freckles combine with various elements of the American dream to produce an automobile out of whose hood the head of a yellow giraffe emerges."

What a laugh! A river of laughter so violent it opened chasms and abysses before them. The bar had filled up, animated Saturday night, swinging. Andre, for no reason, was laughing his belly out. Vico surprised him with, "Hey, who's your inner Haha?"

A few minutes later Vico said, "Guess what? A teddy bear's just been elected President of the United States!"

"Great. Big Mama's coming back --- teddy bears and childhood."

"But teddy bears don't laugh."

"Everyone's going to start laughing pretty soon," said Andre, "because two thousand years of Novocain are wearing off."

"Yeah, no more soul and all that," said Vico. "Well, I'm gonna go back and take a look-see at my piano and see what I can dig up."

"Wait!" called Andre. "How do I get Maya to come back? What do I have to do so she'll respond to me?"

"Can't talk with the dead," said Vico. "Better luck with the living."

"If only she'd make herself dead," Andre groaned. "She won't give me a sign, nothing. Goddamn silence!"

He knew it was useless, a waste. But how to put a blackout on love? How extinguish the imaginary aura that still glows in the head long after the object that has created it has gone?

Vico shouted back at him, as if to give him hope, "Just think, before too long we might see a teddy bear in the White House!"

Andre could have cared less whether a teddy bear or a giraffe appeared on the horizon. He only had one problem: how to deal with the loss of Maya.

"Hey, did you know that in Paris, France, last night some kids climbed up Notre Dame and decorated it with black and red flags."

"And in the morning they found one of them still there, clinging to a gargoyle, and a helicopter had to come to get him down."

Andre wasn't listening. Like a monk, he felt tired of the world, weary of these gestures that led no place. It had been different in 1965 (was it?) in Selma, Alabama. He had been one of the first whites to make the trip to the south, participate in the marches. There had been violence; he had been jailed. He had stayed locked in a cell for two weeks with other protesters. Because he expressed himself so strongly, they had asked him to write letters for them with the hope that their women would respond. Andre felt the same violence in himself again. He was angry. He demanded accounts. He wouldn't accept silence. He would squeeze the neck of Maya's silence like the neck of a chicken. The holocaust of his love required a victim.

Music burst around him, bright shrapnel of sound, conversation bubbles. From nearby: "Soon perhaps technicians will invent a way to insert a phone dial into the human eardrum."

"Yeah, man, and soon fireflies will invade the avenues of New York City."

Andre saw it: the slow invasion of pinpointed lights luminously crossing the screen of his mind. He was waking up. No more wasted time, indecision, dead moments. Time to smash, to shock, to shed his screams. Break the glue: float.

All these people swarming in and out around him were glued to their lives, loves, little habits, thoughts, amusements, as flies to flypaper. Was there anything in this nightmare city that wasn't glue --- men glued to jobs, bodies glued to the sidewalk, dollar bills glued to banks, posters glued to buildings? It was time to break the glue.

Next to him, one elbow propped on the bar, a man with a rasping, prophetic voice went on, "The time's gonna come when everything that's been will be again, and all that is to be will have been."

Andre grunted, coughed. He was sick with uneasy excitement, fever. If only Maya would answer! How to close the accounts that a man and a woman open with each other?

"You don't have to worry about the end, man. It's coming, faster and faster, bigger and bigger, like a snowball, the whole thing's going to self-destruct..."

They stood drinking their beers and fanning the fires of an apocalyptic yearning.

The seagulls and the fireflies would inhabit New York. In Andre's mind that student kept setting himself on fire. Why had he been a witness to that? He didn't believe anything happened accidentally. In the back of the room a woman cried. Imperturbable, forever fixed to the same happy wavelength, Vico jangled the black and white keys. Another dark-haired girl was dancing. Andre saw with exalted horror that while she was moving someone secretly lit a match and touched it to the red fringe of her skirt. More flames! She screamed. Hands beat out the brief fire that threatened to travel up her thighs. Behind Andre, a tall man with a cowboy hat kept shaking his head and repeating, "I don't understand. I don't understand."

Vico surged up before him. "Listen, man, don't stand there like a zombie. Snap out of it. Before the grave gets you, grab for the gusto of life!"

Andre walked out into the night. Gusts of wind machine-gunned the sidewalk. He swerved past a beggar whose hands stabbed at him, begging him for a dollar, just a dollar. He wandered down to the Bowery. It was raining hard. Phantoms of men moved around him, along the walls, like packs of starved dogs. Where was the kid who had tried to set himself on fire? Where were the fireflies someone had promised would invade New York? Police sirens howled. A desire overwhelmed him to fall down on his knees, open his stomach and vomit. But this desire was short-circuited by a new and even more powerful awareness: he would either have to forget Maya or kill her.

Maya had been the oceanic woman in whom the hard, tough forms of his body had been liquefied. The fantastic nights of their love kept hunting Andre down, relentlessly haunting his head. How could he not think about all those days of their love, when he sank into her like a sun into the sea? The more he had loved her, the more he had been liquefied, the more he had convulsed into the slender sluice of her silver infinity. No more.

He turned and, slouching like a beast through the wind, rain and darkness, he ambled uptown past the ruined slums, past closed Italian kitchens advertising "Heroes."

Chapter XXX

Andre was not the only visitor waiting at the St. Regis for Salvador Dali to make his daily appearance at five pm in the elegant tearoom full of mirrors. A group of young kids, hippy style, were eagerly camping out on the sidewalk. A tall boy with blond curly hair had a white band around his forehead upon which was written, "Don't adjust your head, there's something temporarily wrong with reality."

A funny moment occurred when a straw-haired wisp of a girl began to sing, "Life is just a bowl of cherries."

Her companion, who had a guitar, accompanied her with, "And reality is the pips we spit out."

Andre pushed his way past the group and made his way up the steps into the St. Regis, thinking: "No, life is knowing how to ignite God so that he burns like a match and ignites your cigar!"

It was very rare that Dali let anyone come up to his suite. But Andre, who had become friends with Dali through Maya, was invited to come up. "I want you to see how furiously I have been amusing myself!" Dali told him. "Gala is away and psychologically I am a little child in her absence. Come and see. What a revenge I am having! How I am enjoying myself."

With Gala gone, it looked as if a riot had taken place in the hotel suite. Socks flooded the carpet and traces of toothpaste could be found on mirrors and the backs of chair. A huge stuffed rhinoceros dominated the disheveled bed. Andre burst into laughter. Dali, twirling his moustache and searching through the sea of socks, explained, "It's the psychological revenge of being free from the woman-mother."

"Is anyone ever free from that?" Andre wondered.

"Most men marry their mother, though some settle for their sister. But I am so glad, Andre, that you settled for nothing less than Maya. What a superb creature! What a divine woman! She has the gift to live above the family, and therefore above the nation and any flag or cause. Maya is magic, sometimes I think she is our memory."

"She was my memory!" cried Andre. "But now she is trying to forget me. Look, I have a letter from her that says, 'Will you please have the politeness to take me out of your mind!'"

Dali snorted and picked up his solid gold cane. "Impossible! There is only one woman, Gala, of which every woman is a part, and she is dreaming us all." He tapped his cane. "Don't you know that a woman is the primordial dream without a dreamer that creates all the other dreams and dreamers?"

"Well," sighed Andre, "I'm in the process of being evicted from the dream of Maya."

"As you know," said Dali, pontifical, "there is only one thing I prefer to women and that is the railroad station in Perpignan, which is the navel of the world."

Dali lifted a monocle and examined Andre through it. "I always look at men as if they were pictures. Most men today are filled with nothing but ideas, without which they would starve, shrivel at once. They would do better to amuse themselves! The only thing that counts is personality. And of course imagination, which is the personality in action. That is rare, like gold. It's easier to amuse yourself if you have a passion like I do: I hunt down stupid people, to confuse, panic and bewilder them."

"Blow their minds."

"Yes, blow into their heads," Dali smiled. "Not such an inglorious idea. As some people collect gas in their bellies, I think others have wind in their heads!"

"Brain farts," said Andre.

"You are not joking as much as you think," proclaimed Dali, twirling his moustache. "What astonishes me in the way people live is how little attention they pay to the act of defecation."

"I wonder if anyone's ever studied the effects of the flush toilet on the soul of modern man."

"That is why I worship gold so much," said Dali. "It is the frozen excrement of the sun."

"Tell me," said Andre, point-blank, "what would you do if Gala left you. Or died."

Dali didn't hesitate. "It has already been planned: I would eat her."

"All of her?"

'I have a few friends, who are witch doctors, who assure me they can shrink her into eatable size."

"Cannibalism"

"Don't forget that cannibalism is a mark of respect. You only eat what you love."

"But the agony?"

"Remember that I once tied a dying dog to a microphone, so the sounds of his agony would be multiplied."

Dali finished getting himself ready for his descent into the tearoom. With his cape and gold cane, he looked like a grand magician.

"I suppose the Christian ceremony is symbolic cannibalism. You eat the wafer which is the body of Christ."

"I've always thought," said Dali, moving majestically toward the door, "that if you love something eating it is the best way of making it a part of yourself and keeping it inside you."

Dali strolled out with his gold cane, which, Andre thought, was probably a symbol of all he had eaten, defecated, and turned into gold. But a new thought had come to him, a drastic solution to his troubles. His energy demanded a sacrifice. Because so much had been given, something had to be taken away. He would return to the country and "eat" Maya. Thank you, Dali.

Chapter XXXI

Maya's head appeared above the bushes. Pain and pleasure began shooting through Andre. He had been waiting for her to come out for at least an hour, crouched down in a cramped space between the tree and the fence. The sudden sight of her had made him think for a moment that everything was beginning again. It wasn't. Yet this had once been his cottage. One happy summer after another had piled up there. How idiotic to think he could end it all by strangling her! Even if she were dead it would take him years to eat and digest all of Maya!

It was late in the afternoon. Maya had lovely blue flowers that formed a superb crown on top of her head. She was wearing a long, pale, flowery gown. It made her look precisely like some medieval queen, Florentine perhaps, who had gone through the fields to pick flowers. Seeing her inviolable delicacy, a knot of hatred formed in Andre's stomach. Was there no trace left of the nights they had lived, of the love they had shared?

He waited. His nerves were coiled. He could have bounded toward her. Perhaps he had misinterpreted her silence. Just because she had said "no," what did that mean? Days of suffering had split Andre, scraped him like a razor blade. It was no wonder he felt a little crazy.

The late September sun was just setting over the potato fields. Hidden in the bushes with a .38 "Saturday Night Special" in his pocket,

Andre was grinding his teeth. Maya had once told him, "Do you know that when you sleep you grind your teeth?" Now he had to accept the brutal fact that everything they had lived together no longer counted for anything at all. Maya of course didn't care. But Andre felt he had to "win" at all costs. His father, the one-time cycling champion, liked to remind him, "In a race it's easy to know where you are, whether you've won." Andre didn't know. He was still tormented by this idea of being a champion. Once at three in the morning he had made Maya call Brussels to talk to his father and hear in his own words how he would have won the "Tour de France" race in 1933 if an automobile hadn't knocked him down. Andre's head buzzed with an inflamed glory he had never achieved.

Now he approached with murderous intentions the graceful figure of Maya. The indigo flowers in her hair shone like an electric aura around her head. She looked more slender than usual, also taller, and even more majestic. The voice of Maya talking with Louise and Robert drifted out over the porch, past the rose bushes where he was hidden. To his left the lush willow tree pitched its canopy of leaves up to the sky. Everything that evening seemed so calm, peaceful, shaded. God! Andre cursed himself for the images of Maya that still sparked in his brain. Why was he making such a big thing of her? A woman was a woman was a woman; why did he think Maya was anything more? The romantic illusion! He had all these images of love, whole shoeboxes of them, floating around unattached in his head, and Maya came closer than any woman he had ever known to meeting them, being one with them. How could she have guessed what a dangerous path he was on, how tragic and futile the quest?

Feeling like a slug, Andre crawled through the garden, heavy with herb scents, lavender and thyme. He tried to pinpoint his thoughts on what he had to do, the death he had chosen --- that had perhaps chosen him. Everything came back to him --- the way Maya smelled of "L'Heure Bleue" in the morning, the lace curtains in her room, the framed Russian icons by her bed. Robert would be there with her now, both of them bathing in a happiness they had not suffered enough to deserve. To flame with energy, explode above life hardly ever touching the ground, to fulgurate... That was Andre's dream. How could he allow a woman he had loved to continue to exist as if nothing had ever been?

He saw Maya stand up and incline her head slightly, her long Nefertiti neck. Was she bowing to Robert, saluting him? Andre had hoped to find her alone, but he couldn't wait for the right occasion. Had Robert replaced him? Andre refused to believe that Robert had any reality. He saw Robert as just an unworthy substitute for himself.

Andre wanted to show his authority over this woman. If he was going to kill her, let there be witnesses! Maya's body had once been a sponge for the violence of his love. Now that violence had no outlet, no lightning rod to absorb the shock. It wasn't even violence, rather an abundant flow of energy, exuberance that nothing could contain. That's why Andre loved Vico, because there was a guy who literally flamed with energy, you could see it crackling around his head, in his shoulders. But Vico had no evil in him, no conscious good. He was simply a creature, wild American barbarian, living at the maximum of his powers. His intensity wasn't willed, he did nothing to get, achieve it; it just came. As if he had amphetamines running naturally in his blood, he was always high.

But for Andre the time had come when the pure expression of vital energy wasn't enough. He had to be able to act, to prove himself through an irrevocable gesture. Only the victim of his love could prove the intensity and truth of that love. In order for Maya to be faithful to what they had lived, it was necessary for her to be sacrificed. This was the last taboo of love that could be broken, the final frontier that demanded to be crossed.

Between the porch railings he could glimpse her graceful body bedecked in a flowery gown, shimmering in the dying light. They were drinking tea. Maya seemed happy; joy was shining on her face like a million drops of water. Was it Robert who gave her that bliss? Or was she simply triumphing in the delight of her new possession? Andre dug his fingers into the ground. He was like a crouching animal, a bull pretending to be a panther, a rhinoceros with his heart in flames among the flowers.

At last Andre Cordier had found a purpose: he was going to "eat" her. All his senses were attuned to that purpose. Should he himself die? He had always felt that life wasn't worth enough to be worth dying for. If he killed himself, as that kid near 42nd Street had tried to do, wouldn't that prove the value of what he rejected? Yet living in peace wasn't enough either. He didn't want to become like Hoppy, a happy vegetable. What he really would have liked was to have been consumed like a meteor at certain very intense moments of love with Maya. How beautiful had been their affirmations made without any ulterior motive! He remembered their laughter, their electric spasms, and Maya saying, "The only thing that counts for me is finding joy every day!"

His belly clenched. How long could he go on living under this strain? A few more minutes and he would reveal himself. He would step out and confront her and put the snub-nosed barrel to her head and pull the trigger and then... If only he could get Louise out of the way! She had stepped in front of Maya and was blocking his view of her. "Have the kindness not to remember anything about me," Maya had once whispered to him. What would she cry out in terror now when she saw him leaping toward her?

A stab of regret hit Andre. What was the terrible force that made him want to bring Maya down, to trap her like a bird in the depths of his own mud and despair? Was his "cannibalism" simply a revolt against all that was refined, superb, poetic in her? He had believed in Maya as if she were a goddess, a shining, royal sphinx, a soaring, spider eagle, and inimitable companion of sensational nights. He had loved her so intensely, literally trying to bury himself in her flesh, that now, at this moment of truth, he couldn't bring himself to destroy the idol his ardent love had created.

He heard Louise scream. He saw Maya's beloved head, crowned with the blue flowers, turn in shock and surprise toward him. Andre had a vision of her rising, aimed like a huge, mystical arrow toward the sun. There was no place for him to go anymore but toward himself. He realized it with a sudden, suicidal clarity that stimulated him by its very desperateness. He took one more step toward her. Then he stopped becoming. He pointed the gun toward the side of his head and fired.

Chapter XXXII

Andre Cordier was dead. His body was cremated, and after a small ceremony, his ashes were dispersed over the Atlantic. A few of his friends gathered afterwards at Ben's house. "I still can't believe he's not with us," said Ben. "It's my fault. I should have done something."

They walked down to the bay. Maya wandered ahead of them on the sandy path. She was barefoot; over her shoulders a Spanish shawl floated in the evening breeze. The last light flowed over the grass, grazing the land. A lonely yellow rowboat drifted back and forth next to the weeds. From time to time Maya stopped and sniffed at the honeysuckle. She picked up a few strands of grass, put them between her teeth, and bit them. They could smell the salt sea scents. It was a strangely calm evening.

"Stop," Maya said. "Look at the water. How it's alive."

The surface of the inland water looked as if it were in perpetual vibration.

"What makes it do that?"

"It's the insects."

Robert thought of all the vibrations of that summer, the tense, quivering surface they had lived on. Finally the tension had proved too much for them. They had all wanted to live without compromises. It was an old idea and death was the price they were paying.

The light vibrated in a bouquet of colors. To the right, the road became a pebbly path drifting down to the water from the dunes. When Maya took it, Ben said, "How can you do that? You must have brave feet."

As she followed the path down to the water, Robert followed her bare brown feet with his eyes.

Ben said he had just bought a pair of shoes. His sandals were falling apart. He held them up to show them to Maya. The loop through which his toe was supposed to fit had come undone. "That's not the way sandals are meant to be," said Maya.

"No, they're not," said Ben. They laughed. Ben put his arm around Maya's waist and held her for a second. "I'm so sorry about Andre. I know in your heart you loved him."

The evening surged, reddened like fire over the large stretches of water. A lighthouse beyond the breakwater began to go on and off. The cool night lit itself up with early stars as the calm water splashed lazily.

"He never belonged to me. He was wild and beautiful in his own way but too crazy for me."

Robert caught up to them, took Maya's hand in her own. He wanted to tell her, "You belong to me now," but he wasn't sure if she could ever belong to anyone.

Maya and Robert embraced as the light over the bay dropped and the shore's whiteness faded. Then they turned to go back. Ben was waiting for them on a plank stretched over a narrow creek. "What do the little fish do in winter?" Maya wondered.

Good question, thought Robert. Would his passion for Maya prove as ephemeral as the summer or durable and lasting into the winter and beyond?

"They freeze up in the ice which keeps them alive till spring when they float loose again in the thaw."

"Haha. Deep freeze for fish."

Ben seized Robert and pulled him aside. "This time, you know, it's real." He didn't wait to hear his answer. "Let's go back to the house and drink."

"Bonne idée!" said Maya. Too many things had happened for her too. She was anxious for any chance to get away from the horror stories.

Lights shone like spears thrown into the bay. Further away the bridge of Sag Harbor glittered. Robert grabbed the barefooted Maya and pulled her toward him. She didn't resist. Entangled, they ambled clumsily along.

They came back and sat down on the big leather chairs on Ben's veranda. Beyond the screen dark leaves were undulating.

"Ben, what you really need is a woman." It was the first time Maya had permitted herself to make an allusion to his private life.

"Women!" Ben grunted. "You know what they say in Spain: a wife is a whore who's agreed to wash dishes."

Ben poured himself another White Label and soda. His deep, gravelly voice wavered around them like the lapping of waves. "When I first moved into a studio in New York I found in a closet an old sealed silver vase. Something made me suspicious; I called a friend. We opened the vase and found the ashes of the previous tenant's mother. What a discovery!"

"How morbid!" Maya echoed.

"It's not easy to get rid of your ghosts," Robert remarked. If they weren't careful, all the phantoms and wraiths of that summer would come back to haunt them. In a strange way, the evening had already become a mass for the dead, for Andre and Carolina. A glorious requiem resonant with secret vibrations echoed separately in each one of them.

"In about a month I'm going to Africa," Ben announced. "They've invited me for an exhibition of my drawings. Do you see? An artist gives an exhibition: the exhibition consists in the cannibalization of the artist. The artist, however, has written the menu. His intelligence has foreseen his destruction."

"But the menu," Robert added, "was a phony. It was written in such small letters that no one could read it. This only whetted their appetite."

A glass of scotch in his hands, Ben moved unsteadily across the porch and kissed Maya on both cheeks. Then he came up to Robert, embraced him and said, "Good luck. Be happy together."

Later, Robert would try to put the thoughts of Ben and that lunatic evening out of his mind. Ben like a great Gatsby of the art world; Ben his substitute father; Ben who wrote an indecipherable menu for his own cannibalization; Ben the alcoholic; Ben the last of the noble artists; Ben the man with no love, the funny man who said he couldn't speak English anymore, only the local language of Sag Harbor; Ben who said he really didn't like whiskey and only drank it (a bottle a day) as a souvenir of earlier days; Ben who said, "All my life I've spent building for a future which, at bottom, I don't believe in; Ben who, half-teasing, half-serious, said as they were leaving, "Maya, you know very well the only thing that could save me would be your marrying me. The reason I feel so good is that I've been taking life from you. I've been having blood transfusions from you!"

"Oh, no wonder I've been feeling so exhausted, so drained!"

Back in the car, under stars scurrying through the sky like mice, Maya said, "If only someone could stay with Ben, guide him, control him!"

Another responsibility that Robert couldn't worry about: he had one already --- Maya.

Chapter XXXIII

When the lamp flicked on in the kitchen, bathing the window blanketed by night with sharp reflections, it became immediately apparent that two bodies, naked as worms, were cavorting on the living room floor in front of the fireplace where a few flames still flickered. There was a furious tangle of blind arms and bare legs.

Her instincts triggered Maya to flee. Once Robert might have said, "What energy! It's like a midnight sun!" But he couldn't do that anymore. He couldn't accept such unlimited freedom. It had already led to two deaths.

Oblivious to everything else but themselves, the two bodies of Marthe and Vico revolved round and round in a bright, Rubenesque merry-go-round of flesh.

In the doorway Louise's head popped up, blushing like a ripe apple. "They don't pay any attention to me!" was her chagrined cry. "It's as if I didn't exist."

"Get away! Get away!" Maya pushed back Louise.

"Wow, I feel wild!" Vico exclaimed, while Marthe scrambled to get up.

Maya was getting hysterical. "Ick! How I hate this. In public, like zoo animals! You can be naked as much as you want, but love's a thing that only concerns two people."

"They started doing it when I was here," moaned Louise. "As if they didn't see me. As if I were invisible."

"Get out of here!" frantic, agitated, Maya shouted.

Robert moved her away, guided her up the stairs into her bedroom where he locked the door and tried to calm her. She was fidgeting nervously, hysterically, on the verge of a breakdown.

"Listen," he said, "before we go any further, I just want to tell you how I feel ---"

"Will you please shut-up!" she cut him off. "Whatever you may have done in the past with Carolina or whoever concerns only you. Not us. But I warn you: while you and I are together, we're completely together. This relationship must be absolute or I'm not interested."

"I know that, dear Maya," he said, hugging her. "I would never behave like Marthe and Vico, those savages." How far he had come from the days when he thought of Marthe as a liberator, a trailblazer of the body as Carolina had been of the mind. All that was over. A new life had begun.

Still nervous, upset, Maya was saying, "They can make love all day long if they like but do they have to choose my living room? It's not a sports arena after all!" Her voice rose, became passionate, severe, angry. "Imbeciles! Because they penetrate each other they think they know what passion is. Idiots! The pistons of a machine have more passion than those two!"

Louise came up, furious, stimulated and embarrassed by what she had seen. How could she forget that day in the dunes when Vico had touched his hand to her bare thighs? The times she had been naked with a man she could count on her fingers. Now she felt her own loneliness. She could never forgive Vico for opting to go "all in" with Marthe.

Robert went downstairs. Marthe and Vico had just finished getting dressed, putting themselves back together again.

Combing his wavy shoulder-length hair, Vico tried to apologize. "We didn't know you guys were coming back so soon and when you came in we were so far gone it was hard to stop on a dime."

"Please," said Robert with icy courtesy. "It's not important."

Marthe threw herself at Robert and clumsily embraced him. "Please tell Maya not to hold it against me. You must understand.... with Hoppy gone it's so difficult. Besides, I know he would have wanted me to do whatever I felt like doing. He always tried not to make things into problems, to live without problems because there is no problem."

She started to cry. After all that had just happened it seemed ridiculously melodramatic. Robert held her, wondering what would happen next. It was two in the morning.

But Vico was ready, raring to go. "What a freaking weird place this is," he declared. "I mean, weird! Let's get out of here once and for all."

"Where?" asked Marthe without any of her usual enthusiasm.

"Santa Fe!" chortled Vico. "Injun country!" he laughed. "Let's take our chances and run. Let's go and find the gods that leap out of the cactus!"

"Best of luck," said Robert sincerely, but with a cool, understated irony.

Marthe nodded her head. She started to speak sadly about Hoppy. "He never knew what he wanted anyway. He could have waited all his life and he wouldn't have known."

"He did have a few fantastic ideas," said Vico. "I'll never forget how he wanted to tie kerosene lamps onto the horns of the bulls."

They packed their duffel bags. Upstairs the light had gone off in Maya's bedroom. Robert went outside with them. It was quiet and cool. The moon hung like a slice of cantaloupe above the fields. Marthe climbed on the big motorcycle behind Vico. They would get to New York just as the sun was coming up.

Vico revved up the bike and turned to Robert. "It's really too bad about Andre. That dude never thought life was important enough to be worth dying for."

Marthe shook her head and then began to laugh richly and raucously.

"I'll give him a salute," Vico said.

He roared away, Marthe on the back of the bike, blowing bubbles of kisses at Robert.

He stood helplessly, sadly, waving, and heard Vico crying "Goodbiiiiiii!" Great voyaging barbaric American, talented pianist, intelligent idiot, Vico hit the road again with his wild roar and insolent yawp and the sickeningly innocent, paradisiacal cry of his "Wow!"

A few minutes later, in the clear, already chilly night, Robert heard the sounds of "Boom! Blam!" It was Vico with a gun, shooting out the lights on the porches of abandoned farmhouses, thus saluting the spirit of Andre.

Chapter XXXIV

Stretched for the last time on the beach in the short, shining October afternoon, he said to Maya, "It's wonderful but a little sad to be here alone. Everyone's gone. Look at all the footprints in the sand; it's like a battlefield. It's as if we alone had survived."

The sky, jeweled with blue, hung above them. The waves burst into the cool, large light; the sun tried to shake away memories. He thought of Ben, who had been a "papa" to them all; of Louise, with her secretive refusals and furtive arousals; of Andre, who had found his happiness in destroying himself, and Vico, the wild one; of Marthe with her lazy, voluptuous appetites, and Hoppy, who had drifted away; and finally of Carolina, his first love, who could never reconcile the yearning of the body with the hard facts of the mind.

A gull cried; Robert felt a fugitive vibration in the air, a subtle hint that happiness could be seized. The sea became as one with the sun. The world dissolved in a wave.

Robert felt so happy he could have killed himself from joy. How many men were given a true love, a love that remained on the surface of the body, where it played, yet at the same time descended into the very core of inner experience, the concentrated, hidden sources out of which arose in flashes, from time to time, poetry and religion and sex and love? The simple desire a man has to find, something that might be true, that he can believe in for a moment, even though it may disappear tomorrow --- Robert knew he had found it.

The sensation he had living with Maya was that he had returned home, at last had become his real self. He was no longer the lost soldier, the anguished warrior, "ghosted" with memories. His strength came from inside, he was a new man, perhaps half-man, half-animal ---but not a beast, rather a friendly creature, a sympathetic Minotaur.

They bicycled back. Bare, brown, the potato fields lay around them. The summer that had been harvested was going up in smoke, in the bonfires already burning, and how strange it was for them at last to be experiencing this fullness that carried them far beyond their expectations. How could they complain when, with Marthe and Vico gone, they were left with nothing but themselves? It was what they had wanted, yearned for, spent a summer of deadly intrigues trying to get, and now they had it. In a few days they would have to leave Wainscott. The nights were getting cold and there was no heat in the cottage.

Louise hovered in the shadows, whimpering like an abandoned dog. There seemed no reason for her to exist anymore. Ben took her out to dinner a few times.

They had this inner hunger and they had each other to satisfy it. They "ate" the flesh of their passion. They had reached a kind of ultimate glorification and apotheosis of mind and body. They forgot the dry, burned out days, the mist that rolled in and licked the roof, the damp cold that had begun to haunt the corners of the house.

Waking in the morning Maya would say, "Should we poke our noses outside?"

Instead Robert would thrust his nose into her neck. All that he hadn't lived, or had failed to live, with Carolina, came back and flooded him now.

In this fantastic freedom from and for life, united through sleep and more, held close together, they rustled around the quiet cottage in the early morning.

Louise had gone off to do laundry that didn't need to be done.

"How silly," said Maya. "She invents things for herself to do."

"Look at this!" In the room next to the kitchen, which had been Louise's, there was no longer any bed.

"How did she manage to move all these heavy things by herself? What kind of mad impulse forced her to do all this? Here she is all the time, arranging, arranging!"

"Maybe Ben stopped to say hello and helped her."

"I hope so. If she doesn't get a man or something soon she's going to go crazy!"

Robert had won. Through him Maya had been wrested away from Louise and from the dark, destructive forces of Andre. Louise now put all of her energy into organizing and running the house. She had carried her bed upstairs, placed it in the alcove outside Maya's room. "Probably so she can hear our love sounds," Robert said.

Outside it was overcast, windy. They sat at the table in the kitchen, eating lemon cake, drinking coffee. "I know I've been really tough, angry, with Louise at times, but I think she's had a good summer. I've tried to make things good for her."

"It's been better for her than it has for others."

The morning limped on. They talked for a long time about Louise. Maya still couldn't forget her, but she was fading fast. And he and Maya were growing closer and closer together. In the end, perhaps they would be drawn so closely together, so tightly, narrowly bound, that they would be overwhelmed by the sadness and ecstasy of it. When Nietzsche talks about the "sadness of profound happiness", how close Robert felt to him!

"Wet around here, wet," said Maya as she hopped over the puddles on the porch. The morning was silent, heavy, still with the full weight of autumn. A pearl-grey mist floated over the fields. They walked out to the road, feeling full and alone, overcome with the fatigue of a dangerous joy. The grass was wet; the road deserted, the air dry, the furrowed fields bare.

"Marvelous," he said.

They held each other. No birds, no sounds. Could the entire universe be reduced to this: a man and a woman?

Robert squeezed and kissed her.

The potatoes had gone; even the farmers had disappeared.

"How much do you want? What do you want?"

"I want everything. I want the moon!" Maya suddenly cried. "Don't want to lose anything that belongs to me and there might be so much."

Her wild spirit delighted Robert. He hoped he could keep her from being bored.

They began with themselves. Each night fulfilled them and each morning they set out, fresh apprentices, raging to learn.

When Louise came back, she lit the fire and wrapped herself twice in "woolies." Toward the end of the afternoon it cleared up. The sun came out with a cool, autumnal, lazy splendor.

Robert taught himself to move very slowly in time, to be very patient when he was with Maya. It was his way of defying reality, of forgetting his past, the guns and the war and sit-ins and the demonstrations.

He tried to register in himself all of her reactions, to know at each moment how she felt. How many days had they to live with each other? He could put no dates on it, no limits. He allowed himself the liberty of not worrying what would happen.

He never had enough of her. They kept going higher and higher. When she slept, he said she smiled like the sea. When she took a siesta, he would sit beside her on the bed and watch her, like a sentinel. It was lovely the way her nudity was spread out before him. Here, asleep, was the splendid trophy he had spent all summer hunting.

One day they went walking on the beach. The black sea cracked against the shore; the waves shiny like razor blades. Maya lit a Benson and Hedges, smoked a little, turned to him with a smile and said, "Do you want to see how much I love you?" Before he had a chance to answer or grab her, she had made the gesture of popping the lit end of the cigarette into her lips.

Chapter XXXV

Elegantly dressed in a pink Japanese robe, Mrs. Mellon sat on her sun porch surrounded by a spray of bright flowers and gorgeous green plants. On the pastel walls were a few minor impressionist paintings. Robert was surprised to find her alone. The big house with the pointed gables known as "Sunny Hours," had a look of crisp, cool clarity about it, as if, after months of summer agitation, it had returned to itself.

Robert had never felt even as a child that he had any accounts to render to his grandmother. He had taken advantage of being without a mother or father to grow up as he pleased. But now his own life was going off in another direction and he was happy and it gladdened him to come and see this remarkable old lady who had survived so many things and yet managed so eagerly to remain herself. He wondered what she had summoned him for.

The moment she saw him she surprised him with her rich, radiant joyfulness. "Robbie!" she jumped to her feet. They embraced.

"Bless you, bless you, my darling," Mrs. Mellon murmured.

Robert was astonished.

"Sit down. Would you like some iced tea? Coffee?"

Robert shook his head. She rang for one of her maids anyway.

Sitting there on the paisley divan with the sunlight illuminating her bird-like profile, Robert couldn't help but admire her beauty. Even though she was almost eighty, she had kept her girlish charm and enthusiasm. He was aware that this could very well be the last time he saw her.

"Remember when I was a little boy and you would take me to the zoo in Central Park and I kept asking you if animals had a soul?"

She smiled at the memory she recalled all too well: the cute blonde-haired boy toddling along beside her down the zoo path.

"I hope you're happy with Maya," she said abruptly. "I would very much like to have you both over to dinner. Would you be free tomorrow?"

Robert hugged her impulsively.

"You're not living the way I wanted you to live," she continued. "That troubled me for a long time. But I think I can accept it now."

It was Robert's turn to ask, "And you?"

She shook her head and smiled. "Not me," she declared, "no more for me! At my age, no!
After three wonderful husbands, I've had a full life. I'm satisfied."

"How fantastic to hear someone say they're satisfied."

"As if there were any need for me to make myself ridiculous with Phillip Poindexter."

"But I thought you loved Phillip. I thought you were so close together."

"I did. But I was crazy. I wanted too much to let myself be crazy one more time. You know how they say, 'One last fling'. I thought there was something but there was nothing, not even a 'fling'. Illusions of summer! When he started growing a beard, then that thing with the motorcycle, idiotic, and soon, you know, he started to do yoga, sitting out there by the pool with his legs crossed pretending to meditate while my maids brought him lunch on a tray! Haha, what a laugh! To think I was so amused by him I almost married him. Well, let's call things by their name: he wanted to marry me. You know what? Phillip is bankrupt. Remember his computer scheme for cosmetics? Talk, my dear boy, nothing but talk. His limousine? Phony appearances. What do I care? Through friends I learned he lost his apartment in New York and fled the country to the Bahamas."

"I wouldn't be surprised if he found a handsome young man to take along with him."

"I wouldn't be surprised by anything anymore," she answered. They laughed. "Not even death could surprise me. What a wonderful feeling to know that nothing, nothing in the world can take me by surprise anymore! I'm alone in the house now. It feels good. Oh, you can't imagine how good it feels! I'm not going to fight my age anymore. I lived with pride. I'll die with it too."

"With that attitude you'll outlive us all."

"If I were to go to sleep at night and never wake up again, it wouldn't matter one damn bit to me," she affirmed with a strange, soft weariness in her voice. "I've had my life. It was wonderful. Here's to you!"

The grand old dame raised her glass; they clinked; something was tugging at Robert's throat. "Ma, Ma," he wanted to say, the name he had called her as a child. He wanted to grasp her bony fingers in his hand and tell her how happy he was.

"I think you have a beautiful life ahead of you," she said.

He kissed her. "I've been going around in a circle for awhile but now the line's beginning to straighten out."

"The errors of youth don't matter. It's what happens later that counts. And I'm glad you found a woman more substantial than Carolina, who was a real will-o-the-wisp."

"I know you'd love Maya. In many ways she's like you."

"No more slip-ups now!"

Robert laughed. He would never forget that phrase, "No more slip-ups!"

Where did she come from, this strange, eccentric woman who was his grandmother? She had no roots; her way of life was vanishing. At least she would be able to say this about herself: she had been unique.

"One more thing, dear Robbie. I think you know but I should tell you again. After I die, there's nothing. This house, the apartment on Fifth Avenue, the money, it all goes back to the other side of the Mellon family."

There were times, as a teenager, when Robert had wished her dead, just to be free from the powerful influence of this woman. It was like a hidden undertow in his life, he couldn't quite get away from it. Had his fascination with his grandmother, her personality, her life-style, led him to his obsession with Maya? Was he simply repeating with Maya the love he had wanted to live as a child with his grandmother?

As rich in character as in life, generous in her judgments and her style, what could he reproach this woman except his own hunger? It wasn't her fault certainly, if some inner, unspoken rage had led Robert to break off all contact with her. Returning home, he envied her serenity, which wasn't just, as they say, that of her age: she had always it. What did she know about suffering? Perhaps more than Robert thought. She had lost three husbands, and her daughter. Somehow those losses never seemed to have affected her, to strike at her guts. Did she accept life to that degree? Was it a kind of Buddhist wisdom that Robert ignored?

How beautiful it had been to hear her say, "I've had a good life!" She meant it, he knew; she didn't regret anything and she didn't desire anything. Robert realized he loved her. She was his only blood connection, the only being in the world that had cared for him no matter what. Now, just as she said she could accept him, he could accept her.

With a feeling tinged with emotion that gradually approached awe, he sat in front of her as the light faded and heard her repeating again, "No more slip-ups," and then telling him about her projects: she had decided to do one of the few things in her life she had not done but had always wanted to do --- she was going to take a trip to India.

Chapter XXXVI

Drops of rain clung to the trees. Louise was cutting flowers. Then she sat on the porch, covering her legs with boiled bee's wax, peeling it off. Upstairs Maya lay in bed. She was tired. The last two days she and Robert had pushed themselves to the limit.

After waxing her legs Louise went out to the shed for firewood. She shuddered; before she carried the logs inside she had to scrape the spiders off.

"Spiders burn," she said, "but you wouldn't want them running around the house if the fire didn't burn quickly enough."

Robert made some coffee; Louise wanted some too. The moment Robert ate, Louise ate. "I don't eat much by myself but whenever anyone else eats, I eat. I guess I'm just a monkey eater," she said.

The morning light faded and Robert's soul leaped toward the horizon. To think that in two days they were leaving, another departure! For once Robert had what he wanted; he'd gotten what he'd come to the country for. He had Maya.

The light clung to the trees. Some things began, and others stopped. Every instant changed; V-shaped flights of geese going south appeared. Louise put the lard they had left over up in a tree. "That way," she explained, "the birds that aren't migratory will have something to keep them warm during the winter. Not all of them will survive," she added sadly.

He went back upstairs to see what Maya was doing. She was in the bathroom. He scratched softly, almost inaudibly, on the door. "Maya," he whispered. "There's a cat to see you."

She moved her head from side to side, kissing him lightly several times. Her fingers scratched his shoulders. She was naked, a cigarette lit in a pale-blue ashtray on the sink, next to pewter cups and glasses filled with marbles. He stood watching as she gazed at herself in the mirror, looking to see who she was, what she could be. Was it man who had the key to a woman, who could unlock her and reveal her to herself, or vice versa? They both revealed each other. What was love but a self-reflecting game of mirrors?

"Sometimes when I look at myself, I see my face changing. I see this eagle coming out of the mirror at me, threatening to replace my own head."

"Does it?"

She laughed, puffed her cigarette. "The other night I dreamt I was a 'spider eagle'. I wanted to soar so high, but that damn spider stung me! Anyway my dreams don't matter. Only my life."

"You're a mystery woman. I feel I'm always searching for clues, hints, anything that might help me to know more about who you are."

"Don't try," she pleaded. "Don't try."

That morning Louise stayed outside, fiddling around in the garden, digging with a spade.

When Maya came out of the bathroom they went back to the bed. They searched for freedom in themselves, going deeper and deeper. They never had enough of themselves, never had enough of saying "You." Afterwards, they got up. Barefoot, Maya ran in the grass. Her features radiated happiness as they walked down the road to the beach for the last time.

Robert trailed behind her. Maya turned and, "Bang bang," she said. "You're dead."

"I die in you."

"Then I make you rise again."

All their resurrections! All their nights, all their mornings of glory! And the two pumpkins they saw lying in the fields like fallen suns.

"Tell me," she asked, "how did you arrive at loving so much?" She frowned and became somber. "I just hope you won't be disappointed by me." She hesitated. "I hope I don't do evil to you."

He thought of the spider eagle, taking wing toward the sun; he thought of Louise saying, "Just watch out. Maya is a terribly powerful woman. Andre, who was like an ox, was no match for her."

"It's a risk I have to take," he said. "I can't do anything about it. Besides, I choose it."

"You're very strong."

"It's not a question of being strong. Not at all. I just know what I want."

"I guess that was one of my problems. I never knew what I wanted."

He was quiet.

"Please be strong, baby blue," she urged him. "Please be strong. Always. Always."

In the middle of the night it often seemed to him they were two adversaries struggling obscurely toward death. Her body startled and frightened him with its savagery. His breath pounded; he abandoned himself; gradually the knot of his body was unbound in this true delirium. Something new, never before known, was being born in him.

Were they striving for a state of total permeability, where bodies opened like flowers, and completely porous, flowed one into the other? Intercommunicating vases, where the contents of the one were poured into that of the other, and they each were gradually delivered of themselves?

Not quite, for when Robert tried to take her she fought, she wrestled, she bit him as she could, nibbling, nipping at him with her teeth until, after his dream of porous pervasiveness, he drew back, a little astonished.

"Ever see a sea urchin?" she asked. "They're like porcupines of the sea and you eat them --- I'm like that."

Later she shared this intimacy: "Andre and I, we were happy for a while. We loved that happiness so much we were willing to throw it away. I guess that was the highest value we could put on it, the knowledge that it wouldn't last. With you it's different."

"We won't throw it away. We're going to live it and make it last."

"Yes, and I promise I won't lose it like that ring."

She pulled him down toward her.

Chapter XXXVII

If some roads lead to love, many are the roads that also lead to death. How could Robert begin to understand the rupture between the miraculous delicacy of Maya's days and the blazing chaos of her nights? He didn't know whether he was living or dying, perhaps both at the same time. But if death came now, he wouldn't be afraid of it anymore; he could say he had lived, participated, flowed, and been rolled in the stream. There was only one thing that worried him: looking at photos he had begun to perceive some identity between Andre's face and his own.

Once, waking at night, he had seen Andre's head – complete with the bullet lodged in his brain -- grinning and glaring back at him, as if it were his own. For a second, it was as if their identities merged, their heads transposed. But this was quickly forgotten in Maya's seismic spasms, her volcanic violence, her abrupt transitions between sensual cruelty and exquisite tenderness. She was like an erotic sphinx that posed impossible questions to a man and helped him solve the riddle of himself.

How many times did he burst into her? Everything that he had been and that made him what he was, came alive and was renewed in her. How much happened in the miniscule space that separated their two eyes!

Their bodies sang songs. "Let's do everything," she urged. "Leave no song unsung, come like the waves!"

So they burst in sprays and sounds of love. He soared into her as she bit his ears with her teeth. He furrowed her flesh. She tossed her head back, cried out with her gorgeous shrieks and moans, conveying her wish to be fully consumed in the fire.

He penetrated her more than she knew, more than she could go; he penetrated her further than herself. They kept going and going. There were no limits, no boundaries. The waves that shook their bodies as they lay next to each other imitated the great ocean.

One thing is born out of another. People are born out of each other. Lovers keep reproducing themselves.

They fulfilled the law that Maya had announced at the start of the summer, the grand imperative: be happy. 'Make' joy.

In another way Robert felt they came close to Carolina when she said, "There's nothing but change, evolution, destruction, and growth."

Love had carried them on this slow and difficult ascension toward the light. Although the warmth had withdrawn from the day, they baked on the heights of this luminous sensuality that was forever surpassing itself. They rose into rapture.

"How high can we go?" wondered Maya.

"Ben sees the world as a pyramid. When you get to the top, when you hit the summit, you explode."

To her fascination Robert opposed his willpower. He no longer was afraid of resembling Andre, whom he had already gone far beyond

Louise lay in the alcove next door, pretending to read but listening to Maya and Robert. She spent her time hunting down spiders hidden in corners. Maya and Robert were now so close that Louise had become useless, a dumbwaiter.

The day before they left she announced, "Guess what? Ben invited me to come and live with him. He wants me to take care of things and help him with the house and ---"

"And I think it's lovely!" exclaimed Maya, jumping up and down with childlike enthusiasm. "Do it, do it! You can have a lovely relationship."

Louise packed her bags. Ben had moved back to his house in Connecticut. They drove Louise to the ferry. It was just leaving. Amid a flurry of kisses, embraces, well wishes, Louise jumped onboard. Maya was very happy. "Ben has exactly need of you. I'm sure he'll drink a lot less if you're there. You've got to control him."

"Just make sure you control yourself," Louise said significantly. "No more madness."

"No, Robert controls everything now."

They kissed. Louise was almost crying. "Thank you for the summer," she said. "We all ended up with something we didn't expect."

"Maybe it will end tomorrow. But for now it's wonderful. Good-bye. Be happy."

The ferry pulled away. Beyond was the breakwater against which the waves slapped. They left the wharf and went down to the beach. Sailing boats at anchor bobbed, almost immobile. The light shone on the huge white tilted pier stakes. Upon one of them, a gull slowly descended, fluttered and perched. Robert saw him but said nothing. A few minutes later Maya saw him. "Hey, you saw him but you hid him from me!" He laughed and embraced her. "It's the first thing you've hidden from me!" She pinched his cheeks with her fingers, punishing him.

She stopped and drew a line in the sand with her feet. "That's as far as we go and no further."

They got back into the car and left the white light and the wind on the water and drove back to the cottage. The shutters had been closed; it already looked abandoned. They got out of the car and he took her arm and they walked up the road.

"All gone," she said softly, still looking at the brown fields but thinking of something else.

"All gone. But beautiful. Bare."

She darted away. He ran after her, caught her and seized her by the waist. He ran his fingers down her neck, just below her shirt. Just as the autumn fields were bathed in a clear, simple light, so he wanted to lose himself in her. Once again he had the sense of gambling. At last he had done something to lose his life; perhaps he had done something to win it as well.

"I'm very glad Louise found something. I hope Ben and she find each other. I think it would be marvelous."

"Yes, I know, she was getting more and more upset about us. Our unity shut her out. There was no room for her anymore."

Beyond them at the end of the field, behind the wire fence, the two bulls were dozing, lying in the grass. "They're happy now too," Maya said. "Too chilly for the flies."

On the other side of them the stripped corn stalks were already beginning to rot. Maya Alvarez (née Kahle) and Robert Lord stood in the middle of the road and embraced. Maya put her arm around his back, squeezing him to her. "I think we've earned this solitude."

Robert felt weightless, both the future and the past slipped out of his mind. For once he had no anticipation, nor regrets, nor nostalgia. Everything was pure and fine, and he and Maya were one. The pale sun warmed them; the fields expanded, drenched in the amber light. The wind rustled. It was beautiful, he knew, and the thought of its being so fleeting, that this moment was for now, for now only, and no more, never again, crossed his mind.

He had mastered his desires; they had led him to this serenity, this understanding. He was not sure about being there next year, or even tomorrow, knew he could promise nothing. Suddenly he thought with acute pain of Carolina. She had been a lesson, a lesson in love, and now perhaps wrongly, even terribly, he was applying what he had learned in this lesson toward Maya.

She whispered something in his ear, he couldn't quite understand what it was, but he caught enough of the drift to know that he was hers, hers more than ever, hers for this moment at least, that was all he could say, all that anyone could say.

Sunlight fell on their shoulders; brown velvety caterpillars crawled over the grass. The air smelled of nothing, not even the sea. There were no telltale fragrances of things past. Robert thought of Maya, of nothing but Maya, she filled and spread through and illumined his mind. His hands touched her bare shoulders and warmed them. She had a few freckles. "The winter will come and take them away," she said.

Clouds floated overhead like magic carpets. They kissed each other for a long time, lost in their kisses, and then walked back.

"Let's not marry each other," Maya said. "Let us just be ourselves and marry happiness."

"I think we've already done that."

That evening he thought of Marthe, the night she and Hoppy went rampaging on the beach; of Maya slipping into the wild, silver, silent sea, shouting she could swim to England; of Vico shooting out the farmhouse lights; of Andre, leaping out of the rose bushes, revolver in hand. He thought of that time three months ago, almost inaccessible now, when it had all begun, when he and Carolina had arrived in Sag Harbor for a big party at Ben's on the Fourth of July.

Looking back, Robert could say with a sigh, "Well, that was the way it had to be." Whereas, during the time they were living it, they had absolutely no idea of how it was supposed to be at all.

The next morning they piled up and packed the car and left for New York City.

Sag Harbor, 1969

Wade Stevenson was born in New York City in 1945. He now lives in Buffalo, New York with his wife Lori, his daughter, Annawade, and his dogs Daisy and Toshi.

Made in the USA
Charleston, SC
07 October 2013